Other Books by Tejas Desai

The Human Tragedy
Good Americans (2013)

The Brotherhood Chronicle
The Brotherhood (2012)
The Brotherhood, Second Edition (2018)
The Run and Hide (2019)
The Dance Towards Death (2020)

Selected Indie Authors and Artists
Recommended by The New Wei

Allan Avidano	Vijay R. Nathan
Richard Livsey	William J. McGee
Brienne Walsh	W. Lance Hunt
Brontez Purnell	Lancelot Schaubert
Olena Jennings	Catherine Manett
Anthony Veasna So	Annette Brown
Lynley Shimat	Lorraine Schein
Ishy Christine Degyansky	Chris Stylez
Rajiv Mohabir	Jay Sizemore
Raj Tawney	Kacper Jarecki

"The distinction between a dated book and a timeless book emerges in whether or not its subject matter hits upon universal notes. This is a book about Covid and Trump and many other soon-to-be dated subjects. And yet Tejas has focused his real ire upon death, his real hope upon love, and his deepest reflections upon the meaning of life itself."

> — Lancelot Schaubert,
> author of *Bell Hammers* and *Overmorrow*,
> songwriter of *H.A.L.T.S.*, filmmaker for *Alaska*

"With *Bad Americans*, Tejas Desai poignantly describes the effects of Covid on NYC through a compelling fictional storyline ... All twelve of the character stories are so gripping that you'll want to know what comes next."

> — M.C. Allison, librarian & blogger

"Tejas Desai, one of the nation's boldest and most innovative writers, tackles the nature of American identity in *Bad Americans*, a panoramic tale of exploration and survival during the Covid-19 pandemic. Channeling Boccaccio and Chaucer, Desai sets his novel on the Gatsbyesque estate of dating-app magnate Olive Mixer, who invites each of twelve diverse guests to share their stories on consecutive days. What ensues is a poignant and often hilarious commentary on social experimentation and the individual's search for meaning in a world that co-opts and commodifies identity. *Bad Americans* is a daring novel as compelling as it is intellectually challenging."

> — Jacob M. Appel, author of *Einstein's Beach House*

"The fictional characters' sentiments are carefully crafted, offering an intriguing range of realistic reactions to the Covid-19 Pandemic. An illuminating ... exploration of recent history and the people who lived through it."

> — *Kirkus Reviews*

BAD AMERICANS

PART I

THE GREAT AMERICAN PANDEMIC NOVEL
IN TWO PARTS

THE HUMAN TRAGEDY
VOLUME 2

Tejas Desai

New York

BAD AMERICANS: PART I by Tejas Desai

Contact the author at his website: http://tejas-desai.com
More about The New Wei: http://thenewwei.wordpress.com
ISBN # 978-1-7347278-2-1 (Hardcover Edition)
ISBN# 978-1-7347278-3-8 (Paperback Edition)
ISBN # 978-1-7347278-4-5 (eBook Edition)
Library of Congress Control Number # 2025909947
Copyright © 2025 Tejas H. Desai
Cover Design by Fena Lee
All rights reserved.

The New Wei, LLC
P. O. Box 650411
Fresh Meadows, NY 11365

Dedicated to
all my fellow Americans

Release Schedule for BAD AMERICANS

"On the Frontlines" (aka "Andrea's Story," novelette)—March 15, 2025

"Immigrants Unite!" (aka "Cathy's Story," spoken word poetic tale)—April 15, 2025

"Corona Chaos" (aka "Taylor's Story," short story)—May 15, 2025

"Black Boy's Ballad" (aka "Rashan's Story," novella)—June 15, 2025

"Mason Mayhem" (aka "Ricard's Story," novelette)—July 15, 2025

"Love Liability" (aka "Nalini's Story," novelette)—August 15, 2025

BAD AMERICANS: PART I (novel with stories)—September 15, 2025

"Barcelona Blasphemy" (aka "Lisa's Story," novelette)—October 15, 2025

"ISIS Crisis" (aka "Khassan's Story," short story)—November 15, 2025

"A Model Citizen" (aka "Hayley's Story," novelette)—December 15, 2025

"Cape Conundrum" (aka "Pritesh's Story," novelette)—January 15, 2026

"The Manchurian Algerian" (aka "Sylvania's Story," novelette)—February 15, 2026

"Dope Double Ditty" (aka "Angela's Story," novella)—March 15, 2026

BAD AMERICANS: PART II (novel with stories)—April 15, 2026

Note on BAD AMERICANS: PART I

Inspired by classics like *The Decameron*, *The Canterbury Tales*, and *1001 Arabian Nights*, as well as reality TV shows like *The Bachelor* and *Big Brother*, *Bad Americans* is both The Great American Pandemic Novel and a collection of 12 stories, novelettes, and novellas within a frame narrative. Like its predecessor in *The Human Tragedy* anthology series, *Good Americans* (2013), it seeks to present a panoramic portrait of contemporary America in a dynamic way.

In the summer of 2020, following the Covid lockdown in New York City, billionaire tech entrepreneur Olive Mixer summons 12 diverse Americans to his Hamptons, Long Island, mansion to rekindle their humanity and find love.

Each day, the guests date, argue, fight, compete, and dine. Every night, one guest must tell a story. These tales, while fictional, depict a different aspect of the American experience and vary widely in subject and style. Many respond to one another. And while they function within the greater narrative of *Bad Americans*, they also stand alone and can be enjoyed as single reads.

Due to its length, *Bad Americans* is being released in two parts in multiple formats. Each part contains the frame narrative and six stories. The individual stories are also being released as Kindle eBooks a month apart before the publications of the two whole volumes.

Table of Contents

"What is any Nation, after all—and what is any human being, but a struggle between conflicting, paradoxical, opposing elements—and they themselves and their most violent contests, important parts of that One Identity, and its development?"

— Walt Whitman

"I begin to sing about Poseidon, the great god, mover of the earth and fruitless sea, god of the deep... A two-fold office the gods allotted you, O Shaker of the Earth, to be a tamer of horses and a savior of ships!"

— Homeric Hymn

Introduction

If you've lived more than a decade, you may have heard of a book called *Good Americans* released in 2013 by a publisher named Tejas Desai that bears his name. And if you've read that book, then you've encountered its introduction by a literary agent that describes the strange process by which she acquired it and assisted with its publication into the world.

Its deliverer, a vague figure known only as The Jester, promised another short story collection within a few years, which, once again, like that first anthology, would compile several stories reflecting the human condition in this great but troubled nation, written by anonymous authors.

This series would be known as *The Human Tragedy*, perhaps named after the French author Honore de Balzac's magnum opus, and, according to The Jester, would consist of an endless series of books delivered every few years. *Good Americans* had focused on the diseased aspects of our society and, perhaps to the hope of both the literary agent and publisher who had pushed it out into the world despite the objections of the literary elite of its time, would focus perhaps on a gentler and nobler aspect of the human condition.

However, years passed, and despite a combination of rave reviews and severe put-downs by those offended by the chutzpah of that chronicle, neither the literary agent nor the publisher heard anything from the Jester. Five years elapsed, and not a word. Mr. Desai moved on to publish the sequels to his popular book *The Brotherhood* through his company, The New Wei, and, having received awards, accolades, and even Amazon #1 bestseller statuses in various categories, understandably moved on from the project, perhaps even considering the existence of The Jester to be a joke itself.

But the literary agent, Ophelia Gibbs, who had placed such a powerful emphasis on the publication of that collection, was distraught. Unlike Mr. Desai, she did not lack means, and she was not young. She had passed through that "suspension of twilight" that William Faulkner's character Quentin Compson had referred to in Faulkner's underrated story "A Justice." She had resources and a continuous flow of royalty revenue from a backlist that was decades in the making. Her exasperation with the literary elite of that time, uninterested in diversity, in challenge, in exploring the inner lives of people of color and the external realities of the dispossessed, had given her life meaning, and the absence of The Jester's promised manuscript left her in a distressed state, so much so that she decided to retire. In fact, she gifted her agency's brand to her assistant, Aeneas, the author of this Introduction.

Sadly, having tired of living in her lonely apartment in Flushing, Queens, venturing out only for the occasional pho or hotpot or meal of soup dumplings and bok choy, Ophelia moved into a nursing home on Northern Boulevard to play endless games of bingo with her fellow elderly. That was not long before the Covid pandemic hit Queens, and it was here that she acquired the deadly virus and passed away in April 2020.

Having heard of her passing and even more moved by the inheritance of her entire backlist revenue, I, Aeneas Sokratis Alexopoulos, decided I could not simply let her legacy go unfinished. I had, of course, created my own backlist by this time, several non-fiction titles and select upmarket fiction, along with the ONE BIG AUTHOR who paid my bills.

But now, free of financial burden after being gifted Ms. Gibbs' backlist through a trust, and even with a large and expanding family with my beautiful wife Adrianna filling bigger homes in Whitestone with even costlier mortgages, I decided to dedicate myself to tracking down the Jester and the manuscripts he had been keeping from Ms. Gibbs, Mr. Desai, and the world. Sure, my wife insisted the Jester must have died, moved on, or been a phantom of Ms. Gibbs' imagination, but I was determined to find him (if he existed) nevertheless, even a full three years after my mentor's passing and a full decade since the publication of the initial volume.

Still, times had seemingly changed. #Ilovediversebooks had been successful to some extent, and with the push of DEI programs, despite the political backlash by half the country, it might have been possible to publish such a book through a major publisher in the 2020s, especially now that the pandemic was on its heels, even as the virus was not. I did not have those contacts, but it was possible I could find an agent who did. Self-publishing had put *Good Americans* out into the world, but it had doomed the book to a limited readership and cult status as well.

First, I needed to track down The Jester and the next manuscript or to find out why it had never been produced or delivered. My first clue lay in the email address The Jester had used to send *Good Americans* to Ophelia. As her assistant, she had forwarded it to me at the time, and using a dubious service recommended to me by a friend of a friend, I was able to track down the IP address used when that email was first created and registered.

This hunt led me to an apartment in Elmhurst, Queens, where, after an analysis of housing records, *White Pages,* and *Spokeo*, I found myself face-to-face at a Zoom meeting with a young editor named Tracey Gomez, who explained to me the complexities of her situation.

You see, in 2013, she had been a college student who had worked part-time as a publicist for an independent author, and it was this author who had commissioned her to send the manuscript to Ophelia and even drafted the emails himself. And yes, this author's name was Tejas Desai.

Surprise, surprise, that it was the eventual publisher himself who had compiled the collection, or perhaps written it himself, and had sent it to Ophelia via Ms. Gomez. Was it simply luck that some-how Ophelia had found Mr. Desai's Facebook page and blog and decided to contact him, or had he laid another egg for her to catch? Well, some mysteries may never be solved.

I decided to confront Mr. Desai and set up a meeting without revealing the reason. He told me he was out in the Hamptons, staying in Sag Harbor. I could wait until he returned to Queens, but I decided to make the long drive out, past Riverhead and I-495, onto that lonely road that leads to the backwoods of the elite.

Yes, it was a strange circumstance to meet a struggling writer in a place filled with wealth, even though Sag Harbor itself is judged lower on the Hamptons spectrum, being known as the Black Hamptons. But it was possible, given his recent successes, that Mr. Desai was no longer as poor as he had been. And certainly, I was shocked when this son of a traffic cop and lab technician—first responders during both 9/11 and the Covid pandemic—arrived at Page at 63 Main dressed in a polo shirt, khakis, and Calvin Klein shoes, projecting the aura of the uncaring and relaxed rich.

He explained; however, that he was staying at an Airbnb when not being shown around town by a college friend. I asked if this was research for another book, and he said it certainly was. Another murder mystery? An international conspiracy thriller? No, he stated. Something more important, something closer to his heart and to the lifeblood of our nation.

Then he revealed that he understood my intent: he had spoken to Ms. Gomez, and he knew that I knew of his deception. He was slightly ashamed, he said as he sliced into a poached egg, but he insisted that it had been a white lie, no different than the essence of imaginative realistic fiction itself. Lying to tell the truth: isn't that what we all did? There was no way, after all, that in 2013 a major publisher would have released a book of short stories filled with various races and different subjects when a brown guy's name was on it. Even outside of the fact that no one would read it, and no one could market it, wasn't it "appropriation?"

So, he had sent it anonymously to Ms. Gibbs, hoping she could place it with a publisher, any publisher, and when she couldn't, he claimed she just happened to find him, and when he placed his name on it and put it out into the world, there was a kind of poetic justice to it. After all, there were no anonymous authors: he had written the stories himself.

What was the reason The Jester had not fulfilled his promises, then, I asked him. Well, that was simply life, he answered. He had been consumed with *The Brotherhood Chronicle* trilogy, his work as a public librarian, traveling the world, exploring other indie talents for his New Wei literary arts movement and collective, etc. But he was still dedicated to *The Human Tragedy*, and that's why he was here, completing some final research for the next volume.

But why The Hamptons, I asked? That didn't sound like the setting of a typical story from *Good Americans*, which had been characterized by grit and set among the lower elements of our society. Mr. Desai reminded me that one tale had been set at the University of Oxford, another upstate, a third in Manhattan. That said, he admitted I was somewhat correct: *Bad Americans*, its sequel, was different than its predecessor. For one thing, he had done extensive research, even more than for the first book, and while the volume had 100% been written by him, he had gotten feedback from many, many Americans of every stripe.

I returned to Queens, hoping he would send me the full manuscript within six months. Finally, in November 2023, it entered my inbox.

Certainly, *Bad Americans* was far different than the original volume. It contained 12 short stories of phenomenal diversity and innovation, yet they were set within a frame narrative in the Hamptons during the Covid pandemic of 2020.

The book was amazingly vivid and realistic. It brought me back to the time of lockdowns and food shortages, police killings of Black people, targeting of Asians and riots in masks, political turmoil and social upheaval, the questioning of our origins and destruction of heroic statues. Granted the virus and the social reaction to it exacerbated issues that already existed, but they were put forth in such a forceful and extreme manner that one could not help but pay attention and influence the decade that followed.

This volume was also massive: about 260,000 words, more than twice the length of the first book. It was also, in its own way, superior.

Just as the 14th-century Boccaccio responded to the Black Death in his city of Florence by exiling his fictional aristocrats to the countryside to tell 100 stories, so too had Desai, who had lived in Queens and acquired the virus during its darkest days, placed 12 diverse Americans, along with a large staff, at the home of a billionaire tech entrepreneur in the Hamptons, just a car ride away from the afflicted city of New York, to craft their own. Yes, that melting pot and salad bowl that we love was the perfect setting to dissect this contemporary catastrophe and all the issues that surrounded it, within tales rich in diversity, crisis, suspense, and ironic resolutions.

In addition to literary predecessors like *The Canterbury Tales* and *1001 Arabian Nights*, the book also resembles reality shows of this time: *The Bachelor*, *Big Brother*, maybe even *Survivor*, but unlike those, the structure of the frame story is loose and negotiable, the relationships fluid, unforced, and believable. The competitive elements are downplayed. Therefore, we encounter a new kind of "reality" altogether. And the class elements among participants and staff also resemble a show like *Upstairs Downstairs*, but set here, in America.

Mr. Desai polished the book, and, through our contacts, the book was submitted to publishers over the next year. However, even this effort was unsuccessful. The novel and short story collection in one was an unheard-of concept for a risk-averse industry, and how could a book with a different subject, style, and structure for each story possibly be marketed? DEI efforts were also ending with the (correct) anticipation of the re-election of Donald Trump. Once again, the publishing effort was fruitless.

Ultimately, Mr. Desai decided to embark on one of the most ambitious publishing plans in literary history: to publish each individual story in *Bad Americans* as a Kindle eBook a month apart, starting in March 2025, and then publish the whole volumes—novel with stories—in two parts, in September 2025 and April 2026.

To prepare for this, Mr. Desai did a final rewrite of the frame story. All the books were copyedited and proofread. Author blurbs were enlisted. Despite all the odds against it, *Bad Americans* was placed out into the world through more than 18 individual publications.

Time will tell if *The Human Tragedy* receives the accolades it deserves and whether it garners sufficient readership, but I will not be responsible for that. I've done my part to assist the passage of *Bad Americans* into the public sphere, and, as Ophelia once said, I am proud of that.

Sincerely,
Aeneas Sokratis Alexopoulos
March 2025

The Americans had arrived in the Hamptons and now stood in the den of the Saggplex—12 of them, hanging out in the groups they had naturally formed after arriving and finding their rooms. They were waiting for their host, Olive Mixer, the reclusive billionaire who owned dating apps and had created the competition that had chosen them.

They had been locked down by the government for months; now they hoped to be free. Two weeks of eating, activities, and dating in a secure environment. Finally, they could forget about the virus and death. They could be among people again. This was The Getaway.

Sung, Head of Security, stood at the center of the main den, next to a table filled with hors d' oeuvres. The Conservatives were discussing the illegals and the great things the President had done. Meanwhile, the Liberals were gossiping about the Rogue Two—the Quarantined Girl and the Skinhead.

Sung was thinking about the Rogue Two also. He had rapid tested them upon arrival. Both had come directly from Connecticut after quarantining at home and uploading tests. But Nalini, the corporate lawyer, had been driven by her father, so Sung needed to clear it with the two doctors, Alexa and Rashadi, before she could join everyone else.

Her father was sitting at a local restaurant nearby for word in case she needed to be sent back.

The other ten had been picked up in limos—five had quarantined for two weeks in a different complex of bungalows on the North Shore that Olive owned, while the other five had self-quarantined at their homes in and around New York City, uploading regular tests. All were tested before they were cleared.

Now they waited for Olive Mixer as they munched on food and drank cocktails served by Ares, one of the house staff. The Liberals, lounging on beanies, included Rashan Hall, an African American teacher; Lisa Applebaum, a Jewish American blogger; Cathy Wei Quan, a Taiwanese American social worker; and Andrea Mendoza, a Filipino American nurse. The Conservatives, clustered around the bar, included Taylor Williams, a white Financial Analyst; Khassan Murdashev, a Chechen American dental hygiene student; Angela Diaz, an Ecuadorian American hair salon owner; and Sylvania Trainor, an Asian American transgender seamstress.

The Skinhead, Ricard Shaw, munched on a cracker alone in the corner near a TV and PlayStation, and in another corner by an ornate curtain was an uncommon pair—Pritesh Lakshmi, an Indian computer engineer, and Hayley Clark, a young model. Everyone noticed they seemed to already have a great rapport.

Through that curtain on the right side of the den, a man emerged. He was tall and had an olive complexion. He wore a traditional black suit with red tie. In each hand he held a book; one was *The Decameron* by Giovanni Boccaccio, the other *The Canterbury Tales* by Geoffrey Chaucer.

He approached the center of the room and placed the books on the table where the hors d'oeuvres had been placed. Suddenly everyone realized a book was already there, but no one had seen it: *The Arabian Nights*.

Olive clapped two times, and the second time he held his hands together flat as if he was praying to the crowd, or perhaps waiing to them in the Thai manner. It wasn't clear.

"Thank you all for coming. I'm Olive Mixer. I'm so happy you decided to be here with us. When this awful pandemic started, I knew it was going to be something we'd never experienced. Not only have we seen so many of our fellow New Yorkers get sick and die, but we've seen life as it was collapse. The isolation, the homeschooling," he said, looking at Rashan. "Even I have lost so many friends, so much so that my staff here has become like my family, and you will treat them as such, or I'll hear about it."

Some of the guests laughed at that; others looked at each other quizzically.

"In any case, my goal is for everyone here to have a good time and perhaps find love."

"Numbers don't seem to add up for that," Rashan said. "My gaydar is at zero. Except maybe you and that guy." He pointed to Ares.

"Are we being recorded?" Taylor asked. "I didn't sign up for a reality show."

"That might be cool though," Hayley said, touching Pritesh's arm as he folded them across his chest.

"Yes, I could have made this into a reality show like *Big Brother*, or *The Bachelor*, or *Survivor*, or any number of other copycats. But I don't want to do that. My goal isn't commercial; it's holistic. Trust me, I'm rich enough that I don't need any more money."

"Bullshit," Ricard muttered. "I see cameras everywhere, Big Brother."

"That's just for security," Olive explained. "Sung and his team, Darnell and Micah, will be monitoring the area to make sure no one else who isn't cleared gets inside, or for other funny business."

"Getting back to the romance, though, how will this work?" Rashan asked. "Will we be set up?"

"I find it's better for these things to work organically," Olive said. "Every day you will be fed three meals, and every morning and afternoon there will be activities, some of which will have prizes, others not. But the main thing is that you have fun and socialize without worrying about getting sick. And every night, one of you will each have to tell the group a story."

"A story?" Lisa asked.

"Hence the *Canterbury Tales*," Cathy said. "Now it's clicking."

"Yes, a story," Olive said. "This is a safe space. There's no length, content, or style requirement. In fact, I prefer it if you push the boundaries of content and form. And that you try to stick to the re-alities you know, though I'm not mandating that."

"What's the purpose of that?" Khassan asked.

"The main goal is to enjoy ourselves during the time we have together," Olive said. "You are all lucky. I hope you find friendships and love. But we will live in a deeply divided nation, and not just politically. I deliberately picked as diverse a group as I could—people of many ethnicities, sexualities, professions. This is our chance to hear about each other, and perhaps understand each other, in a narrative format, and hopefully even about Americans who are not represented among this group."

"So we are lab rats in some social experiment," Ricard said. "I knew it."

"If you ever feel that way," Olive said, "you are welcome to leave."

"I don't know, I think it sounds pretty cool," Cathy said. "I performed spoken word in college, so maybe I can incorporate that."

"Fantastic," Olive said. "And I did pick people who could tell stories—not like Pulitzer Prize winners, but like real people. For example, Angela is a hair stylist—she specializes in gossiping and BS. Khassan does stand-up comedy and drives Ubers on the side. Lisa is a blogger. I could go on. Are there any other questions?"

"I was in this so I could find a partner after breaking up with my boyfriend," Rashan said. "Doesn't seem like that's gonna happen for me here."

"That's not all that's suspicious," a voice said from the grand foyer connecting the front door to the den. When the crowd turned, they saw a beautiful Indian American girl in her late 20s wearing a suit.

"Hope she didn't come in like that," Lisa whispered to Andrea, who laughed; Sylvania and Angela, who were both ornately dressed, whispered to one another, "What is she wearing?"

"No, the suit was originally in this long dress," Ricard, the skinhead, said to Lisa as he came up behind her. Lisa glared at him with horror and backed away a bit.

"Nalini, welcome," Olive said. "I'm sorry to have held you up."

"I followed procedure, so I don't know why I was punished, unlike everyone else here."

"We had to make sure you were okay since you came with your father," Olive said.

"I mean, he quarantined too, so what? I told Security that."

"It was a mix-up. But we have cleared you."

"I guess I missed the whole spiel, but I did get the latter half of that," Nalini continued. "So, you're telling us that we're here to tell lovey-dovey stories like 'We are the World.' 'Cuz I also came to get a man. I'm not getting any younger."

"There are plenty of possibilities for you," Olive said. "But I don't want to be Big Brother, setting people up. Sometimes things work better without a push."

"Yeah, we don't need Big Brother," Taylor concurred. "I'm waiting for these activities. Already getting restless."

"I mean, it's still better than being out there," Rashan noted. "Even with the soft opening."

"Well, we can always confer with the lawyer if we have any issues," Lisa said.

"Okay, moving on," Olive said. "I want to introduce some of our team. You might have already met some of them. Sung here is Head of Security, and the two security guards are Darnell and Micah. They live on-site here at the Saggplex—Sung in the basement where his office is, and Darnell and Micah on the sixth floor."

A tall, muscular African American man, his fingers dipped into his pockets, came forward and nodded at the crowd. Hayley winked at him. She had already flirted with him and his partner Micah on the sixth floor since the three of them were the only ones staying there. She remembered seeing them from afar during her brief outings while quarantining at the bungalow complex—they only got an hour a day to walk around the grounds—and earlier today, wowed by the bathing possibilities on the sixth floor, she put on a bubble bath and invited them to soap her, but then Darnell was called away, and Micah had been the one to rub some lotion on her shoulders before he had been summoned for office duty, which meant monitoring the cameras in the basement. That was before Hayley hit it off with Pritesh after coming down freshly bathed.

"Micah is busy, but you'll meet him eventually," Olive said. "Next, we have my staff that mostly lives at the White House, another home I own near Sagg Beach, a spot that you will all enjoy later. This is Ares and Rabia, who drive my two limos and double as handypeople."

Ares, behind the bar, waved, while Rabia carried in some more hors d'oeuvres from the room on the left and acknowledged the crowd with a brief head nod.

"You'll meet Nick and Temple another day. They will help with some of the activities and bringing over supplies. They are tested and cleared; you don't have to worry."

"Our two maids who will do all the cleaning here are Maja and Zahra."

Two women came into the room, with traditional white aprons over their plain dresses, nodded, and smiled.

"Our two doctors, who will be making sure we are Covid-free and healthy, are Alexa and Rashadi."

The two doctors, who had tested everyone but the Rogue Two, dressed then in full hazmat suits, came into the den from the foyer and waved. It was the first time the guests had seen them in regular clothes.

"They will also be in and out, but they are cleared, so you don't have to worry about contamination.

"Last but not least, our amazing cooks who will be feeding you: Thiago and Abeo, our two chefs. Plus Rafael and Bom, our two assistant cooks."

The four cooks came out from the left entrance wearing chef whites. The two assistants were pushing carts with more food.

"Holy shit," Khassan said. "You're Thiago de Silva!"

Even before the rest of the crowd recognized the famous chef, known for his show *Thiago Inferno* and his stints on *Iron Chef*, another guest, Taylor, perked up and approached Thiago. The two men hugged warmly. Then Taylor hugged Rafael too.

"What the fuck is going on?" Lisa asked.

"Sorry, let me explain," Thiago said. "Yes, I am Thiago de Silva. You know me from my shows, but I have also been in the fight to feed the hungry in this country. Specifically, I formed and led the Universal Kitchen that fed so many essential workers and desperately hungry people when the economy collapsed following the lockdown. Olive asked me to be here, so this is a kind of short break for me. And Taylor, here, volunteered to help me and Rafael run food lines in Corona, Queens during the worst days so far of this pandemic."

"You seem as selfless as Elon Musk," Cathy quipped at Taylor.

"Well, some of us say and others do," Taylor said. "I'm a former NATO soldier, deployed in Afghanistan and Iraq before becoming a financial analyst. Charity is in my blood. I just don't think the government should do it."

"I ate so many wonderful meals at Elmhurst Hospital," Andrea said. "Thank you so much."

"No, thank you," Olive said. "I forgot to mention, we have a hero here. Andrea Mendoza is a nurse at hard-hit Elmhurst Hospital. A true essential worker. Let's give her a round of applause."

Everyone started clapping. Andrea seemed embarrassed initially, but eventually, she bowed and waved in appreciation.

"Thank you so much," Andrea said. "I wish I could forget some of the things I experienced. But I wouldn't trade my role for anything."

"Maybe we'll hear about it soon," Olive said. "Which reminds me of some ground rules. First, you will find out if you are telling a story on the morning you are to tell it. I am doing this to keep things spontaneous. You can choose to skip meals or activities on that day to work on your tale. Otherwise, I do expect everyone to attend meals and activities, though I understand things happen. During off times, you are welcome to enjoy the entire place and the amenities here—our library, our gym downstairs, our indoor and outdoor courts, gaming systems, board games, karaoke bar, fun room. This is a big complex, so I won't give you a formal tour, but you can feel free to explore on your own.

"Finally, while I'm not banning the use of phones, devices, and social media—in fact, the next room has several devices you can use—it is stipulated in the contract you signed that you cannot post or write about the experience. What happens here stays here. That said, we will not tolerate unwelcome behavior, and anyone who engages in it will be banished from the complex. You have my word."

"Tough contract," Nalini said.

"You can re-review whatever you want," Olive said.

"I have to post daily to keep up my social media feeds, or it could drown my career," Hayley said.

"Yes, I'm aware," Olive said. "I don't mind you posting your body or some backgrounds, as long as it's not specifically related to things that are happening here."

Hayley gave him a thumbs up. Then Abeo, the other chef, began explaining the spread of food.

"To start, we decided to do a fusion of Indian, Japanese, and Spanish cuisine. We have three different types of maki with samosa-style tops: one with lobster, cucumber, mango, and tamarind chutney; another with salmon, avocado, sweet potato, and mustard; and, for the vegetarians, maki with teriyaki tofu, avocado, carrot, red bell pepper, and green chutney. We have six selections of tapas: papayas bravas, gambas al ajillo, croquettes, a salmorejo, empanadas, and boquerones en vinegre. There are also three types of cheeses: brie, muenster, and gouda, along with Ritz and salt crackers, as well as three types of bread: raisin-encrusted pumpernickel, spicy naan baked with jalapeños, and focaccia with tomato sauce inside.

"In addition to the full bar we have in the corner here, to drink we have a special bottle of champagne for this occasion and some after-dinner brandy too. I hope you will enjoy."

"We're starting you off light," Thiago joked.

"Enjoy, everyone," Olive said, turning to leave through the library. "I will see you tomorrow for breakfast. And feel free to peruse these volumes for inspiration."

~ DAY ONE ~

Andrea woke with a start. She had dreamt about being at the hospital, swerving around people on gurneys in the hallway to try to save a patient in ICU—but as soon as she arrived, she saw the man wore a Oton gold death mask.

Then she remembered where she was. Two weeks in the Hamptons—a break from the madness.

Not everyone had been so lucky. For months they had been denied vacation, but then, there was nowhere to go anyway, unless you wanted to sneak out on a flight to Florida and never come back. Or you could get the virus yourself, which often happened—then you would get 10–14 days off, assuming you survived.

The light was shining through the window. She preferred the natural light to the shade—and as she waded to the bathroom, she noticed a small red envelope under the door.

"Is it Chinese New Year?" she wondered to herself, remembering her days as a maid in Hong Kong.

She picked it up. The envelope, surrounded by gold trimming, was sealed with a small gold heart. She picked it with her nail, opened the envelope, and removed a plain white card.

Inside was written:

> Thank you for serving
> Of all, you are deserving
> To sound the first siren call
> Do remember the tall
> Order of your calling
> When crafting your story
> You can focus on the glory

Or the absolutely appalling
Failures of the elite.
Or make something up
Life is short and sweet
Or long and corrupt
Now let's eat!

An hour later Andrea heard the call for breakfast and took the elevator down to the den, where she met Rashan and Lisa. Taylor, Angela, and Sylvania were also there. Sung spoke to someone over his headset, then he led them through the three rooms on the left of the complex. The first featured an endless amount of electronic equipment, from iPads to iPhones to e-readers. Against the far wall were tabletops and chairs to plug in devices. A collection of board games rested on shelves in a corner shaped like a beehive. Espresso and vending machines were present too. And the middle was an empty area where presumably people could play the board games or horse around.

The next room included a large kitchen closed off with a separate wall, windows, and door, so only staff could have access. Peeking through the windows, Andrea noticed Bom and Rafael putting some final touches on breakfast. Behind them was a wood-fired oven and a massive refrigerator. On the open side, a large wall doubled as a handball and racquetball court. In the left corner was a basketball hoop, along with shelves filled with various balls for play.

The third room featured a long brown wooden table with ornate baroque and rococo chairs that Sung told them Olive had purchased from 18th-century homes. A few cabinets featured fine China dinnerware and silverware. In the far corner was a restroom that included two sinks, two toilets, and two showers. There was also an external flowing sink.

Passing through thick, dark blue, faux silk curtains, they came outside to the patio. Ornately designed porcelain tiles, etched with quotes by literary figures, supported wicker tables and chairs. Beyond that were beanies, futons, and couches. The patio ended at a fireplace. Hanging over them was a large awning with a sunroof, and panels that, while raised now, could come down during bad weather.

Andrea noticed Hayley and Pritesh were sitting at a table, holding hands, but Hayley appeared to be flirting with Thiago, the chef, while Pritesh looked on jealously. Meanwhile, at another table, Ricard and Khassan were arguing about some 9/11 conspiracy theory involving Israel and Free Masonry.

"Shit, let's sit far away from the skinhead," Lisa said to Rashan. "Makes my skin crawl."

Taylor, Sylvania, and Angela sat with Khassan and introduced themselves to Ricard, who nodded at them humbly. Khassan explained that he and Ricard had discovered the gym that morning and lifted weights. There they had seen Hayley running the treadmill, without Pritesh.

"She's definitely the hottest commodity," Khassan said to an eye-roll from Angela. "How that Indian dweeb got her is the main mystery of this enterprise so far."

"I'm just looking for relaxation, darling," Sylvania said. "Leave the drama on the outside."

"I see you're dressed more humbly today," Ricard said to Angela and Sylvania, who both wore robes, like sisters. The day before, Angela had worn a low-cut black lace blouse that showed off her cleavage, with a neat white jacket on top, along with stiletto heels and white stretch pants that went down only half her calf. Sylvania wore an immaculately sewn, tight-fitting dress with a feathery spike ball on her right shoulder, slight shoulder pads, suit-like lapels that displayed a V on the upper chest, a belt across her waist with a large buckle and a slightly more flowing hemline that ended just above her knees.

"Good first impressions are a must, chico," Angela said. "Don't they say that where you're from?"

"Where I'm from no one can afford to dress like that," Ricard said. "Unless you're a suit like Ms. Fairfield County over there."

Angela followed his eye line and saw Nalini and Cathy jogging towards the patio from the grassy field next to them. They were both wearing tank tops and short shorts.

"Shit, Cathy's with that spreader," Rashan said to Lisa.

"She was cleared," Lisa said unconfidently. She glanced at Andrea, who shrugged.

"I don't know what exact protocols they followed," Andrea said. "There's no fool-proof method with this crazy virus. I guess we just have to trust."

Cathy, breathing heavily, sauntered over to their table, with Nalini following.

"It's beautiful around here. We jogged to the beach and back."

Lisa and Rashan nodded at Nalini.

"I see you made a new friend," Rashan said.

"Yeah, Asian sisters," Cathy said, high-fiving Nalini.

"We figured running, even in this heat, was better than being cooped up in a gym," Nalini explained.

"I should go with you next time," Lisa said, rubbing her stomach. "Believe it or not, I used to be as skinny as her."

She pointed at Hayley, who had finally finished her flirtation with Thiago and was now sitting on Pritesh's lap while clasping his hand.

"Must have been a long time ago," Rashan quipped, to a hard shoulder punch from Lisa.

At that moment they saw Olive enter through the curtain. He wore a white short-sleeve lace shirt, khakis, and a Panama hat.

"Good morning, everyone. I hope you all had a restful night in your new rooms. Thiago will introduce this morning's breakfast and then you can take the entire morning to do whatever you wish. There are plenty of activities out in the field, in the rooms you passed through, and on the other side of the complex, in the karaoke bar, the game room, and more. We will have lunch around 1 p.m., and then go out to the beach, where again you can feel free to do as you please. Today is a day to get to know each other before we have planned activities."

Thiago explained that the breakfast was "traditional American."

"Anything you can think of: scrambled eggs, pancakes, cereal, bagels, and all the rest. Enjoy it while you have it because the other days, we might go kind of crazy."

"Kind of crazy?" Khassan asked, examining the food as it was rolled out by the chefs. "It's a good amount, I guess."

"More like a Motel 6 continental breakfast than the Ritz Carlton," Taylor quipped to Thiago, "but I guess you can't be fancy every day."

"We'll leave you in suspense, Taylor," Thiago responded.

"My uncle owns a Motel 6 in Maryland," Pritesh told Hayley, which Khassan overheard. "That's where I quarantined before I got into The Getaway."

"I hope their breakfast was better," Hayley said, kissing him on the cheek and hopping off his lap. "Oh, I'm going to eat too much." But she only took a small bowl of muesli, blueberries, strawberries, and yogurt.

"Gotta watch that figure," Khassan said.

"Yeah, for what?" Taylor muttered.

Meanwhile, Pritesh, a vegetarian, took a bagel and cream cheese, while Ricard loaded up—pancakes, scrambled eggs, sausages, the works.

"I can't eat pork," Khassan said while taking plenty of other food himself.

"There are plenty of vegan, vegetarian, gluten-free, non-diary, non-pork options for everyone," Abeo said.

"I'm paleo myself," Thiago added. "We'll have plenty of options in every meal for every dietary need."

The ladies tried not to eat too much. Afterwards, some guests, like Hayley and Pritesh, went up to their rooms, while others explored the place. Angela and Sylvania entered the game room, where they played arcade games, while Taylor and Khassan threw around a football in the backyard.

Soon enough, lunchtime rolled around, and everyone gathered at the patio for sandwiches—everyone but Hayley and Pritesh.

"I just saw the model by the pool," Lisa said, a disgusted look on her face. "Her bf is taking pics of her."

"There's a pool here?" Rashan asked.

"Yeah, it's on the other side of the building," Nalini said. "Cathy and I saw it while we were jogging."

"The building's shaped like a T," Cathy clarified. "Like Tetris."

"We were just playing Tetris in the arcade room," Sylvania mentioned.

"Makes sense," Khassan said to Ricard. "Is that the gay sign? QAnon?"

"There's something going on," Ricard responded.

Taylor was shaking his head, but he said nothing. He took a hero with salami, ham, prosciutto with vinegar, salt, and pepper. Ricard kept it simple since he had over-eaten at breakfast—bologna and cheese with mustard and mayonnaise between rye.

"Bologna and cheese," Khassan said, looking at Ricard, but his gaze fluttered over to Rashan. "Isn't that what they serve in prison?"

"Why are you looking at me?" Rashan asked.

"Pretty boy. Figured you hadn't been."

"My dad did time," Rashan said. "Framed, though."

"Please, divulge."

"Maybe when the time is right. We have a story to tell, don't we?"

"Yeah, that's what they serve in the hole," Darnell said as he passed by. He had just reminded Pritesh and Hayley about lunch as he passed the pool while on his rounds. He intended to check out Hayley again but realized he might be too late in the game to triumph.

"So glad security has been in prison," Taylor said.

"Never said I did time, brother," Darnell responded. "Guess you'll keep guessing."

Taylor appeared embarrassed. Ricard seemed uncomfortable. Meanwhile, Hayley fluttered through the curtains in a bikini, dragging Pritesh with her. She took a sweet potato patty with green chutney, cucumbers, and sumac between wheat bread. But then she split it in two and gave the other half to Pritesh.

"Oh, how sweet," Lisa said to Andrea bitterly as Pritesh bit into it from her hand.

"Shit," Darnell said. "Eating out of each other's hands already."

A few of them packed freshly squeezed fruit juices in to-go cups as they prepared to travel to the beach. Olive had given them several options: walking or biking along a trail on the right side of Sagaponack Pond, or kayaking, canoeing, or paddleboarding on the pond itself, which led to a dock in front of the White House that fronted the beach.

For the most part, the guests traveled to the beach with their new friends. Andrea excused herself to work on her story. Lisa and Rashan took a walk. Taylor and Sylvania commandeered a canoe and talked Angela into sitting in the middle of it despite her fear of water—she wore a life vest. Ditto for Hayley and Pritesh—Pritesh donned the vest and did the rowing.

Khassan and Ricard, while trying to get bikes, ran into Cathy and Nalini in the garage. As Ricard marveled at Olive's extensive collection of fancy vehicles, Cathy began flirting with him. Ricard mentioned he did maintenance work on cars along with plenty of other part-time gigs.

"Everyone loves a biker," Cathy had mentioned to Nalini shortly before. "Daryl from *The Walking Dead* is a badass."

"Yeah, they're sexy," Nalini had agreed, not revealing that she had developed an immediate attraction to Ricard when she had seen him yesterday morning while he was parking his bike. That was before he had been cleared and she had been, briefly, quarantined.

The four of them biked to the beach, with Cathy and Ricard talking and laughing. Meanwhile, Khassan tried to speak to Nalini, but she only responded in brief quips.

At the beach, Pritesh took pics of Hayley against the waves, while Taylor threw the football around with Sylvania. He had been impressed by her rowing skills and learned she had been a high school and college quarterback before she had transitioned. She could still throw a mean spiral, that was for sure.

During a down period, they noticed Darnell, the security guard, flirting with Angela.

"You better get on that, darling," Sylvania told Taylor. "He's stealing your girl."

"I do like her," Taylor acknowledged. He and Angela had spoken briefly about how they agreed with the President's approach to Covid and saving small businesses.

"Who are you interested in?" Taylor asked. "No offense, but I haven't known many people like you."

"Trannies," Sylvania said in a mock tone. "I consider myself a 'her,' if that's what you mean."

"So, a man?" Taylor asked awkwardly.

"I could go either way. But it's all a joke, isn't it?"

Eventually, they joined a volleyball game with Khassan, Ricard, Cathy, and Nalini. Taylor saw that as an opportunity to ask Angela to join the competition with the intention of breaking up her conversation with Darnell, but Angela told him that she didn't want to play.

Taylor naturally took charge of the volleyball match, so much so that, despite shifting players after every game, his team won every time. Sylvania was the next best player, and Taylor made sure to get her on his side whenever possible.

Around 6 p.m., the attendees were summoned to the White House, where they were able to shower if they wished and change or rest in some guest and staff rooms that had been cleaned just for that purpose. Then at about 8 p.m., they sat at tables in a large space next to a pool that overlooked the beach. The sun was starting to descend to their left, but it was still fully light outside—the sound of singing cicadas was dying down as faded songs of the Eastern whip-poor-wills began to clash with cricket chirps. Fireflies began to appear, hovering around with infrequent flashings. Occasional mosquitoes buzzed around.

Cathy and Nalini rejoined Lisa and Rashan at their table. Apparently, the latter two had been chatting with the maids Maja and Zahra at a patio on the other side of the White House, near the pond, and claimed they had gotten juicy dirt on Olive.

"Apparently Olive's been a bad boy," Lisa whispered to Cathy with a wink, but she seemed to be primarily speaking to Nalini, the lawyer. "Fired a bunch of maids when Covid hit."

"Do tell," Nalini said. But then Andrea joined them too, a print-out in her hand. Apparently, Ares had driven her over from the Saggplex.

"I can't do phones," Andrea said. "Ares helped me print my story out."

"Well, maybe we'll talk about it later," Nalini said to Lisa.

The dinner was an orgy of Peruvian cuisine. Though Angela was of Ecuadorian descent, she was ecstatic but also easily critical, something Thiago and Abeo took with grace. Still, she enjoyed guinea pig with papa a la huancaina, which was boiled yellow potatoes in a creamy sauce. Others had ceviche, rotisserie chicken with aji verde, the spicy green sauce, salchipapa, or sliced hot dogs with French fries. The vegans had lomo saltado, the beef made with seitan, and quinoa salad, among many other offerings.

Rashan was complaining again about the lack of another gay man when Olive appeared, now dressed in a striped, purple suit with yellow tie.

~ DAY ONE ~
INTRODUCTION TO ANDREA'S STORY

Olive spoke from a mic that had been set up in front of the pool. "I hope you've all had a great day today. I am proud to introduce our first storyteller: Andrea Mendoza, heroic nurse at Elmhurst Hospital and first responder. She immigrated from the Philippines many years ago and now saves American lives. I believe she also lived in Hong Kong for a time too. In any case, without further ado, here's Andrea Mendoza!"

Andrea got up among another round of applause. She made her way up to the front of the pool, looking back to make sure she didn't fall in.

"Wow, I am so nervous. The first one!" she exclaimed, her hand shaking as she looked down at the printout. "Well, you might guess what my story is about, so I won't keep you waiting. Here it is!"

~ Day One ~
Andrea's Story
(*AKA "ON THE FRONTLINES"*)

This story is going to be about how ordinary people who work essential jobs stood up to this horrendous virus and tried to help people despite the incompetence of the Establishment.

You've probably heard about a Chinese American scientist who, before the virus was in the Kirkland retirement home, had figured out it was spreading in Washington state. But no one listened to her because our incompetent lying selfish President was already calling it the China Virus and no one was going to listen to someone who was descended from Chinese, and the CDC and the bureaucratic people were spinning lies too.

It's funny because in any society there is a class of people the privileged look down on even though, and maybe because, they are doing the essential work no one wants to do. I am from the Philippines, but I lived in Hong Kong as a maid to a rich family. Hong Kong Chinese people looked down on Filipinos and thought we were dirty. But we are what made the city run. On Sundays, we sat beneath the trains, bridges, and highways having a great time eating and partying. Because the other days we were working.

I bring that up to give you a basis for the rest of the story.

Nurse Beatrice

We are going to start with a nurse. This is not because I am a nurse but because nurses were on the front lines of the pandemic so it is good to have their perspective. I am going to call our Nurse Beatrice because it is a neutral, holy name, and it protects the innocent. She immigrated to America in her early 20s without a nursing background, but she worked hard to finish a college degree here and go through all the courses, tests, "training," and the ridiculous bureaucratic procedures an immigrant needs to complete to get on par with an American-born citizen.

Eventually, she became a CNA, or a Certified Nursing Assistant, and worked in the Neonatal ICU at Elmhurst. That's a prestigious job for a CNA—you are dealing with just-born babies so that is very heartwarming indeed.

However, there's also a lot of politics in nursing, so I'm going to explain the nursing hierarchy and Beatrice's situation before we get to our main drama.

An RN, or Registered Nurse, is a licensed nurse who has years of education and has passed the NCLEX-RN exam. A CNA has no license, but she is certified—she must take a nurse aide program and pass a test. CNAs are bossed around by the RNs and do a lot even though they technically should not. The Nurse Practitioners are on the highest level and make much more money than the Registered Nurses. This hierarchy causes bitterness, and you can only imagine the backbiting when there are babies involved.

Beatrice was quiet, honest, and straightforward. But a troublemaking Jamaican CNA named Claire was always trying to instigate the CNAs against the RNs and the Nurse Practitioners. Most CNAs like Beatrice would agree with Claire's complaints to her face, but only a minority followed her lead to disrupt activity. It was a union job, so they used passive-aggressive resistance: using sick time and vacation time, evoking seniority to do as little work as possible, and passing it on to the hardworking people like Beatrice.

Since she was doing much of the work anyway, and needed more money—bank account, pension, 401(k)—Beatrice decided to become an RN herself by going to school, completing a program, and taking the test. It was a Catch-22 as she needed to pay money for her education and testing with no guarantee she would get a higher paying RN job, but what else is new in America?

After starting her Clinicals, she realized that she needed to create a better relationship with her RN bosses, and their bosses, the Nurse Practitioners, who are not unionized and make their money based on their "performance" which basically means tricking their staff into working harder for less. RNs were kind of in the middle—they were unionized but also needed to please their non-union bosses without pissing off their union CNAs too much. Since she was going to be an RN one day, she thought she had to understand their mentality.

Her direct supervisor was an RN named Oxana, originally from Ukraine. When CNA Beatrice told her she wanted to take on a higher workload, Oxana was happy—every class here likes it when someone wants to join their ranks. It spurs loyalty and strokes their ego until it becomes a threat to them. Then it becomes a problem.

Oxana kept Beatrice working hard, thinking she would get promoted to RN once she was licensed. She had Beatrice complete evaluation and assessment plans, give IVs, and dress wounds. By the time Beatrice finished her degree, passed her test, fulfilled other requirements, and got licensed, two years had passed.

During those two years, two RN openings in Neonatal were filled by outsiders. Unbeknownst to the newly licensed Beatrice, one RN position was about to open due to retirement, but by now Oxana's thinking had changed, and she preferred to hire a distant relative from Ukraine.

Oxana thought her relative would be easier to control as she was ignorant of union rules, plus she spoke Ukrainian and Russian so they could communicate without others understanding what they were saying. More importantly, Beatrice was admired by Oxana's own supervisor, a Ghanaian Nurse Practitioner named Kosima, so Oxana thought that Beatrice might ultimately displace her.

To get rid of her, Oxana told Beatrice about an RN opening in the general ICU. She called Human Resources, and an ICU Nurse Practitioner named Carol, talking up Beatrice's skills.

Human Resources departments tend to not be well-organized. They often post jobs that don't exist and take them down just as fast, or they call employees up to offer random jobs they've never even heard of, let alone applied to. That's what happened with Beatrice—she had heard horror stories about the ICU, so she was hesitant to apply, but an HR rep called and convinced her to interview for the newly posted position. She ended up applying by the closing date. As usual, the interview was just a screen, and the panel already knew who they wanted. Carol, the other Nurse Practitioners, and HR were so pleased by Beatrice's rep as pumped up by Oxana that they gave her the job despite a weak interview.

Nurse Beatrice in ICU

Once she got to the adult ICU in January 2020, Beatrice realized that the environment there was very different than Neonatal.

Even though she had worked in Neonatal ICU for years, newborn babies rarely passed away. In the adult ICU, patients died all the time. The pace was much faster too, and they worked closely with the ER, their primary pipeline for patients.

Becoming a supervisor only increased her stress. While she had studied Oxana and Kosima's tactics, she found being in that position was quite different. She had to learn a whole new set of skills to be a fair and effective supervisor, and the political situation was the opposite of Neonatal.

The CNAs here, especially her favorites, Mihai and Euna, were gung-ho. There was no other choice in ICU, so she didn't have to motivate anyone or deal with subversive idiots like Claire. But more people meant more problems and personality conflicts were abundant.

Mihai and Euna would constantly joke around and even pretend to be sexually attracted to each other, tapping bottoms and all the rest (out of the "vision" of supervisors, of course), and they would get each other Christmas presents even though neither was religious. Last Christmas, Euna got Mihai a toy giraffe since he complained about being short, and Euna received a toy koala bear mother and daughter because she didn't have a boyfriend or kid. But the two would fight like hell when it came to scheduling vacations: Mihai liked to visit his native Romania and Euna preferred cruises to the Caribbean (despite being Korean American and born in Seoul, she had never been to Korea after immigrating as a little child and didn't want to return).

Winter and summer dates, long weekends for barbecues and weddings, it was all in play, and sometimes Beatrice felt like a referee—they both had the same date of hire, so they fought over who had seniority—Euna claimed first dibs because she was slightly older and had allegedly put in her paperwork first. They were also competitive about doing things correctly at work. Still, Beatrice felt lucky to be able to delegate in an environment where staff was happy to do other people's jobs and often did them without being asked, even though that could potentially get her in trouble.

She adjusted, and within two months, she was an effective though awkwardly aligned member of the rapid response team. She relied on Mihai and Euna's judgment, and they relied on her leadership. This was her situation when the city changed in early March 2020.

Normally the ER would get a few hundred patients a day and ICU would admit a fraction of that. Car accident victims and patients with cardiac arrest were the norm. When they heard about the outbreak in the nursing home in Kirkland, Washington in late February, they began to talk about whether the new disease could possibly, unknowingly, be in the city.

However, the hospital administration offered no guidance, so while many workers wore normal PPE, including N-95 masks, gloves, and light gowns, they weren't required to and had no protocol about it. Still, Beatrice took the lead and told Euna and Mihai to suit up, and there were no arguments from them.

The first suspicious cases were rushed in with high fevers, dry cough, and shortness of breath, often progressing to pneumonia-like symptoms. However, Covid testing was not rapid then, so they isolated the patients in ICU, testing and treating them as well as they could, usually with antibiotics to make sure the disease didn't get worse. If the patients had trouble breathing, they used Bi-Pap machines, often employed for sleep apnea, but if the patients clearly could not breathe on their own, they progressed to using the few ventilators they had available.

One day in early March, an eighty-year-old man living nearby in Elmhurst was admitted with a fever, cough, and shortness of breath. But, while transferring to ICU, he suffered cardiac arrest. Dr. Sullivan McCanny started CPR with the help of Nurse Beatrice and her team, but they were unsuccessful, and he passed away.

The body was isolated and tested for Covid, but that would take time. Meanwhile, more patients were admitted. A young man in his 20s, a pizza delivery man, was riding his bike when he was side-swiped by a bus—his leg had been sheared, requiring IVs with fluids and antibiotics, blood transfusions, closing of the wound, and a central line. But when Mihai suggested to Dr. McCanny that they scan his chest, they discovered pneumonia and opaque-looking lungs. Again, he was isolated and tested.

The normal influx of ICU patients kept coming, but a week later, the volume started to get worse. Dr. Sullivan McCanny and her fellow ICU physicians began to worry that they didn't have enough ventilators, BiPap machines, and PPE to keep up.

Mihai and Euna expressed the same concerns, and Beatrice relayed them to Nurse Practitioner Carol. Meanwhile, Carol told Beatrice that the administration was planning to cancel all planned vacations coming up (Mihai and Euna weren't too happy about that, as they lost money on their scheduled trips abroad) and Beatrice was already struggling with sick leave callouts (but not from Mihai and Euna—they had to pick up the slack). The mayor had just announced that schools and all non-essential businesses were to be closed. Cruise lines and many flights had been canceled too. The city, the country, and much of the world were going into lockdown, and ground zero was about to be Elmhurst's ICU. Lucky Beatrice.

Doctor Sullivan McCanny
(*from her point of view*)

What first got my radar up was the pizza delivery man sideswiped by a bus that veered into the unprotected biking lane. Here was a guy in a relatively minor traffic accident, who needed all the typical ICU treatments like a central line to administer vasopressors to get his blood pressure up, blood transfusions, antibiotics, and the stitching of a wound. I know that doesn't sound minor, but we deal with this stuff all the time. I usually order all tests, so we did a scan of his chest and discovered this random man in his 20s with a leg injury had lungs looking like the eighty-year-old who had just passed away. Later we received the test results. He was positive for Covid-19.

By that time, the ICU had been inundated. People of all ages and ethnic backgrounds came in with symptoms from cough and fever to fatigue and stomach pains, to chronic pneumonia and shortness of breath. Soon the entire ICU was filled. We even had to keep patients on gurneys in the hallways. We made makeshift ICUs in other areas of the hospital, but the waiting room was still packed every day. Eventually, the ER stopped admitting anyone who didn't have symptoms, isolating the sick from their families.

Meanwhile, we developed a better testing regime that was faster than the original one for the pizza delivery man which took like a week (and which we had to ship out to a special lab). As I biked from my apartment in Sunnyside, I would see lines outside Elmhurst Hospital Center every day. People wanted to get tested for even minor maladies because any symptom could potentially become Covid. You could literally have no symptoms and still have the virus.

Given the high demand and short supplies, we started to tell people only to come in if they absolutely needed to because coming in could mean never coming out at all. But that was often a self-fulfilling prophecy because the longer someone waited for treatment, the more likely it would be that they would not survive the virus.

Patients started coming in even sicker and needing advanced care. The BiPap machines delivered oxygen to patients who had pneumonia-like or cough symptoms, but we started running out of them. Some patients' lungs were so weak that they couldn't breathe on their own, and the ventilators kept them alive. At one point we only had five ventilators left, and I knew that would last only a few days, if even that.

In addition, I became concerned with the lack of PPE we had, from N-95 masks to gowns, gloves, and shields. We had to protect ourselves in order to keep patients alive, and without equipment, we couldn't do either. The main problem was that we still did not know exactly how the virus spread, whether it was through respiratory droplets within six feet (or possibly more) or if it survived on surfaces and could be spread by touching orifices like your eyes. Protecting ourselves was of paramount importance so that we could keep our team motivated and coming to work to treat patients and save lives.

I emailed different members of the administration asking for additional ventilators, BiPaps, CPaps, and high flow machines, but I kept getting responses which asked how many we had left, how many patients were occupying the ICU, and other statistics meant to stall the process; officially, they were telling the public we were well-stocked. Meanwhile, the president and the CDC were repeating the same things: this was not a big deal; we would get out of this soon.

When I realized we would not get help, I contacted a local news station, which agreed to do a story on the situation at the Elmhurst ICU. I took an iPhone video, without showing faces or revealing identities, of the condition in the ICU, of patients on gurneys in hallways, the number of ventilators, the lack of PPE, etc. I told them I wore the same N-95 mask on successive days and that my staff did the same.

Once the story aired, it was picked up by larger stations and newspapers, which did their own segments on the situation. I told them I didn't care if I got into trouble for revealing the truth if it meant saving lives.

Suddenly things began happening. We started getting ventilators, CPap machines, and PPE from other hospitals. We started coordinating with them for future deliveries. Considering that we were all run by the same corporation, you would think this would have been done from the beginning.

Even the CDC, Surgeon General, and other administration officials started changing their tune. The only person who didn't change his tune was our President. But nothing can be done about him.

I was ready for a backlash by the administration for speaking out, which is what I heard usually happened in these situations, but the response to the coverage was so positive they couldn't dare. By this point, the public was appreciative of the "health care heroes."

Pizza Delivery Man
(about him after hospitalization)

The pizza delivery man was named Ricardo Torres. He was an undocumented immigrant from El Salvador who worked for a neighborhood pizza place. For generations, it had been run by an Italian American family, but they had moved to Long Island, and it was now operated by a Chinese family. He was lucky to work at that job full-time, and he would supplement his income through UberEATS at odd hours to provide for his wife and five children who had braved the harsh trip across the US-Mexico border.

He was making a routine pizza delivery to an apartment in Rego Park when he was sideswiped by a bus as they both entered an underpass; the bus accidentally swerved into the unprotected bike lane, crushing him against the wall as they both exited the tunnel. The bus driver, an African American man named Vernon Bodsworth, kept going and was later flagged down by the police. He explained that he didn't realize he had hit the man, and no charges were filed.

Ricardo had a large wound on his leg; it could have been much worse but since he was exiting the tunnel at the time, he was spared instant death. Still, life-saving support had to be administered by Nurse Beatrice's team.

But his opaque lungs and Covid diagnosis threw the staff for a loop. Contact tracing was just beginning at that time, and the sheer number of Covid cases made it difficult to discover origins. But this case was particularly disturbing, so it was reported to the State, which then sent it back to the City.

The City traced it to the Chinese family. Only the wife tested positive, but they all had to quarantine. It wasn't clear if she had given it to Ricardo or vice versa. She had not left the country in years, nor had he. When they tested Ricardo's family, his wife and one of his sons both tested positive. Somehow, they maintained a quarantine in their tiny apartment away from the other kids. Even though they were here illegally, the City shielded them from ICE.

The City reached out to the Chinese family's friends and other pizza delivery drivers. It took two months, but they traced it to a family that had visited Italy a week before. They had ordered a pizza. But who knows? Was a quick pizza delivery enough time to transmit it? The virus was all over the city at that point. Ricardo could have acquired it anywhere. Maybe they just needed to draw a conclusion.

Meanwhile, the federal government still did nothing about people bringing Covid into the country on airplanes. But either way, wherever he got Covid, Ricardo was in ICU, dying.

Since his lungs were weak, they had him on a ventilator via an endotracheal tube from his mouth, and they were infusing antibiotics, vasopressors, and steroids.

Ricardo was alone in his ordeal, but Beatrice, Mihai, and Euna tried to make his environment as homey as possible, even while dealing with Covid patients going into respiratory failure and cardiac arrest every hour. They decorated his room with balloons, teddy bears, and cards. On his birthday, they got him a cake and ate it privately on break, isolated and shielded by barriers in different sections of the dining area.

When Chef Thiago's non-profit began delivering meals to hospital workers so they wouldn't have to go out, Euna felt bad that Ricardo could only eat via the nasogastric tube, so even though he was sedated, she would eat her meals in front of him, waving her spoon at him as a psychological tactic, hoping that he would subconsciously want it enough to snap out of it.

With ventilators running low, Respiratory Therapist Sarmili, and X-ray Technician Marcos, each skeptical Ricardo would make it due to the progression of the disease and how dependent his lungs had become on the ventilator to function, suggested to Doctor McCanny and Nurse Practitioner Carol that he share a ventilator with another patient because his case was not likely to succeed. But Doctor McCanny had developed a sweet spot for him due to his unique case, so she decided to assign other patients to share while they waited for more ventilators to arrive.

Suddenly, Ricardo got much worse. He developed acute respiratory distress syndrome (ARDS), which occurs when the lung's air sacs, alveoli, fill with fluid, not allowing oxygen to flow to the rest of the body's organs. The ventilator alone wouldn't help him breathe at this point. Nurse Beatrice, a devout Catholic, took out her Bible and began reading him soothing psalms to ease his passage into the next life.

But Doctor McCanny had an ace up her sleeve. By mid-April, she had enough clout to place Ricardo on an ECMO machine, which functioned as an external lung, taking blood from Ricardo's heart, oxygenating it, and returning it back to the heart to send to his lungs and other organs. The ventilator stayed in place but was set low, so that it didn't put too much pressure on his lungs, allowing them to slowly recover to their former glory.

Since Ricardo was undocumented, he had no clear medical history, so it wasn't even known if ECMO would be a good option, but Doctor McCanny decided to take a chance—it was still only a 50–50 possibility that ECMO would succeed even in an ideal case. Only a few other hospitals in the country had tried such a procedure on a Covid patient, so an entire team of surgeons, physicians, and specialists became involved in his care.

Nurse Beatrice and her team were happy that Ricardo was given a chance to live, even though they were partially pushed out of the picture by the additional professional attention on him.

The Bus Driver
(*the guy who got away*)

Meanwhile, Covid patients on gurneys filled the hallways. Some patients would, unnoticed, wake up from comas and naturally take off their oxygen masks, then head to the bathroom and die—sometimes they would be found an hour later, documented as "bathroom codes." Euna and Mihai felt terrible about this, but they could do nothing. Most other CNAs were out on sick leave, and they were overwhelmed.

Then Vernon, the bus driver who had sideswiped Ricardo, ended up in ICU himself with Covid.

Directly after being questioned, released, and passing his two-week paid administrative leave, Vernon was driving a city bus when a passenger boarded, maskless, and coughed directly into his face. Vernon asked him to leave, but the customer had stayed maskless until his stop, and Vernon, as usual, had no way to force him out. In fact, he could have gotten in trouble if the spotters noticed anything askew in his route.

But after his shift, Vernon posted a now famous video where he complained about how "people don't care" about the quarantine and mask policies, nor about their fellow human beings. He didn't mention hitting Ricardo, though he had privately expressed regret to Ricardo's family even as he had blamed Ricardo during the investigation, saying that he had carelessly swerved into the bus lane.

In the video, Vernon also complained about people at his local basketball court in East Elmhurst playing maskless, without social distancing, which ultimately spurred the NYPD to remove the baskets. That did stop people from playing basketball, but it didn't make people follow the rules.

A few days later, Vernon began developing symptoms, waking up to extreme fatigue and a major cough. He was rushed to the ER by paramedics, then given a CPap machine and placed in ICU's hallway while awaiting admittance. A few days later, after enough people had passed away, he was admitted to ICU and placed on a ventilator.

At first, Nurse Beatrice and her team didn't realize Vernon was the one who sent Ricardo to ICU, but even with endless, exhausting days, gossip traveled fast, and then the media got wind of it too. But though they felt conflicted, even angry, the staff couldn't treat Vernon any differently.

Their attitude changed as they got to know the family. Vernon's wife called Nurse Beatrice to get updates, and after her quarantine ended, she and Vernon's entire extended family began coming to the street across from ICU. Nurse Beatrice, Mihai, or Euna would come to the window and post signs about his progress, and the family would respond by asking specific questions, which the nurses would answer in kind.

About three weeks after he was admitted, Doctor McCanny and her team thought Vernon was improving, as his lung scans showed less congestion than Ricardo's did during the same period, and they considered taking him off the ventilator.

But the day before they were scheduled to remove it, Marcos informed Sarmili that Vernon's scan showed that the congestion had progressed. Only a couple of days later, Vernon developed ARDS, but because of his history of medical conditions including diabetes, high blood pressure, and cardiac stents, Doctor McCanny wasn't confident enough to put him on the ECMO machine and hoped that an experimental steroid and antibody treatment would work instead.

Unfortunately, Vernon was too far gone, and he passed away the next day. Euna held up a sign to the family that he was finally at peace.

The General Picture

The days wore on. Every day people were lost, every day they were replaced by others on ventilators or life support. The hallways were still filled with people on BiPap and CPap machines, and the staff was exhausted but still pressed on.

There was little Mikala Jackson, only eight years old. He was one of the first to develop the severe reaction called Multisystem Inflammatory Syndrome that some children got from Covid, at a time when most people didn't believe children could get Covid at all. His organs became inflamed, and so did his skin and eyes. He died shortly after being admitted to ICU.

His little body was placed in one of the refrigerator trucks outside the hospital, which was our makeshift morgue, where he remained for two weeks while his mother and stepfather made the necessary arrangements to have his body marked for transportation to a funeral home. They were in quarantine and had symptoms themselves, making the situation even more difficult.

Burying him was another story. All the funeral homes, mostly located in Middle Village, were backed up, and it took weeks, sometimes months, to get a proper burial with only socially distanced immediate family members allowed to attend. That was for the lucky.

The unlucky, who were not claimed or even identified, were kept in the refrigerated trucks for weeks. Then their bodies were placed into simple wooden coffins and given a letter-number identification. They were driven to the northern coast of Queens, loaded onto the ferry, and taken to Hart Island off the Bronx, to be buried anonymously in mass graves. The site had served as a mass grave for the forgotten, unclaimed, and dispossessed for hundreds of years, from previous epidemics like tuberculosis, the 1918 flu, and AIDS.

Nurse Beatrice and her team lost several unidentified and unclaimed patients. The one that haunted her the most was a homeless man in his forties who held onto a rosary even as he was wheeled into ICU with severe bronchitis. Doctor McCanny and her team tried to save his life by performing CPR, and he lasted a few hours in ICU. Nurse Beatrice, with gloved hands, twirled the rosary for him and said her prayers as he passed away.

One of the ER staff told her that he had whispered his name was Thomas before being sedated. Nurse Beatrice told Jerrie and Chevron, the men who carted him away, who carted them all away, but they said the body had no paper identification, so they had to give him a number until he was claimed. They did put "(possibly Thomas)" on the tag. Ultimately, he was buried on Hart Island with the number, not the name.

A woman with feces wiped on her face was rushed into the ER, then ICU. She was screaming for Rihanna and Chris Brown to save her as she violently shook from chills. Her cough wasn't too bad, but Covid had apparently gotten to her brain—the chills led to a horrible fever that caused her to vomit her internal gastric secretions, and aspirate on them, despite the efforts of the staff. She looked to be in her thirties, but Mihai surmised this was due to bodily abuse and she could easily have been in her twenties. She was also buried in an unmarked grave on Hart Island.

A successful Bangladeshi American hedge fund manager in his forties named Naeem had severe fatigue causing almost total immobility, though his cough wasn't terrible at first. His wife began calling Nurse Beatrice and told her that they had just bought a two-million-dollar home in Dix Hills out on Long Island and were set to move when he became afflicted. They had three children, and it wasn't clear what they could do now.

Ultimately his lungs deteriorated, and he had to be placed on the ventilator, but that might have exacerbated his condition so that by the time he was placed on the ECMO machine, it was too little, too late. They seriously considered allowing his wife inside ICU, suited up to the total degree, for a last goodbye, but the Administration rejected the request at the last second. Once again, he died with Nurse Beatrice, Mihai, and Euna at his side, with Beatrice giving the bad news by phone, and Mihai the sign to his extended family outside.

Home Life

It was exhausting—all the patients, all the deaths. The nicknames staff gave to patients, sometimes their only identity, didn't matter much. Soon the patient was dead and shipped away.

After completing a shift, Beatrice and her colleagues would shower with disinfectant and take off their PPE carefully in the same pre-planned way, making sure each piece—shield, mask, gown, cap, gloves—were removed in the right order so they wouldn't be infected. After a while, they had enough supplies that they didn't have to wear the same stuff again the next day. But they still carried the nagging worry that they could contract the virus themselves.

Beatrice and her team worked the early morning day shift—Tuesday, Wednesday, Thursday, 6 a.m.–6 p.m.—so at the beginning of the pandemic she would reach home in Maspeth around 7 p.m. when all her neighbors would hit together their pots and pans letting her and the other essential workers knew that their work was appreciated.

Her husband was an RN at a Jamaica hospital. They decided at the beginning of the pandemic that the kids, nine and seven, would be safer living with their aunt and uncle in Connecticut, and they would videoconference with them at 8 p.m. every night.

Beatrice and her husband lived in different parts of the house, used different bathrooms, and separated the kitchen, even half the stove, with a curtain. Sure, it was a little extreme, but they felt better about it, and their only contact was the video conference with the kids at 8 p.m. This strained their relationship, and that was before they were forced to work longer hours.

Eventually, the virus began infecting more staff. Two nurses on the night staff called out. Carol and the other Nurse Practitioners were told by their bosses that shifts would have to be combined. Beatrice, Euna, and Mihai began to work sixteen-hour shifts, sometimes even longer, depending on call outs. Sometimes they would be called in on their days off too.

Nurse Beatrice and her team didn't have much of a choice—they knew they were in a war against an invisible enemy and that they were the soldiers on the front lines. They began hearing reports that, in other states where Covid rates had temporarily fallen, hospitals were closing, and long-time staff were being laid off, since there "wasn't enough to do" and not enough money, even though the administrators seemed to be eating well.

What else is new in America? But that was reason enough for them to put up with long hours. They were paid overtime for their trouble, but it was exhausting, and they knew they could ultimately lose their jobs even after heroically risking their lives for their fellow New Yorkers.

Around this time morale was falling—our incompetent President was talking about injecting disinfectant into people and preemptively taking a drug that had no proven effectiveness against Covid while his team of medical experts slavishly looked on. Still, the declining Covid rates and the Firechat-style leadership of our Governor kept up hope.

Beatrice would get home around midnight sometimes, exhausted, fall into bed and wake up the next morning for another shift. Sometimes she would sleep in the hospital, like the Resident doctors. She had become an RN for the money, yet the additional education had only put her in more debt. Now it was all about the mission, and nothing else mattered.

Nurses began returning from quarantine, sometimes too soon. The normal quarantine length was fourteen days at minimum, but nurses on other shifts were returning sooner. Beatrice became suspicious. Was the administration forcing them back to make up for low manpower? At the same time, other RNs and CNAs were calling out sick too, so their shifts weren't getting any lighter.

And soon her own staff was about to be afflicted.

Euna's Illness

One day Beatrice noticed Euna coughing, and she advised her to go to the lobby to get a test—by now they were free and relatively rapid for staff. Euna resisted, saying she needed to tend to her patients. But later in the day, her coughing became worse, and even through the mask and shield, Beatrice could see her skin had paled.

Beatrice insisted Euna go home. Euna did go downstairs and got the test before she left.

Euna was out for several days. Then she called in, saying that the first test was positive but that she was feeling better and had been cleared to come back to work within seven days if her symptoms disappeared. Beatrice asked if she had to get a negative test first, but Euna said it wasn't required.

This shocked Beatrice. The normal quarantine time for Covid exposure was fourteen days—that was true even for people entering from a state or country with high rates of Covid-19. Yet Euna was only given a seven-day quarantine and told she could come back without a negative Covid test.

Beatrice checked with HR, and they told her the same thing. She loved Euna but hoped she wouldn't expose the rest of the staff to Covid. Mihai expressed his reservations too but acknowledged it would be great to have Euna back—they were stretched thin and could use all the help they could get. Doctor McCanny and Nurse Carol were also skeptical, but Nurse Carol didn't feel she could complain. Doctor McCanny would have, but was too busy.

On the day she was meant to return, Euna called and said her condition had worsened—she was feeling major fatigue, and her cough had increased. Beatrice was secretly relieved. She told her to rest and feel better.

But Euna deteriorated. She became too weak to get out of bed. Her roommate Matt would check in from behind her bedroom door in their cramped apartment in Woodside.

Matt contacted Euna's parents in Douglaston. Her mom decided to move in and let Matt live in their basement until Euna got better. But as soon as Euna's parents and brother Joon got to the apartment, they realized the situation was too dire to care for her through a door. They decided to call 911.

Euna was rushed to the Elmhurst ER, where a scan revealed that her lungs had developed a fungus infection, probably aspergillosis, and there was some atelectasis, or partial lung collapse. They also noticed blood clots—her right leg had turned blue, possibly associated with a cut she had suffered.

They immediately placed her in ICU, put her on IV antibiotics, and tried to treat the infection on her leg, but it seemed the spread had put her in septic shock. The only way to save her life was to remove the leg through surgery.

Doctors had to place her in a medically induced coma. The day before the surgery, Beatrice and Mihai visited Euna. It was early in the morning, preceding their long shift, but they were determined to give Euna support. Each held one of her hands. Mihai even brought the koala bears that Euna had left in her cubicle. He told her he would take care of them like his own kid if she got better.

That night, when Beatrice got home, she spoke to Euna's mother. According to her, Euna never had any medical problems. She had been a perfectly healthy woman in her late twenties. Despite being a different type of Christian, Beatrice prayed with Euna's family on speakerphone. Then she cried through the night, hoping Euna would make it.

The next morning, after several hours of surgery, Euna's right leg was successfully removed, but she remained in a coma while the doctors decided what to do about her lungs. She was now on a ventilator. They considered whether to remove one of her lungs too if it didn't heal, or to place her on the ECMO machine.

Beatrice couldn't believe she was now taking care of one of her own. Her spirit was nearly shattered after all the hardship and travail. She wondered if she could make it through her shifts. But she prayed with her rosary every night and tried to avoid the news about our President.

The next morning, she sat with Euna and began to pray for her. As she was singing a Biblical song, Euna's finger twitched. Then one of her eyes opened slightly. Beatrice called her name.

"Euna! Euna!" she whispered. She called to Mihai, who rushed over too. Euna moved her eyelid again a bit. Then the other eye opened. Her other finger moved too.

Nurse Carol and Dr. McCanny advised Nurse Beatrice that it was ok to lower Euna's sedation. Once fully awake, she was aware of her surroundings but still was too weak to move. Her muscles had started to atrophy due to the bed rest.

They extubated her and placed her on the ECMO machine.

"If she makes it," Doctor McCanny said, "or that is, when she does, she'll have a long recovery process ahead of her."

But Doctor McCanny was just being positive. There was no guarantee she would live. But they hoped Euna would be like Ricardo and not Vernon.

Ricardo's Comeback

Because Ricardo had survived, he was now Covid free, awake from his medically induced coma, and off his ECMO machine. In fact, he had been admitted to a medical floor and was placed on the long regimen of physical therapy he would need to recover fully. The virus might have left his body, but it had left destruction in its wake, plus weeks on the ECMO machine and the ventilator meant that his lungs were weak and would take time to function fully on their own.

Even sitting on the edge of the bed was a major task for him; once he was able to do that, going to the bathroom still required a walker. Then he had to learn to dress and feed himself and walk continuously for several minutes on his own.

Initially he would be out of breath fairly quickly. He shifted from a wheelchair to a walker; he alternatively tried squats, weight lifts, and climbing steps. After several weeks, he was able to walk down a hallway for several minutes and climb a few stairs before giving out. That convinced his therapists he was well enough to be discharged, though he would need more therapy and training at home to be anywhere close to where he was prior to hospitalization.

Doctors, nurses, physical therapists, surgeons, x-ray technicians, occupational therapists, and countless others who had helped him lined the hallway as he was wheeled out of the hospital and into the waiting arms of his wife and children. He stood, hugging them in front of the cameras, despite the potential threat of an ICE raid. Nurse Beatrice, Carol, Mihai, and Doctor McCanny were there briefly to cheer him on, before returning to their other patients.

Euna's Transplant

The surgeons consulted with several lung and heart specialists before deciding a double-lung transplant would be best for Euna. Given the poor state of her lungs, it was unlikely she could recover to Ricardo's level without one. Euna's mother made the difficult decision to have the surgery to give Euna the possibility of a normal life once she recovered.

They would need two healthy lungs from someone with a similar body size and matching blood and tissue types. Most potential donors would be brain dead or recently deceased. The lung transplant team entered her information in the database with all her specs and waited for a match—and for her turn to come up.

It usually took several months for a donor to be located, but her situation was dire, so she couldn't wait too long.

Thankfully, she matched with Heather, an African American girl in Philadelphia who was brain dead after a fall had cracked her skull. But there was a catch—Heather was classified as an increased risk donor since she had Hepatitis C, and Euna could be infected if they went ahead with the transplant.

Euna's mother decided to reject the lungs and wait for another donor, saying it would defeat the purpose to infect Euna with something else.

By this time, Euna was Covid negative, out of ICU, and admitted to a medical floor. She could speak a bit, but the virus had taken its toll, and she still couldn't get out of bed or even sit on its edge like Ricardo had. Beatrice and Mihai would visit her before and after their shifts, each bringing a different set of balloons each day to adorn the tables next to her bed. Mihai would show her the koala bears, and even the giraffe she had bought him, which he had never brought home.

Doctor McCanny had been fighting for Covid survivors' relatives to be able to visit them after they were Covid-negative and out of ICU, but this had still been rejected by the administration. However, Beatrice and Mihai hatched a plot to have Euna's mother visit her while wearing the full regalia that nurses did, without the administration's knowledge.

They snuck her in through a back staff entrance, dressed her up in a gown, cap, double masks, shield, and gloves, and brought her to the floor. As they neared the room, they heard the roar of the flatline. Within seconds a team of doctors and nurses surrounded Euna, trying to revive her from cardiac arrest. Wailing, her mother tried to run to her, but Beatrice and Mihai held her back. She crumbled as she realized her young daughter was lost. She was only twenty-six years old.

Mihai and Euna's Family

A week after Euna passed, Mihai took Beatrice aside and, through heavy PPE, asked for a leave of absence, claiming depression. Nurse Beatrice informed Carol, who refused to grant it, telling him they needed everyone on the floor. Without bothering to give a two-week notice, Mihai quit.

Beatrice needed to assemble a new team of CNAs. But by now, the Covid cases were decreasing due to the lockdown, so while the situation was still busier than usual, it was also more manageable.

At this time the administration told the staff they would get paid vacations to different places in the USA, including free airline tickets and hotel stays. But there was a complicated way to redeem this offer online and a separate payment for taxes due to the complex laws on the books. And the bosses still weren't granting time off due to Covid, so it was another Catch-22.

Mihai went to his native Romania for a few weeks, then returned to the U. S. While the state had a quarantine policy upon return from foreign travel, no one at the TSA or Customs told him about it.

Then Mihai tried to reevaluate what to do with his life. Beatrice urged him to return to service, saying she would gladly convince Carol to reinstate him, but Mihai told her that part of his life was over. He went on unemployment benefits (he claimed he was laid off), spending his time streaming TV shows, listening to audiobooks, and singing along to songs on Spotify.

Delayed by almost two months due to the backup at the funeral home, Euna's funeral was about to be held at Flushing Cemetery, and it would be limited and socially distanced. Euna's mother asked Nurse Beatrice to invite Mihai. She reached out to him—he was reluctant to come, but she emphasized that it was the last time he would get to see Euna above ground.

Neither Beatrice nor Mihai could hold back tears as Euna entered the earth. Afterwards, outside the cemetery, Mihai connected with Euna's brother Joon. They talked about sports and TV shows. Joon told Mihai that he had been playing a lot of basketball since Euna's death, even though it was essentially outlawed to play close to people.

A day later, Mihai decided to meet and play Joon at a park in Douglaston. They both wore masks at first but soon ditched them. They started playing with other guys and eventually Euna's former roommate Matt, still living in Euna's parents' basement, decided to join too.

Mihai no longer cared about his own health or protection, and Joon had adopted a similar philosophy, but for a different reason. He was a serious Christian, unlike his free-wheeling sister, and while he had initially followed the quarantine mandates, ultimately God decided who lived and died—he wouldn't abide by Man's dictates on how to behave.

His goal was to convert Mihai and save his soul. Mihai was technically an Orthodox Christian, but he didn't practice his faith. Joon began to talk Mihai into becoming an evangelical Protestant.

Joon was studying to be a pastor, and he had a young, attractive Korean American friend named Karen who would come to the basketball games to hang out, watching the men play while listening to Korean Christian music on her headphones. Joon noticed the way Mihai looked at her. One day, he told Mihai that if he wanted Karen, he would have to become a Protestant.

Playing basketball helped alleviate Mihai's depression, and he started equating Karen with Euna. He decided he might as well claim to become a Christian because he liked Joon and Karen's company and felt closer to Euna that way.

Joon invited him to a church meeting on a Sunday morning, in defiance of State orders, where Mihai began praying with Karen and their fellow young Korean Christians while listening to Joon's sermons—Joon was practicing to one day become an official pastor.

The sermons were like entertainment—interesting on the surface but mostly an escape from Mihai's secular life (Netflix and Hulu shows), and an excuse to be with Karen. He wanted to believe in some Higher Purpose, in the Gospel and to spread the word of God, but another part of him couldn't accept a God that had destroyed his friend Euna, a saver of lives. It didn't make much sense to him.

But Joon was not discouraged. He had successfully converted Euna's former roommate Matt, and he persisted on the mission. Although Mihai behaved like he was buying Joon's sermons, Joon could tell he was not totally sincere. Karen could tell that too—she wouldn't agree to spend "alone time" with Mihai at his apartment, relegating their courtship to brief conversations at the church and the basketball court. Joon was telling her to hold off from deeper dealings until Mihai's heart was converted, but meanwhile, Karen began having feelings for Matt and they started spending "alone time" with each other in Euna's parents' basement.

Mihai could sense things had changed between him and Karen, but he couldn't put a handle on why. One day after church, he confronted Karen, then tried to kiss her; Matt stepped in.

A scuffle ensued. Ultimately Matt revealed his love for Karen and asked Mihai to respect it. Mihai smiled, then punched Matt in the face. When the congregation tried to intervene, he fled.

Joon's calls to Mihai's cell phone went unanswered. The next day, Mihai's mother decided to clean Mihai's room, and she found him hanging from the fan in the ceiling. She tried to cut him down, but it was too late. He was dead, at thirty-one years of age.

Beatrice's New Struggle

News of Mihai's death hit Beatrice hard. She tried to distract herself by focusing on building her CNA team. The hospital said it didn't have money to hire new CNAs, so they were rotated in from other departments for a month at a time.

The first batch she got was from the Neonatal unit since they had slowed down—people were leaving the city and dying, so births were down (despite the large immigrant population that made the birth rate higher at Elmhurst than at other hospitals). Even new mothers with Covid who ended up in ICU were birthing Covid-free children who were soon discharged to spouses and families.

Beatrice was livid when she got Claire, the complainer and whiner. In ICU there was no room for laziness when death was at every turn.

From the first day, she was blunt with Claire, telling her there would be no forgiveness for error. Of course, Claire had already complained to the union, HR, Oxana, and Kosima that she did not want to be transferred to ICU, but she couldn't get the temporary transfer changed.

The situation had lightened from the toughest spring months of the pandemic, but people were still coming in with severe symptoms and ICU was still often at full or near full capacity.

Beatrice was still losing patients she cared deeply about, and she was still seeing Chevron and his new partner Tori carting away bodies to the refrigerator truck or the morgue. (Jerrie had contracted Covid and was recovering at Queens Hospital, closer to where he lived.) Often, Beatrice would cry on the nearly empty bus going back to Maspeth, traveling only with other essential workers or the occasional homeless or mentally ill person, trying to get through this situation with her soul intact. The only thing she had was her faith in God, but she felt that she was being tested for some legitimate reason she couldn't understand.

She certainly needed a good team to keep people alive.

At first, Claire wore her gear as tightly as possible and was hesitant to go all the way with tasks when dealing with Covid patients. The other transferred CNAs, Komora and Leah, whom Nurse Beatrice nicknamed the sorority sisters, behaved similarly.

But one day, when Claire was hesitant to change a recently deceased patient's bed, Beatrice had a fit. She asked Nurse Carol and Doctor McCanny to come around to reinforce the work order, and they did. Ultimately Claire and the sorority sisters realized they had no choice but to comply. They would never leave ICU unless they quit, so they had to work at full capacity, or at least as far as they were capable.

That wasn't enough for Beatrice or Nurse Carol, who were used to Euna and Mihai routinely doing RN-type tasks, like changing IVs, without asking, whereas these new CNAs stuck to their work assignments. They began to feel that the new CNAs were liabilities bringing down the level of care at ICU.

But when Beatrice ordered Claire and the sorority sisters to change IVs and give CPR, she crossed the line. The three complained to the union, and this time it seemed like the administration didn't want to take a chance with grievances. They realized that their staff, with all their losses, might have been burnt out, so they decided to make another switch. Now Oxana would be transferred to ICU since she had already supervised Claire and the sorority sisters, and Beatrice would be back at Neonatal.

In a way, it was a boon for Beatrice. Kosima admired her, and Beatrice was exhausted. She wouldn't have to deal with death daily. But she also didn't really want to go. She had gotten used to the hectic pace and the sense of duty at ICU. Yet the administration made it clear that if she fought the transfer, she could lose her supervisory position. Nurse Carol complained but to no avail—as non-union, she could be terminated if she pushed too hard. Even during Covid, the complainers won and the dedicated lost.

On her last day at ICU, Beatrice took her husband's car out to Flushing Cemetery, where both Euna and Mihai were buried, side by side, and placed their favorite animals on each grave—Euna's koala bears and Mihai's giraffe. She had kept them when the respective families had cleared out their stuff—in Mihai's case, he had never returned to his cubicle after quitting.

She knelt there for a long time, directly in between their graves, rotating her rosary as she prayed. Despite all the travails, the sudden, random, senseless deaths, and sad burials, she still chose to believe that God had a purpose for all this suffering and that there would be a meaning to it—that despite their sins and disbelief, she would see her beloved CNAs again when she passed away herself one day.

Then she made the sign of the cross on her chest. She got up to go back to her car. She would prepare for her latest assignment. For a new day outside ICU.

~ DAY ONE ~
REACTION TO ANDREA'S STORY

A long pause followed the conclusion of the story. It appeared everyone was waiting to see if it was finished. Finally, Khassan spoke.

"Man, that was depressing shit," he said.

"Reminds us of why we're here, at least," Lisa said.

"Powerful story," Rashan said.

"Just this Trump hate has got to stop," Taylor said. "The President did all he could to get ventilators to the hospitals."

"He also keeps saying the virus is just going to go away," Cathy said. "Well, we're opening up again but that wouldn't have happened if we hadn't closed down to stop the spread."

"You know, I was helping feed the hungry," Taylor said. "Food lines in New York City. It was unbelievable. I never thought I would see that in my life. In Afghanistan, in Iraq, sure. But in Queens?"

"I'm amazed you've been to Queens," Cathy said. "You know, my parents run a deli not far from Elmhurst Hospital. They get harassed every fucking day with people calling it the China Virus, saying that 'you people' brought it here. Just because of your favorite politician."

"Okay," Olive said. "I think that's enough feedback. Very powerful story, Andrea, thank you. Let's keep it going tomorrow."

"She doesn't get a Twinkie or anything?" Khassan asked. "Man, this sucks."

"Trump is a man of the people," Ricard said. "This suit, Taylor, is a fake though."

Cathy gave the middle finger to Taylor as she passed him and sat next to Ricard. Angela and Sylvania approached Taylor to console him. He initially brushed them off as he gave Cathy and Ricard the evil eye, but the triumvirate did walk back to the Saggplex together.

53

"You were a maid?" Maja asked Andrea, with Zahra close behind her.

"Yes," Andrea responded. "It was a good time in Hong Kong. Better than here."

They laughed. "There used to be a lot of us," Maja said. "Maids I mean."

"There's other stuff too," Lisa whispered. Her crew huddled and began to gossip anew, with Nalini taking notes.

~ Day Two ~

Cathy awoke and immediately checked if she was about to fall off the bed. This was her natural response when sleeping on her single bed in her Elmhurst apartment, where she had taught herself to rest in one position. But now she realized she was in a big, spacious bed. No more quick starts, for two weeks, anyway.

She got up quickly, put on her jogging clothes, and was about to run out the door to join her Asian sister when she saw the envelope on the floor. She had short nails, so she used her teeth to pluck the seal.

> Roses are red
> Violets are blue
> Stories need to be told
> And today that teller is you.

"Lame." She thought she could do much better. But then it dawned on her. She would have to prepare and tell an entire story in spoken word that night. That was her challenge to herself after taking a hiatus from slam competitions to focus on social work.

She immediately started cramming. What would her subject be? Were there any books that could help her? She had never told an entire story in spoken word. Was it even possible?

By the time she heard the call to breakfast, she had created a draft about her experiences with homeless and mentally disturbed People of Color. Those experiences mostly took place at her practicum at Elmhurst Hospital, which was near her parents' apartment. She realized she needed to change the location so it wouldn't be too similar to Andrea's story. She also wanted to check some resources, so she was happy when she was informed when entering the den downstairs that the breakfast would be held in the tea garden near the croquet court, which was on the other side of the Tetris "T" of the Saggplex.

She cruised through the library, making a note to return to check some titles, then entered the karaoke bar and the game room. After jogging past the pool and the shuffleboard court, she finally approached the tea garden.

"This feels more like the Hamptons proper," Taylor was saying to Andrea and Sylvania as Cathy found a seat next to Andrea and Rashan. Then Taylor continued a whole spiel about how he loved immigrants, but that illegal immigration was ruining the fabric of the nation by letting crazy people over the border. Angela seemed to be lapping that up.

"For your information, most crimes are committed by American-born citizens," Cathy shouted, to which Taylor rolled his eyes. Nalini came jogging in from the opposite direction, just as they had the day before, except this time Lisa followed a ways behind her, huffing and puffing.

"I guess you found a new jogging buddy," Cathy said.

"Where were you?" Nalini asked.

"Plotting my tale," Cathy said. "I'm next."

"Sweet. Well, honestly, I wish I was with you. The hippo couldn't keep up. I had to stop and wait a few times."

Lisa was still huffing as she approached and sat down.

"Have some lemonade, honey," Rashan said, putting it next to her. She flushed it down.

"I'm going to look like her again," Lisa responded, staring at Hayley, who was nibbling Pritesh's ears. "Jeez, get a fucking room."

Olive appeared. He was wearing all white, including a V-neck polo T-shirt and chino shorts. He held a croquet mallet in his hand.

"We're going to give you a taste of the good life this morning," he said. "A croquet competition. Two teams. Winners get an advantage at the next competition. And there will be voting during the storytelling tonight."

"How about yesterday?" Khassan asked.

"Andrea is a healthcare hero. I didn't think it was appropriate to judge her tale."

"Us mere mortals will have to be assessed," Taylor said.

"So how will that work?" Nalini asked.

"Well, each guest will have a vote," Olive said. "That's 11 people. They will either vote Yes or No in a secret ballot. If the storyteller gets a majority No, they will be isolated at the North Shore complex for the day. But they can return that evening to hear the next story."

"I have an issue with that," Ricard said. "Seems to reward storytellers who please the crowd rather than telling a truthful story that might not."

"I agree," Olive said. "That's why I beseech you to consider the quality of the tale when voting rather than whether you 'liked' it. But I guess we won't know for sure why people vote as they do."

"Is that enough of a punishment, honey?" Sylvania asked. "Why not just banish them from the house?"

"I told you; this isn't *Survivor* or *The Bachelor*," Olive said. "I'm not sending you out into a pandemic. You've had enough isolation for months that I don't think you want to spend even part of a day alone."

"I raise a glass to that," Rashan said, acknowledging Nalini. "As long as they're Covid-free, I'm happy mingling."

Thiago and the chefs rolled out the breakfast, which consisted of Indian snacks: uttapam; samosas with green and brown chutney; samosa chat which included chickpeas; sev usal, a dried peas curry with sev, onions, chutney, and an assortment of crunchy bites; pav bhaji, a thick vegetable curry served with a warm roll; and idli samba. For drinks, in addition to the usual array of coffee and espresso drinks, there were two blends of Yerba Mate, one from Brazil and another from California, along with classic chai with milk, and an assortment of chai tea bags.

Since the meal was fully vegetarian and partially vegan, no one should have had a problem with it, but for those who couldn't handle spicy food, a smaller sample of the breakfast from the day before was also laid out.

Ricard and Lisa made a strange couple this way, both opting for the bland "American" meal, and awkwardly getting up for it at the same time—Ricard once again piling on the scrambled eggs, and Lisa skipping the bagel for the oatmeal and almond milk, as she saw Hayley taking muesli, yogurt, and berries. Lisa grabbed some berries too.

Almost everyone else enjoyed the spicy breakfast. Pritesh made fun of Hayley for not being able to handle it. Hayley claimed she just wanted to remain healthy; Pritesh noted the meal was vegetarian.

"That doesn't mean it's good for you, Pri," she countered.

Olive allowed guests to pick their own teams but warned it wouldn't always be that way. So, Lisa, Cathy, Rashan, Andrea, and Nalini were on one team, while Taylor, Angela, Sylvania, Khassan, and Ricard were on the other. Pritesh and Hayley were not picked.

"Can't we opt out?" Hayley asked Olive. "I want Pri to take more pics of me. Maybe by the creek?"

"Why don't you play?" Olive asked. "You'll have part of the afternoon to do whatever."

They reluctantly agreed and split up, Pritesh on Taylor's team, Hayley on Lisa's team. Taylor was the only guest who knew how to play croquet, so he explained it to his team, particularly Angela, including the correct order of shots, roquets, and bonus shots, how and when to place your foot on a ball, and general strategies on hitting bonus shots. They had all seen it in the movies, a man standing behind a woman, holding the stick with her, teaching her to play it right. And that's what he did, playing that stereotypical role.

Angela seemed to enjoy the attention he gave her and told him she would need him to advise her on good business practices to make her recently reopened hair salon solvent. That was enough to cause Darnell, manning the security perimeter, to feel a little jealous.

Lisa's team had to learn from scratch, and they got better as the competition went on, but they were no match for Taylor's team, even as they took turns striking. Sylvania also caught on fast, as did Khassan and Ricard. Cathy played the best on her team, but Taylor's team won easily.

Olive announced that Taylor's team would get a bonus during

the next competition, a prize he didn't reveal. Next, they got a break before lunch. Hayley was a little pissed that Pritesh didn't give her a hand during the croquet competition, considering all the attention Taylor had given Angela, even though Pritesh explained that they were on opposite teams. She asked Micah, the security guard, for his assistance in keeping the Asian and Hispanic fishermen, who would often crowd the bridge in front of the complex, away from them while they snapped pics. Pritesh, upset by this request, went up to his room, leaving Micah to snap the pics of Hayley by the creek.

Meanwhile, an ornate Japanese fusion lunch was served near the pool, including oyakodon, a donburi rice set with chicken, egg, tofu, edamame, sliced scallions, and onions; a tuna, salmon, and avocado salad with seaweed, kaiware sprouts, and shichimi togarashi to kick up the spice; uni mazeman made with temomi ramen noodles, buttery uni (sea urchin), braised bamboo shoots, chive oil, and a locally caught Black Sea bass; chicken and beef teriyaki (made with premium Washugyu beef) served on a variety of rice dishes including garlic fried rice, basmati, jasmine as well as thick wheat noodles; an udon noodle dish with a gastronomically cooked egg yolk on top, along with tuna sashimi, grazed pork belly, sea urchin, mountain yam, and mekabu seaweed; grilled octopus; yaki tori; tuna tataki; five other types of sashimi and sushi; twenty types of special rolls; five types of maki including California rolls and Philadelphia rolls. They also had miso soup, mushroom soup, kani salad, and lobster salad.

There was a large vegan menu too.

All the guests tried to eat as little as possible, but Andrea and Lisa couldn't help themselves. Cathy had more discipline and quickly escaped to the library to do some research for her story. Khassan and Ricard went to check out some of Olive's motorcycles in the garage, while Lisa, Andrea, and Rashan decided to take a walk to the White House again to speak to Maja and Zahra about the revelations they had made the day before about Olive. But soon, it started raining, and they changed their plans, heading back to their rooms to dry off. Ricard rushed to put his motorcycle, which was parked out front by the main entrance, into Olive's garage, and the chefs covered the food and headed back inside.

Pritesh was in bed reading a news article about Indian politics when someone knocked on his door. When he approached the door and opened it, he saw it was Hayley. She was soaked.

"What, that Micah couldn't dry you off?" he asked.

"Isn't that your role, buddy?" she snapped back.

"I don't know, is it?"

She pushed him out of the way and waltzed inside.

"You could pretend like you care," she said, turning around. "You should have fought me when I said I wanted Security to come out. I mean you're the one who's supposed to protect me, not him."

Pritesh slammed the door shut.

"Of course, we're all supposed to be mind-readers. But you came crawling back, didn't you?"

She shook her head and smiled. Then she approached him and clamped her hands against his cheeks, her thumb massaging his lower lip.

"You know, you really should get an arranged marriage, you dumb weirdo."

They kissed. Ultimately, it became a ferocious kiss. Meanwhile, Nalini was in the fifth-floor den relaxing alone in her robe. She had just taken a bath in the Jacuzzi. Khassan was staying in the room next to her, while one room was empty since no one else had wanted to room next to the "quarantined girl." Ricard was staying on the second floor, but he was waiting in the fifth-floor den while Khassan got some playing cards from his room.

"You smell nice," Ricard said after Nalini had waited for what seemed like forever for him to finally say something to her, despite all her hints.

"Thanks. Just took a bubble bath in the Jacuzzi."

"I've never been in a Jacuzzi. Didn't realize they had one."

"Every floor has one. I could go back if you wanna try it."

"You're probably used to it. Being a suit and all."

Khassan returned with some playing cards, and the three played some poker. They each won one game. Soon they were called down to the den, where Olive revealed the afternoon activity, which was racquetball on the indoor court. Since Taylor's team had won the previous battle, his prize was that he got to choose who on each team would compete in this sport, as only two rounds were allowed with one player on each team competing. Taylor, of course, chose himself and Sylvania, who he considered the most athletic after him. But Khassan advised Taylor that he had played racquetball before, so Taylor changed his mind. Meanwhile, Taylor also got to choose who would compete with them—since the other team was missing Cathy, who was still working on her story, he chose Rashan and Andrea.

An additional wall was extended from the existing one to make it a true racquetball court—Taylor easily beat Rashan. Khassan had a harder time with Andrea, but he was triumphant too, so a final round was not needed.

"What's their punishment?" Khassan asked, somewhat giddy.

"Tomorrow morning the losing team will have to clean some of the rooms in the White House, where the staff lives," Olive said.

"No worries," Lisa said. "Andrea used to be a maid. And I want to help Maja and Zahra. They have a much larger workload since you fired their coworkers. Apparently, you had no problem sending a bunch of poor maids out in the middle of a pandemic."

A big silence filled the room.

"Who told you that?" Olive asked. "Maja?"

"I thought you loved your staff," Lisa said. "Instead, you did what every businessman does during a crisis. Consolidate and eliminate waste. Even human waste."

"It was complicated," Olive said. "I couldn't keep everybody. The stock market was crashing. I wasn't sure how my business would do. I didn't realize it would help my dating sites. And frankly, the terminated workers were liars. And traitors."

"Traitors?"

"Were they here illegally, or something?" Taylor asked. "I bet that was it."

"Was that it?" Lisa asked.

"I don't need to tell you," Olive said. "And if you don't trust the process ..."

"I know, I can go, right?" Lisa said. "Maybe I should."

"This whole thing has been sketchy since the beginning," Nalini said. "Like the discrimination against me when I got here."

Olive held up his hands. "Dinner is served in the dining room. Anyone who wants to leave, can. Good luck."

Olive marched out. Thiago, who had been listening as he readied dinner in the kitchen, gave a speech about how Olive was a good man.

"I'm on a contract here, and I certainly don't condone firings, but Abeo and Bom have told me that he treats his workers like family. If he had a reason to terminate people during a pandemic, then I trust his reasons were good."

Lisa and her crew went to the den, where Cathy joined them. She was excited about her story. She certainly didn't want to leave before getting her due.

"I say we stay to help Maja and Zahra," Andrea said. "Plus, I had a planned vacation; I don't want to go back to the hospital yet."

"Yeah, well, it's just more isolation for me until school starts, and then it's probably going to be hybrid teaching," Rashan said. "It is nice to be around people, even though there are no dating prospects here for my queer ass."

"I'm a blogger who quit her day job during the pandemic," Lisa said. "Makes no difference either way to me. But you have a point, Andrea. We can help the workers. Maybe even unionize them."

"Stay for my story!" Cathy urged, and they agreed. They went into the dining room, where Taylor and his companions were already seated around an ornate table. Hayley and Pritesh finally came down too, now hand in hand.

"Abeo and I are in competition," Thiago said, with the other cooks flanking him. "Abeo is Olive's long-time cook, whereas Olive asked me to come for this Getaway. I have important work to do on the frontlines but even I needed a vacation, and I figured, why not get a paid one?

"Tonight, I will give you one favorite ethnic spread of mine, and Abeo will go tomorrow. Personally, I went with a Swedish meal. As you may know, and if you've ever read *The Girl with the Dragon Tattoo*, the Swedes are a boring people, always drinking tons of black coffee and eating meatballs. Where I am from in southern Brazil, we have lots of Scandinavians. I dated all these Swedish girls when I was younger, and I can tell you, they are pretty and tall but not that exciting. So, we thought we would try to make the Swedish experience fun. It's ironic because Abeo has cooked in Sweden, whereas I've cooked in Denmark. Ares, I'll cook some Finnish food for you next time. Or, maybe, some other time..."

Ares winked and pointed at Thiago with mock indignation.

"First, we have a traditional Swedish meal, artsoppa, a pea soup with a little pork, and pancakes with lingonberry jam. Then Swedish meatballs in a creamy sauce with pickled cucumber and mashed potatoes. Reindeer, which they eat in northern Sweden and which we got imported from there despite the global supply issue, is served with chanterelle, one of Sweden's best mushrooms, fried with onions and sauce on a braided cardamom bread. We have pytt I panna, which is a fried egg on top of roasted and seasoned potatoes. A version of Jansson's temptation, which they also eat in Finland: it is a potato casserole with pickled sprats, or a kind of anchovy, along with onions, breadcrumbs, and cream. There's boiled and marinated crayfish with dill weed, served with sauerkraut, and, yes, more potatoes.

"For the vegetarians, we have: greve, hushallsost, and svecia cheese with knackebrod, or crisp bread, filmjolk and yogurt, muesli and blueberry soup. For the vegans, we have more pea soup without meat; a variety of fruit soups including rose hip soup; mixed carrot, potato, and rutabaga dumplings served with sauerkraut and lingonberry jam. There's also a Jansson's temptation without sprats or cream. For dessert, we have thin pancakes with mustard, new potatoes with pickled herring, chives, sour cream, and strawberries. There is also a smorgastarta, a kind of layered sandwich cake, but made with almond-based cream for the vegans.

"We have all the typical drinks and cocktails, along with

Swedish coffee if you would like, and an imported Mariestads beer from Sweden. I hope that satisfies you."

Once again Lisa tried to imitate Hayley's intake of yogurt, muesli, and soup but couldn't help trying the dumplings and pancakes. Ricard said he preferred to just have a burger and fries but tried the reindeer and thought it was weird. Khassan avoided the pork soup. Angela was unhappy with the bland nature of the offerings, but Thiago put some salsa sauce on her meatballs, so she felt better.

Everyone did eat heartily, after which Olive snuck in, wearing a navy blue robe.

"I see no one has left," he said.

"Nowhere else to go," Rashan admitted.

"Food brings everyone together," Thiago claimed.

"More info about the firings will be needed before a decision is made," Lisa stated.

"You won't get it from me," Olive said. "In any case, the rain has ceased, so I figure Cathy could tell her story on the patio, next to the fireplace."

They all went out into the patio. Ares let the roof and sides down so that the patio was open again. The air was cool, a welcome change from the heat and humidity of the prior days. Rabia turned on the fireplace, and everyone grabbed chairs and placed them around it.

Cathy stood on the side of the fireplace, perusing the notes on her phone, using her left hand to deflect fireflies while one of her legs shook nervously. To show solidarity with Andrea and other essential workers, she had put on an Elmhurst Hospital Center T-shirt that she had been given during a practicum there before the pandemic. She also wore short pink shorts and flip-flops. Her hair, normally shoulder-length, was tied back in a simple ponytail.

"Our second storyteller was one of the first to apply for The Getaway, and she caught my eye immediately," Olive said. "A first-generation Asian American, she is a child of immigrants from Taiwan and has been an exceptional student throughout her life. She just earned her bachelor's degree in social work will try to get her master's and ultimately become a clinical social worker, which is no easy task in New York City, or so I've read.

"She was born, raised, and still lives in Elmhurst, Queens, right by the Elmhurst Hospital Center, so like Andrea, she's seen the misery of the pandemic first-hand. She wrote in her application that she has worked with vulnerable populations, from the homeless and imprisoned to victims of domestic violence. I was also impressed by her background as a spoken word poet, and she's participated in national slam competitions. That's primarily why I chose her next for this exercise, the first to be judged. No pressure! Now give it up for second storyteller, Cathy Wei Quan!"

Olive receded to the side of the fireplace as Cathy awkwardly replaced him among applause from most of the crowd, though her friends were louder than the rest.

"Can everyone hear me?" she shouted as the applause died down.

Lisa, Rashan, and Andrea assented.

"Sorry, it's been a while since I performed spoken word, and normally I've got a mic." There was laughter from the crowd.

Rashan shouted, "Don't apologize, girl, just kill it!"

"Thanks, Rashan. I am nervous because I usually have more time to prepare. Also spoken word isn't really storytelling, it's more about evoking a mood and perpetuating a point, but I'm going to try to tell an entire story in spoken word, so bear with me. It might be a little rough, but I've got notes on this phone in case I slip up.

"I was struggling this morning with what I should focus my story on, given all the issues we've faced during this horrible pandemic. As Olive said, I have done practicums with vulnerable populations and studied some of the social consequences of the pandemic, so I do have insight into the disproportional suffering and death of African Americans due to Covid, as well as depression and domestic violence due to the lockdown. But unlike Andrea, I wasn't face-to-face with Covid deaths, something I feel a little guilty about as I was primarily forced to work remotely most of the time.

"All that said, I decided not to make those issues the focus of my story because I don't want to appropriate. There are other People of Color in our house, so they can address those issues if they want. Instead, my story, or poem, is closer to home. My parents are immigrants from Taiwan, and they own a deli in Elmhurst near my home. Sometimes I help out, which I've been doing on and off since I was a kid, and I've experienced first-hand the discrimination Asian Americans have had to face due to what our President disgustingly describes as the 'China virus,' because I've seen it and experienced it.

"And while my parents came legally, there is a significant undocumented population in Queens too, so I thought I would share some compassionate description of their lives because they are our hardest workers who are also our most vulnerable population of all, unfairly demonized, and they have the least voice in our society."

"They've also done the wrong thing," Taylor shouted.

Cathy's friends gave him a dirty look.

"Let her tell her story," Olive said, now standing in the back. "You'll have time to comment afterwards."

Cathy rolled her eyes but controlled her anger. She began her tale.

~ Day Two ~
Cathy's Story
(AKA "IMMIGRANTS UNITE!")

Illegal
A word
That cuts off
Speech
Illegal
A concept
That snaps off
Feet
Illegal
Why even say it?

Some will always
Blame others
For their problems,
Easier than pondering
The entire situation.
Illegal
A word without meaning,
Definition or feeling.
Illegal,
Let's kill it.

Now let me tell you a story
About a strong woman, Asian.
Is she that model minority,
Perpetual foreigner,

Bad Americans: Part I

Slanty-eyed best friend
Of a white chick on Hallmark
Stamped on a bamboo ceiling,
Floor mat of white victims?
That Asian? Not quite.

Forget your biases,
What do you think?
We're talking about
Some chink?
A mysterious beauty
Foreign but domestic,
Slippery but friendly,
That China girl who is the object
Of your desire, David Bowie?
Not quite.

She's her own woman,
College-educated,
A girl without boundaries
In China they call her Sheng nu,
Leftover woman,
Diseased and used,
A Choubi.
Nope.
She's not that either.

She came to the USA as a tourist
But she's no anchor baby whore
In China she was leftover,
Here she's reborn,
Pristine, educated
But undocumented.
That's the complication,
That's the predicament.

Is she scheming
On street corners
Talking weird men
Into dubious exchanges?
Nah, she's hustling
Making cheap car parts,
At an underground factory
Working for a fat Korean guy
Who hires Chinese chicks
Cuz he likes their asses.

I'm not making excuses.
Look at this situation.
Here's a beautiful girl,
Smart, promising,
Harassed at work
Raped in her hometown
Escapes to America,
Land of the Free,
Home of the Brave,
Looking for a resurgence.

How's she welcomed?
She's told she's not welcome.
So she's slaving in Flushing,
Another Brick in the Wall
Of the consumer economy,
Sleeping on the floor of a two-bedroom
With 15 of her coworkers.

Do you remember another time
When European immigrants
Did the same shit
Living in tenements
Ghettos too

Bad Americans: Part I

Nativists called them
Southern races
Well guess what?
Now they're the fucking racists.

She could have stayed in China
Lived in her own place.
Better, she was a princess
Nice apartment, good family
But she wasn't free,
Not in body. Not in mind.
She wanted a new life.
Now she's in a different type
Of Prison in the capitalist cycle.

Heteronormative, binary shit
Cisgender slavery.
Not a good fit.
Granted, it could be worse.
At least she's not in debt
Like those poor girls
From Central America
Crossing the Rio Grande,
Ducking among tall weeds
Avoiding wacko lone wolves
Waving guns and yelling God.
Acting like they own a country
That can't be owned.

I admit, she's privileged
Among the unprivileged.
She had a choice,
She made the plunge
Of her own volition,
But did she?

In China cops are everywhere
So are cameras
Your every move is surveilled,
Yes, you are documented.
Would you have a choice?

In America you should have a choice
And you shouldn't be controlled
Let's say this in a chorus:
Undocumented is Freedom.
Undocumented is the America way.

That definition is accepted
By the majority of Americans
But not by the vocal minority
Of Trump-supporting assholes
So now she's in a new slavery
Born of his zero-tolerance bullshit.

Sorry to bore you
With this political wit
But it's the menu of the day
Speaking of which
Let's return to our story.

Back at the factory
Around lunch-time
The fat guy called her
To his office
Because he can.
She's his slave
His meal of the day
He told her to kneel
And stick his ding-dong
Inside her mouth.

Bad Americans: Part I

Déjà vu, but in a new country,
That's why she escaped
In the first place.
She wasn't taking that shit
Fuck this, she bit it
Ran out, Flew away
To Flushing Creek.

Crying her eyes out
She couldn't believe it
Same bullshit as China
In the land of the free.
Staring at the water,
Not knowing what to do
Your own people exploit you
It's fucked up but it's true.

She couldn't go back
She couldn't stay here
No way she could win
She thought she would jump in.
Tell me, sincerely,
What would you do?

This is the crisis she faced
She was debased and erased
But it's the same shit faced
By undocumented people
From anywhere and everywhere
All over our country.
Put yourselves in their shoes.
WHAT WOULD YOU DO?

Now that I've got you riveted
I'm going to shift this shit

To another girl in this story
Call it Sister Sister 2
She IS that model minority
Perpetual foreigner,
Barbie Doll desire
Of every 60-something
White Man on OK Cupid.

She IS that over-achiever
American-born and weird.
Likes bubble tea and Hello Kitty
Perfect score on the SAT
Didn't need her mommy
To bribe the University
To get into an Ivy.

Cherise was her name,
Yeah, her parents were funny,
Wanted her to fit in.
Not even gonna tell you
Her Chinese name
Cuz you can't pronounce it.
You racist motherfuckers.

Sister was at Skyview
Aimlessly wandering
Bubble Tea in hand
She goes out for air
Along Roosevelt,
Under the Van Wyck
There's a girl crying
Staring at the water
Dead-eyed, desperate.

Bad Americans: Part I

Yeah, she looks like her
And she thinks
THAT COULD BE ME.
Anyone think that
Anymore at all
In our selfish society?
THIS COULD BE ME.

Cherise ran over
She calmed her down
Heard her story
Hugged her too
Wiped her tears
Talked her out
Of the Fall.

Told her to report it all
But the girl didn't want trouble
Didn't want to call the cops
She's afraid of deportation
A messed-up situation.

And by the way,
Cherise gave her a name.
Forget that Chinese shit
You can't pronounce it.
Call her Emily.
From now on
Yes, verily,
She has a name.
So show some respect.
Her name is Emily.
Cherise took her home
On the subway to Elmhurst
Put her in a basement
Her parents owned the building

It hadn't been rented out
Due to an asbestos problem
That had been fixed already.

She brought down bedding
Food and drinks too
Even bought a mini-fridge
From Target and a cold brew.

Cherise realized though
She couldn't keep her forever
She needed to out her
To her parents or someone else
Maybe get her a job
A hard-sell to a couple
Of Trump-supporting assholes.

I mean her parents
She loved them but come on
Immigrants from Taiwan
Hard-workers, Catholics
Own a deli and store
They sell trinkets for practice
Typical immigrant types
America First!
They did it the right way
Those postage-stamp Asians
You see on Life Insurance
Commercials on TV
During the Super Bowl party
Slanty-eyed foreigners included
For diversity purposes only.
That's who she needed to convince.
But she had some arguments.
She'd been on Speech and Debate
In high school, Specialized.

Bad Americans: Part I

Along with every other club
The well-rounded applicant.
That was the fucking rub.

You were renting the basement
Before asbestos—that was illegal.
You're taking money in cash too
Hiding your profits,
Like your favorite President
Who won't even show his taxes
And complains about the undocumented
Not paying their fair share.
What the fuck is the difference?

Plus, she could help out
Financially and morally too
Running the store
Another hand around
Is what you need
You can pay her less
Cherise already helped out
When one parent couldn't make it
Cutting into homework time.
So Emily working in the store
Would help Cherise study more
An education argument
Works every time
In an Asian household.
Doesn't it?

With this arsenal
Cherise made the reveal
Her parents weren't convinced
Ready to call ICE, even DHS!
Wait, Cherise said,

Meet her first
She's not scary,
She's a human being.
She looks like us.
She could be us.
She's escaping the CCP.
Just like you two.

Mention the Chinese
Communist Party
To a Taiwanese American
And you might get a response.
She took them down
Made the introduction
Her parents couldn't call
The Feds on this poor girl
A human being in front of them
She spoke Mandarin
She complained about China
She was beautiful
And she could work
They were convinced now
Let's try to make this work.

Still, talking in private,
Her mom was skeptical.
What if she takes our money
And runs to some other world?
Where would she go
Her dad asked seriously.
Canada? Mexico? Another deli?
Even the homeless drunk man
Who wanders into the store
Every morning can't make
His way back home to Mexico.
How can she?

They decided to take the plunge.
Sanctuary City score!
Everyone's doing it
So why not them?
They'll help someone out
It's what God wants now
So let's get with it.

Emily starts working in the store.
She's an immigrant,
She works hard there.
Shelving, helping customers
Register, inventory
You name it.
Everyone loves it.

Now the story takes another turn
Because a pandemic makes its return
Not since 1918 have we seen
A virus this mean
And it comes from China
Or maybe a CIA lab
Depending on who you believe
But people are willing to deceive
Themselves and others
If they could blame someone else
Whether it's undocumented or Chinese.

We've got the best scientists and doctors
But Republicans are still making elixirs
Churning out fake news and shitty fixers
Taking pills meant for other diseases
The virus is a hoax, don't believe it!
Masks under their noses, wearing no masks
No lockdowns, protesting a potential vax

Fucking morons, how dumb can they be?
Can we live in a society more free?

That's a joke, but seriously
They can't read so they watch Fox News.
CNN is too complex for their views
Forget MSNBC, that's tyranny
Don't get me started
On Trump's villainy
Supporting Putin
Praising white supremacists.
He's created this vortex
Through his stupidity.

Now let's get back to the story
The virus came to town
So smart people locked us down
But with caution comes consequences
Racism and xenophobia emerge
Everybody loved the model minority
Until the President called the germ
The China Virus in his first term.
Now we're the #1 enemy.
They want cheap prices from Asia
But tariffs too. You can't win.
But it's a-ok to pardon
Corrupt sheriffs in lieu!

The lockdown caused shortages
Even toilet paper was scarce
So where they gonna get that shit?
At the deli of course!
They lined up outside
Social distanced too
But you always got assholes

Who are stirring the brew.
Once inside they start shouting at you!
"You people brought it here"
"It's your fault"
"Go back to your country"
"Oh, I'm born here"
"Don't care, get me some salt."

It never ends
The perpetual foreigner
When will we be accepted
For the Americans we are
Three generations, four, five, six
Makes no difference!
You are how you look
And are we supposed to forget
The Chinese Exclusion Act
The Japanese Internment Camps
Lynch mobs in San Francisco
Laws helping the Irish
Most Americans are ignorant
Of our racist history
They say we're the model minority
But when things get bad
You see nothing's changed
The positives are just a fad.

Worse than these racist psychos
Are the people standing around
Doing nothing to help out
The victims of discrimination
They don't even frown
Maybe cuz they agree
We don't want to believe
Inside they cheer with glee.

Or the bystander effect
Like Kitty Genovese
And I know that's been disproven
But whatever, please,
Plus there are no cops
Take forever to come
And EMS busy carting bodies
Go to the hospital and the morgue.

One day Emily was shelving
Spices in the corner of the store
Customer asked her for more
She stood up and smiled
So happy to be working
His eyes were red and bore
Into her soul and he tore
A heavy cough right into her face
Like a smack of mace
She tried to cover herself
But it was too late,
It was all over her face
Even with the mask on
There would be a trace.

Customer pushed her into the spices
Called her a chink and a whore
Said he'd be back for more
If they called the police
It would be worse
A deliberate hate attack
A wretched curse
People stood around,
No one helped her up
Until Cherise's dad came over
They put her in a closet,

Bad Americans: Part I

Told her to wipe her face
Called Cherise up
She was on a Zoom call
Told them to isolate her
In the basement apartment
Until they got word.

Cherise slipped her food
Twice a day and once for fun
Hoping nothing would happen
But just as they feared
A few days later
She developed a fever
Violent coughing
Congestion, fatigue
The whole catalog of
Covid-19 disease.

Her parents didn't want
To call 911
Afraid they'd get tapped
But Cherise knew the law
They didn't have to hand
Her to immigration
This was a
Life-and-death situation
So she called EMS
They came several minutes later
And took her to rest.
Now you know the situation
The hospitals are war zones
No one allowed in unless
They are equipped for battle.
But Cherise was resourceful
She got the nurse's number

So she could text for updates
Plus she drew some pictures
Yes she could draw
Just like all her other talents
And every other day
She would text a pic to the nurse
To show Emily if she wasn't adverse.

And she'd hold up signs
From the street corner
Standing next to
Refrigerated trucks
Full of bodies
And long lines
For Covid testing.
Thanking the nurses for their work.
Those essential workers
The HealthCare heroes
We owe them our lives
Let's show them our support.

The main nurse
Was an Ethiopian woman
Call her Nurse Edna
She was loving and devoted
To the cause of life.
She was a Christian
But not in a bad way
I mean she kept texting
About God's love
It didn't creep Cherise out
Not right away, anyway.

She was Cherise's only
View to the inside

Bad Americans: Part I

And she told her
Emily got worse
Her lungs filled up
Got put on a ventilator
Cuz she couldn't breathe
On her own. Cherise cried
Thought it was the end
Edna said she prayed
Every day. Even Cherise tried
But couldn't get it up.

I emphasize this to say
All Christians aren't bad,
The ones who understand
The religion aren't sad,
In fact, they're glad
To help the unfortunate
As their religion dictates
And we should be mad
At the Evangelicals
Who have poisoned
Genuine faith.

Now all this stress
Was getting Cherise
Into a hot mess
I mean internally
With the lockdowns
And the social distancing
The online classes
The bullshit meetings
The store beatings

It gets to a person
I've noticed this

On my practicums
The negatives of lockdowns
Are true, depression
Domestic violence,
Bogus detentions
Of our most
Vulnerable populations.

Cherise handled this—
Tadda! Through dating apps
Thanks Olive
Ladies you know
We get a lot of attention
But good men are hard to find
Cherise talked to a lot of guys
IChat, WhatsApp, Facetime
Finally found a Taiwanese dude
Who seemed to have
The right attitude.

Around this time
The texts started
Getting better
Nurses gave a thumbs up
From the window screens
When Cherise lifted up
The thank you signs
And drawings.

Apparently, Emily
Received antibodies,
An experimental treatment
That worked in her case
She began to recover
And breathe without

Bad Americans: Part I

The ventilator
That Trump took forever
To deliver.

When she was finally released
Emily met her in the lobby
Wearing full gear
Provided by the hospital
She air-hugged Edna (rare!)
As she wheeled out Emily
She got a standing ovation
From the healthcare heroes
Who got their share of fanfare
At the 7 p.m. hour
Pots and pan clanking
As they showered and cowered
But these were real claps
By people who had saved her
Friend and confidante
Who could blame her
For feeling perpetual debt
For their healthcare saviors.

Emily rested in the basement
Cherise wasn't afraid
Of being around her bed
Without a mask on
Emily had tested negative
For the antigen
But she wore one in case
Emily had Covid long-haul
But a milder type
She just felt fatigue
So she avoided the hype
Of the hospital for this easier life
Of the stress-free type.

Meanwhile the cases got lower
Deaths were slowing down
So Cuomo opened the city
And Cherise was able to meet
Kenneth, the man of her dreams.
Kenneth had a friend
Also Taiwanese American
Aren't we amazing?
His name was Stanley
He lived with his parents
He was a good Asian son
Didn't mind that Emily
Was an immigrant.

So both were happy
But is that the moral
Of this story?
Unfortunately
There's more to be said
There's that quote
From Orson Welles
The end of the story
Depends where you stop.
I'm gonna give you
A little more
On which
To chomp!
Ha ha
Don't you love
My sometimes rhymes
I think I'm having
Fun this time!

So it turns out
That Kenneth

Wasn't perfect.
Cherise moved in
With him
In an apartment
Her parents
Objections aside
Given the situation
Of staying inside
Tensions began
To form and rise.

Emily meanwhile
Was still living
In the basement.
Stanley paid no rent
So they avoided
That inflation
He would only
Come by
To cuddle
Or watch Netflix
In style.

But Emily
Noticed Cherise
Starting using makeup
Over her eyelid
Maybe hiding
Some shit
So she asked
What's with this?
Cherise denied it
So Emily
Told Stanley
He defended

His best friend
Kenneth certainly
Wasn't violent.

Situation changed
When Cherise
Facetimed her
One day
Crying, bleeding
From her mouth
Emily called
Stanley
He had enough
Wanted to go
Over to confront
The toad
But Emily
Stopped him
I'm undocumented
I don't want overload.

So Stanley called
Domestic Violence
Rather than 911
After the delay
They contacted
The authorities
Descended on the lair
Better late than never
Cherise was alive
Kenneth was nowhere
Put her in a shelter
APB on him
Found him
At a Paris Baguette
Eating an éclair.

Cherise spent a lonely
Night in the place
Afraid she would get Covid
Though she'd likely
Been exposed already
Probably saved her life
Not so lucky for her man
For Kenneth caught
Corona virus in jail
Brought it to his parents
While out on bail
Killed them promptly.
He had mild symptoms
I feel bad for them
But at least he got
Justice and his due
A guilty conscience
For the rest of his
Miserable existence.

Now switch to Emily
She'd saved her sister
Just like her sister
Had been there for her
But she realized
She was lucky
Her hesitation
Not calling 911
Directly
Could have
Doomed Cherise.

She was sick
Of being illegal
Working in the store

Was too much for her.
She ditched America
Took a flight back
To Communist China
Where no one knows
What became of her.

She was probably
"Re-educated"
In one of those camps
Rehabilitated
To a working member
Of Chinese society
Maybe she earned a star
On their morality bar.

Stanley fled too
Back to Taiwan
Where he was born
And got a job
Teaching kids
Got caught up in
Their Covid protocols
Meant to ensnare
Anyone spreading
The deadly virus there.
He quarantined
On arrival
Where he Zoomed
With Cherise
If there's a happy ending
It's that they fell in love
But now they couldn't
Be together or move
Cuz Cherise's father

Bad Americans: Part I

Fell ill too
Not enough to
Be hospitalized.
But she was exposed
Again and didn't want
To leave her abode.

And while Cherise
Could Zoom in
Her classes
They said
In-person
Practicums
Could be
Coming soon
A wish-list
Who knows
If it's true.

Yes Cherise
Was training
To be a
Social Worker
Like me
An idealist
A do-gooder
But one without
A filthy mouth
Your doppelganger
Can't be exactly
Your cup of tea.

What's the moral
Of this Story?
That we should

Be more caring
And inclusive
Of everyone
In our society?
Look what Emily
Was able to contribute
What more she could
Have done and become
If she hadn't been
For our bad laws
And Trump-supporting
Racist fascist scum.

Isn't that
What America
Is all about
Letting people
Fulfill their potential
Having their clout
Let everyone in
Eventually the shit
Will be found out
And given the boot
The Ethiopian nurse
Saved lives and then some
For every Stanley
There's a Kenneth
The assholes abound
They are usually born here
Like Kenneth and Taylor
Oops did I say that out loud?

Anyway I think
You get my point
Now let's get loaded

And smoke a joint.
Ha ha! Just kidding!
Kind of ...

Lisa and her crew were standing, clapping, hollering. Olive came up. He was holding a wooden mug containing hot chocolate laced with coconut rum.

Cathy bowed, then rejoined her friends, who were patting her on the back.

Taylor was standing too, but not to praise the story.

"That's two to one," Taylor said. "When are we getting our perspective, Olive? Because this is a rout. I'm not saying what she said was inaccurate, but it's hardly telling the whole story."

"No one can tell the whole story, Taylor," Olive said. "That's why we'll have 12 stories."

"I just think it was too one-sided."

"How?" Lisa asked.

"I mean, let's look at it from this perspective: this girl purposefully stayed in the country illegally to escape the oppression of the Chinese Communist Party, got free medical care while she was dying, and apparently never had to pay it back. She was never reported to the authorities. She had wonderfully selfless Americans helping her. The domestic violence hotline saved another woman's life.

"I'm not excusing racism, but the virus did originate in China, and note that the CCP and even crazy American conspiracy theorists are incorrectly saying the CIA cooked it up in a lab. For all we know, the CCP created it in their own lab in Wuhan. Our country, unlike Taiwan, let this guy Stanley have dual citizenship. Kenneth, the abuser, got off easy. Sure, his parents died, but nothing really happened to him. And I've got to say, the lockdown has hurt people well beyond the domestic violence uptick. Our most vulnerable citizens, our low-wage-earning laborers, and yes, illegal immigrants, lost their jobs and were waiting in food lines to eat. Thiago and Rafael can tell you. That has nothing to do with race. The cure can't be worse than the cancer, as our President has said."

"Why can't the CCP and the CIA be in on it?" Ricard asked. "It might be a worldwide conspiracy."

"You tell it!" Khassan said.

"Yeah, the Jews are behind it, right, Khassan?" Lisa asked.

"You said it, not me."

"Cathy, do you want to respond to anything Taylor said?" Olive asked.

Cathy looked like she wanted to, but Rashan whispered to her that it wasn't worth it.

"Okay, so let's vote," Olive said. "I've given you a cell phone number. Please send your vote to this number, which I have. So only I will know who is voting how."

Lisa had already told her crew that if they stuck together, they had an automatic four votes and only needed two to put them over the top. That could be Hayley or Pritesh. Maybe even Ricard or Khassan. She didn't have faith in Taylor or Angela. She wasn't sure why the transgender Sylvania was friends with the conservatives, but she figured she was hopeless too.

They all sent their texts. Olive tallied them.

He shook his head.

"I'm sorry Cathy," he said. "It was close. But you lost, 6–5."

"That's bullshit," Khassan said. "Maybe not my cup of tea, but it was solid."

"I liked it too," Ricard said, which seemed to shock everyone.

"Okay, let's not reveal how we voted," Olive said. "It's supposed to be anonymous."

Lisa was confounded. If it was true that Khassan and Ricard had voted for Cathy, then she should have gotten six votes, even without Hayley or Pritesh. So, either there was a dissenter in her group, or Khassan and/or Ricard were lying.

"That means I'll be isolated tomorrow," Cathy said, shrugging. "Sucks for me."

Her group consoled her while shunning the others. Meanwhile, Ricard approached Cathy and told her he liked her story, even though he didn't agree with illegal immigration, masks, or the lockdown, it was still a free country, and he liked how she stood up for the People.

They went up to the second-floor den and hung out there, and then Lisa decided she wanted to go out to the White House because Maja had texted her that she had some weed. Andrea said she was tired and went to sleep; and even though Ricard and Cathy were getting along splendidly, Ricard said he didn't feel like going, which pleased Nalini until she realized Ricard was going to sleep, by himself.

Still, at least she would have Ricard to herself the next day, with Cathy out of the way.

Outside, near the creek, they were surprised to see Ares, who they thought might rat them out—instead, he was apparently in on the weed run and led them to the edge of the woods near the pool, where Maja and Zahra handed out the tokes.

They sat on the moist ground, leaning on trees, smoking.

"It's gonna be legal soon," Cathy said. "No biggie."

"You're the one who suggested it," Rashan said.

"I did?"

"At the end of your story."

"Oh yeah. I forgot."

Maja and Lisa were talking about the firings, how they seemed to come out of nowhere and left the entire workload on them. But Ares defended Olive as the best boss ever.

"Of course, you would say that," Maja said. "You've sucked his cock."

"Really?" Lisa asked. "Spill the beans, baby."

"He was Olive's pet," Maja said. "The only reason Ares is in the country."

"My visa situation's complicated," Ares said. "But that does show you how great a person Olive is. Even after we broke up, he wasn't bitter. He still supported my J-visa."

"How was he in the sack?" Rashan wanted to know. Ares hinted that he was big. Rashan didn't want to delve too deep, so he changed the subject and complained about his ex-boyfriend Josh, who had left him at the start of the pandemic to go to his ranch in Montana—without him.

"Lots of shit happened at the start of the pandemic," Ares said. "My J-visa is babysitting Olive's lawyer's kids in Chappaqua, but Olive pulled me out here as another full-time chauffeur, even though Rabia already had the job. I mean I was out here a lot anyway, but he saved me because Covid was spreading a lot over in Westchester."

"Maybe he just wanted you close so he could fuck you," Cathy said.

"Well, he's not fucking me now," Ares snapped back. "Anyway, you get ready by 8 a.m. tomorrow, and I'll drive you over to the North Shore."

"Shit, what am I gonna do all day by myself?" Cathy asked. "Is he gonna starve me too?"

"Nah, Olive'll provide, he always does. Just relax now. Reminds me of my childhood in Finland, just chilling out. We will forget this sick American culture for now."

They all tried to stare out into the woods. Nalini had the hardest time concentrating. She started having a rambling conversation with Zahra, one she had forgotten by the next day.

~ Day Three ~

Taylor went down to the basement early and got spotted on the bench press by none other than Darnell, who was technically on Big Brother duty in the security office next to the gym. Sung was sleeping on a cot in the office. Darnell snuck out. He got lonely all by himself. Hayley, the only other person there, was running on the treadmill, so Darnell chatted with her.

The night before, Taylor felt things were going well with Angela, but when they approached her room after hanging out, he had awkwardly blown it.

"Carino," she had said, "I had a good time tonight."

She had kissed him on the cheek and hugged him. He could have kissed her back or said something so she would let him into her room, but he had chickened out.

"You'll have another chance, man," Darnell said. "But you can't keep on blowing it."

Taylor knew he shouldn't be complaining to his competition, but then Darnell seemed to like all the girls, so maybe it was okay. Anyway, Darnell was staff, an essential non-factor.

Upstairs, as he was entering his room, Taylor saw the card. He used a letter opener he had in his briefcase to open it. The card said:

Stories can move us
But they can also unnerve us
They can make us open our eyes
Or close them and reopen them anew
Think about what you want the audience to experience
And give it to them tonight, like a special brew...

"Sure, I'll give it to them," Taylor thought. He would counter Cathy's story for sure, finally give them a conservative voice, correct the wrongs uttered, even if it was brutal and not popular. He didn't have to be popular. But he did want to win.

It was a beautiful, sunny day, not a cloud in the sky, so breakfast took place on the patio. Today's spread included many pastries, divided into vegan and non-vegan sections: chocolate croissants, puff pastries, cinnamon rolls, apple Danishes, cannolis, strudels, eclairs, flaky pastries, kouign-amanns, mille-feuilles, and much more.

Abeo was stationed at a thin pancake station, ready to take orders to produce a variety of crepes, from Nutella-banana to pineapple and cherry. Thiago was at a waffle station, but he also made fresh French toast in whatever style the person requested. Muesli, oatmeal, yogurt, apples, oranges, blueberries, and bananas were available, but no eggs, cereal, hash browns, bacon, sausages, potatoes, or other usuals. For drinks, there was an assortment of coffee styles, yerba mate, a few teas, and fresh orange juice.

Ricard wasn't too happy with the lack of meat, but then the liberal crew came in from cleaning the White House rooms, their punishment for losing the racquetball competition the day before, and Nalini suggested it might be healthier to eat fruit for a change. So it was French toast for him and oatmeal for her with yogurt, apples, and oranges. Then he made the startling admission that he was a bit of a nature fiend, especially fond of birds.

"Wow, I wouldn't have taken you for a birder," Nalini said.

Lisa, huffing, was trying to "eat healthy" with muesli, yogurt, and blueberries, but not happily—frustrated, she tried a strudel and a Danish. Nalini laughed to herself. That morning at the White House, while cleaning the staff's rooms, Lisa told Nalini she had been blacklisted from the art world after blogging about a Me Too incident. While jogging back to the Saggplex, they had connected over Nalini's decision to switch to defending the disadvantaged, but, being exhausted after toking weed all night and cleaning rooms that morning, they couldn't complete their whole routine. Cathy had been spared that punishment since she was banished to the North Shore—but that meant Nalini would have Ricard to herself that day.

Pritesh had been sent to clean the rooms by Hayley because she didn't want to mess up her exercise routine that morning.

"You really are pussy-whipped, aren't you?" Nalini had teased Pritesh as they double-teamed a bed. "That was fast."

"She's a nice girl."

"Enough to bring back to your parents in India?"

He didn't respond to that. "How about you? Don't you like the skinhead?"

"That's different. I'm American," she said.

"You look Indian to me. Your rich parents won't care that you're dating a white biker?"

Nalini didn't respond. She knew that would be an issue, but she didn't care anymore. She was sick of the city lifestyle, even with her lockstep six-figure salary and sweet apartment in Long Island City overlooking the Manhattan skyline. Representing powerful interests wasn't her cup of tea anymore. She wanted to understand and defend the people she had ignored for most of her life. The pandemic had forced her home, but she was rather relieved that it happened.

Now Nalini devised a plot to spend time with Ricard, but first, she had to participate in the morning activity, which was a basketball tournament.

Instead of the court inside the Saggplex where they had played racquetball, the basketball competition took place in the backyard past the patio. The guests followed Sung, who had woken up, past a porcelain-tiled path that led to a large marble statue of the Greek god Poseidon, a trident in one hand and a dolphin in another. Water flowed out of his mouth into a marble pool.

Beyond the fountain was a Jacuzzi shaped like a heart, surrounded by beach chairs. To its left were two sauna rooms. To its right was a barbecue station. After that was a manicured field with a small miniature golf course on the left and a batting cage on the right. Several yards after, the basketball court stretched out with two hoops on either side, with a slightly elevated maple wood floor, and beyond that, a thirty-yard field seemed to double for football and soccer, marked by yardsticks and end zones, with both field goal posts and soccer nets on either side. Following that, in the far-right corner, was a baseball diamond and a field large enough for a softball game; to the left was a miniature racetrack full of a collection of small RVs and bicycles.

Woods surrounded the manicured area. Sung informed them that Olive owned a large portion of the woods to the right of the manicured property. It was ideal for games like zip-lining, bungee jumping, laser tag, paintball, or even rock climbing if one installed a portable wall. The woods were not fenced off from the roads on either side, so anyone could come through or even camp there, but that was unlikely in such an affluent area.

Without Cathy, they were short one person, so Ares, who had just returned from the North Shore Complex where he had dropped Cathy off, decided to sub for her. Still, only five people could play at a time, so one would be on the bench as a sixth man. Lisa decided that would be her, and she never actually came into the game. Pritesh sat as the sixth man on Taylor's team.

Most guests wanted to stick to the same teams, but Khassan noted that there were more women on Lisa's team, making it lopsided. Lisa said that was sexist, but still, she welcomed a change, considering she was exhausted. Khassan and Ricard switched with Andrea and Rashan.

During the game, Rashan was annoyed at Taylor's bossy behavior but even more at Khassan, who was guarding him and frequently asked him about his Islamic-sounding name.

"My dad was flirting with Islam when I was born," Rashan finally explained. "Gave it up in prison, went back to his African roots."

"Back to your dad. What was he in prison for?"

"Don't know, don't care. My mom says he was framed by the New Black Panther party. He did his time. Now he's teaching on the West Coast."

"You still talk to him?"

"That's a negative. My mom and my sis, they're the only ones to me." That brought back memories, but Rashan was more interested in muscling up against Ares when he had the ball.

But it didn't matter. Sylvania's size made her a formidable force inside. If she was triple-teamed, she would pass it out to Taylor for an outside shot. Their team won again easily.

"What's our punishment?" Khassan asked Sung.

"Not yet," Sung said. Then Rashan realized he hadn't seen Olive at all.

"He has some business to take care of," Sung said. "Just relax until lunchtime."

Nalini wanted to talk to Ricard, but he quickly went into the Saggplex with Khassan. Lisa and Andrea were tired, so they decided to just lounge by the pool after taking showers. Nalini followed their lead.

Up in Pritesh's room, Hayley asked if Pritesh wanted to come into the shower with her, but he declined. When she came out wrapped in a towel, he told her he was pissed.

"Do I just exist to do your work for you?" he asked. "The beds, the photos. Meanwhile, you're flirting with everyone from the security guard to that celebrity chef."

She unfurled her towel.

"They don't have this."

"I don't want to do your work for you."

She put the towel back on.

"Okay, so don't. I thought you wanted to."

"No, and I certainly do not want to see you flirting with other guys. Was your last boyfriend OK with that?"

"My last boyfriend was my promoter. It was a different situation."

"Sounds the same to me. He did your work."

"He took my money," she said. "And he was cheating on me. I wanted out. The pandemic gave me that out."

"So now you're out, and I'm your new boy toy?"

"What the hell is this about? Okay, next time I'll clean the fucking beds. I thought you felt guilty about yesterday."

"There's nothing to feel guilty about. That's what I was trying to say."

He looked out the window at the creek. "Look, I think I'll feel better when I'm out with those fishermen at the creek. Meanwhile, you can hang out with the jet set at the pool."

"Dude, now you're making it a class thing? Whatever, do what you want. You're annoying the shit out of me."

She threw the towel on the bed, took a thin red bikini, and put it on. Pritesh left.

He went down to the creek and watched the Asian and Hispanic men fish. The quiet rhythm calmed him a bit. It made him think about his on-and-off-again failed dating life throughout the United States as he had made his way through a variety of consulting jobs on his H-1 B visa. Sometimes he felt he was doing this just to submerge himself into American culture and get away from his parents' archaic expectations of him marrying in his caste, maybe to lure him back to India, or at least to settle him into Indian culture in America. But he didn't want to go back. And he wasn't sure he wanted to settle into anything.

Being in a relationship so soon upon coming to the Getaway astonished him. He'd made a quick pass at Lisa in the limo, he'd been so desperate, but when she had rejected him, he'd laid off, only to be approached by Hayley in the den. Now he realized she had probably flirted with Darnell and Thiago and Micah and all the guys, and maybe he was just the easiest patsy. He knew everyone thought of him as a pervert, a twenty-eight-year-old man with a nineteen-year-old woman. But who was using whom?

Meanwhile, Hayley marched down to the pool where Lisa, Andrea, and Nalini were already lying on sunbeds munching on some lunch options: paninis, fried chicken, and fresh watermelon slices as they sipped on lemonade, mimosas, and Bloody Marys. Her tiny nipples were barely covered and her panties were a thong.

"Shit, she might as well be naked," Lisa said to Andrea.

"Is that why you didn't invite me down here?" Hayley asked, overhearing her comment. "I'm your teammate."

"You didn't want to hang out with us mere plebeians at the White House while we were doing actual work," Lisa countered.

"Is that what you call blogging?" Hayley asked. "Actual work?"

"Calm down, ladies," Nalini said, immediately feeling fake as she said the following: "Everyone's work is valuable."

"Actually, there is a difference because I don't blog for monetary reward," Lisa said. "I do it for the public good. To expose things the public needs to know."

"Are you calling me a hooker?" Hayley asked. "Because, you know, modeling is an art too."

"If anyone can take your pictures, it can't be an art," Lisa said. "What? Are you going to have the chef take them now?"

"At least he knows something about it. Cow."

Lisa immediately started to get up but couldn't do a sit-up to get out of the chair. Nalini flipped up instead.

"Calm down, sister," Nalini said, as she followed Hayley to the trays where the lunch options were laid out by Thiago and Rafael. The main offering was fried chicken cooked Cajun style. There were other styles of fried chicken with sauces, including honey mustard, sweet relish, and barbecue bonanza. The paninis included ham and cheese; turkey club; mock duck with duck sauce; tofurkey and crispy fried vegan bacon; tofu, cucumbers, and green hot sauce.

"There's nothing here for me," Hayley said. "Better not to eat before a session."

"Are you okay?" Nalini asked.

"You know, my mom drove me across the country when I was 16 to live in a cramped apartment, all by myself, taking any shit job I could get for years and working clubs late night to survive. I always wanted to be a runway model. Then social media started working for me. It's taken a lot of work to get millions of followers on IG and TikTok. Without Terry, I've got to get fresh content up and restart my feeds with new pages. Since he owned the accounts, he took the brands with him, the deals with him. Maybe Lisa's on vacation, but I can't afford to be."

"Who's Terry?"

"My promoter. My ex-boyfriend. My everything until we broke up."

"Shit. I'm sorry."

"This is the ideal backdrop. Hamptons. We were on the North Shore hiding out, but I can't go back there now."

"I'll take your photos," Thiago said. "I know how life in the limelight is."

"Let's make up with Lisa first," Nalini said, taking Hayley's hand.

"I appreciate the effort," Hayley said. "But I don't think I'm ready."

Ricard and Khassan came down. They were both shirtless and in swimming trunks. They ate lunch as Hayley and Thiago started taking pictures by the croquet court, and Nalini considered her move.

"I heard the woods are peaceful," she said to Ricard. "Lots of birds singing and hiding out."

Ricard snickered as he munched on his fried chicken. "Sure, let's go."

Khassan was going to come along but got the hint from Nalini that she wanted to be alone with him. They strolled out into the woods just as Sung made the announcement that they would head back to the beach for the afternoon activity, which was sailing.

"Mainly you hear the whip-poor-wills out here singing," Ricard said. "We should see warblers, cardinals, blackbirds, starlings, and sandpipers. Problem is the ecosystem has been disrupted by human elites, some caused by hunting, I admit, but also industrial. So you mainly just see sparrows and robins in the cities and the suburbs now, and that's one of the reasons for this theory that somehow there was an animal transmission that caused Covid to emerge. But that's BS. It is true that the lack of diversity of wildlife is contributing to more diseases in general, but Covid is different. It really is a plan to lessen the diversity of humanity by killing off a certain number so only the elite can survive and mold humanity to their image. It's kind of like that Poseidon statue that Olive has. That's the model that people like Olive and his brethren want to mold us into. That's why the Jackson Club and others like it exist. We love freedom, and we don't want to be molded into nothing else. We'll be free like a bird."

"You really love your biker brothers, don't you? But then why come out here with the suits?"

"Long story. My ex has been trying to stick me with child support and not let me see my daughter, and the online court sessions have been annoying as shit. The lockdown shut up my employment prospects, even out there in the dunes. Normally I refuse to take unemployment or any other government handout, but I need it for the support. I'm embarrassed as shit to take it. I figured maybe I'd find somebody or something to take my mind off it here. I got my bros, but they got their own stuff going on too."

"You can't be that close-minded. You're here with me."

"Who said I was close-minded? I'm more open-minded than you, suit."

They both laughed. It was a nice moment for Nalini to feel she was finally appreciated by Ricard.

"When I moved back to Connecticut, I was so relieved," she said. "I hated my life in the city. Empty dates with empty guys. All the money in the world can't buy happiness; it's true. You need a greater purpose—to feel you're doing something. Just seeing the bikers pass my house in a line, I realized I didn't even see an entire world that was right in front of me due to my privileged upbringing."

"At least you own it. That's a step."

Nalini felt good about her time here. She had found some binoculars in Olive's collection of random stuff he kept in the game room. Ricard was doing what he loved, and Nalini liked being in a place where she wasn't a "suit."

Meanwhile, Cathy was exploring the empty bungalow complex where some of the guests had quarantined, let out for only an hour a day to walk the grounds for an entire two weeks. She had been lucky, or maybe not so lucky, to have quarantined in her apartment in Elmhurst, but now she had the complex to herself—the winery, the vineyards, the gardens, the lanes of the bungalow complexes, even the beach on the Great Peconic Bay with its calm, almost lake-like water and view of the South Fork across it. Being alone after the story and the drama wasn't such a bad thing—she could munch on the sandwiches provided to her for a light lunch and still make it back for dinner.

The rest of the guests made it to the beach, where they boarded two boats that sailed them out to the ocean. Olive warned them about the increasing prevalence of sharks due to the warming temperatures and, ironically, the cleaner water and the proliferation of sea life closer to the shore. Still, Khassan and Taylor had a diving competition. After one dive, they felt the waves suddenly increase and became freaked out that it was a shark, but when they boarded the boats and looked back, it was Ares and Thiago driving two speedboats with parasails attached.

This time, the two teams would choose three people—one to drive the boat, the other two to parasail; Rabia and Olive acted as judges, assessing two factors: whether the boat was sufficiently fast and moved around the water with enough maneuvering and whether the parasailers maintained a good height and posture and performed any moves, which were bonuses.

Area and Thiago remained in the boats as copilots in case of mishaps. Taylor chose himself to drive for his team and encouraged Sylvania and Angela to be his parasailers, even though Angela had a fear of water and couldn't swim. She would be wearing a life jacket, and the other options were Rashan, Andrea, and Pritesh, none of whom were particularly enthused about the exercise—so ultimately, she agreed. On the other team, Khassan wanted to drive. Hayley was down for anything, and while Lisa didn't want any part in this, her team was missing Cathy, Ricard, and Nalini, so there were no other choices. Thiago offered to drive, and Lisa could be his eyes and ears, while Hayley and Khassan were the parasailers. But at the last moment, not wanting to be shown up by Hayley yet again, Lisa decided to parasail and let Khassan drive.

So the boats were lined up side by side. Olive took out a small starter pistol and pointed it in the air. As he fired, Taylor revved up, and Khassan jolted right after. The parasailers were pushed from the back of the open boats onto the water—Lisa and Angela let out screams, but their feet skirted the ocean only for a few seconds, after which the sails that trailed them inflated and were hoisted into the sky.

Lisa started enjoying the heights—Hayley, only a foot from her, began doing a dance with her hands and feet. Lisa started to copy her and put in her own variations. Every few seconds, they were jolted left or right as Khassan tried various maneuvers and turns to best Taylor. At one point, he even started swerving around in a circle, making a kind of whirlpool in the ocean while Lisa and Hayley lifted their hands in the air and screamed from the rush.

Meanwhile, Sylvania tried to control the moves of the parasail with her body and performed a more rhythmic dance, while Taylor, despite the trash talk, tried to make smooth and controlled turns so that he primarily moved in an "S" shape. Angela got over her nerves and turned on her Latina moves with her hips.

A few minutes later, they drove back to shore. The ladies crashed into more shallow water and were able to stutter onto the sand as the speedboats slowed down onto the beach itself. The two sailboats were nearly there too—tables, chairs, a bonfire, and a feast awaiting them.

After they unharnessed, Lisa and Hayley hugged—their differences apparently assuaged by the fun they had together, at least for now. Then Thiago and Khassan high-fived them. Angela and Sylvania embraced too, but Taylor paced, worried. Olive and Rabia tallied their scores—and announced that Khassan and his team were victorious. The four engaged in a group hug as Taylor berated his friends. Sylvania snapped back that she did her part and that Taylor should have driven more ornately. Angela didn't say much. She just headed towards the food.

Meanwhile, music started blasting—it was traditional sub-Saharan rhythms, what they learned was Atilogwu, mixed with modern dance music. Currently DeBarge's "Rhythm of the Night" was playing. Maja and Zahra, apparently off work and holding bottles of

Umqombothi, a traditional South African beer, danced around the bonfire. Soon Lisa and Hayley joined them.

Darnell noticed Angela was upset and tried to console her, while Micah stared at the women dancing around the bonfire. Andrea joined in the fun.

Rashan was impressed by the inclusion of African music. As he approached the trays of food, Abeo was announcing, "It's a paradise! It's a paradise!" in his Nigerian accent.

His spread was his response to Thiago's Swedish-themed meal the night before, and it was a magnificent combination of African cuisines—in this case, Somalian, Ethiopian, and South African specialties.

Darnell heaped his plate with some of the Somalian food—hirib ali, roasted goat with basmati rice, and basbaas sauce—along with chicken suqqar, a spicy chicken stew served with chapatti bread. Angela took the South African boerewors, a type of sausage containing beef, lamb, pork, and a number of spices. This was barbecued by Bom on a braai and served with pap, softly ground maize, and shee-ba, a cooked sauce made of tomatoes and onions.

Meanwhile, Micah, the security guard, tried the Ethiopian food, taking a large round injera bread and, following Abeo's direction, placing on its perimeter some tibs, or meat chunks sauteed in butter with onions, garlic, hot peppers, and rosemary; misir wot, red lentils cooked in a spicy berbere sauce; shiro, ground chickpeas; and yater kik alicha, yellow split peas.

Pritesh tried to ignore Hayley's continuous flirting with Thiago and took the injera bread too, but he surrounded it with gomen, or steamed collard greens; enguday tibs, or crimini mushrooms; keysir selata, or sautéed beets, carrots, potatoes; and butecha selata, with butecha and kale. He saw Hayley leave the bonfire and take some South African shangaan spinach, served with ground peanuts, an almond-based cream sauce, and spices, plus a dessert of fruit salad including navel orange, mango, papaya, blueberries, bananas, and strawberries. She sat down with Micah, Darnell, and Angela. Thiago sat next to her a moment later. Since he was a paleo, he had made a special plate for himself of lean cod, fruits, and vegetables.

Pritesh was joined by Khassan, who came with two drinks: Witblits, a grape-fermented brandy, along with its fruitier alternative, Mampoer, which he gave to Pritesh. He had also taken South African bobotie, spicy minced meat baked with an egg-based topping and served with yellow rice and chutney. Nalini took some Ethiopian vegan biryani with mock chicken covered with a mango curry sauce and sat with them.

"I didn't realize you were vegan," Pritesh said.

"I eat meat; I just hate meat," Nalini said. "Maybe I should go back to being a veggie."

"Where were you?" Khassan asked. "I kicked ass for us in parasailing."

"In the woods," she said.

"With Ricard? Because I don't see him."

Suddenly they did see him. His motorcycle came roaring down the path from the Saggplex and stopped at the intersection of the White House and the Sagaponack Pond. A helmeted rider behind him held his hips. When she jumped off and removed her helmet, they saw it was Cathy.

"Yeah, that," Nalini said.

"Wow, he picked her up from the North Shore?" Khassan asked. "That's cold."

"He volunteered to go," Nalini said, "instead of Ares."

"So I guess the woods weren't lovely, dark, and deep?" Khassan quipped.

Nalini punched his shoulder. "Fuck you. I think he just likes to help people."

Pritesh was listening but mostly minding his girl at the other table.

"You just gonna let her flirt with other guys, man?" Khassan asked Pritesh, who didn't respond as Ricard and Cathy approached.

"Yo, how was the quarantine?" Khassan asked Cathy.

"Actually, kind of nice," Cathy replied. "It was good to debrief.

The beach is smooth there. The water is so calm, you can go like a mile out and still be standing in waist-high water."

"So I guess it's good to lose," Khassan said. "But I gotta tell you, I switched to your team, and we won. Don't know what our prize is, though."

He described the activity to her as Ricard got them food: the boerewors; hirib ali; beef, chicken, and vegetable sambusa patties; and sabaayad, a vegan dish where chapattis were filled with vegetables and cilantro aioli.

Meanwhile, Taylor rolled around and joined them too. He had the injera bread with various sides, but in the middle, he had placed a dessert—South African malva pudding made from apricot jam with a spongy caramel iced texture, cream sauce, and served with ice cream. He had chosen chocolate, but they also had vanilla, strawberry, green tea, red bean, apricot, and mango.

"Living large," Khassan said. "Are you telling the story tonight?"

"Yeah, that's why I don't want to get too tanked."

Spotting Angela at the other table and Sylvania dancing with Andrea and Lisa, Taylor saw he had alienated his friends, so he wasn't clear what support he would have for his story.

"Have you practiced?" Nalini asked Taylor.

"I don't need to," he said. "It's instinctual. Like telling stories around the campfire in Iraq."

"Quarantine wasn't bad," Cathy informed him. "Just in case you wanted to know."

"Doubt I'll be quarantined," he said.

"Sure," Cathy said. "You're such a popular guy."

Rafael came around with some drinks, including tej, an Ethiopian sweet honey dessert wine, which Taylor took; spiced black tea, tried by Cathy; rooibos tea, taken by Lisa when she finally stopped dancing to eat; lassi, which Nalini tried; and amasi, a South African-based sour milk that Andrea sampled. Van Der Hum liqueur was also available to mix with cocktails, and this was poured into existing glasses by several guests and staff.

Olive finally announced that the story would be starting in

fifteen minutes and that they could gather around the bonfire to hear it. Meanwhile, guests and staff could try several African desserts as they listened to it, but some of them opted to wait until the next story was done. Some took their chairs; others decided to sit or even lounge on the sand. Most of the staff, except for Sung and the doctors, were there too.

Hayley took a moment to look out into the ocean and saw a bottlenose dolphin jump out of the water, then another. She clapped.

"Thought it was a shark," a voice said behind her. She turned and saw it was Pritesh.

"Dolphins are much prettier," she said. "Don't you think?"

He stood there uncomfortably for a few seconds. He wanted to say sorry, but the words wouldn't come out.

She put out her hands. "Well, are you gonna say anything?"

He reached down to kiss her, and she reciprocated. They kissed softly but deeply. She extended her fingers, and they matched hands, finger to finger.

"Actions speak louder than words, right?" she asked as they wrapped their fingers together.

~ DAY THREE ~
INTRODUCTION TO TAYLOR'S STORY

Olive came up before the bonfire.

"Welcome to the third story and the third night of our great Getaway. First, I want to address the elephant in the room. Since each team won a competition today, they will cancel each other out, and there will be no punishment or handicap for that. We will have the voting after this story; however, and there will be consequences for defeat.

"Tonight's storyteller is Taylor Williams, a great champion who has given service to our country. He's a graduate of Brown University, a descendant of an old Rhode Island family that has sent generations to Harvard. Yet he signed up to serve in Iraq and Afghanistan, and when this pandemic hit, instead of sitting in his country home in Cold Spring, NY, he volunteered to help Thiago and Rafael feed the hungry at breadlines in Queens, NY, something we never thought we would see in the land of plenty.

"Of course, Taylor has some strong opinions that come with his great education and sacrifice for our nation. I don't know what kind of story he will tell, but I have no doubt it will factor into the flavor of his tale. Please do welcome Taylor Williams to the stage!"

Taylor approached, his hands behind his back.

"I want to start out by saying, repeating even, that I didn't have a problem with Cathy's story; I just think we need to look from a different point of view here. Sure, maybe some illegal immigrants have legitimate reasons to break the law, but Cathy's character didn't, and many people overstaying their visas and crossing the border from Mexico don't.

"Most are middle- or upper-middle-class in their own countries

115

who are paying agents and taking advantage of the lax enforcement of our laws or of lax laws themselves. They lie to get free lawyers paid for by our tax dollars. They have anchor babies and create all kinds of BS to stay here.

"I love cultural and ethnic diversity. I've been on the front lines of the fight for freedom around the world, from Afghanistan to Iraq. I helped Thiago and Rafael and so many other selfless Americans give out food to starving immigrants of all backgrounds during the pandemic, but there is right and wrong, and coming here illegally is wrong. I guarantee you, you won't be able to do that in Germany, or China, or Thailand, or wherever else and get away with it for long.

"My story focuses on true Americans, immigrants who came here the right way and are doing the right thing every day and are being punished for it due to selfish politicians who want to reward bad behavior and overplay a pandemic to get votes. This isn't just the internationally privileged who come here selfishly; it's also the drug gangs, human traffickers, and other criminals who have penetrated our southern border to bring misery to working families; the BLM 'protesters' taking advantage of a true tragedy to foment insurrection; and the politicians playing up an annoyingly contagious flu-like virus as if it's the Black Death.

"My heroes are hard-working immigrants from Ecuador. Maybe you've known some immigrants from Ecuador. Many have settled in Corona, Queens, especially, and they understand and appreciate our capitalist democracy due to the failed socialist policies of their own country that devalued their currency so much that they use U.S. dollars. Unfortunately, those who have settled in primarily Hispanic neighborhoods have to send their children to overcrowded, underperforming public schools that are failing our children, while politicians like AOC are more interested in their popularity than actually helping people. But, like Cathy, I digress ...

"Here's my story," he said, telling it from memory.

~ Day Three ~
Taylor's Story
(*AKA "CORONA CHAOS"*)

A man named Xavier Zambrano immigrated from Ecuador to Queens through his much older brother, Eduardo, waiting over 20 years to come legally. His family owned a farm back in Guayas Province, but he made his living as an agricultural engineer. When he immigrated to the U.S. with his family, he lived briefly with his brother in his modest home in Corona, but given that can-do American spirit, he immediately decided to make his own living and branch out.

His brother Eduardo owned an Ecuadorian restaurant in Corona, and Xavier's wife Ana worked there as a waitress. Xavier's two children were very young, and he wanted to bring them up as strict Catholics, so he borrowed money from his brother and sent them to Catholic school. He rented his own apartment in a three-story home in Queens, and he bought a medallion by borrowing money from the bank, which allowed him to work as a taxi driver.

This was in 2013 when medallions were nearly a million bucks and right before Uber became big in New York City. As you might imagine, as the years went on, Xavier eked out a living, but he regretted his decision to get a medallion when he could have just waited and become an Uber driver. In debt to the bank and too proud to ask Eduardo for more financial help, he decided his only bet was to keep driving.

As the years passed, his brother Eduardo got sick of New York City. He was much older. His kids had graduated from college, and his wife had passed on years before. He decided to sell his restaurant and his house. He moved to North Carolina's Outer Banks, where he bought a cheaper house, lived off his investments, and settled into a peaceful life. As a favor, the new owner of the restaurant kept the current staff, and, thankfully, Ana retained her job.

Now around 2016, some illegal Mexican gangs became prominent in one part of Corona and western Flushing, and they wanted to expand their money-making ventures. Associated with El Chapo, they would stop at nothing to sell their product. One of the gang's leaders, Hector Lopez, set up shop in a house next to Xavier's. He noticed Xavier would park his cab nearby in the evening and take it out in the morning. He got an idea—the cab would be an ideal way to transport their product without being suspected.

Hector befriended Xavier, acting like a concerned fellow Hispanic who could look after Xavier's wife and kids, protecting them from gangs and other predators. Of course, he was buttering up Xavier for the kill. One day, Hector was in his cab, getting a friendly free ride to "work" in Woodside when he got Xavier to pull over in a deserted spot and stuck him up with a gun. His amigos came out of the woodwork and surrounded the cab, armed too. Xavier was forced to agree to transport Hector's product from his home where it arrived through Mexico after a circumvented route to different distribution centers around New York City and Long Island.

Xavier was a good man, a devout Catholic, but he had a family, so he felt he had no choice but to comply. He knew he was doing the wrong thing. He would pull his taxi over and cry when he was alone, but he didn't know a way to get out of his predicament. Granted, Hector did pay him, but it was a pittance. The real reason he kept doing it was the threat to his family if he veered away from his job even a bit.

This kept up for more than two years. Soon Hector no longer paid Xavier and even demanded money from him for continuing "protection." Xavier felt like giving up everything and moving back to Ecuador where at least he could live his own life with his family. But then, given Hector and El Chapo's connections, it was distinctly possible they could hit him there too, and he didn't want to take that chance. He loved his family too much. He wanted to protect them.

One day, after holding it in for years, he confessed to his priest. His priest advised him to go to the Feds and hope that he and his family would be placed in witness protection, which might have been the best alternative for him rather than continuing to live in fear and endless debt. Xavier thanked the priest for his advice but decided it was still too risky.

However, after a year of confessing and receiving this advice, inspired by President Trump's zero tolerance policy on Mexican drug gangs, he decided to contact the Feds. He received the number from the priest, who got it from his own contact. He spoke to an agent named William Davis who said he would help him, and they agreed to meet in a remote spot in Nassau County's Hempstead after one of Xavier's drug drop-offs, which Davis said he would monitor and record.

Xavier was extremely nervous during the drop-off in Hempstead, but he tried not to act any differently around his contact, with whom he made small talk in Spanish every time he delivered the supply of cocaine, heroin, and meth. He did look around a few times, checking for any cars he didn't recognize, but he didn't notice anything amiss.

Everything went smoothly at the drop-off, and Xavier drove to the meetup point, a deserted spot near a LIRR railroad station. As a train cruised past, a car drove up swiftly and braked abruptly. A man got out, but it was not a white man. Briefly Xavier noticed Hector Lopez's bloody eyes as he unloaded several shots into the cab, killing Xavier instantly.

It's sad, isn't it? A hard-working immigrant, who did everything the right way, trying to obtain the American dream like anyone else, extorted for years and meeting his end in such a sad and shocking fashion. It's not right, but unfortunately, this is what turning a blind eye to the Mexican border for years and these well-intentioned but ultimately disastrous Sanctuary City policies have done to our great nation and the greatest city on Earth. It turns out the priest's contact was a turncoat, in on the payouts, and "William Davis" was not a Fed agent but just another illegal with an appropriate accent and authoritative manner.

This shocking murder, however, is only the beginning of this great tragedy. Hector Lopez and his associates drove the cab to a remote beach on Nassau's southern shore and torched the car in the middle of the night, but they knew that Xavier would eventually be missed, and an investigation would start. Better to abandon their "home" and operations for a bit, and let a new illegal crew continue the enterprise. After destroying the evidence, Hector and his fellow illegal pals drove back to Mexico for a siesta while another crew snuck into the country and came up to carry on the enterprise in different locations.

When Xavier didn't come home that night, his wife, Ana, became frantic. She called friends to inquire if they knew where he was. She even called Hector, but he didn't pick up. Finally, after waiting the entire night for him to return, she contacted the police.

The police, as usual, didn't take it seriously until more than 48 hours had passed. They figured a Hispanic taxi driver missing overnight could be doing any number of things, including going on a drinking or adultery binge, even though Ana insisted Xavier was a God-fearing man and wouldn't partake in those pursuits. Finally, the missing persons case became more urgent, and someone eventually found the burned cab and reported it. Investigators were able to match the VIN number on an alloy plate to Xavier's cab, and then dental analysis and the DNA results of charred bones confirmed Xavier's remains were inside.

Ana was shocked at the murder, grieving enormously and considering suicide. But she needed to be strong for her children. She tried to help the police—soon she realized Hector was no longer living in his home, and detectives were able to surmise, while they had no direct proof, that he was here illegally and that he may have had something to do with the murder. Still, they were not able to prove it, and the case went cold.

Meanwhile, Ana tried to continue to live her life, with some financial assistance from Xavier's brother. She declared bankruptcy to avoid paying off the medallion. Even though it had been in Xavier's name, someone needed to pay it, and she was his surviving spouse. She had no choice but to pull her girls out of Catholic school and place them in public school. At this point, they were in junior high school, and as you might imagine, even the typical middle school experience is fraught with anxiety, but the public school in Corona, which won't be mentioned by name, was filled with bullies and gangs, and her children weren't happy there.

Then the pandemic arrived. Not only were the public schools shut down, but the restaurants were banned from having indoor dining. So the kids were left at home to do bogus "remote learning," regressing their education even further, and Ana was laid off from her job, as the restaurant owner cut all unnecessary staff.

She couldn't pay her rent, and she had to look after her two impressionable young teen daughters. Eduardo offered her the chance to move to North Carolina, but she was a proud woman, and she had a sense of national responsibility too—she did not want to spread the virus to another state since New York City was the epicenter. She was also afraid she wouldn't be able to return to New York if there was a more extreme lockdown.

She used the few savings she had, the money Eduardo was sending her, and President Trump's $1200 payment, to cover some basics. She was too proud to apply for unemployment benefits, like a true American, but the rent moratorium helped, one of the few things local leaders did right. She found out they were giving out free food in western Queens, so she made the long trip by bicycle (she did not own a car, and the subway was too dangerous) in the cold and waited for hours to get food for her family every day. The girls were eventually able to pick up meals from the junior high school once Mayor de Blasio's turtle-like administration got around to it, but everyone needs more than one meal a day, and Ana did the best she could with the help of compassionate Americans.

Finally, months later, once the Covid cases went down, even though Governor Cuomo and Mayor De Blasio were still fighting publicly and refusing to lift some restrictions, Ana was able to get a job through a connection, working at a Latin fusion restaurant in midtown Manhattan.

The restaurant had been able to survive through President Trump's loan program and by serving takeout. Even though local leaders hadn't yet allowed outdoor dining, the restaurant already had a sidewalk outdoor dining area and was preparing for the possibility, since the warm weather was here, and people were already gathering outdoors despite the slow lifting of restrictions.

The restaurant hired additional staff they could train and use once the go-ahead came. Since most of their former employees had left the city, Ana was lucky and got the job through her contact. She would ride her bicycle there sometimes, but she became a bit more comfortable with the subway, even though it took her a good forty-five minutes to an hour to get to work every day.

Unfortunately, this new job coincided with the murder of George Floyd and the resultant Black Lives Matter protests. Let me say, I was as shocked and appalled as anybody by that senseless murder—yes, Mr. Floyd had drugs in his system and yes, he had a record, but that type of force was totally unnecessary in that situation. Still, did that justify widespread looting and chaos? I know, there were many peaceful protestors, but thugs took advantage of the unrest, looting and destroying property. But that wasn't all. The liberal media turned a blind eye, but worse happened than that.

Ana would work until the restaurant closed at 11 p.m. every night. She was usually accompanied by the owner, Carmela, a delivery man, Carlos, and another coworker, Alicia, but that Monday night, June 1st, the owner Carmela decided to stay home. Alicia had the key and could lock up.

Throughout the day, the protestors marched past. Carmela called Alicia a couple of times, keeping up with the evolving situation and trying to decide whether it was dire enough to board up the shop and go home. But they only observed a few incidents of disorder, like people running up to the restaurant windows and flashing Ana, or rushing inside and demanding food, but they were able to assuage the various situations, and some police were around at times. Plus they were getting service calls and making deliveries, so it made sense to stay open.

However, when night fell, the situation completely changed. They began to see protestors hitting police and police smashing back with their shields and batons. Soon the incidents became calmer, and the turmoil seemed to move further up the streets, where police were trying to control the crowds. Ana and Alicia began to feel better. Carlos was on a call, and Ana was taking another order.

But this was the calm before the storm. Suddenly they noticed six men and two women, wearing masks and hoodies, enter the restaurant. But they weren't there for an order. Two men wielded guns and the others had shovels, wrenches, hammers, sticks, and pickaxes.

Ana was at the register, and when they demanded the money, she quickly put down the phone, opened the register, and gave them everything inside. Another man asked who had the combination to the safe, and Alicia insisted only the owner did and that she wasn't present. But this man wouldn't take no for an answer. He made Alicia go to the back to open the safe, and when she couldn't, he forced her to call the owner and ask for the combination.

Meanwhile, the other members of the crowd were ransacking the restaurant, taking statuettes, paintings, flags, and anything else that could be of value. As Alicia was calling Carmela, Ana was begging for her life from the other armed man who was still counting the money from the register, when one of the woman robbers noticed that the phone was on speaker.

"Puta," she exclaimed. "She's recording this."

This woman was carrying a pickaxe, and in anger, she swung it at Ana, who raised her arms to defend herself and got stabbed. In fact, the pickaxe stuck in her arm and splashed blood all over the two robbers and the counter. As Ana screamed, the other criminals freaked out. Not knowing what to do, wanting to end the screaming and the chaos to regain control, the man fired into Ana's stomach several times, but that only increased the screaming, so that like a pack of hyenas, the other robbers dropped their stolen goods and began beating Ana until she stopped screeching permanently.

Meanwhile, Carmela heard this commotion and began yelling herself over the phone. The man sticking up Alicia lost patience and shot Alicia in the head. The robbers decided to extricate the safe and take it with them, like the morons that they were, to try another day. They took the other items and what cash they could, loaded it into a getaway van that pulled up and sped off. Fifteen minutes later, Carlos returned from a delivery to find the bodies. And the police finally showed up a few minutes later. They had been called by Carmela and the person giving her order, but they were undermanned due to the protests.

I only give Ana's story as an example. She was hardly the only person to be terrorized, beaten, and even murdered that night, or on the nights that preceded and followed. Interesting how the stories of responsible Asian American business owners in the Bronx being beaten within inches of their lives were only shown on the more conservative-leaning local stations like Pix and Fox. There's a problem when the news is tilted in favor of certain causes and not truth. But these are the lives of real people, ruined by stupid, irresponsible, and cruel criminals and the politicians who give them cover, who used one true tragedy to prey on innocent others.

Xavier and Ana had an American dream. They pursued that dream like many immigrants before them, but they had their lives snuffed out by their own people, so-called People of Color, who refused to live by our laws. This isn't about race, it's about right, but Xavier and Ana's race did affect them because they were targeted by these criminals as they were believed to be vulnerable.

I don't have to tell you, Xavier and Ana's murders ruined the lives of their daughters, two sweet girls who were forced to survive in a crappy public middle school and now lost both their parents senselessly. Eduardo thought of adopting them and brought them down to North Carolina after the funeral service. He settled Ana's accounts, but despite being a good man, he didn't feel he had the ability to raise two teenage girls alone, with his wife having passed many years before.

So he put out a notice for adoption on a GoFundMe campaign to raise money for the girls, and a nice Christian family in Kansas came to the rescue. They were wealthy people who were dedicated to resurrecting the lives of troubled youth. They visited the girls, and despite initial pushback, the girls became enamored of their warm ways. The adoption is still being completed; it takes time, but I have no doubt the girls will have a loving home for the future.

But let this be a lesson to all Americans. Immigration is good, it is the American way, but we should not turn our backs on lawlessness and misbehavior, simply to check off politically correct boxes. Lives, especially of vulnerable immigrants, literally hang in the balance. I'm sorry I had to share with you such a disturbing and sad story, but I think it was necessary to educate you and give you a check on reality, given the slant in the media against conservative viewpoints and the stories of real, responsible people.

~ Day Three ~
Reaction to Taylor's Story

"Overall, it was an effective story," Cathy said. "But all the political stuff is such baloney. Do you realize that the Democrats passed the $1200 stimulus, that they were responsible for the rent moratorium, and that they also passed an unemployment bill giving people who were unemployed $600 a week, $2400 a month, so they could survive if they lost their jobs through no fault of their own? Trump has ignored the pandemic; he said it was going to go away with the warm weather, yet only the lockdown helped bring down the numbers."

"President Trump's name was on the checks, last time I checked," Taylor said. "But that's not even the point. A woman like Ana had too much honor to keep sitting at home and collecting a government check. I didn't even mention the fraud schemes with unemployment benefits, meant for good working people, including essential workers, being cashed in by criminals to defraud our government. They're investigating them in upstate NY but I'm sure it's in NYC too."

"For every example, there's always a counterexample," Lisa said.

Nalini concurred and noted, as Cathy had in the past, that most crimes were committed by American citizens, not by illegal or legal immigrants.

"That's my story," Taylor said. "I'm sticking to it."

Rashan finally got up—he had been quietly fuming.

"The biggest bullshit of all, Taylor," he said, "is about BLM. We're getting killed every day by bad cops, yet your focus is on a random murder committed by losers who took advantage of mostly peaceful protests? Get your priorities straight, man, we're not all criminals."

"I didn't say 'you' were," Taylor responded. "I didn't even mention an African American."

"I'm working every day to make sure BIPOC are being raised right, are being educated," Rashan continued. "We aren't exactly the privileged, man. You know we were the most disproportionately affected by Covid. Your white privilege is so strong you don't even notice it."

"Whatever," Taylor said. "I know I'm privileged, but I'm not sure it's because I'm white. Either way, I'm not telling a story about my yachting trip off Cape Cod. I work with vulnerable populations when I'm not racking up the dough. I don't think you should judge me so harshly."

Rashan waved dismissively at Taylor and sat down. Olive seemed to be listening and absorbing all this, but when no one else spoke, he came up and asked if anyone else had a comment. Not even Khassan said anything.

Olive shrugged. "Okay, I guess we're ready to vote?"

Taylor braced for this banishment. He figured Angela and Sylvania had abandoned him and that the others wouldn't support him either. But when the votes came through, Olive reported it was 5–4 for Taylor.

"You're lucky because the punishment was going to be worse than quarantining at the North Shore Complex," Olive said. "You were going to have to clean all the rooms with Maja and Zahra's advice, in both complexes."

"Glad I was spared," Taylor said, looking at Angela. "Maybe Lisa will be next, and she'll actually have to do some work after she bombs her tale."

"Ha ha," Lisa said, giving him the finger.

"Do you ever get tired of being a dick?" Cathy asked him.

Taylor didn't respond to that. Olive reminded everyone about the desserts and told them they could stay out there as long as they wanted.

Pritesh turned and looked for Hayley. She had been sitting next to him, but she wasn't there now. He saw Thiago slapping Taylor on the back and Darnell talking to Micah. The usual suspects were accounted for.

Meanwhile, Taylor approached Angela.

"Thanks for not punishing me," he said. "I know I can be harsh when I lose."

"Well, you didn't lose," Angela responded, tugging his shirt. "It was a good story. Thanks for representing people like me. It's tough to tell the truth in America, especially about Latinos."

This time he didn't have to think. He kissed her naturally. He even pecked Angela's nose.

"Carino," she said, holding him close. She could feel Darnell's jealous eyes on her back.

As Nalini took some malab iyo malawax, a Somali crepe drizzled with honey and shuk shuko sugar duster, from the dessert cart, Rashan approached, having grabbed some Ethiopian baklava made up of filo layers filled with dry fruits and chopped nuts and bound together with honey.

"Yo, did you vote for Taylor's story?" he asked.

Nalini shrugged. "It was a solid story. I voted on the merits."

"It's also about content. I thought we were all a team. Did you vote against Cathy too?"

Nalini didn't answer at first. "The votes are anonymous," she said.

Ricard approached. "Freedom is the American way, my friend. Let her vote as she wants."

"Or what? You'll lynch me?" Rashan said. "You're a brown traitor, Nalini. I can understand Pritesh wrapped around the white model's finger, but you?"

"Don't worry about him," Ricard said as Rashan went away to talk to Cathy. "It's funny how a biker can outargue a lawyer."

"How was picking up Cathy?" Nalini asked.

"Why, are you jealous?"

"Imagine spending all afternoon with a guy in the woods, and then suddenly he chooses to pick up another girl on the other side of an island. Sure, I'm thrilled."

"We can go on a ride now."

"Are you sure that's allowed?"

Ricard laughed. "Allowed?"

"Sorry, I am the quarantined girl," she said. She put down her dessert, and they went off.

Pritesh was still looking for Hayley as he saw Rashan, Cathy, Andrea, and Lisa starting to walk along the dark beach to the right. Sylvania and Khassan were preparing to throw around a glowing night frisbee. Taylor and Angela were headed back towards the Saggplex.

Suddenly Pritesh heard a large shriek on the left side of the beach. Another scream confirmed it was coming from the water. In the darkness, illuminated only by the moonlight, he could see two figures that seemed to be dancing in the water.

He started moving towards it, but suddenly he was eclipsed. Micah and Darnell rushed into the water. As Pritesh got closer, he saw it was Hayley struggling with what looked like a big fish about ten feet into the ocean. He realized it was a shark.

Darnell punched the shark, then grabbed it, trying to pull it off her, but it wasn't working. Then Micah held it too. Darnell picked up a surfboard floating nearby and started hitting it.

Finally, the shark let go. Hayley was no longer screaming. But she was convulsing. Micah held her above the water as he carried her to shore. Darnell was still swinging the surfboard, but the shark had swum away.

Soon Thiago was there too. As Micah lay her on the sand and pumped her chest to make sure she ejected any water she might have swallowed, Thiago flashed his light on her and saw the injuries: on her torso, upper thigh, and lower calf were jagged bites patterned like curving semicircles that looked like they were made from arrowheads.

He turned off the light and started to call 911, but suddenly Olive's hand was on his phone.

"What are you doing?" Thiago asked.

"You want her to get Covid and never leave the hospital?" Olive asked. "Because that's what's gonna happen if we call an ambulance and they take her. I'll call Alexa and Rashadi. They'll be here right away."

"She'll bleed to death before that."

"We have a nurse," he said as Andrea ran up with the rest of her crew. Andrea tried to close the wounds with her hands as she commanded Rafael to fashion a constricting band from the dining cloth. The men took off their shirts to use as constricting bands too. Abeo brought some bottles of whisky, which Andrea applied for a quick sanitizer.

Soon Ares and Rabia were using the flashlights on their phones to illuminate the wounds. Bom was helping close them with the constricting bands while Olive called Alexa and Rashadi.

Pritesh was crying as he stood over the scene. He was too shocked to help or do anything.

"Just talk to her, bro," Micah told him, so Pritesh knelt and tried to say some encouraging words to Hayley through his tears. She had thrown up some water and seemed to be in a semi-conscious case of shock.

Meanwhile, Thiago looked at his watch. "I swear, Olive, if she dies ..." he said, but then they noticed Alexa's van pull up on the beach. The two doctors, wearing their PPE, sprang out.

While Alexa checked her vitals, Rashadi got some gauze, sutures, needles, antibiotics, morphine, an oxygen tank, a saline tank, IVs, a defibrillator pump, and some other supplies from the van.

They hooked Hayley up to the IV.

"See, we have plenty of help," Olive said to Thiago, who rolled his eyes, his arms folded.

"How is she?" Olive asked Alexa.

"The wounds don't seem too deep, but I'll confirm with an X-ray at the clinic," Alexa said. "She fought back, so the shark probably went for different areas—it missed the artery but got some muscle and light veins. She's in shock, she's lost some blood, but I'm pumping some saline into her. And morphine for the pain."

Andrea was stitching up the wound on her lower calf as Rabia and Ares brought out a stretcher. Darnell and Micah were prepared to lift her onto it once Rashadi gave the word.

"You can treat her on your own?" Olive asked.

"If she regains full consciousness, yes," Alexa responded. "If not, or if she develops gangrene in the affected areas, we might need to go to a hospital, unfortunately."

As Andrea, Alexa, and Rashadi finished dressing the wounds, Hayley began moaning.

Pritesh rubbed her forehead, but he was still shaking and was unable to speak. So Thiago knelt down too.

"You awake, princess?" he asked.

She didn't respond, but her eyes were open now, and she was breathing.

"Hi, Hayley," Andrea said. "This is Andrea. We're going to take care of you, okay?"

"It's Alexa, Hayley. Tell me, do you feel pain?"

"No," she finally said. "Where am I?"

"You're on the beach in Sagg, okay?" Alexa said. "I'm going to take care of you."

She instructed the men to lift her onto the stretcher. Thiago and Pritesh tried to help too, but Pritesh only got the tips of his fingers on her torso.

"I can go with you," Thiago said to Alexa.

"That's okay. I can use Andrea's help, though."

"Moral support, Alexa. She needs moral support."

"Shouldn't that be Pritesh?" Khassan noted, slapping him on the back, but Pritesh seemed paralyzed.

"I don't want any distractions, Thiago," Alexa said. "Maybe bring over food later. If things go well, we might be back at the Saggplex tomorrow afternoon. But the X-rays will tell us the extent of damage, if there are bones involved, etc."

As Rashadi began to drive away, Olive felt a raindrop fall on him.

"We'd better clean up and get everyone back," he said to Thiago and Ares. "It's gonna pour."

"I still think it's about your wallet, Olive," Thiago said as he headed back to the carts.

Ares hugged Olive. "I know you're doing what you think is right," he said.

Rashan was watching this too, clustered with Lisa and Cathy.

"He should've called an ambulance," Lisa said.

"I don't know," Cathy said. "The hospitals are overloaded."

Rashan felt the raindrops falling with increasing rapidity. "We should go back," he said.

He looked back at the dark beach and the sea behind him. He noticed Lisa staring into it too.

Rashan awoke with a start. He could hear rain pelting against the windows and the sounds of occasional thunder. He'd dreamt about being in a perpetual whirlpool, the circular wave twirling him towards a black hole, and no matter how desperately he fought back against the current, he couldn't make gains against the power of the jet stream. As he neared the black hole and whatever its contents, or lack thereof, portended, he prayed to an invisible God he deemed Poseidon—but only Ares appeared, holding up a palm.

It was like how he felt in a relationship with Josh, the white hipster he had lived with until the pandemic hit. He had always ignored their differences, placed them in the back of his mind, but when the pandemic came, he realized the security he had envisioned in Josh was a mirage. Josh had returned to the farm in Montana to quarantine, said he even met a woman to settle down with. That was just to please Dad, Rashan thought. He'd never pictured Josh with a woman, only another man, and that only in his most jealous moments.

Josh had given him a fig leaf, allowing him to remain in his apartment in Fort Greene to quarantine. But now the lease was ending, and Rashan had to decide where to go. The pandemic wasn't over yet. Would schools be open? Much would depend on that. Maybe he could live with his mom if he did remote work. He didn't want to teach remotely, but it was probably the safest option.

But even during the lockdown, Rashan began to wish he was with his mom in Bed Stuy, even though he knew she was elderly and that he should avoid her. His sister was living with her husband in New Rochelle. That was the epicenter of the pandemic at one point, and he had been very ill at home. Thankfully, he hadn't died. But many people Rashan knew had.

That's why he was furious at Taylor's story the night before—the scenes of faceless criminal rioters attacking civilians were so racist and didn't even touch on the main killers of BIPOC during the pandemic, which was the virus itself. So, when he saw the card next to the door, he was elated. He could tell a story that wouldn't just depict Black people as stereotypical criminals and rioters. They were sensitive people too. They could feel; they could live; they could be complex and human.

Gently, he unfolded the flap, which was surprisingly easy to lift as it was only lightly sealed. He read a poem:

> Stories are like birds
> Expand wings and fly anew
> Now show us, can you?

It was a haiku. Would he tell a story in poetic form like Cathy? He doubted it. In college he had done improv comedy, so he considered making something up as he went along. But that might not guarantee the impact he wanted the story to have.

Downstairs in the dining room, everyone was waiting around tensely, hoping to hear about Hayley.

Pritesh wasn't there. Rashan wondered if he was with Hayley. He noticed Thiago pacing around near Taylor and Angela, who were wearing robes and holding hands.

"Cowards, both of them," Thiago muttered. Rashan assumed he meant Pritesh and Olive.

Soon Olive did appear, wearing blue silk pajamas. His hair seemed slightly disheveled.

"I'm sorry about everything that's happened; I hope you are all okay. I'm happy to report that Hayley is doing well. Her wounds have been treated by our doctors, and she's resting at their office in Southampton. If all goes well, she should be back at the Saggplex this afternoon."

Thiago huffed and turned his attention to the breakfast, a combination of omelets and Lebanese options. Rashan and Khassan both took the same plate of Lebanese nabulsi cheese, a few jams, zaatar, dukka, and olive oil. Khassan winked at him, reminding him he was an honorary Muslim.

"We're not all terrorists, just some of us are," Khassan joked. "And we're ugly. Small penises, big noses," he added. "Not as big as the Jews, but ..."

Lisa came in a bit late, which surprised Rashan. He thought maybe she would have gone down to the gym to work out, but she was also in her pajamas—hers were pink. The disheveled sisters included Nalini, who was in her robe. Rashan looked at Cathy.

"Yup, I was the only one in the gym," Cathy said. "Guess they thought jogging was off the table because of the rain."

"Or maybe the tragedy," Taylor commented. "Sorry to hear it."

Nalini was sitting with Ricard. Rashan assumed she had spent the night with him. He had relayed his suspicions about her voting patterns to Cathy, Lisa, and Andrea—she was basically excommunicated from their group, as far as he was concerned, but maybe she didn't care because she had finally hit it off with Ricard, who they also didn't like, except Cathy, for some reason.

"It's unfortunate that it's supposed to rain the whole day, except perhaps the evening," Olive said. "So we will have a couple of indoor activities today. And we'll see about tonight for the story."

Lisa and Cathy took sliced falafel, manakish, fatayer, hummus, baba ganoush, pita bread, and ka'ak. Also, some specially made Turkish coffee and some Middle Eastern teas as well, including zaatar, black, and mint teas. Abeo was at the omelet station, and Ricard took some scrambled eggs and old-fashioned southern grits served with home fries and buttered corn. Meanwhile, Taylor had some deviled eggs with hollandaise sauce, and Angela tried the eggs Florentine.

Olive explained the competition would be a Dance Dance Revolution in the den. Because of the tragedy, he wouldn't make everyone participate, but the winner would get a treat.

Rashan wanted to opt out to work on his story, but he loved DDR and would stake his rep on it. So, he decided to participate against Khassan, Taylor, Ricard, Sylvania, and Cathy. Angela said she would be Taylor's cheerleader. Nalini decided to cheer on Ricard but immediately regretted not participating when she learned Cathy and Ricard might go head-to-head based on the randomizer's matchups. So she decided to get into the competition, despite only wearing a bikini underneath her robe, and that meant one extra player—Ares— volunteered to compete, but then Olive decided he would enter instead. A randomizer picked new matchups and new songs for each. The difficulty was placed at three out of five.

Rashan figured since he had eaten a light breakfast, whereas Taylor and Ricard had eggs in their tummies, he would be lighter on his feet. Even Khassan had downed a bagel and cinnamon roll, not being able to contain himself.

Rashan faced off against Khassan—the randomizer chose "Clarity" by Zedd featuring Foxes. Rashan noted he hadn't grown up playing DDR in strip malls like Khassan, only having access to it at the public library where his mother was a security guard. But he astonished Khassan and beat him easily, hitting the bonus points on cue.

Against her arch-enemy Taylor and dancing to Dua Lipa's "New Rules," Cathy started off down, but she came back and pulled off a remarkable upset to Taylor's usual frustration. Rashan slapped her hand emphatically. Sylvania's height might have been a crutch against Olive as he cruised to victory dancing to David Guetta's "Playing Hard" featuring Ne-Yo. Then Ricard and Nalini went head-to-head to "Sky High" by Haruki Yamada, a DDR classic and a remix of the Jigsaw tribute to their 1970s song. It was a difficult track, and Nalini's athleticism was no match for Ricard's knowledge of the song. While she hoped he would go easy on her, his natural competitiveness led him to a narrow victory.

Next, Rashan faced Olive to "Party Rock Anthem" by LMFAO. Rashan thought he would be naturally good at it due to the song's mostly electronic beats, yet Olive stayed with him and finished with a flurry of moves to beat him. Ricard matched up against Cathy, and after the embarrassment of losing to Ricard on a song about cheating, Nalini had to see Ricard and Cathy match up to "Something Just Like This" by Chainsmokers and Coldplay, a song about getting together despite differences. Nalini was so frustrated that she made an excuse to get a drink and instead went up to Pritesh's room on the third floor.

She found him despondent.

"It's not your fault," Nalini said. "I mean, what could you do in that position?"

"Something. Anything. It's too late. I have lost her."

"She might be scarred for life," Nalini said. "I don't think losing her should be your biggest worry right now."

He agreed he would try to be there for her when she returned. He got up and hugged Nalini, crying into her bosom. She was taken aback, but then she rubbed his head of hair. She recalled rubbing Ricard's bald head the night before, after they had driven to Sag Harbor and checked out the ships sailing to the North Fork, oblivious to Hayley's tragedy.

Back in the den, Ricard and Cathy had a close competition. But Cathy won on the final sequence, to Ricard's chagrin and mock bow.

The final match was between Cathy and Olive. The randomizer picked "Rising Fire Hawk," an exceedingly difficult song that used to be expert level in an older version but was now available by default. Yet it was the perfect song to decide the champion.

"Ready to go up against the girl you banished?" Cathy asked.

"I didn't banish you," Olive replied. "Your peers did."

"It was good to be alone for a day, I have to say. If you win, Olive, do you get the prize?"

"Of course," he said. "I'm just another guest now."

The brutal volley of multiple steps in the initial sequence showed Cathy was way out of her element. Even though Olive struggled too, he had enough experience with the song to win easily.

"Big Brother gets the big prize," Ricard said bitterly.

"It's not so big," Olive said. "I get a lunch; you don't."

"We don't get a lunch?" Ricard asked.

"We ate a little bit late, and Thiago is planning something big for dinner," Olive explained. "And with the Hayley tragedy, I'm giving him and the chefs a bit of a break. You can have some more of the leftovers if you want. But otherwise, just wait until the bigger dinner."

"So, what are you eating?"

"I think I'll make myself a croquette, madame," he said.

"Qui, qui," Khassan mocked him.

"I bet Thiago's making it for him," Taylor said.

The group broke up. Ricard and Cathy headed to the game room to play some arcades. Meanwhile, Angela consoled Taylor on his latest loss, and they went up to his room on the fourth floor. Khassan found himself joking around with Sylvania as Rashan went to the library to pick up some books before he started to practice his story.

He picked up Saeed Jones' recent book *How We Fight for our Lives* and Jericho Brown's poetry collection *Tradition*. He looked for Roxanne Gay's *Bad Feminist,* but apparently Cathy had taken it out and hadn't returned it. Joan Didion, just because; crime authors Walter Mosley and Chester Himes; gay author Andrew Holleran. As he was leaving, he picked up some Chelsea Handler and David Sedaris, thinking he might make his story funny anyway.

The afternoon announcement was for the karaoke tournament. Ricard and Cathy were already in the game room, so they were the first to arrive. There they were confronted by Sung, Darnell, and Micah.

"We noticed you went somewhere on your motorcycle yesterday," Sung said.

"Yeah, to pick up Cathy at the North Shore," Ricard explained. "Ares said it was okay."

"How about in the evening? Coming back late at night with the Indian girl?"

Cathy looked intently at Ricard.

"It's a free country," he said. "I don't see the problem."

"We just wanna make sure you weren't exposed, brother," Darnell said, holding up a swab. "Where'd you go? Were you around anyone?"

"Nah, it was bare," Ricard said. "We just went up to Sag Harbor. Nobody was close to us."

"That's a high-volume area, compared to the rest of the Hamptons," Sung said.

"You waited long enough," Cathy said, trying to give Ricard some cover. "Everyone could have Covid at this point, given your logic."

"We review the cameras periodically," Sung said. "We don't always catch everything right away."

"Whatever, just test me," Ricard said and got the swab. "If I got it, maybe you all got it now."

"You'll be in big trouble then," Sung said. "Per the agreement."

Ricard wanted to say, "Fuck your agreement," but he held his tongue. Between Nalini and Cathy, things were suddenly going well for him here.

"Negative," Sung confirmed as Nalini arrived with Pritesh.

"What about her?" Cathy asked.

"We already got her," Sung said.

"Sorry, brother," Darnell told Ricard. "Just protocol."

Ricard locked eyes with Nalini, but she pretended like she didn't care and kept talking to Pritesh, who seemed nervous, watching the door intently as the others filed inside.

Many eyes were on Pritesh, but no one muttered a thing.

Those who missed the DDR competition didn't realize they weren't getting a lunch. Lisa asked about it, and Olive told them they could have the leftovers of the breakfast if they wanted.

"We're not paying anything for this, true," Lisa said. "But I didn't come here to starve."

Micah guided her towards the leftovers in the tech room. In the meantime, Olive announced that karaoke wouldn't be a competition.

"It'll be difficult to judge. So, this is going to be a team builder."

Yet immediately, best buddies Angela and Sylvania got into a heated competition.

Angela sang Mariah to perfection, and Sylvania mastered the offbeat "Gay Thoughts" by The Growlers. Angela continued with Selena and Beyoncé, and Sylvania with selections from *The Book of Mormon*. Cathy and Nalini tried to keep up, countering each other with Lady Gaga's "Poker Face" and "Fight Song" by Rachel Platten, and the tension seemed palpable for a continued faceoff, but ultimately, they deferred to the more passionate Angela and Sylvania.

Darnell suggested the guys get in on karaoke, but no one wanted to sing, not even Khassan. So, he took it upon himself and focused on gangsta rap, mimicking 50 Cent's "In Da Club" to huge applause. Angela countered with Rihanna's "Rude Boy," and a competition seemed to flourish between the two. Darnell answered with "Lose Yourself" by Eminem; Angela decided to sing a duet with Sylvania, the 90s song "The Boy is Mine" by Brandy and Monica. Essentially Sylvania bowed out after that, and Darnell and Angela went back and forth.

Tupac's "Hit Em Up," Celine Dion's "The Heart Goes On" ... the songs were so disparate that their contest was almost comical despite their mastery of the material. But the two finally collaborated on a duet when they sang "Promiscuous," with Angela as Nelly Furtado and Darnell as Timbaland. They got so into it that Darnell started sweating her with his dance moves, and while she responded to some extent, she rebuffed his attempt at grinding, and that almost resulted in a charge to the dance floor by Taylor.

To make peace, Sylvania suggested they each sing one song, and the group would vote on a winner, irrespective of Olive's wishes. Angela chose Toni Braxton's "Unbreak My Heart," and Darnell picked Nelly's "Ride Wit Me." Angela had just started singing when she saw Andrea wheel Hayley into the room, and she ceased abruptly, as did the music.

A poncho covered Hayley's head and body. She was somewhat wet from the rain, but it was just drizzling now. Andrea helped her take it off. She was wearing a hospital gown underneath. An IV was in her arm, and a clear bag was mounted on a pole sticking up from the wheelchair. Her injury was well-bandaged at both the thigh and the calf. It bulged around her midsection.

Hayley held up her hand as Andrea wheeled her to the center of the room.

"We're so glad to have you back, Hayley," Olive said. "How do you feel?"

"I've been better," she said, sounding tired. "I need to thank Andrea, Alexa, and Rashadi for taking care of me. And to everyone who helped me with the shark. My memory's a little fuzzy, but they told me a lot of you helped."

"Darnell beat the shit out of that shark," Khassan said. "And Micah pulled you out."

Darnell shrugged. "All in a day's work, girl. Glad you're feeling better."

She put her arms out. He bent down to hug her.

"Where's Micah?" she asked. Darnell informed her that he was with Lisa.

"And Thiago," Hayley said. "Alexa told me you helped. Come give Momma a squeeze."

Thiago bent down to hug her too. "You know, you could go home," he said.

"This is my home now," she said. "You are my family."

Everyone looked at Olive. It was a strange statement, but then, it was also a strange time.

"I'm glad you feel that way," Olive said with a mysterious grin.

Pritesh had been silently weeping. Hayley looked at him, but Pritesh couldn't return the glance. Instead, he rushed out of the room.

"So how long until she recovers?" Taylor asked aloud to break an uncomfortable silence.

"The wounds will take a while," Alexa said, "and she'll have to avoid strenuous activities, at least for a few days."

"Probably better to take her to her room to rest," Olive said.

"Of course," Alexa said. Andrea started to wheel her away.

"We really have to thank you, Andrea," Olive said. "I know you're not on the clock."

"Nurses are always on the clock," Andrea said as she wheeled Hayley through the curtain. "When people need us, we are there."

"I noticed you all aren't wearing your whole getup," Darnell said to Alexa and Rashadi, referring to their PPE.

"We're going to stay on the fifth floor to help monitor Hayley for the next week and a half," Alexa responded. "We've been wearing the PPE and testing twice a day. We've limited ourselves to telehealth appointments. We don't plan to be outside this safe zone."

"Olive paying you extra?" Darnell asked.

"Something like that," Rashadi said as they turned to leave, with Thiago tailing.

"Wonder what's going to happen with her and Pritesh?" Cathy asked Ricard.

"That's their problem," Ricard replied.

Everyone decided to wrap up the karaoke session and reconvene at dinner—Darnell and Angela's battle would be postponed. It was still raining outside. Upstairs in Hayley's room, Andrea, Alexa, and Rashadi helped Hayley into her bed. Thiago assisted with the IV equipment. Alexa explained they would be pumping her with morphine for the next day or two to help with the pain, but after that, they would transition to pills.

"That could get a little dicey, yes, doc?" Thiago asked.

"We don't want to overmedicate," Alexa responded. "But you don't want her to be in pain, do you?"

"Andrea, please, get some rest," Rashadi told her. "We will take it from here."

"Glad to help," she said. "If you need anything, Hayley, let me know. I'm so sorry this happened to you."

Andrea hugged Hayley and left. Alexa and Rashadi went to ready their room, leaving Thiago alone with Hayley.

"Thank you again for saving me," she said. "I'm not surprised it was you."

"You're very welcome, Momma. I do whatever I can to help my fellow man."

"Listen, can you see how Pritesh is?"

"That coward did nothing to help you."

"I want to make sure he's okay."

"He should come see how you are."

"I know; I always choose the worst men," she said, rubbing Thiago's hand.

"Believe me, my delicious momma, I am tempted by you, but I do not want to get a bad reputation with Me Too and everything else. You cannot even legally drink."

"Oh, is that the reason? Or maybe it's these fucking bandages?"

"Don't worry, my dear, you will recover in time."

"My career is ruined, Thiago. How am I gonna post pics with these scars?"

"There are surgeries, I think," Thiago said. "But modeling was always going to be finite for you. Better to branch into something more sustainable."

Thiago left soon after, saying he needed to prep the big dinner they had made.

Lying there alone, Hayley took out her phone and followed the Instagram stories of other models, including former friends who, like her, had left traditional modeling and tried to form a partial IG and TikTok career.

Very few girls had been as successful as she had; one even supplemented her income through OnlyFans, telling Hayley that nude pay-per-view was the way to make money these days, but Hayley wouldn't lower herself to that level. She was a real model who happened to be successful on social media.

Now she didn't have many options. Her career was already handicapped by her breakup with Terry, her former boyfriend and promoter, who had taken his team, along with the brand deals and her follower pages, with him. Her plan had been to sue him after leaving The Getaway, since he had used their "friendship" to leech off her success. She had never even read this contract that had given him control of everything except her personal pages—thankfully, the latter was where she had the most followers.

But now her injury made it impossible for her to post pics from the chest down. She could rely on face shots, but her body was what people wanted to see. Reposting old pics, which Terry's team did with her other pages, would only hold followers for so long. Eventually they would start dropping off. Reels were necessary to get fans in bulk. Competition was fierce, even for someone as successful as her.

While lying in a delirious state in Alexa's Southampton office, pumped full of morphine, she started thinking of ways to make money. The injury could be a compelling media story: she could start a GoFundMe; it could be big. But Olive's lawyer, Larry Summers, had nixed that possibility, calling her at Alexa's office to remind her not to speak or post about the incident, even after leaving The Getaway, or she would be in breach of contract.

Olive would pay for her medical care if she kept her mouth shut—maybe even the surgeries to come. That was a lifeline, as she was already broke and didn't have health insurance—she'd had coverage in Cali under her mom but had never bothered getting it under the ACA in New York due to the exorbitant prices, and now her mom needed all she could get under MediCal because she was in the "nut bin," as Hayley called it.

Yes, her mom had gone cuckoo after she had dropped her off to model mayhem in New York. Hayley sometimes blamed herself for moving out there, but this was always her mom's ambition for her, since she had never made it herself.

Delirium, pain, shock, pending confrontation, litigation decisions to be made, her mother in the loony bin in LA, and Terry on the lam. The Getaway was the best place for her. She really had nowhere else to go.

A few hours later, the rain stopped. It wasn't forecast to start again, but then, the forecast was usually wrong. Still, the powers that be decided to have dinner on the field past the patio, setting up tables on the wet grass, with a bonfire on the football field, the flames flickering.

Little did everyone know that Hayley, Alexa, Rashadi, and Andrea had been flown in by helicopter that afternoon by the service Blade (the pilot in a contained space and masked) at that very spot.

"At least we're less likely to get bit," Rashan said, referring to the mosquitos that might swarm on a humid evening. But they still saw the fireflies and heard the cricket chirps along with the whip-poor-wills and dying sounds of cicadas.

Of course, he was thinking about himself—he had prepared his story, not based on the books he had selected, but rather on the African "experience" that Abeo had set up for them the day before—the Atilogwu music, the dance, the atmosphere that seemed to correlate with some of Rashan's improv comedy performances in college.

Their dinner was Brazilian. Thiago stated proudly that he had outdone Abeo's spread the evening before by going straight to his national origins. Abeo begged to differ, claiming he would counter by cooking Nigerian at some point.

Traditional rice and beans, a staple dish for everything, was served with Brazilian pasta, in this case a combination of Japanese yakisoba and spaghetti; Brazilian pizza, wood-fired in the kitchen with a thin, flexible crust, a light tomato sauce, guava, minas and catupiry cheese for the vegetarians, chicken for the meat eaters. There was picanha barbecue; a feijoada stew made a little quicker than the 24 hours normally required, though Thiago had started the process in the early morning shortly after Hayley's injury; a Brazilian variation on Russian beef stroganoff, sauteed and served with Brazilian sour cream; empadao, a chicken pie; farofa, a dish of bacon and tapioca flour; and moqueca baiana, a fish stew.

Appetizers included boil hot de bacalhau, a little ball of deep-fried, salted cod; pastel de queijo, a fried pastry with chicken for omnivores and cheese for herbivores; pan de queijo, a cheese bread served with minas cheese and jam; a vinaigrette salad; extra sautéed collards; curcoxinha, a chicken croquette; and acaraje, black-eyed peas mashed with chopped onions and deep-fried.

Thiago started mimicking Abeo, repeating, "It's a paradise!"

Abeo and Bom rolled their eyes; Rafael laughed.

All served Thiago's meal as he rushed back and forth telling guests they could order at the tables if they wanted. Maybe Hayley's entrance had made them more reflective or self-conscious because most guests were dressed in their best and almost looked like attendees at a wedding. Sylvania was wearing a rather classy outfit, a slithery red cocktail dress made from silk velvet with sequins on hexagonal flaps that floated down each leg. Even Ricard was wearing a decent shirt as he sat with a sundress-draped Cathy, who was with Rashan, Lisa, and Andrea.

Rashan, wearing a clip-on bow tie, still considered Nalini a race traitor, so she, wearing a halter dress, stuck with Pritesh, even as she eyed Ricard constantly. Pritesh had apparently recovered enough to come down, but it wasn't clear what he would do if Hayley came out.

Then Alexa relieved his tension by approaching with a takeaway box. She began attacking the vegan portion of the cuisine. She put in small amounts of vegan sausage, tofu, and collard greens; a vegan version of farofa, with vegan bacon; and a vegetarian lasagna. There were also a couple of stews, a little too messy to carry up: vatapa, a thick stew made with vegetables rather than the traditional shrimp; and feijao tropeiro, a stew made with tropeiro beans.

As she was finishing up, Pritesh got up and told her he would carry up the food. Nalini wasn't sure how to feel about this about-face because it left her alone again.

Upstairs in Hayley's room, Rashadi was measuring the morphine they were administering, but upon Pritesh's entrance, and at Hayley's request, she left them alone.

He placed the box on the drawer next to Hayley and began bawling again.

"Enough with the crying, Pri. It would have been nice to have an assist."

"I choked," he mustered up. "I'm sorry."

"It wouldn't have mattered anyway. I'm a freak now. So go and get some other girl."

He started shaking his head wildly.

"No, no, no," he said. "You're not a freak. You're a princess to me."

"I wish that was a good thing."

They were both tickled at that. She made room on the bed. He curled up like a ball, put his head on her upper chest, and caressed the bandage on her lower abdomen.

"Does it hurt?" he asked.

"With all this shit pumped into me by the dear doctors? Nah, I'm in paradise."

Downstairs, the dessert and drinks were brought out, but in the meantime, Rashan told everyone he preferred if they sat on the grass in front of the bonfire, in a circle around him, to mimic African dance. "There's no distance between dancer and watcher, actor and participant," he said. Most groaned at that, since they didn't want grass stains on their clothes. Plus, they were eating dessert and drinking. Taylor, in a tuxedo, was enjoying a brigadeiro, a chocolate truffle, with a spiked Brazilian lemonade. Khassan ate a beijinho, a coconut fudge ball, with guarana, a soft drink made from the fruit; Lisa couldn't help herself and had the quindim, made from sugar, ground coconut, and egg yolks spiced up by Rafael through gastronomy, with a vinyl quente, a mulled wine; and Andrea ate a sonho, a cream doughnut, with cajuina, made of blended cashewed apples. Others had curau, a Brazilian corn pudding, and crème de manga, a mango cream cup, with varieties of cachaca, a sugarcane juice made in both alcoholic (caipirinha, caju amigo, rabo-de-galo, etc.) and non-alcoholic versions.

The progression into Rashan's preferred circle was slow, but little by little, it was accomplished. Nalini made a play for Ricard by sitting near him, only separated by a conciliatory Lisa, with Cathy on his other side. Taylor and Angela held hands, with Taylor maneuvering them away from Darnell. Khassan hung with Sylvania.

Olive approached the circle. He was wearing a seersucker suit.

"You're wearing that after a rainstorm?" Sylvania asked. "You're not gonna sweat out or anything. How about this: I'll make you a funky suit tomorrow, dear."

"Sounds good," Olive said. "Okay, so are we all ready for Rashan's story?"

"Ready as I'll ever be," Taylor said sarcastically.

~ Day Four ~
Introduction to Rashan's Story

"Thanks for coming in your best following a trying night and day," Olive said. "I hope you haven't drunk too much. In addition to the Brazilian hard lemonade, I think we have some South African liqueurs left from yesterday too. They can be pretty buzzing. And if you haven't been to Cape Town or out on a safari in Kruger, I recommend trying it before you die, which might be sooner than later the way things are going.

"We have the perfect storyteller for the occasion, I think—Rashan Hall (he/him/his—gotta get those pronouns right!), a proud gay man dedicated to a life of service, an elementary school teacher in a rough neighborhood in his native Brooklyn. He once did improv comedy in college, so that's why I thought he might tell an interesting and possibly funny story. That said, I don't know what he has in mind for us. Anticipation is part of the fun, but I'm excited to hear it. Please welcome to the de facto stage, Mister Rashan Hall (he/him/his)!"

The liberal crew went wild. Khassan and Sylvania gave him grudging respect.

"Thanks, everyone," Rashan said as he slowly came up to the bonfire and got a backslap from Olive. "It's funny, all afternoon I was working on my story: I read through a bunch of books and thought about what I read about my historical roots when I was hunkered down at my apartment in Fort Greene after my boyfriend, Josh, left me to move back to Montana at the beginning of the lockdown.

"I think that the key to putting our painful past and present to rest is comedy. And I do think it's important to understand history to properly appreciate the present. As William Faulkner once said, 'The past is never past,' and that's especially true for African Americans.

"But then I remember listening to that fucking Atilogwu mix yesterday and watching these impromptu dances. I planned a story, but then I scrapped it. And forget about history and comedy too. I'm settling in for some long-form improv.

"In typical short-form improv comedy, you're with a troupe; someone in the audience has a suggestion that starts things off, and then somebody else in the troupe starts a gag, and you've just gotta follow along, respond, and improvise on your own but in a way that meshes with the whole. There's a cardinal rule: 'Never deny, always agree.'

"In long-form improv, especially if it's one person doing it, you're starting off with a concept, character, or setting and then building off that. Like Cathy was versed in spoken word but never told an entire story in spoken word, I've never done long-form improv, so I've set that as my challenge for tonight.

"I'm starting as my basic premise: a character named Stephen, who is a queer, Black librarian in Brooklyn who gets into a relationship with a hot hipster from Montana. Stephen is nearly a decade older than me, though —I decided to make it a little personal but a little distant too.

"This is a tough time for African Americans and for queer people too. The pandemic has accelerated this, but it didn't cause it. I'm hoping to tell a story that will make you understand a bit of what some of us are going through, the pain we feel as a people who have been systematically oppressed yet also trying to grapple with present realities, attempting to be normal and ourselves simultaneously beside all that necessary political noise.

"I read that in African music and dance, there is no distance between dancer and watcher, actor and participant, so that's why I asked everyone to form a circle around me so you can be one with the story as I tell it."

Taylor rolled his eyes but didn't comment. Then Khassan did blurt something out.

"Since the audience can make a suggestion in improv, can I?"

"Maybe we can all make suggestions throughout," Taylor requested.

"That could get complicated, Taylor," Rashan responded.

"Yeah, we could be here for hours," Cathy noted, staring at Taylor, "and the story could get pretty disjointed, especially if the haters try to mess you up."

"Let's compromise," Rashan said. "I'll take one suggestion before I start, Khassan."

"Fine. Put in a Black Panther who is in prison like your dad was."

The suggestion seemed to make Rashan uncomfortable, but he assented.

"Okay, Khassan," he said. "You got it. Here I go."

~ Day Four ~
Rashan's Story
(AKA "BLACK BOY'S BALLAD")

~ Stephen ~
The Black Kid from Bed Stuy

So, there was this sensitive kid from Bed Stuy named Stephen. He was black and he grew up in the hood where no one gave him a chance to express himself. But he stayed true to himself in this macho world, and it was through education and caring teachers that he got a chance to escape that prison of the mind.

He earned that BA at Brooklyn College and even went ahead and got his Masters at Queens College. He worked full-time so he took a few years to get that, but not as long as some of these knuckleheads do—and by his late 20s, he was a librarian at a public library in Bushwick.

Stephen had struggled with his sexuality. He was too afraid of reprisal to tell anyone while growing up, even while queerness was becoming more accepted. He tried to stay away from that toxic negativity from the gangbangers and other fools who are dumb enough to play into the white man's prison, literally and figuratively.

Stephen did know the deal literally, as his dad was in prison for murder. His father had been a Black Panther in the 70s and many say that when he joined the Nation of Islam in the 90s his former brothers, now a bunch of informants, got mad and framed him for killing a cop when in fact they had done the deed themselves in an inside job.

It always made Stephen angry, but then he never knew his dad so he steered clear; his mom had stopped taking him to Sing Sing when he hit puberty. She was a hard-working custodian at the local library, which is how he got to reading and was inspired towards his path.

He'd come out to his mom when he was in grad school; she was disappointed, but she had accepted it. He could never tell his old pals from Bed Stuy; they'd probably cap his ass. So, he cut all ties with that world and moved into a tiny apartment in Bushwick that was walking distance from the public library where he worked.

~ Stephen ~
The Queer Cat

Thankfully, the library was the place where he could be in a safe space. He could read queer lit that made him feel heard and be among people more tolerant. Yet even in a profession open to LGBTQIA identity and expression, he sometimes felt the Other when talking to straight people and even with other queer folks.

But check this, I want to step back a bit and chart Stephen's inroads into this environment so we can really step into his shoes. Stephen guessed he was gay as early as middle school, but he fronted for a while. He did bogus shit like holding hands with girls and dating in groups. He kissed a couple of girls and went "steady."

By the time he got to Brooklyn College, he was watching gay porn, but he was still shy about chilling at the queer club, cuz he found them cliquey. So, he went online and tried to meet up with guys, usually in Manhattan or sometimes down in Sheepshead Bay. The last thing he wanted was to date a brother, not because he didn't like chocolate but cuz he didn't want to be outed near his hood.

Fast forward to grad school, and he'd found his stride a bit more. He came out to his mom, started dating brothers and made gay friends in Queens, particularly in Jackson Heights. But still, he found a lot of these cats were ignorant and just into hard sex. He didn't mind it at first, but like all people, he wanted to find love. Even in his late 20s (and don't confuse him with me, please, I'm a lot younger!), he was still very impressionable and had starry eyes for a better life.

So, once he got that full-time gig and started visiting the other side of Bushwick, his fantasies about being loved by someone mature, emotionally stable, rich, and yes, even privileged, exploded.

~ Bushwick ~
The White Part

Here's the deal if you don't know Brooklyn. I'm gonna be specific to Bushwick but this goes for much of Brooklyn these days, at least pre-pandemic. You've heard about gentrification, but do you know it's reality? Do you know that the architect of this city, a man named Robert Moses, arranged this city to isolate African Americans and make sure we couldn't access beaches, pools, parks and other amenities that so-called civilized white people could? Sorry, I did my thesis on this topic, so I thought I'd throw that shit in.

This so-called gentrification of today is a direct result of that Grand Design, so that we have two neighborhoods in every part of the borough, the part where whites and other "accepted races" like Asians live, and the other part which is mostly black and Hispanic. This is where whites and Asians who aren't as wealthy (maybe they are also librarians and educators or work in non-profit or something) are making inroads, displacing minorities even further out into southeast Long Island, Valley Stream and faraway places like that.

The gentrified part of Bushwick is kind of like in Lena Dunham's bogus show about white privilege, *Girls*. It's the area where Roberta's is, near Moore Street and Bogart, and the other section along Knickerbocker Avenue, Maria Hernandez Park, Myrtle and Central, that's code for White People Central, a small area where everyone is white, and there are pretty much no cops.

But if you make inroads into the hood, go down Bushwick Avenue and Malcolm X Blvd, you'll see the real Bushwick, where the most sophisticated restaurants are bodegas and broke taco spots, where there are cops every few blocks, and constant traffic lights, and speed cameras, and dollar stores, and laundries, and all other money traps to make sure people of color stay poor. And if you don't think this ain't on purpose, you ain't paying attention.

Anyway, if you're an educated brother living in one of these areas, your best bet is to escape and try to fit into the gentrified area. You might feel awkward being one of the few people of color there, but then white people will accept a certain percentage and might even think you're kind of cool, as long as you fit in the box, fill the quota, and make them feel good about supporting "social justice."

Gentrified Bushwick's got a lot of weird shops and museums, and some events are just put on temporarily. One week a large warehouse near Roberta's had a performance art installation on triggering incidents. You would go into a room that presented things that happened in New York once upon a time, like the Kitty Genovese stabbing, or the barbershop hit on Albert Anastasia, or the Abner Louima desecration, or even mundane shit.

After each experience, you would get a card that leads you to a different room: it could further incite you or calm things down, or it could alter your perceptions completely. You could leave notes of your own explaining your feelings or if the trigger was too profound you could leave as well. Of course, like all art aimed at white people, they included one assault on a black person by the NYPD from like 25 years ago, just to make it seem like they're not racist, and focused mostly on shit that happened to white people in the "good old days" from the 50s and 60s.

~ Jacob ~
The Connector

While writing down his triggering experience to the Abner Louima presentation which shook him to the core but was insufficiently whitewashed (I won't even describe the sketchy "acting display;" it's too ridiculous), Stephen met Jacob who was watching him write, agreed with his assessment, and sympathized with his concerns. They decided to revolt and left the warehouse together to eat a late brunch at a local hole-in-the-wall, and that's where he made his first white friend in Bushwick.

But he was hardly done. Jacob knew lots of people—kind of like that lady, Lois Weisberg from Chicago that Malcolm Gladwell wrote about in *The New Yorker* one time in the late 1990s—that was around the time I was born and my dad was screwed during the Million Youth March due to his association with Khalid Abdul Muhammad—y'all know now I do research, but anyway, I've said too much: Stephen is not me.

Point is, Jacob was an extrovert; he loved people and knew lots of 'em, and unlike some of those dense kids, he was an urban half-Jew and an emotionally available cat, so he understood the black experience not just actually but emotionally. These two bonded over brunch and Jacob invited him to a house party he was having the next weekend.

Now Jacob's wife, Rebecca, was the same way; she was a strong Christian originally from the Midwest so she took charity and connecting people seriously. They invited tons of people to monthly parties, even homeless people they'd met on trains and people with Down Syndrome who lived next door or whoever. They cooked up a big meal, and they served everyone a million times over, and everyone was playing video games or card games or board games, or they were chilling or making out or whatever people did at house parties.

Now Stephen would've normally gone to one of these white boy parties and been a shy fly on the wall, wearing his coat half the time until finally being persuaded to stack it with those other coats in the host's bedroom by some drunken weirdo, and then, fearing someone would steal it, like expected from the hood, he'd grab it and leave.

But Jacob welcomed him in and made him feel right at home in the beginning so that his coat went down on the bed right away, and Rebecca offered him some beer and homemade cookies so he forgot about his jacket pretty fast, and he got introduced quickly to other people. And that's where he first met Max.

Mag(nificient) Max

I've got you close together because I want you not only to understand but to feel Stephen's attraction to Max. Here was a tall, handsome, man in his late 30s with a beard and tattoos; he drank craft beer, and he could talk about the ingredients and process because he owned the actual fucking brewery that made it! Together with a friend anyway, who I'll also be introducing.

So Max fucking had tattoos. And big muscles. And a beard that filled up his big jowl. Did I mention that? One of his tattoos had a big Buddha extending down his arm, the other one had a sketch of Jesus. He had both a Star of David and a Swastika tattooed on his chest and a cross on his back. He said they're all the same; who gives a fuck.

And he told Stephen about his trips to Southeast Asia: Vietnam, Thailand, Laos, Cambodia, and Angkor Wat. South America: Patagonia, Chile, and the Aurora Australis. Europe. The Northern Lights. Ibiza, Santorini. I mean Stephen had barely left New York City except for trips up to Sing Sing and the occasional visit to relatives on Long Island, New Jersey, and once to South Carolina which he could only vaguely recall. So that was eye-opening.

Right now, it's in vogue for queer peeps to ascribe to asexuality, and non-binary identifiers, and shit like that. To each his own, but let's face it, it's a puritanical movement within LGBTQIA. Let me tell you, Stephen was a passionate soul who had a strong sexuality, and it was burgeoning. I mean he couldn't wait to kiss Max and get his beard scuffing over his soft cheeks and be under his powerful muscles.

Long story short, remember I mentioned the coat room; well, that's where these two ended up late at night, making out on those coats, until someone came in to retrieve theirs; Stephen and Max had to flip back up, acting like it wasn't a big deal. Max went to talk to other people. Stephen was kind of embarrassed and wanted to leave the party, but he didn't want to walk back through the hood this late at night, so he called an Uber.

The next day he was hung over; for a few days he let the experience ride, but he became kind of obsessed with Max, so he started stalking him through Jacob's friends list on Facebook. You know how fraught and neurotic shit can be when you're not sure how or whether to approach someone you like.

Stephen was just about to friend him when he got a request from Max. He accepted right away, and Max messaged him; they decided to have brunch at a different hole in the wall that weekend and visit a quaint museum dedicated to displaying obscure artifacts from alternative music festivals in the 1960s (meaning alternative to Woodstock).

Stephen learned that Max was originally from Montana, but had gone to college in Philly, moved to California briefly, and then to NYC with some college friends.

"Montana, that's far away," Stephen said.

"Yeah, it wasn't very diverse; everyone looks like me!" Max said, laughing. "I like being in NYC, a cosmopolitan place where people don't have narrow viewpoints and small minds. Sure, there are hip places in Montana too, like Missoula and Bozeman, but I grew up on a ranch. Not exactly poor, but somehow I was the first in my immediate family to go to college, so maybe that tells you something."

That's really where they bonded. Because while Stephen had heard that his father's side of the family had been fairly educated, he never knew his father; his mother only had a high school diploma, and most of his extended family had, at best, a two-year associate's degree. The Library Science Masters was a big deal.

Max and Stephen talked about books and culture, even about this weird museum with obscure artifacts from old hippies. When the date was over, Stephen told Max he had a good time, and there was that awkward moment when he wasn't sure if he should go in for a kiss or wait. So nervously, he turned away and said he would call an Uber, but Max offered to give him a ride home. He said he would have done the same the weekend before, but he was too drunk.

Stephen was floored. Who in Brooklyn has a car? Stephen and his mom even used to rent a car to go up to Sing Sing or visit relatives. No permanent car was the reason she gave for stopping visits to his dad, not that Stephen believed her.

"We have cars in Montana," Max noted. He had driven it over; the car had Montana plates. Stephen wasn't sure he had ever seen Montana plates before.

Stephen was initially going to refuse Max—he was embarrassed to tell Max where he lived—and it was also slightly possible that Max was a serial killer or some #Metoo style rapist harasser. But Stephen felt safe enough, so he got in Max's car, a freaking Mercedes Benz AMG, and asked how Max could afford that.

"Better to bring this than dad's Lamborghini," he said. "I'm not driving faster than 80 anywhere here."

Stephen was impressed but also intimidated. No wonder Max could afford to own a brewery (with a partner, granted); he probably hailed from generations of money. Almost all the sweethearts Stephen knew in Queens didn't have much bling: they were immigrants or came here within a few generations.

"Do you really want to drive me home?" Stephen asked as he sat in the luxury car.

"Of course, Stephen. Unless you don't feel comfortable."

"I'm just not sure you'll feel comfortable where we're going."

Max laughed. "I drive through Brooklyn all the time. Give me the address, I'll put it into my phone."

Stephen did as he was requested; they crossed Flushing Ave and cruised down Wilson, stopping at all the lights.

"You pass one of these, a cop might stop you," Stephen said, pointing at a cop double-parked a block over. "Well, maybe not you."

"I'll be careful," Max said. "But I know what you mean. I'm aware of my white privilege."

Then Max expressed anger at the life People of Color were forced to live, making notes about the neighborhood, the delis and the dollar stores. Stephen lit up; by the time Max pulled up to his place, Stephen wasn't shy anymore. He jumped Max, and they made out for a few minutes before Stephen got out, asking Max to text him when he got home.

They had similar weekly brunches for a bit, went to more weird museums and performance shows, even to concerts and readings in cheap apartments by cult figures like Cuddle Cat and Wonky Woman, who still sold their singles on CDs. CDs!

Like all good romances it went slow, and months passed before Stephen let Max enter his shitty tiny apartment, but when he did, they went deep into each other, in more ways than one.

Prancing and Romancing in the Echo Chamber while Popping the Bubble

For a while, though, their romance existed in a bubble. I don't just mean the Brooklyn bubble, or the gentrified bubble, but more specifically, Jacob and Rebecca's friend bubble. Because even though that couple was constantly moving more people into their circle, it was mostly the same crew that hung out weekend after weekend, and Stephen and Max were mainstays.

Which doesn't mean Stephen wasn't over at Max's place. In fact, the opposite was true, and after a while, Stephen's apartment was just a place to keep some stuff, and he was essentially living in Max's crib.

But check this, Max didn't live in Bushwick. No, he lived far away in Greenpoint, closer to his brewery in Williamsburg. Which is why the car was helpful. Still, Stephen ended up using Uber a lot, and Max would pay the bills.

Max lived in a loft apartment on the water. He did have a roommate named Clay, also his business partner. Clay was originally from Savannah, Georgia, and he had some southern macho tendencies that annoyed Stephen, but they got along okay. Max and Clay lived on different floors, attached by a rickety ladder. A roof was above the apartment where they could get some further privacy.

In addition to attending Jacob's parties in Bushwick, after which they would usually drive drunk back to Greenpoint (which was safer than driving drunk to Stephen's place) and sleep in the next morning. Then they would either cook brunch or go out for eggs and mimosas with a whining Clay. They would also, occasionally, take a trip upstate—mainly meaning along the Hudson River Valley—to places like Peekskill and Croton-on-Hudson. They hiked in Harriman State Park or Bear Mountain, or fished at Jones Point Park, and tried to never visit Donald Trump State Park, good God, I hope that name doesn't last long.

On these journeys they passed Sing Sing a lot, but Stephen never mentioned that his dad was incarcerated there for a murder he possibly didn't commit. He tried not to think about it and focused instead on pretending to enjoy the outdoor activities that Max loved. On their initial excursions, Stephen found that being in nature freed him and was a welcome change from Brooklyn, but soon he realized he wasn't as rugged or used to the physical exertion that Max found natural.

Sure, it was nice hiking to a remote spot, making love wildly in the dirt, buck naked, or smoking some strange, crazy, inappropriately-laced pseudo-weed while fishing for some eel, but when they started camping overnight and shitting in the dirt, it became a little much for Stephen.

Still, he loved Max and didn't want to disappoint him. He liked how Max always introduced him to new things, but mainly, he found Max safe. He loved being in his arms. He adored the sweet moments when they would wiggle their noses, staring into each other's eyes, knowing they would be each other's forever. Stephen had had plenty of hookups he had regretted; he never had a relationship enduring past a few dates, but this relationship had lasted many months.

Summertime Gladness

That was in the spring of 2019, before the pandemic. In the summertime, they saw Shakespeare in the Park, a couple of concerts at Barclay Center and Forest Hills Stadium, and made some beach outings to the Rockaways, Jones Beach, and Long Beach, but never made it this far out in Long Island. Still, these excursions reminded Stephen of his relatives in Valley Stream. He realized maybe they had reached the point in their relationship where he should introduce Max to his family, and he thought organizing a family barbecue might be the best bet.

Max had yet to meet Stephen's mother. That seemed to be a preliminary step before introducing Max to his greater relatives, whom he rarely saw. But Stephen was concerned. While his mother had accepted that her son was gay, introducing her to Max would crystallize this concept. White people share shit all the time, but Stephen and his mom had never discussed his sexuality in depth. Its actuality would only sink in once he introduced his first gay partner. And frankly, Stephen was scared; this was his first real relationship, and he didn't want to jinx it or scare Max away.

His relatives, on the other hand, didn't know Stephen was gay and likely didn't suspect it, and that made him more nervous. On the other hand, no one had said anything against homosexuality outside of a few random political comments, so he wasn't sure how they would react. One had been to prison on a soft drug charge and one for a domestic violence incident, but he never felt uncomfortable around them, at least not for that reason.

No, the main discomfort was cultural. They were suburban, he was city, and Max was elite, at least in Stephen's mind. How would Max react to being at a family barbecue where fried chicken and waffles, collard greens, Mac and cheese, fried okra, watermelon, jambalaya with jerk chicken were the offerings? (Yeah, he had a Cajun and Caribbean wing that married into the family too; will explain when I get to it.) And how would they react to a muscular white hipster with tattoos and a big beard who lived in Greenpoint?

Stephen's mind started churning. To make the reveal more indirectly, he could combine friends and family so he could arrive together with the guests, and his mom would already be there. Maybe not mentioning that Max was his partner but gradually making it clear through hand holding and some cuddling. Or would his family feel betrayed that he hadn't been straightforward?

He thought further. To diffuse cultural tension, they could hold the event at a park in Greenpoint, Williamsburg, or Bushwick. Then Stephen could invite his relatives to the city, controlling the agenda in their gay-friendly turf and providing them food. But his relatives might not want to come deep into Brooklyn, and they might not like the food. And wasn't the point to introduce Max into their African American culture and make him comfortable in it, rather than pulling them into his hipster world? Or did it make more sense since Stephen had already moved into Max's world and wasn't interested in leaving it?

Stephen's experience dealing with diverse groups of people at the public library helped him. He decided he would compromise in a way that would make sense for all parties. He would call his family out to his turf, but make it a potluck, so they could bring their own food too, diversifying the selection and keeping everyone happy—in the stomach, at least.

His mother would bring her stuff with the intention of meeting family (granted, she didn't always get along with everyone, and that was a reason for limiting interactions, but whatever) and would be introduced to Max at the same time. It seemed as foolproof a plan as he could make, given all the elements at play, and he kind of felt like a genius for coming up with it.

First, he needed to see if Max was open to it. In bed one night after making love, resting in Max's arms, he brought up that he hadn't seen his mother or his relatives in a while.

He hoped Max would say that he would be open to meeting them. Instead, Max gently encouraged Stephen to visit his family. While this wasn't the response Stephen wanted, it was encouraging and sweet. So, he told Max that the family was having some issues and wouldn't it be a good idea to have an event where they could bring his mom and her relatives together for a potluck so everyone could meet again after so long and become whole?

Max was silent for a bit but then agreed that it would be a good idea. The next evening, after they had both arrived home from work, and Clay was busy cooking (it was his turn—he and Max were competing to prove who was the best), Stephen told Max he wanted to invite all their friends to make it into one big smash. That would also repay Jacob and Rebecca because finally, now they would be the party makers.

Max said, "Sure, sounds like a great idea." Even Clay concurred and was excited to cook for it.

The Great American Potluck

East River State Park is now called Marsha P. Johnson State Park after an LGBTQIA activist who was important to the Stonewall uprising. It was renamed in early 2020 by Governor Cuomo right before the pandemic hit, and I heard that any day now they're going to do an official ceremony and announce some big improvements.

In Summer 2019 it was chosen by our friendly couple for their first major event because a) it was very close to the brewery and not too far from Max's apartment and b) It was on the East River and featured a great view of Manhattan. It was bigger than WNYC Transmitter Park and had more public space and tables for picnicking than Bushwick Inlet next door.

It was also near Smorgasburg, a large market open on Saturdays, so if anyone didn't like the potluck, they could always go buy stuff. Parking was tough, especially when Smorgasburg was operational, which is why Max had argued for McCarren or McGolrick in Greenpoint or even Maria Hernandez in Bushwick.

But the lure of the beach was too big, and East River won out. In fact, they chose to do it on a Sunday when Smorgasburg was closed so they wouldn't have the congestion—the guests would just have to like the food. Max offered to pay for some collective Uber rides from Bushwick, but Jacob and Rebecca dismissed them, saying they would take the L train and walk.

Most of his relatives from Valley Stream agreed to come. Stephen picked up his mom, driving Max's car—he had taken the driving test in the early spring after being taught by Max and was now a licensed driver. Stephen's mom's first comment when crossing the street from the housing development as Stephen carried her homemade cuisine was to ask Stephen how the hell he could afford a Mercedes Benz on a librarian's salary. Had he started dealing drugs?

"No, Ma," he said, kissing her cheek. "It's my friend's."

"Of course. I was just testing you, sweetie," she said, with a grin. "But what kind of friends do you have now?"

"You'll see, Ma," he said, as he put four trays and one wrapped pie in the trunk.

He had to circle a few times, but he found parking only a few blocks away. It was a nice day, early Sunday afternoon—no Smorgasburg, no active meters, or alternative side block-offs. He carried the trays into the park, making the long walk past the bathrooms and dog run to the beach area, where Max and Clay had said they would find a spot.

Stephen looked around for them. His mom was carrying a couple of drinks with her.

"Lots of people," she said.

"Not as bad as Saturdays."

"But a great view."

"That's why we chose it, Ma," he said, when he finally spotted Max and Clay. They had nabbed a picnic table right next to the beach, a prime spot, and had brought their own foldable table and a barbecuing grill. Max rested the trays on the table as Clay boasted about how he had already taken a few trips from the brewery and his own car to get stuff.

Max and Clay had brought a casserole, meatloaf, some linguine and clams, a few artisanal sandwiches and brownies they normally sold at the café area of the brewery, along with some non-alcoholic drinks including green tea, soda, and other caffeinated beverages.

"We could've been douche-y and brought some beers but, I figure we could all go for drinks at the brewery once things die down or they kick us out at dusk," Clay explained.

Stephen hated Clay for acting so perfect in public while being an insufferable whiner in private. But he caught his lip as he introduced both to his mom as good friends.

"So wonderful to meet you, Ma'am," Clay said, bending a bit as he took her hand lightly. For a second, Stephen thought he was going to kiss it, but he didn't go that far.

"My, what a gentleman," she said. "It's Patricia."

Clay nodded. Stephen glanced at Max, uncertain how to approach the issue at hand.

Max took the opposite approach, shaking her hand effusively, smiling and calling her "Ma."

Then he placed his arm around Stephen and held him by the waist.

Stephen leaned into him shyly, then pulled away just as fast, clapped his hands and said, "So, when's everyone else coming?"

Max didn't seem happy about that, but he didn't say anything. Instead, he moved to unwrap the smothered chicken, fried fish, cornbread, black-eyed peas, and pecan pie that Stephen's mom had made.

"Damn," Clay said. "Is that Pecan Pie? I'm from Georgia originally and that's my favorite."

Ma smiled. "My family has roots in North and South Carolina mainly, but I've been down to Georgia a few times. We'll talk, young man."

Then Ma pulled Stephen aside. Now she was frowning.

"This is why you invited me?" she asked, aiming her eyes at Max. "Invited us?"

"Sorry, Ma, to lay it on you like this."

"I just wish you had been more straightforward about it."

"I was embarrassed. I thought you might take it the wrong way."

"Stevie, I accepted it long ago."

"How about the others?"

"They might not be as receptive. That's why you should've consulted me first. But now that I know, I can steer them. Your aunt Gladys and Phil are hopeless, but the others, I can work on."

She hugged him tightly. Then she turned to Max. "So what? Are you two engaged?"

Max looked at Clay, then smiled. Stephen was embarrassed.

"Ma, no. We're just—"

"Oh, 'in a relationship.' Please. Work on that, young man. Now let us get to preparing this food. We've got a big crowd coming."

She helped Clay prepare the canned heat, racks and portable hot plates as Stephen and Max stepped aside and talked about how they were glad that Ma had accepted their relationship.

Family Fusion

The first to arrive were the aforementioned Aunt Gladys and Uncle Phil.

Gladys had texted Ma several times about parking, which Ma finally referred to Stephen, saying she couldn't deal with it. But when Stephen responded, Gladys went silent, meaning she didn't need assistance anymore. Gladys was originally from Jamaica (the country), so she had a natural attitude, but her insecurity among African Americans sometimes led to total bitchiness.

Ma's brother Phil owned a car mechanic business out in nearby Elmont, earning enough that his wife Gladys could be a homemaker, though she would help at the business if needed. He was the one with the domestic violence charge, but honestly, with Gladys as his wife, could you blame him?

When they arrived, Gladys was bitching about how hard it was to find the place, but the view calmed her down. Phil was carrying most of the food they had brought, which was jerk chicken with fried plantains, rice, and peas; another tray had curry goat with stir-fry; and on top, some roti and Jamaican patties separately wrapped in aluminum foil. Gladys held a smaller tray of ackee and salt fish with coleslaw.

"Took you a while to get here," Ma responded, taking the small tray out of Gladys' hands and giving it to Max. Then she showed Phil where to put his trays.

Gladys held back and changed direction to avoid confrontation. She focused on the view.

Phil moved towards Stephen and held out his arms. Stephen hugged him.

"It's been a long time, boy. How you?" he asked.

"You know, chilling," Stephen responded.

"Not too much, I hope. You don't wanna end up like…"

"He'll never end up like Brant," Ma said.

"Brant's doing well now," Gladys countered. "He's in school…"

On and off, this conversation continued about their kid Brantly, the one who had been in prison on the marijuana possession charge and, by the way, had two baby mommas and had survived a drive by, too. But everything was behind him now, Gladys insisted: he was working at Best Buy and going to some obscure technical college to do some computer thing.

Stephen was looking forward to seeing Brantly because growing up he got along best with him, as opposed to his Aunt Clarice's children, daughter Imani or son Devonte, both of whom used to bully him. Devonte was now a prosecutor in the Bronx, and it wasn't clear if his schedule would allow him to come, but Imani, her husband, young kids and mom were due.

The next to arrive, though, were Jacob, Rebecca, and a couple of their other friends, Robbie and Gia. Stephen was relieved they seemed to get on with his family, his Ma being the friendly glue.

As Phil, Jacob and Clay were discussing basketball, Max pulled Stephen aside and they took a walk down the shore.

"So how will they feel if we hold hands?" Max asked.

"I guess we can find out," Stephen said. "My mom says she's more worried about Phil and Gladys, but I'm more freaked out about my cousin Imani because she's apparently this big evangelical now."

"Honestly, Stephen, I wish you had been a little more upfront with me too, but I get it. Not sure how we'll deal with my family either."

They held hands on their walk down the beach; when they returned and approached, still holding hands, Imani and her family were there. Phil didn't look happy; he turned away. Gladys stared at him, wide-eyed.

"Well, brother Stephen, I see you have a friend," Imani said.

She smiled and hugged Stephen. He was shocked.

"Yup, he's a very good friend. This is Max," he said, introducing Max, who held out his hand, but he got a hug from Imani too.

"My religion tells me to love all people," she said.

"That doesn't mean you approve of that stuff, though," her husband Gabriel, a man of Filipino descent originally from Louisiana, said. But he did hold out his hand to Stephen, who shook it reluctantly.

"Anyway," Clay said, holding a spatula. "Some more jerk chicken, anyone?"

Stephen was surprised it was Clay of all people who broke the ice and united everyone through the meal. Stephen gave him props, though; in public, at least, he was smooth. He had adroitly put himself in charge of serving the now diverse cuisine. The hipster crew had brought some breakfast items: scrambled eggs, sausages, bacon, hash browns, pancakes, and fruit. Meanwhile Imani's family brought some fried chicken, okra, collard greens, buttered corn, watermelon, jambalaya, and po boy sandwiches. Combined, it was all a hit, and everyone was constantly going back up to get more.

Jacob and Rebecca worked their usual social magic, despite being a bit out of place. Robbie was a little neurotic, but he and Gia did their best to avoid awkwardness.

As the afternoon wore on, the group was able to carve out a space to put up a portable volleyball net that Imani's family had brought. Everyone had a great time, and Ma worked on Phil and Gladys with the issue.

"I was kind of shocked when you were okay with me and Max," Stephen later told Imani. "Aren't you big time into Jesus now?"

"Maybe you should be too. Then you would know why."

"You still think I'm going to hell, don't you?" he asked.

"You really want me to answer that? All we know is we're all going to perish. And then, the Lord will decide..."

"Please, don't give me the Jesus lecture," Stephen said, laughing. "Where's Brantly?"

"Funny you should ask," he heard a voice behind him. He turned around; Brantly was approaching with a grab and go box from Popeye's.

"That's what you brought?" Imani asked, focusing on the box.

"What, I figured someone would forget the fried chicken," Brantly said. "Also got some biscuits and Cajun fries. What's not to love, Momma?"

"I got the fried chicken, moron," Imani said. "And you think Cajun fries makes you...Whatever, it's good to see you."

After they hugged, Brantly performed a weird handshake with Stephen, one they did when they were younger. Then Brantly hit Stephen hard on the shoulder.

"Been a long time, brother. How you, man?"

"Stephen's gay. We just found out today," Imani said before Stephen could respond.

Stephen rolled his eyes.

"What?" Brantly said, laughing. He looked at Imani, then Stephen.

"For real?"

Stephen nodded.

"His man is over there," Imani went on. "The big white guy with the tattoos and muscles. Oh yeah."

"What, you met him in prison or something?" Brantly asked, looking at Max talking to Gabriel in the distance. "And he's friends with Gabe now?"

"Funny stuff," Imani said. "You want me to introduce you?"

"She playing right? Stevie?"

Stephen shook his head. "Nah, man. I'm a fag. And that's who I hope, is my future beau."

Brantly kept staring at Max. "Alright," he said. "This is kind of a shock. Haven't seen you in so long. Guess people change. Were you like that..."

"Yeah. But no, obviously not around you."

"Don't get me wrong man, I'm just trying to process. I mean I guess it's cool. Hold up, let me put down my shit."

He labored over to the table with the food, but there wasn't any room to put it. He examined the table, then took the tray of fried chicken and shoved it off the table. The tray hit the grass, and everyone turned around. Brantly put the Popeyes box there instead.

"See, I did bring the fried chicken!" he shouted to Imani, then put up two middle fingers and stalked off back towards the inner portion of the park.

Max, Clay, and the others looked at Stephen. He thought of running for Brantly, but then he thought better of it.

"Sorry for that," Phil apologized to Ma. "We'll clean it up. It's getting late anyway, maybe we should be leaving."

Ma shrugged. "You wanna go, tell Stephen, not me. And Jesus, control your son."

"My son isn't the disgrace," Gladys said, coming over. "You can keep the food and the trays. Let's go, Phil."

"We should clean up," Phil insisted.

"They're keeping our food, aren't they?" she replied.

"It's alright, Uncle Phil," Stephen said. "If you don't feel comfortable, you can go. We'll clean up."

Phil turned to him. "I'm not uncomfortable because of you," he said, looking at Max. "Take care, son. Maybe he'll get over it."

They left soon after. Jacob and Rebecca helped Stephen, his mom, and Max pick up Imani's food and throw it out.

"At least he did bring the fried chicken," Stephen quipped to Imani, who shoved him.

Everyone played a few more games of volleyball. Max and Stephen became a little more comfortable holding each other around Stephen's family. Clay grilled a few burgers but there was so much food that only the kids ate them. But everyone was eager for dessert: pecan pie and watermelon with soda and green tea drinks.

Then the sun started to descend below the horizon. Unlike many other parks, East River State closed at dusk, so they had to high tail it soon. Clay invited everyone to head to his brewery nearby for an after-party.

"Not exactly our spot," Imani said, gathering her kids. "But I'll pray for you, Stephen. It was so nice to see you again."

"Same here," Gabe said, shaking Stephen's hand. "Let us know if you need anything."

With that, they left, taking their net, volleyball, and trays. The hipsters helped clean up and took the remaining things—hot plates, canned heat, table, grill, racks, trays, etc.—to Clay's van, which they would take to the after-party, where Clay said he would cook some more burgers, since he had patties left.

Stephen took his mom's empty trays back to Max's car and began to drive her home. He planned to return to the brewery. As they took a left onto Harrison Avenue, his mom apologized for Brantly's behavior.

"You know he's a troubled one. Phil and Gladys should've taken him to the library more when he was younger. But that Gladys has this perverted vision of Jesus. She doesn't talk about it much but it's even worse than Imani, I think that—"

"It's alright, Ma. He'll come around, just give it some time. It'll probably be more of a challenge with the Carolina side of the family."

"That's a whole 'nother chapter of the story. And imagine if we still kept in touch with your father's side. Jesus, that would be a show."

"I haven't been around them since I was too young to talk, right?"

"Yup. It's for the best I divorced myself from them. And him."

He heard sirens behind him. That was a common sound in this part of the hood, but when he heard a robotic voice asking someone to pull over, he realized the cop was right behind him.

He kept going because all the parking spots were taken, and he wasn't sure if he should double-park. The voice commanded him again. He began to panic and put on the brake. But the voice commanded him again, even though they were both stopped.

"What the fuck does he want?" Stephen asked.

"There's a fire hydrant there," Ma said. "Hopefully that's what he means."

Stephen pulled a little forward, but someone jumped up ahead to jaywalk, so he stopped abruptly. The voice sounded again—this time exasperated.

"Pull over, sir. I'm not going to ask you again."

Stephen finally pulled next to the fire hydrant, which was in front of a bus stop. The cop double-parked.

Stephen waited in the car for what seemed like 15–20 minutes.

"Do these people specialize in wasting people's time?" Stephen asked.

"Be patient, Stephen," Ma said. "You don't want to agitate them."

"They're supposed to be serving us."

"Don't behave like your father," she said.

Finally, the cop came over. Stephen had the AC on, so he rolled down his window.

"When I ask you to pull over, you pull over," the white cop said, sticking his flashlight into the car.

Stephen wanted to argue but he remained silent. The cop shined the flashlight on Ma, then on the backseat.

"Where are you going?" he asked Stephen.

"Just dropping my Ma off at home."

"Where's home?"

Stephen told him the name of the complex.

"Rough spot," the cop said.

"I don't live there anymore. Now I'm in Bushwick. My boyfriend lives in Williamsburg. We were just having a family barbecue in East River State Park."

"Didn't drink, did you?"

"No, sir. That's not allowed in the park. I'm a librarian, sir. I follow the law."

"Uh, huh," he said. He flashed his light through the car again, almost for show. "Can I have your license and registration, please?"

Stephen gave it to him. The cop went back to his vehicle.

"That was good, Stevie," Ma said. "You didn't give him any reason to get upset or suspect you."

"We'll see," Stephen said. "Why's there a different rule for us, though? If it had been Max driving, he wouldn't have pulled us over at all. And Max could've given him so much smack, and it wouldn't have mattered."

About twenty minutes later, the cop returned and handed Stephen back his license and registration.

"Alright, Stephen. You know, you ran that red light," the cop said. "That's why I pulled you over. But I'm gonna let it go, since you're with your mom. Be more cognizant of how you're driving. You sure you haven't been drinking, right?"

"Yes, sir. Not even a sip."

"Alright. You take care, ma'am," the cop said. "That's a rough spot. Think of moving her out."

"Thank you, officer," she said. Stephen rolled up his window. But he didn't move immediately, even after the cop had driven away.

"I didn't run no red light," he said. "Maybe by a split second. He just pulled me over cuz I'm black."

"Well, he didn't even give you a breathalyzer. I think you should be happy with the result."

"And giving us a lecture. Get the fuck out of here."

Stephen eventually got over it. Pulling up to the complex, he noticed the usual suspects were hanging outside.

"The trays are empty," she said. "I'll get them from the trunk and go inside. You don't want to be recognized by your old friends. And don't leave this Benz alone."

"They were never my friends. But, yeah, I guess that's for the best. You sure you can handle it?"

"Sure, Stephen. It's for the best."

He popped the trunk from inside the car. Ma paused.

"I'm glad you told me. He seems like a nice man. A very nice man. Let me know if it becomes something more serious. I'm hoping this lasts for you."

"Sure, Ma. I'm so glad you understand."

"I'm here for you, Stephen. And I'll work on our family. Maybe this will bring us closer. These things can be a blessing in disguise."

Stephen kissed his mother's cheek, then hugged her. She got out of the car and walked towards the trunk. He felt bad for not helping her, but then he didn't want to have to talk to those knuckleheads he grew up with. At the least they'd waste his time, maybe give him a hard time, if history was to be a judge.

Pop Da Brew

By the time he found parking near the brewery, tons of emotions were stirring inside him. How would his father have reacted to being pulled over for such a dumb, made-up reason. Or how would Brantly? Brantly. Wasn't he more like those knuckleheads Stephen had avoided?

He was still deep in thought as he entered the brewery, so a loud shout utterly shocked him; then confetti was being thrown at him. Confetti? Was it his birthday?

He looked around. The people throwing the confetti were Jacob, Rebecca, Robbie, Gia, and several of their friends who hadn't been at the park. Plus the staff, a few regulars at the bar, and some customers he had never seen before.

"What's the occasion?" Stephen mumbled. Then Max approached, a huge smile on his face. He got on one knee and opened a box. A ring was inside.

"Stephen," he said. "We've been dating for less than a year, but you're the light of my life. I want to spend the rest of my life with you. What do you think, should we give it a shot?"

Stephen was shocked. He hadn't anticipated this. But he started to cry. How could he say no?

"Yes!" Stephen shouted. "Yes! Yes! Of course!" They hugged. A makeshift sign was put up, "Max & Stephen." The stranger customers congratulated him. They had some shots. And beers. And more shots. Clay congratulated him too but warned him to treat Max right. And he got drunk. Very drunk. He made out with Max in an Uber. Or so he remembered. Because soon it was late morning, and he was hung over. Clay was making them breakfast.

Fall Foliage

In the fall they started going upstate again to take advantage of the beautiful foliage, the fall fish, and the crisp air of the woods. Max had apologized for not proposing at the park, but after Brantly's explosion, he hadn't felt it was the right spot. Stephen had informed Ma, who had informed everyone else. She claimed everyone was on board, even Brantly and his parents, though they hadn't contacted Stephen about it.

But Stephen didn't have much time to care about random relatives he rarely saw. Life became busier: the library was getting packed with kids again in the afternoon, and after a relative respite, they were again having incidents with the emotionally disturbed and homeless, occasional book challenges, and all the rest. The brewery was bustling too, and Max sometimes had to stay late.

Max got ambitious on his hikes, especially in Hook Mountain State Park above Nyack. Stephen could barely keep up. Max said hikes in Montana were more rugged and challenging, if you could disassociate yourself from the forest fires, and Cali. Yeah, that was a nature trap right there, but it was the same problem—he just hoped it wouldn't get hot enough to burn. And Stephen felt out of place, but whatever, no couple could have everything in common.

But whichever hike they took, they always stopped on the same cliff overlooking the Hudson River, with Sing Sing right across, and Stephen was forced to think about his dad. He considered asking Max to change the route, but perhaps secretly he wanted to stop there and make out with Max as if his father could observe him from a distance and scowl. It was the ultimate act of defiance against the neglectful old man, who, like so many black fathers, was never in his life.

One day they stopped on the same spot; it was like mid-October and Max started to make out with Stephen, but then suddenly he stopped and looked out over the water at Sing Sing.

Stephen suspected that maybe he knew something. But Max

said, "I want to go back to Montana. I want you to meet my family. It's about time."

"You haven't told them about me, have you?" Stephen asked.

"I'm sorry," he said, looking back at Stephen. "I have no excuse. But then, you weren't exactly upfront either. My family's old school. They wouldn't even think anyone in the family could be gay."

"You proposed to me for a reason."

"Of course, sweetheart. I want to be with you forever."

As they made out. Stephen could see Sing Sing in the distance. If he was finally going to meet Max's family, maybe Max should meet his father. But then, he hadn't seen his father in years either, would that make sense?

The Visit

They planned to visit Montana in two weeks, giving Stephen enough time to request an impromptu change of vacation request from his manager. Normally this would've been frowned upon, since they were required to plan vacations a fiscal year in advance, but early November wasn't exactly a popular time to vacation, and thankfully no one at his branch was attending the popular NYS Library Conference at the same time.

One day at dinner, Stephen told Max about his encounter with the police officer in Bed Stuy; he concluded that if his mother hadn't been present, things would've gone much differently.

Clay said he didn't buy that: normally "pigs" wouldn't have a problem busting an old black lady either, as she could be carrying drugs in her snatch.

"That's a fucked-up thing to say, even for you," Stephen said.

"What, it's true. That's the way pigs think."

"You're talking about his mom, Clay," Max said. "That's what he means."

"I'm just saying, pigs always think the worst."

"Yeah, I'm sure that's what you meant," Stephen said.

~

Stephen couldn't sleep that night. In the early morning, after both Max and Clay went off to the brewery, he walked over to a local rental car spot that he had found on Google Maps and drove upstate to Sing Sing.

His belt buckle set off the metal detector, leading to a more intrusive search, at which point he somewhat regretted coming; but he stuck through it and was cleared, unlike the lady before him who had to be strip-searched. He gave his full name and hoped his father would recognize it and agree to see him, but he couldn't be sure because he hadn't written in advance.

There weren't too many visitors in the middle of the week, so he got a table quickly. He waited for what seemed like half an hour; he remembered his visits as a child being delayed just as long, so he didn't fret but was still nervous. Finally, an elderly prisoner came through the door wearing a Taqiyah, or a Muslim skullcap. He had a drawn face, angular and large, reminding Stephen of his own. His eyes and nose took after his mom, but her face was round—now he realized how his head had gotten its angular shape.

As his father approached, he perused his son with a groping gaze, which made Stephen uncomfortable, but also made him feel, oddly, appreciated.

"As-Salam-u-Alaikum," his father said. "I can't believe it. You're grown. After so long." He opened his arms. "Give me a hug."

Stephen wasn't sure he wanted to, but he got up anyway and hugged the old man for what felt like many minutes. The thick mass of arm muscles against his back and chest enveloped him fully and he realized that his father could have pressed and easily crushed him to death, making Max's caresses seem like those of a skinny dweeb. The guard finally told them to disentangle, for the rules only allowed a brief period of contact.

They sat, both teary-eyed, but his father's tears were running down his cheeks.

"You're the first person who's visited me in fifteen years," he said as he wiped them furiously. "I can't believe it. My son. You've grown up. Tell me, how are you? What are you up to?"

Stephen told him what he did for a living. Then he mentioned his mom.

"That woman. I guess I can see why she stopped coming."

"No one for fifteen years?" Stephen asked. "Not even your brothers, sisters—"

"I call my brother in California, my sister in Texas. Some cousins down south. Occasionally I write to pen pals. But in person? No. No one."

"Why not try Ma?"

"She stopped accepting my collect calls. I got the message."

His father watched a family in the corner playing with kids in a toddler area. "This room has been renovated. I wonder, do I have grandkids you can bring?"

Stephen shook his head. "No Dad. But that's why I came. See, I'm engaged."

"Wonderful. So grandkids on the way?"

"Maybe," Stephen said awkwardly. "I mean it hasn't been discussed. But it would have to be by adoption. See, I'm engaged to a guy."

His father was silent for a bit. His eyes averted to the floor, then to the guard.

"Times have changed," he said. "I haven't been out in almost thirty years. But I do watch the news."

"Do you think I'm damned, or something?"

"Our religion doesn't accept it. At least, we believe the devil has a hold of you, and you should not give into temptation. But, in here, it does go on."

"Like in the movies?"

"Rape happens, but not often. We're monitored a lot of the time. It's difficult to find a chance."

"Have you ever been—"

"I had a rough roommate when I first got in. His crew hounded me at first. But the Black Muslim community put them straight. That was a long time ago. I've had female pen pals, but no one's stuck around long enough to come visit. Twenty years is a long time without female company. I'm still married to your mom on paper, so that complicates setting up a conjugal. I'm surprised she hasn't served me."

"She's been busy with other things," Stephen said. "Like making sure I was raised right."

"I can't fault her for that. I'm happy you came to visit, that you're well. You chose your life, I'm glad you're happy and accept it. You're on the outside. I'm not and never will be."

"Weren't you framed? I've looked up your case. Why you didn't try harder to—"

Stephen's father crossed his arms and laughed.

"You're right. I didn't kill that cop. But that doesn't matter. I got life without parole. My lawyers tried to appeal the verdict on procedural grounds, but they failed. I told them to give up. I'd rather live in peace in here under the guidance of Allah than be a menace."

"I don't understand that. Almost everyone fights forever to get out if they didn't do it."

"Almost everyone fights forever even if they did do it, which most of them did, frankly. Sure, advocacy groups keep telling me they'll investigate my case, but I've refused."

"That makes no sense."

"You don't understand the forces at work here, son. I laugh when I see this stuff about Black Lives Matter. Activism and such. Their leaders are the people keeping me in here."

"The Black Panthers? They—"

"Framed me, yes. With the Feds and NYPD. Because I joined the Nation of Islam, one, but also because I know how they worked together against our community in the 1980s. I'm not saying some of it wasn't justified. It was a tough time: poverty, crack-cocaine, gang warfare. Now Turner Goodson turns up and makes headlines every time a brother is killed by a white cop. You know him, right?"

"Who doesn't?"

"If I make noise, he and the others will make sure the people I love will suffer. If it was just him, you could take care of the problem for me. But it's a whole network of former brothers. They're working with the authorities to make sure I never sing. They left me my life, and I'm living it."

"I still don't—"

"Has your mom ever mentioned fighting for me?"

"No. We don't talk about you much. Except when she lectures me about respecting the police and not being like you."

He laughed. "She is protecting you. Like I asked her to. In fact, I asked her not to come see me anymore, to raise you without me in your life because of that. You were never supposed to know that, but I guess it doesn't matter now. You are old enough to know the truth."

"You didn't want to be in my life?"

"I didn't want to be your burden. You deserve better. You were raised right, you have a respectable job, it seems, and now you're going to get married. That's about the best we can hope for. Because in America, we're the damned group, and we always will be."

Stephen stood up. "He's white. My fiancé."

His father nodded. "You want to move up. Well, I hope it works out for you. Forget about me. I made my decisions for a reason. I'm protecting you and your mom and my entire family without you even knowing it."

"Then why mention Turner Goodson?"

"I shouldn't have. I haven't seen anyone from outside in so long."

His father stood up too. "This was a mistake," he went on. "I should have refused you. If you come again, I won't see you."

"Even if I bring grandkids?"

He snickered. "When, in another twenty years? I'll be dead by then."

"How about Mom—"

His father signaled to the guard that he wanted to leave. Stephen wasn't sure if he should hug him goodbye, but his father turned his back and exited without looking back.

History

Stephen could barely sleep that night either, thinking about what his father had said. It sounded crazy: was he really in danger from some invisible black elite that worked with the authorities to make sure that his father didn't tell the truth about why he was in jail?

It seemed counter-intuitive. Perhaps this was the black man lying to himself yet again about his powerlessness, serving the white man's plan to make sure he didn't change the system because, in his mind, it was unchangeable. And to accuse Turner Goodson, a man Stephen admired among the older black activists, as one of the conspirators, even a participant in murder. Had his father been locked up so long that he was dreaming up theories and scenarios?

He wanted to confront his mother, but he wasn't sure he should. He did read about the case obsessively at work. How Officer Henry Kirkpatrick and his partner Gina Cassidy were lured to a Harlem warehouse by an anonymous 911 call from a nearby pay phone; how a voice later identified as being altered alleged a rape in progress.

How Kirkpatrick was shot as soon as he entered. How police were led to his dad's Harlem apartment based on an anonymous tip from a different pay phone. How footprints at the scene matched those of the sneakers found in his father's living room, and the matching weapon, an illegally purchased gun without serial numbers or fingerprints, had been found in his sock drawer, with the exact number of rounds discharged. How his alibi, being home asleep at the time, couldn't be proven or disproven.

A cop killing was bad enough, but in the revived pro-police, anti-crime crusade of the early to mid-1990s, it was a death by prison sentence—literally. The verdict was appealed, but no new evidence was found, so judges rejected a new trial request. That didn't stop some law students from banding together and surmising a conspiracy.

At the time, his dad had been vocal about being innocent and targeted. The prosecution could never determine a clear motive, other than that he hated the police. Multiple people had lived communally in his apartment over the years. Any of these brothers had access to his apartment and could have worn the sneakers and planted the gun.

Stephen found a short biography of his father on a time machine discovery of the now defunct non-profit advocacy site. George Florence was born in Lake Charles, Louisiana, had lived in Texas as a boy and eventually went to college in California. There he met the founders of the Black Panthers and became a prominent member. He initially was attracted to the militant wing of the movement and was imprisoned twice in the early 1970s. However, in the mid-1970s he moved toward the party's peaceful wing and became a prominent community activist in New York City, fighting for black rights in Harlem during the fiscal crisis and violent uprisings in the late 1970s.

During the 1980s, after the party disbanded, he became an advocate against the crack-cocaine, AIDS, and crime epidemics in New York City. Feeling that he was being held back by some of his former comrades who were both profiting from the trade and working with some corrupt members of the NYPD, he joined the Nation of Islam, which was becoming more militant under Khalid Abdul Muhammad's influence. He changed his name to Aabid Muhammad. But this is where things became murky, as the rumors were that some of his comrades, who were now benefitting from the status quo, along with elements of the FBI and law enforcement, wanted to eliminate him as a potential threat, and so came up with a ruse to do so.

But the crusade for his father's freedom had been short-lived. Searches showed that the law students had moved on and become litigators, district attorneys, real estate lawyers. His father had been silent since, and despite the recent trend in ameliorating the wrongs of the 90s harsh imprisonments, the cop shooting hadn't risen to the same level of interest as recent Black Lives Matter shootings of unarmed black men or even old cold cases like the Central Park Five.

Rather, the most prominent article he found on Google (Brooklyn Public Library was too cheap to subscribe to Lexis-Nexis or West

Law) was by a law professor advocating for all people serving life sentences without the possibility of parole, arguing that it was "cruel and unusual punishment"—a kind of death penalty by life, and giving his dad's case as one example. But even that didn't mention any conspiracy or likelihood that his father was innocent.

Lower down on the Google hit list, he did find a few obscure websites referencing forgotten criminal cases that did talk about holes in his father's case: no voice-altering device had ever been located, the gun and sneakers could now be tested for DNA but never had been. With new evidence, enough reasonable doubt existed for another jury to potentially judge differently. But the original lawyers hadn't been able to overturn the conviction due to there being no provable improprieties or irregularities during the first trial. Judges determined that his father had gotten a vigorous defense and that the prosecutor hadn't done anything wrong. Now the defendant wasn't cooperating either, so the case was stalled. The only thing that kept the case alive at all in the public sphere was his father's former fame.

Stephen was wondering if he should defy his father's wishes to look further into the case, potentially risk his own life, his mom's, his family's, Max's, his friends. What could he possibly find out? He could interview his mother, Turner Goodson, his father's former roommates, Gina Cassidy, his father's first lawyer. He could contact the lawyer who argued for prisoner release, the ones who had fought for his father in the past, the authors of the obscure websites, black social justice advocacy groups—but would that be too conspicuous, given the threat and his father's wishes?

He started making lists, even though he wasn't sure he would ever follow through on it.

Montana

Meanwhile the trip to Montana came up. He decided to consider his plan of action on the trip.

Max's family believed they were good friends, so Max asked Stephen to play along until he sprung the truth on them. Stephen found himself on the opposite side of the fence that Max was on during the picnic, so he went with it.

He and Max took a flight to Missoula through Minneapolis and were picked up by Max's sister, Lucy who had a big smile for Stephen. She wore a down jacket, tight, slightly ripped jeans, boots, and a baseball cap with a University of Montana logo. She drove them to their ranch near Hamilton in Ravalli County in the famed Lamborghini.

"I didn't think you actually owned a Lamborghini," Stephen admitted in the back seat.

"Be prepared for Highway 93—Montanabahn style," Max said, with a wink from Lucy.

"Isn't there a speed limit now?"

"So they say."

Stephen noted there was a speed limit: 80 miles per hour. Lucy went an easy 95-100.

"Nowadays, all caution's to the wind," Max said.

"Fer sure," Lucy said, laughing, revving the engine. They flew past the countryside of flat fields, rolling hills, random cabins, occasional bison, flanked by mountains and the blue sky in the far distance. But they slowed down a bit during some stretches through towns where the limit suddenly dipped to 65.

"I was kidding," Max told Stephen. "Only Highway 90 didn't have a limit, and that was in the 1990s. But we can still go pretty fast."

An hour later, they turned a couple of times and entered the Miller Ranch, the name emblazoned on a big ol' green and gold sign like you've probably seen in a million movies. Stephen noticed the great number of trees; in the distance, he saw construction cranes processing wood, and the smoke they created hovered past the vast mountains and the big blue sky.

They drove through the ranch for a few minutes on a windy road and finally approached a modest home made of thick wood. On the porch a man wearing a flannel red shirt and blue trousers smoked a cigar. He wore a stylish mustache and a cowboy hat. Stephen wondered if he had entered a Hollywood movie.

The man laughed and lumbered down the few steps to the path that led to the road where Lucy parked. He was a big man, with a tanned face and a slight scar on his left cheek.

Max got out and hugged him. The man hit his back several times.

"My boy," he said. "How've you been?"

"Glad to be back home in the fresh air," Max said.

"Why would you ever leave? What do those heathens in New York got that we don't?"

"People," Max said.

The man waved. "It's about quality. The good people are in these parts."

He finally noticed Stephen as he got out of the back seat. The man seemed confused.

"Ah. You brought a friend."

"Yup," Max said. "This is Stephen."

Stephen approached and stuck out his hand.

"Stephen, this is my father, old Cole Miller."

Cole shook his hand. "This your business partner?"

"No, he's my good friend."

"He's a librarian," Lucy said, coming up to them, repeating what Stephen had told her on the ride over. "Public library. The works."

"Librarian. A woman's job?"

"It's a diverse field now, sir," Stephen said.

"I see. So how do you know my son?"

"New York is a huge city, Pop," Max interjected. "I know all kinds of people."

He tipped his hat. "Sure. Well let's get you settled. Shawna's been cooking something special for hours now, thinking you'll need a good meal before you take your rightful place as the man of this ranch."

Shawna, Stephen knew, was Max's stepmother. She had essentially raised him since he was 12. His estranged birth mother, Tami, had moved away to Colorado with a professor she had met in Missoula, and Max had never seen her again as she had died a few years later of cancer. She had apparently agreed to pay child support rather than have visitation with her kids, or so his dad told him when he was older. Max and Stephen had bonded over this as well, since Stephen had never known his father, and Max had never really known his birth mother, though he said Shawna was a fine woman.

Shawna made quite the spread for lunch: Rocky Mountain Oysters (calf testicles, not to churn your stomach), sautéed morel mushrooms, Elk steak, bison stew, mashed potatoes, huckleberry flapjacks, rhubarb pie. They ate around the table, as Lucy mentioned that Skylar, Max's other sister, would be there for dinner—she was attending Montana State University in Bozeman, but would drive over to see her brother.

"I was hoping you'd bring home a girl, but maybe that's for the best," Cole said. "That means you're still not tied down there, and you can come back home."

"Lucy can run the ranch just fine," Max replied.

"Lucy's working at that lab in Missoula. Forensics science, a hot field. Skylar wants to be a nurse. They're not planning to stay here forever. And I'm not going to live forever."

"Skylar thinks she's very shi-shi, living in Bozeman," Lucy said.

Stephen looked at Max, hoping he would pop the info to his father, but he seemed hesitant.

"Missoula's not far," Max said. "And is Skylar really going to be in Bozeman forever?"

"They like their careers. Which I encourage. When they get married, used to the cities as they are, are their husbands gonna be okay with taking care of a ranch? It's not a small job, as you know. You like your brewery, and the big city, but ranching, timber, the land: that's in your blood. You know it, Max. You can't escape that."

Max was fully flushed in the face. Stephen had never seen that color on him, even at the picnic. He was usually so calm, even when wasted.

"So your plan for me, Pop, is to live and die alone here?"

"Alone? No. You won't be alone. You know, Tessa Anderson's a grown woman now. She co-runs her ranch next door. A match means a greater operation."

"I see. It's a business deal to you."

"Don't look at it that way, my boy. I'm saying she's a good looking, hardworking, young woman, from a good family, good values, who you've known since you were a little one. How is that a bad thing?"

Stephen was waiting for him to break the news, but Max was just looking down at his food.

"Just an idea, my boy my boy. Don't have to think about it now. It's a free country, but that's my advice. Especially while you're over here, why not reconnect?"

The Climb

After lunch, they settled down in their respective rooms, Max in his old room on the second floor and Stephen in the guest bedroom on the first floor, near the kitchen.

Stephen was upset that Max hadn't revealed their relationship during lunch, but he wasn't sure if he should bring it up. He wanted to go upstairs to see Max but thought it would be best if Max came down to explain the situation. Stephen read *Call Me by Your Name* by Andre Aciman, which had been on his to-do list for months. Hours passed, and Max never came. But then, Stephen did hear a car pull up outside.

Looking out his window, he saw a girl come out of a Porsche— later he would learn it was an old Ruby Red Porsche from 1975, very rare, and amazing that it still ran. She wore over-the-knee black suede boots, tight spandex pants and a light blue, button-down dress shirt with a couple of buttons undone on top, revealing the very top of her cleavage, under an open, light fleece jacket. She was skinny, with bright blonde hair, and a perpetual smile of sorts.

"Maxxie!" she yelled. Then she switched and called, "Maxine!" And giggled some. Stephen heard a pounding near the stairs. Then Max was outside, hugging the girl and rubbing her hair.

"Looks like you haven't changed much. Just a couple of inches taller, maybe?"

"I haven't grown, you big buttfuck. Just got a little wiser. What the hell you doing back in Montana? Thought you'd gotten away from this hot mess."

"Can't ever get away for good. Need to come back eventually."

"Where's—" she started saying, but then Stephen heard Lucy's voice. "Used to call you a hot mess."

"'Cause I graduated from chaw to mochas and lattes. That what you mean?"

"Shopping at some hipster food co-op doesn't make you better."

"Fer sure..." she said, mocking Lucy.

They hugged too, as Stephen came out.

"You know, 'hot mess' started out as a culinary term," he said.

"Who is this hottie?" Skylar asked.

Max breathed. "This is my friend, Stephen."

"Your friend, eh?" Skylar said, punching Stephen in the chest. Then she hugged him.

"Let me look at ya. An all-around skinny boy."

"Jesus Christ, Skylar," Lucy said. "Getting a little too forward, a little too fast?"

"Sister Lisa over here doesn't have a very progressive view of things. You know this is a divided state."

"Whatever. I voted for Obama."

They all laughed. Skylar continued to flirt with Stephen, but it was clearly just a front for the fact that she knew he and Max were an item, whereas apparently Lisa didn't. They all messed around for a bit, and then decided, in true Montana fashion, to "take a hike."

Like all Montanans, they had about five or six options to choose from, and eventually decided that since Stephen was a newbie, they'd choose a relatively easy hike: Blodgett Canyon Overlook Trail.

"It's beautiful, not too tough, and will be good—to start, anyway," Lucy said.

They were all too fast for him, especially since he was exhausted from the flight, but Skylar was chippier and would wait and hold back, encouraging him onward, while Max and Lucy went ahead like two rebel birds. The views of the blue sky, the river and the canyon were stunning, and he kept telling Skylar that he had never seen such beauty anywhere in New York.

"That's why they call it God's country. It isn't just because of the crazy Bible thumpers."

"I heard that the problem here is the racist separatists and neo-Nazis. Isn't that guy Richard Spencer based here?"

"Yeah, up in Whitehead. Which is, ironically, a pretty liberal spot with lots of Jews."

"They're not the only antisemites in the country," he said, thinking about his dad and the Nation of Islam's own history of anti-Semitism.

"Yeah, it's disgusting. Even my dad's said some things that's made me cringe."

They went up a rough and somewhat snowy stretch. Skylar took Stephen's hand and helped him through.

"I wouldn't worry, though," she continued. "I've never heard him say anything negative about blacks. There aren't that many of you here, so most people think you're pretty cool."

"Good to know," Stephen said, laughing.

"The gay thing, though," she said, in a lower tone. "Not sure how he'll take that."

"What, did Max tell you?"

"Everything. Like the ring, by the way," she said, grabbing his wrist. "Diamonds are a girl's best friend."

"Ha ha. I prefer sapphires, but don't tell Max."

"Why not? He should get you what you want."

"So why not Lucy? Is she like that too?"

"Kind of half and half. You know, not really milk, not totally fake either? Wears flannel shirts, no cleavage, but wonder bras."

"Okay," Stephen said, not knowing how to process that.

"Anyway, don't worry about her. My dad's more important. He's a Republican or whatever, but he doesn't hate gays, just thinks it's weird. Max has never told him, so he doesn't know. Thinks Max went to Cali and NYC to get blue-city Satan worshipping out of his system and is gonna come back into the fold eventually. So, if you guys are willing to relocate here to run the ranch, my guess is that he'd be more accepting. But I don't know that for a fact."

"I mean I told my mom and my extended family. Max hasn't said anything to his dad or even Lucy. Doesn't seem encouraging."

"Have some faith in Maxine. I think he's just trying to find the right time."

They climbed up to the Overlook and the beautiful view of the mountain range. In the distance, they saw Don Mackey Point.

Max and Lucy were already there. Lucy turned to Stephen, with tears in her eyes.

"I'm sorry," she said. "I didn't know."

She approached him as if to hug him but then slipped past him and back down the trail. He watched her disappear, then turned to Max.

"Let her process it," Max said, sounding emotional himself.

Stephen stared at him. "At least you finally told her, right?"

Max nodded. "Yeah."

Stephen hugged Max. Then Skylar joined the hug and congratulated them.

They enjoyed the view for a bit. Then Skylar told Max about their conversation regarding their father.

"He's an old fogey," Max explained. "But like all of us, he's got that Maverick in him."

"So why haven't you told him yet?" Stephen asked.

Max didn't reply.

"I mean, I told my entire family," Stephen went on. "They weren't all happy about it, but I did."

"We should turn back," Skylar said. "It'll be dark soon, and Lucy's waiting."

She left. Max and Stephen were alone.

"I'm sorry," Max said. "I know I've been unfair."

"You brought me out here, baby, to this beautiful place. I just wish you'd be more courageous."

"Courageous?" Max said. "I came to New York City with nothing. I co-own a business in Brooklyn, which is expensive."

"How'd you get that money?" Stephen asked. "Bank loan?"

"Why are you asking me that?"

"If we're going to be married, shouldn't I know?"

Max ignored the question. He went back down the trail. Stephen followed him.

"You're not going to tell me?"

"If you already know the answer..."

"I don't."

"You suspect."

"It's logical. You're afraid to tell him because he'll take it back; is that right?"

Max kept going. Stephen said, "Admit it."

Max stopped and turned back to him.

"What's the difference?" he said. "You honestly believe that's more important to me than you?"

"So why won't you?"

Max shook his head. "I don't know why you're doing this to me. You've always been a sweetheart."

"Yeah, like your poodle."

"That's how you feel. Like you're my poodle?"

"Sometimes. Honestly, yes."

"Okay," Max said, shrugging. "If that's the way you feel."

"I just don't understand."

"I told you. He's old-fashioned. You heard him talking."

"Yeah, I did. But I feel like that's not the reason."

"Enjoy the view down the hike, darling. Check out the wildflowers. And the birds. Some beauties."

He turned and left. Stephen didn't follow right away. He waited a few minutes before he proceeded. He was exhausted now so he began to fall further behind.

A few minutes later, he took a break, sitting on a fungus-covered rock, listening to the soft sounds of birds flying up ahead, seeing them but not really processing them. Or the flowers on the ground either.

He wasn't sure how long he sat there. He got up slowly and stumbled down the path. It seemed easy enough, but on a couple of turns the road split and you had a choice: you could descend, or even ascend, and you wouldn't know if you were going right or wrong.

Gabbing with Skylar on the way up, his muscle memory hadn't captured the exact coordinates of the trail. Multitasking had been common on his previous hikes in New York, but then, he had trusty Max with him. At some point, he started doubting this path was right.

Despite, or perhaps because of the pine trees and the boulders scattered about in a strange symmetry, the yellow, orange, and green foliage of the grass, the occasional mounds of snow, and the big blue sky turning into hazy orange ecstasy, he began to feel disoriented and wondered if he knew where he was or even who he was.

This was God's country, but was he a man of God? He wasn't Muslim like his father, he wasn't Christian like his mother, he wasn't anything. Maybe he was a Deist, like the Founding Fathers who had enslaved his people, or maybe he wasn't sure at all. He wasn't sure in New York, but could he be sure here? In his private moments on his other hikes upstate, he had wondered the same thing: does nature take a person closer to a heaven-like fantasy, or does it just remind him of life's brutality and randomness, of the weird coalition of trees thousands of years old never being moved or harmed, juxtaposed with cute rabbits who eat foliage and have gentle vegetarian diets, who in turn are hunted and eaten by foxes and other predators. And that was tame: here he read there were bears, and mountain lions, and wolves.

He kept going on, though. When he questioned which way to turn, he decided on the widest path of least resistance. He was still tired too, so he stopped again to sit on another rock.

It was getting dark. Clearly sunset had passed, and the orange sky was graying. His heart started racing as he got up and went quickly down the path. Suddenly he started to see downed trees, cut in half, and who knows who the culprit was: wind, rain, snow?

Then he heard a sound behind him. He turned quickly, but tripped and fell backwards. He felt his ankle twist and then a pain in his butt, and then he slowly felt a pain in his head as he realized it was a four-legged creature coming at him. He crossed his arms to defend himself, but the creature kept coming. Then he saw a man. He had a long beard.

"Are you okay, friend? Looks like you took a tumble there."

"Yeah. I guess. I'm not used to this route."

"This trail's as easy as they get."

"At least I know I'm going the right way," he said, as he took the man's hand, a thick hand, to help him up. He yelped as he realized his ankle still hurt.

"Can you walk, man?" he asked. "It's getting dark."

The man whistled and the creature came back. It was a dog.

"Man's best friend. The route's pretty simple. It'll be difficult to see soon. Unless things start to burn. That's always the fear around here. I imagine you're not from these parts."

"No. New York City."

The man laughed. "What the hell you doing out here?"

"Visiting my fiancé's family," he said.

"So you decided to take a hike alone?"

"Not exactly."

"New York. Never been myself. Big city. Like fifty times Butte."

"I haven't been to Butte."

"Used to be big back in the day. Before they had the mining dry up."

He tried to walk, and he cringed. He could do it, but not without cringing.

"I wouldn't advise staying here. We've got to get you down."

"I'll make it. Just slowly."

"I don't have a flashlight or anything. Would love to help you down, but I need to see too. We can see how it goes though."

"Thanks for the help, brother. I appreciate it."

"Sure. Slow and easy, let's go."

He started going down the path, slowly, the man leading him by the hand. The dog would go on a bit, and then the man would whistle, and it would come back. At some point, the man seemed to realize he was holding another man's hand and let go.

"We're near the end. You seem good enough. You want me to stay with you, or you think you got it?"

"I've got it. I think."

"I don't want to see you on the five o'clock news, man. We've got bears out here who might want to have an injured man for lunch. That's why I carry this," he said.

He took out a pistol, and Stephen flinched. The man pointed it at him.

"What do you want?" Stephen asked.

The man paused. He looked at Stephen.

"Nothing, friend. It's for self-protection."

The man put it back. Then they saw a light.

"Stephen!" he heard, and he realized it was Skylar's voice.

She approached. "I'm glad I found you. I was worried you got lost."

"He twisted his ankle," the man said. "But I think he'll make it down. Especially now that you've come with that switch."

"Thanks, sir," she said, smiling.

"Anytime. My pleasure." He nodded at Stephen. "She's a pretty one, you lucky dog. Treat her right, you hear?"

He went on, whistling at his dog as he went.

"Are you okay?" she asked.

"I can make it, I think. Max and Lucy?"

"Waiting. He's talking to her. She seems a little upset now, but don't worry. She'll accept it."

Compromise

I know I've gotten a little philosophical, guys, and maybe a little surreal, but this was a bit of a turning point for Stephen, though it would take some time for him to realize it.

He did make it down to the car, and Lucy did hug him and show concern for his ankle. She did apologize for not accepting it at first and for walking off, but he could still feel tension on the way back. He wasn't sure she had suddenly switched into a fag-lover, although it was strange since she lived in liberal Missoula and talked like some Cali ditz.

His ankle began to swell up, so Max called a doctor, and took him into Hamilton the next day. He got it wrapped and got a brace put on. He was told to stay immobile for a bit.

So, for the next few days, he mainly stayed in his room, reading: the Aciman book, then some gay YA romances, and finally, more about his father's case. Occasionally Max would visit him in his room. They made up for the hike fight with wild love in the middle of the night. But Max also said he wanted to reconnect with Montana, so he took trips to Bozeman, and Whitefish, and a few other places, and went on more hikes.

Stephen became more obsessed with finding the link between Turner Goodson and his father, accessing obscure library databases, other archives, and defunct listservs. He read as many online articles as he could.

Turner Goodson, it turned out, was younger than his father. He had joined the Black Panthers in the late 1970s and was in its peaceful, community-oriented wing from the very beginning.

He had fought for black rights regarding redlining and school access and had defended them for uprisings during the hard financial times of the late 1970s. When the Black Panthers disbanded in the early 1980s, many of his brothers fell into gangs, drugs, or hard times, but Turner Goodson turned into a media celebrity by championing victims of police brutality and white violence. Some instances were controversial for supposedly being staged or rigged, as painted by the conservative white media, but that had never been proven.

When their causes aligned, his father and Turner Goodson would show up at events together. But an ideological rift formed. They both believed that the white man was the oppressive devil, but George also thought that the black man was stabbing himself in the front and back. They lacked discipline by doing drugs, they were followers by joining gangs and chumps for getting arrested. Meanwhile, Turner favored media savvy anti-white vigilantism and police injustice protests. He led marches and protests as incidents occurred, always in the media's eye.

Could Turner Goodson, the anti-police injustice crusader, be working with the police to perpetuate a drug and gang culture in the black community that benefited his career?

Did he have access to his father's apartment? Could he have planted the gun and sneakers to frame his father?

Stephen couldn't find evidence one way or the other. He thought maybe he was focusing too much on Turner Goodson, just because his father had mentioned his name. Former Black Panthers who had become gang leaders might want his father eliminated because he was actively fighting to clean up that racket.

One morning before breakfast, the day before they were to fly back while Max and his sisters were out at the Hot Springs, Stephen was reading articles on obscure Black Panthers turned gangsters when his bedroom door opened and Max's dad walked in, wearing a blue flannel shirt and brown trousers. Cole took off his Stetson hat as he approached Stephen.

Stephen sat up in bed, putting his laptop aside.

"My boy," he said, looking at the floor. Then he was silent for a minute. "Max told me last night. About who you really are."

"Really?" Stephen asked. He was mixed happy and scared. Then he thought maybe Max had chickened out, telling his dad something crazy like Stephen was a wealthy entrepreneur looking to buy the ranch or anything to distract from the issue at hand.

"I was very angry last night," Cole continued. "I couldn't sleep.

In the dead of the night, I walked around this ranch I've maintained with my very being, with no light, no nothing, wondering how I could have raised a son like that," he said. He put his hat back on.

"I couldn't see nothing. Didn't wanna see. I was sitting on some logs waiting to be moved. Then the sun peeked up, and I saw Lucy. She was preparing for a long day of coordinating the logging. Then Max was there too, helping her, surveying, just like I taught them long ago. Even with them going on a trip later, still, they were up and doing it. Because God-damn it, even with the brewery and the forensics, they love this ranch even more.

"And I thought to myself, this can work. God made us free. He made us flexible. So tell me, do you love my son?

"Yes, sir. I do."

He glared at Stephen for a second. "Then I'll give you my blessing," he said, "but I want something in return. I want Max to run the ranch. Lucy loves the land, but she has forensics, Skylar has nursing. Now that Max has a partner in crime, I don't see why he can't come back home. Question is, are you willing to do the same?"

Stephen thought about it. "I mean, I have a job I like, but I can work in a library here too. Probably."

"Create your own library in his room, build one on the land. You'll never have to work another day in your life if you can effectively run this operation. Learn from Shawna how to cook real food, make whatever you normally make in New York too. We're not barren of culture either. We've got everything here if you look for it. Buddhist statues, Yerba matte from Brazil. We're not as small-minded as you might think."

"I didn't think you were."

"Good. Now listen. Max borrowed money from me to buy the brewery with his partner over there in New York. He did this so he wouldn't have to owe some predator bank, but he has barely been able to pay his rent with his proceeds. He's a little spoiled, you see. Half is in my name, half in his. Convince him that selling his part of the business to his partner and coming back here will be better for him. Financially, in terms of family. If you want to adopt kids or whatever, better to raise them here."

Stephen thought. "Sure. I guess."

"I need an affirmative to bless this partnership, son."

"I'm pretty sure it's a yes. But I have to think about my mother and my family there too."

"Bring 'em out here. Shawna and I don't mind."

"Why not keep the share and have Clay do the work?"

"If Max has an interest there, he'll keep having the knack to go back. Because the devil has a certain pull."

"I like giving back to my community, but I wouldn't mind living out here. It's beautiful. Almost a dream come true."

"Good. Then it's settled. Work out a plan to convince him."

Settling

He put his hat back on, tipped it and left the room. Stephen had almost forgotten about Max's decision not to tell his father. Now Cole had accepted it so quickly—it was shocking.

But could he really convince Max to sell his interest in the brewery to Clay, and was it too easy to move out here? Certainly, it was beautiful and peaceful, he could escape the ghetto and the cops and everything else. But could he get used to constant hikes, and twisted ankles?

He continued to read articles, but he was a bit distracted as he formulated an alternative plan. Still, he wrote down the names of a couple of former Panthers who were mentioned in articles involving his father in the 1970s and had run-ins with the law later.

Max and his sisters came home rather late, so Stephen ate dinner with Cole and Shawna. Dinner included trout, pinto bean, and ham soup with fry bread, chillicothe, sirloin mutton, which Shawna had learned to make while growing up in South Dakota, huckleberry pie, and a dessert called kuchen, a cross between cake and pie filled with, in this case, flathead cherries.

Shawna never congratulated Stephen on his engagement and still acted strangely around him as Cole once again talked about convincing Max to stay. Cole also suggested that Shawna teach Stephen how to cook some of her favorite recipes when he returned.

Earlier, Cole had spent the afternoon taking Stephen around in his truck, explaining how different aspects of the timber-mining and farming operations worked. Stephen met and spoke to some of the workers about seasonal process, and Cole even showed him some of the finances and paperwork in the office.

Perhaps Cole thought that by showing Stephen these elements, he would seduce him further into the Montana ranch life and give him more ammunition to convince Max. The problem was, this information overwhelmed Stephen, so that he only retained a bit of it.

When Max and his sisters finally came home, they brought with them some strawberry scones and maple bars, and everyone had a heartier dessert. When they were done eating, Max, his sisters, and Stephen relaxed in the den while Cole and Shawna went up for an early bedtime. Max and Stephen drank some scotch and made cocktails while Max's sisters reminisced about their adventures going to Hot Springs that day, and how relaxing it was.

Lying on a divan next to him, Skylar kicked Stephen.

"Why didn't you come with us? It's your last day and you could have put that ankle in the water. I'm sure it would've helped it heal."

"Sorry, I'm just not feeling any more adventurous for this trip," Stephen said.

"Fer sure, you're gonna have to get used to it," Lucy said. "It's just the way we do it out here."

"Next time," Stephen said, tersely.

They talked a bit more about their trips to Bozeman and Whitefish, enticing Stephen to join them the next time he was in town. Lucy joked that they avoided the Neo-Nazi rallies.

"You would've been fine, Stephen," Skylar said. "Like I said, there are so few..."

Stephen noticed Lucy roll her eyes. Then she interjected.

"Tessa sure hasn't changed much, right, Max?" she said.

Skylar gave her a dirty look. Stephen noticed Max was flushed. He didn't respond.

"Tessa," Stephen stated, processing it. "That's the lady who owns the ranch next door?"

"Doesn't own it yet," Lucy said. "But she's in line. Like Max here."

Skylar looked embarrassed. "So you went to her ranch? Or met up with her somewhere?" Stephen asked.

"You've gotta understand, Stephen, Tessa's been a friend since childhood for Max," Skylar said. "So of course, he's gonna see her before he leaves."

"Of course," Stephen said. "So you went to her ranch?"

"Fer sure, we had dinner," Lucy said. "Trout there too. What a surprise? We're rather predictable here."

"Yeah, she's an old friend," Max said. "So it's rude not to go. We've known the family for my entire life."

"Is she pretty?" Stephen asked.

"Don't get jealous, Stevie," Max said. "She's just a friend."

"Who's getting jealous, I'm just asking. Since your dad had mentioned her."

"Oh, they were an item in high school," Lucy said. "I guess Max didn't know he was gay at the time."

"I see," Stephen said.

They were silent for a bit, then Skylar changed the subject to talk about Stephen's life in Brooklyn. Later Lucy and Skylar went to bed, and Max helped Stephen to his bedroom.

"Your dad said we're cool. Did he tell you that?" Stephen asked as they cuddled in bed.

"He didn't seem to accept it last night when I told him," Max replied.

"Well, he came to my room this morning. Told me he was on board. Said he had a long night of denial, but now he's cool. He even showed me around the farm today."

"Really?" Max asked.

"Yeah, showed me all the details of the operation. Even took me to the office and read off some numbers. Like I was his kid already."

"Wow. That's awesome. I was a little worried."

"Yet you left me here alone. What if he'd come in with a gun?"

"My dad wouldn't do that. Listen to you."

"So I guess you did trust him a little."

"I've got tattoos all over. He knows I'm unorthodox."

"And Tessa?"

"An old friend. Would've been rude not to visit."

"And an old flame?"

"I told you I've had hetero relationships. That was one."

"The one?"

"You shouldn't be lecturing, given your history."

"Not judging. Just natural for me to be jealous."

"Well, I'm glad my dad's accepted it. Relieved in fact."

"Took you a while but you did it."

"Tried to find the right time."

"He's got a caveat though. He wants us to relocate here."

"He said that?"

"Yeah."

"Well, that's our decision. It's got nothing to do with him."

"The brewery. He wants you to sell it."

Max paused.

"I guess he told you about the loan and the partnership distribution?"

"I had already guessed. But yeah."

"Maybe he paid for it, but he can't just sell it. I like the brewery, I like Brooklyn, I like our friends. You're not exactly a big fan of Montana, are you?"

"I can get used to it, probably. Just need to ease in."

"Maybe."

"It's beautiful. Fer sure," he said, mocking Lucy.

"Don't worry about her. She likes stoking the fire sometimes."

"Is there a fire to stoke?"

"She's an old friend, I told you. I'm not hetero. That was a phase. Why are you so jealous?"

"I'm not. Maybe I just think she understands the land more than me."

"Maybe you won't need to."

They made slow love. Then they slept together that night. In the morning Stephen woke up and Max wasn't in bed. Near the front door outside his room were Max's packed bags. The family was having breakfast.

They had a light meal of waffles made from kamut, huckleberries, and chokecherry syrup, along with whole-hog sausages. They made small talk.

Lucy told her father about Max visiting Tessa and the ranch. Cole seemed pleased, but maybe that was Stephen's jealousy kicking up again.

As they were leaving, Cole Miller hit Stephen's back and told him to take care of Max. Max hugged his father as Stephen hugged Skylar, and then everyone said their goodbyes.

Shawna gave him a rhubarb and strawberry pie to take home.

On their way to the airport, Max told Stephen they were first going to drive a bit beyond it to a sacred spot dear to his heart.

Good God, Stephen thought, *I hope it's not where Max and Tessa had their first kiss or something.* Lucy sped along Highway 93. They went past Missoula and turned right onto a rural road. He later learned it was White Coyote Road in a town called Arlee.

When they stopped, Stephen saw the magnificent display of white Buddhas against the clear blue sky.

"The Garden of 1000 Buddhas," Max said. "When I was a teenager, I'd drive all the way out here for some peace. This is where I got into spirituality. And thought maybe I was different."

They walked along the stupas and the statues, the central shrine and, coming back around, along the pond, the black devas and bodhisattvas.

"You rarely talk about religion," Stephen said.

"You know what they say, I'm spiritual, not religious."

"Yeah, but I'd think I'd know that about you by now."

"You never know anyone completely, do you?"

Stephen scoffed. They headed back to the car where Lucy was waiting.

"What, you aren't spiritual?" Stephen asked her.

Lucy smiled. "I've seen it before," she said.

The Plan

For the next few months, life seemed to return to normal. Stephen's ankle took a couple of months to heal, and it was too cold to go hiking anyway, so both Max and Stephen were Brooklyn-bound.

Stephen's lease was expiring at the end of the year, and since they were "fully engaged," he moved out of his apartment in Bushwick and started living with Max and Clay full-time. It was one of those weird three-way associations unique to expensive New York, where an engaged or married couple lives with a single person to save money.

Stephen was conflicted about leaving his apartment, especially given his newfound lifestyle—his transition from ghetto Bushwick to hipster Williamsburg had pleased him plenty. He enjoyed living in the Greenpoint loft and he could take Ubers back and forth from the library. But having the support of Max's family seemed important too—Max's business success had been an illusion. He felt that he needed to pull off Cole's design to have an ideal situation.

Stephen wanted to convince Clay to buy out Max, but first he had to figure out if Clay's situation made that possible. If Clay needed to live with them, maybe it wasn't?

With Max working some nights at the brewery, Stephen spent time with Clay in the evenings. Often offering to cook, he learned about Clay's upbringing in Savannah, which gave Clay both southern gentility and an insecurity that made him drive hard to run the brewery his way.

Despite Max's knowledge of brewing, his love of mixology and his initial contribution to the brewery's finances and planning, these days Clay was the driving force behind its day-to-day operations and aesthetic sophistication. Behind the southern machismo was an adept politician with a good relationship with his staff, who he had recruited, and a realistic plan for the business' progression. He kept up with Yelp reviews and wrote apologies or thanks on Trip Advisor. His persona was different at home from "in the office" but Stephen figured, given this situation, he could talk Clay into taking over the business and could steer Max back to Montana.

One day, Stephen made homemade rigatoni with meatball and tomato sauce with olives. He bought a bottle of wine and some brie cheese and crackers. As they ate dinner, he asked Clay about his ambitions regarding the brewery. Were they planning to expand the operation and maybe open another branch?

"I'd love to do that, but business has been slow. Summer and fall were amazing, but it's winter now."

"So you're barely getting by?"

"Rent's the biggest killer. We could move but it's high every-where. Better to have a premium location."

"Didn't Max's father invest..."

"If you need to know, Mr. Nosy Librarian, Max's father's investment went into all the hundreds of thousands of dollars needed to set up and open a business like this. But the rent still needs to be paid. We might have the ability to expand eventually, but it will take a few years."

"Have you ever thought of taking control of the operation?"

"What the hell are you talking about, dude?"

"I mean, buying them out. Owning it yourself."

"I've got partners for a reason. I own half but my portion is from a bank loan. I don't have a ranch back in Georgia or anything."

"I see."

"What, you want to push Max into the book business or some-thing?"

"No. But his father wants us to move back and run the ranch."

"I can't afford not to have a partner, but I'll be glad to take his salary. Cuz we split that too."

"I see," Stephen said.

"I can talk to Max if you want. If he moves back, I can run the business myself, but I still need a business partner."

"Okay, just don't tell him I put you up to it."

"Sure."

Stephen had never run a small business, so he didn't realize the sophistication of the arrangement. There was a difference between the business assets and the way Max and Clay made their individual incomes, which was by earning a managerial salary through profits. It was even possible that the business itself was losing money, though Max didn't inquire.

Yet it seemed like Clay was on his side. Maybe they could both talk to Max, individually, to get him to see that Montana was his best bet for the future, even if he kept his stake in the brewery from afar

The Inquest

While he considered his next move, Stephen continued to look up articles on Black Panthers. He made a list of former Panthers, once gone bad, now reformed, then checked if they were still living in New York City. Who knew his research skills would come in so handy? His primary responsibilities in the library had been to help care for and educate little kids, and there was little research involved in that.

He narrowed his list to a couple of names. He decided to try to contact one former Panther, Reginald "Reggie" Hanes, who was apparently still living in Harlem.

One day, he scheduled a floating holiday and took the subway to 135th street in Central Harlem. On a library database, he had found a couple of people named Reggie Hanes in their 60s, so he decided to just go up to the apartments in question and knock on the doors.

The first apartment building was a few blocks away in the 130s; he walked through a crowd of brothers on the stoop who looked at him funny. When he rang the bell and didn't get a response, one of them asked what he wanted.

"Reggie Hanes?" he asked.

"Don't know that nigga," was the response (and sorry for using that word, just want to make this realistic). "A bitch live there though; that fine thang at work now."

He thanked them and left quickly. He trekked up to the edge of Hamilton Heights, entering another apartment building. This time no one was sitting on the stoop; the building seemed rather run down.

The front door was ajar, so there was no need to ring the bell. The apartment was on the third floor, so Stephen took his time ascending since his ankle still wasn't 100% healed.

When he knocked on a thick door, he heard nothing. He rang the black bell instead. He waited a few minutes.

Then he heard a rather meek, soft voice.

"Who is it? Clarisa?"

"I'm an old friend who wants to talk."

After a pause, the voice said, "I don't got no friends. No money either."

"I'm George Florence's son. Do you remember him?"

Another long pause. "Old George. He still in the hole?"

"I want to get him out. Even though he doesn't want it."

The door opened. He saw a rather frail old man, wearing a stained gray sweater over a pink button-down shirt, and blue trousers.

"You do look like George," he said. "Of what I can remember."

"Can I come in?" Stephen asked as he began to walk in.

"You wanna rob me, you ain't gettin' nothing," Reggie said as he stood aside. "And if you wanna torture me, I'm gonna go pretty fast."

"I just want to talk. I need clarity."

Reggie laughed as he closed the door. "Sure, clarity. The place is a little cold, so your fingers might need mittens."

"I'll survive," Stephen said. Inside the apartment, he saw a hospital-style bed with machines, tubes, and even a defibrillator.

"Old age means lots of problems," Reggie said, sitting down on a torn armchair. Stephen planted himself across from him a couch. The place smelled like it hadn't been aired out in a while.

"I rarely have visitors, so it'd be good to talk. What do you want to know?"

"Who framed my dad?" Stephen asked directly.

"Framed him?" Reggie laughed. "Why do you think he was framed?"

"I visited him in prison. He says he didn't do it. Says he's keeping his mouth shut to protect me. But I'd rather have the truth than protection."

"What did old Georgie tell you?"

Stephen gave him the run down, during which Reggie coughed some, and laughed some. After listening, he was nodding, and said:

"Back then, the atmospherics were different. More exciting than today, but you've got opportunities because of it. The ideals of the 60s and early 70s, they were gone, and the realities had broken down families and communities. By the late 70s and early 80s we were in survival mode and selling smack to survive. We got busted and became informants. When this new crack-cocaine epidemic came, we tipped off the cops for raids, while also getting protection kickbacks from the gangs.

"It was a crazy balancing act, but we made money both ways, so we took it. We don't how the NYPD got the bread to pay us, maybe they were selling the confiscated smack on the side, I don't know. We respected your dad; sure, his crusade against crack-cocaine worried us, but we didn't think he would ever turn on us. We were his brothers.

"Then he joined Khalid Muhammad's crew. We had always been wary of the Nation of Islam—they were too straight. We feared that conversion would make him more militant and threaten our trade.

"With a black mayor elected, we thought the status quo would be altered, and we were seriously scared of that. But we were wrong— we didn't anticipate Giuliani and the backlash against our people in the 90s that would fundamentally twist this city. Looking back on it, maybe we should have joined forces with George instead.

"But at the time, we got scared, especially when he changed his name to Aabid Muhammad. We had a meeting with our police contacts, then separately with our drug contacts, then with each other. Some of us thought we would talk to him, but his zeal might make that dangerous in itself. We decided the only way to save our business was to get him out of the way.

"We respected him too much to kill him. Our police contacts created a strategy. They wanted some cop out of the way too because he was asking too many questions. If he found out about the money-reward system and went to Internal Affairs, the operation would have been over. Then one day we heard this cop was killed and George was arrested. That's all I know."

"So the NYPD killed one of their own and set up my dad for it?"

"Or they contracted it out. Not sure."

"But your plan put my dad in jail."

"We had nothing to do with the operation itself. Or whether it went ahead."

Stephen was fuming, but he kept his composure. "Okay, so tell me the name of these cops you spoke to."

"I can't. I don't want to die yet."

"They're probably as old as you. Maybe even dead."

"Most are dead. But I was told never to rat about it, and I haven't."

"You told me."

"I haven't talked to anyone in a while. But for your safety and your dad's, I recommend you keep it to yourself."

"Thirty years later, who could be a threat to my dad or me now? Is it Turner Goodson?"

Reggie smirked. "Turner. The most famous brother. Why do you ask about him?"

"Just tell me. Is he two-timing us?"

Reggie moved around in his seat, uncomfortably. "I don't know. Obviously, these days he makes his dough by advocating for us. In this case, Black Lives Matter, and these other atrocities committed against our people, as if it's 1930-something. But was he involved with the cops back in the day? Possibly, maybe even on another level I've heard—the FBI. But I don't squirm around in his skin, so I can't say."

"You don't like him?"

"He's a brother. He advocates without stirring our pot. What could be bad?"

"Why did my father mention him?"

"Maybe because he had access. Turner had gotten divorced, and he had been living with old George. He moved out a few months before, and another tenant came in, but I think he still had the keys."

"So he could have planted the evidence."

"It's possible. Or maybe he made a copy for the cops. Don't know, I made sure not to be inside that day."

"Inside?"

"I was your dad's roommate. But I stayed with my girlfriend that night. Maybe your dad should've stayed with you and your mom that night too. See, we liked having options."

Stephen was silent. He assessed Reggie. "So, you did know something was going down that night. And you could have done it. Maybe you did."

"I didn't. I told you."

"You were the primary informant. You knew my dad the best."

"I also liked him the best. He's not dead, is he?"

Stephen stood up. "I'm going to the papers. Or writing a blog post about this."

"I would advise against that, young man."

Stephen took out his phone. "I've been recording you. I have this on tape."

Reggie smiled. "Whenever we rock the cradle, son, we suffer. Not white folks, but us. That's going to be the result of your heroics. You want to do right? March with Turner and people your age so the cops today stop shooting us and putting us into chokeholds. That's the fight of your time. I told you this history because you need to know before we all perish. Your dad will never get out. He is at peace inside. He told you himself."

"I still need to know who did it."

"Well, I can't tell you that. I advise against mousing around more, but I can't stop you. I'm an old man. Just waiting on my Spanish home aide so I can look at that sweet ass."

Stephen suddenly felt an intense desire to grab something, maybe a kitchen knife, and stab this cat. But then he thought about all he could lose, and as with situations with difficult customers at the library, he kept his cool.

But now that he had the recording, he realized he was in danger. He decided to back away; he could hear Reggie chuckling as he opened the door.

"Come back if you have any more questions," he said. "I can't promise I'll be single, though."

~ The Inquest ~
Part II

Outside, Stephen gathered his thoughts. He checked his smartphone while constantly tracking the activity around him. He put up his hoodie out of a reflexive paranoia. He walked a bit and entered a Starbucks. He looked up the roommate situation again—it was strange that none of the roommates were mentioned in any of the articles of the time.

Then he realized something—his father's former apartment was on the same cross streets as the first apartment in Central Harlem he had gone to—and when he finally located the exact address, he realized it was the same apartment. Now it made more sense that Reggie Hanes had once lived there. Yet who lived there now? Would she give him access to the apartment? At least he could get a better visual sense of the situation.

Realizing that he had a lot of time to kill before the resident would likely return from work, he decided to find the crime scene. Thirty years later, it was no longer a warehouse but an auto-body shop, with mostly Hispanic workers. He moused around a bit, asking for a quote so he could get inside. But despite the visual, he realized it was unlikely he would learn anything.

He needed to wait until the apartment occupant came home. It was cold outside. He avoided shouts from local gangbangers and heard teenage girls getting catcalled, so he tried to find another place to loiter. He wandered around the local Key Food for a while, then stopped at a local Soul Food restaurant for an early dinner, making sure it was a spot for the older crowd so he didn't get into any beef. It was tough for a young black man out and about in the city, you didn't know if you'd get messed with by your own people or the police, so it was the easiest course to hang out with seniors.

After dinner, around seven in the early evening, he made his way back to the first apartment building. Somehow, the stoop was empty—local hoodlums preferred afternoons to harass people, seemed like. He rang the bell; a voice asked who it was.

"I'm sorry to bother you. I'm investigating something that happened many years ago in your apartment."

"What?"

"It was a murder. Almost thirty years ago."

He figured that was it. She would tell him to leave or call the cops on him, that's certainly what a white woman would do, but he had to take a chance that this sister would be different.

"What's your name?" she asked.

"Stephen Florence," he said. "George Florence's son. Do you know who he is?"

There was a pause. "Wait there. I'll come out."

He waited, pleasantly surprised. Through the glass on top of the front entrance he saw an apartment door at the end of the hallway on the first floor open, close, and then someone approached. Through the hallway light he saw that it was not a sister at all, but an older white woman—perhaps in her 50s, with silver hair and a fresh, but heavily made-up, face.

She opened the front door.

"Hi Stephen," she said. "I'm Gina. Why don't you come inside."

"Gina," he said. And then he made the connection—it couldn't be, could it? Officer Kirkpatrick's partner, Gina Cassidy? Living in his father's old apartment?

He went inside, and perhaps against his better judgment, followed her down the hallway. She unlocked the door with her key—several locks, in fact.

"You can never be too careful," she said.

She gestured for him to go inside. He hesitated, but he didn't see anyone else, so he ventured in sideways, still watching her, making sure she didn't do anything—it was what he had gotten used to in the Bed Stuy projects.

"Relax Stephen," she said, locking the many locks from the inside. "I should be more scared than you."

"No one else—"

"My daughter is still at Columbia. She goes to school there. She'll be home soon, but no, it's just us."

So that's the "fine thang" the teens had been referring to—not Gina, he assumed. He looked around and saw there were three bedrooms in the apartment, along with a kitchen attached to a dining room, and a relatively spacious bathroom.

"Not bad for Manhattan, right? Where do you live?"

"Brooklyn. Bed Stuy growing up, now Greenpoint."

"Greenpoint. That must be expensive."

"My fiancé's place."

"I see. So, she pays the rent. Let me guess: rich hipster white girl?"

She dumped her thick set of keys on the dining room table and sat down.

"So how can I help you, Stephen?"

"Did Reggie Hanes call you?" he asked.

She smiled. "Actually, he did. Good thinking."

"So you know—"

"I know you have questions. But unlike Reggie, I do mind being recorded."

Stephen took out his phone. He put in his code, turned off the recording app and showed her it was off, then put it on the table.

"You try to smash it, I'll react," he said.

"I don't work for Reggie," she said.

"So you set up your partner?"

"I wouldn't do that. I loved Henry."

"So why are you here?"

Gina looked down at the table. "Things happen in life that you can't control, Stephen. Sometimes you just have to accept them. Roll with the punches."

"So it's true. The cops killed your partner, framed my father, and gave you this apartment to keep your mouth shut?"

"It's a better commute than Long Island," she said. "Now my daughter is thriving."

Stephen shook his head. "Who was the mastermind?"

"I don't know. Henry's shooting shocked me. I was right next to him when he went down. I thought it could have been me, and I was lucky. I had major survivor guilt. I quit the force.

"But a few years after George Florence's trial was over, a senior officer called me. He told me the department was sad for my loss; someone would be in touch to make it up to me. A few days later, I got a visit, on Long Island, from an anonymous officer who claimed he was undercover.

"He offered me this rent-controlled apartment at very low rent. I was a teacher in the Upper East Side then, so I used to make the commute. Selling my mother's house in LI, my car and coming to live here made sense. Who wouldn't take that deal?"

"It doesn't make sense that they would just give it to you, unless you had something on them."

"Maybe they just felt bad. The NYPD also created a very generous fund for Henry's wife and children. It wasn't easy to do it for me since I had quit. So this is what they gave me instead."

"Who called you? Who visited you?"

"Does it matter?"

She went to the refrigerator and opened the door. "You want some pie? My mom used to make some delicious key-lime. Brought down the generations."

Stephen looked around the apartment at the corners of the living room where the sneakers might have been located and wondered about the drawer where the gun might have been found.

"Where was my father's bedroom?" he asked. But when he turned back towards her, she was pointing a gun at him.

He almost jumped. Reflexively, he put his hands up.

"Don't worry, Stephen, I don't want to shoot you," she said. "And I won't if you play ball."

She picked up his phone and put in his code, which she had apparently figured out by watching him. She went to the app and deleted all the recordings.

"You need to leave this alone, Stephen. No one alive, including your father, wants this pursued."

Stephen continued to leave his hands up because he didn't know what else to do.

"Trust me, word is out now," she continued. "If you keep pursuing this, it won't be good for you, your mother, your father, your fiancé or anyone in your life. So you need to take your phone, go back to Brooklyn, and stop worrying about all this. You need to keep living that privileged Greenpoint life. Take after me, let bygones be bygones. Forget the past."

Debate

That night, he was lying next to Max in the Greenpoint apartment, staring up at the ceiling and thinking about that moment. How he had taken the phone and backed out of the apartment. How he had run into her attractive, smiley daughter in the hallway—he could have taken her hostage if he was able and willing to do that, but he didn't. He just walked briskly to the train station and took the subway back to Greenpoint.

He couldn't sleep. Despite Gina's deletion, Stephen still had Reggie's recording. He had managed to email the recording to himself while in Key Food. But should he use it and potentially ruin his and family's life? And now he had Max to think of too.

He got up and climbed down the ladder to the main floor, scrambled into the kitchen and turned on the light. He opened the refrigerator and considered his options. He remembered the scene in *A Wrinkle in Time* where Charles Wallace and Meg made sandwiches in the middle of the night before meeting Mrs. Whatsit. But he didn't have liverwurst or onion salt for that matter. He did have some bologna that Clay had bought. Still, he decided to go back to his sometimes-vegetarian forays and made grilled cheese instead, using the toaster oven because he was too lazy to grease the pan.

The toaster went off. He opened the door and slid out the pieces using a knife. He put a couple of pickles on the hot cheese, then added some mustard and ketchup. He folded the sandwich and used a knife to cut it in half.

"Can't sleep?" a voice asked behind him. He almost jumped, and turned around quickly, still holding the knife. He thought he had heard Reggie's voice, but instead Max stood there, without a shirt on, his tattoos blazing.

"Oh, hey sweetie," Stephen said, putting the knife down behind him.

"Something the matter?"

"No, why?"

"I can tell, that's why."

Max sat down on a stool. Stephen realized he was shaking. He started to cry.

"What's wrong, pumpkin?" Max asked. He went around the counter to embrace Stephen. Stephen held onto his man. He cried a long time.

"I'm sorry to put this on you," Stephen said.

"That's why I'm here. We share everything. What's the matter?"

"What I'm about to tell you doesn't leave this apartment, okay? Not even Clay can know."

"Sure," Max said.

Whispering, Stephen told Max the whole situation. Max seemed uncomfortable during the telling.

"Wow," he said when it was done. "That's quite something."

"I think it's best if I forget it right?"

"Normally I'd say your family, your choice, but now it's my issue too. They could attack any of us, but you could also be smeared in the papers and online. And if they set up your dad, don't you think they could set you up too?"

"Yeah," he said. "It's like some evil, all-pervasive force. You don't know where it is at any time."

"Don't tell Clay. He hates cops, so he might leak this."

"It's not fair. My dad's been locked up my entire life. And he'll never get out because of them."

"I don't know what I would do if that happened to my dad."

There was silence. "Would you support me if I did go to the media with it?" Stephen asked.

Max appeared uncomfortable. "I'll support you. But I don't think you should."

Stephen nodded. "Are you hungry? I think my sandwich is cold."

"I'll take half, if you're offering."

He moved to put the sandwich pieces back in the toaster oven, but Max recommended the microwave.

Stephen moved that way, but then Max changed his mind, and took out a pan.

"I'll add a light layer of olive oil," he said. "Heating it up will peel its taste, but I don't think a little will matter."

He placed some olive oil on the pan and turned the flame on. "So, Clay mentioned your little conversation to me," Max said.

"He did?"

"You're really taking my dad's advice to heart, huh?"

"Just trying to help."

"My dad's been trying to get me to move back to Montana since my early 20s. Since I'm pressing 40, it might make sense now."

"So you'll give up the brewery and move back?"

"I do miss the land. And it's not as homophobic as it once was. It's not New York, but it's peaceful."

"And you'll have our own ranch."

"My dad always wanted me to be his successor. I guess I can't escape fate. This way, him and Shawna can just do as much or as little as they want."

"So you've settled on that?"

"I'm thinking more that way. Maybe I'll change my mind tomorrow."

"I didn't realize your managerial salary was your main profit base."

"It's complicated."

"I like the library, but I can give it up."

"What about your family?"

"Maybe my mom can live on the ranch? The rest I don't care about."

Max pressed the sandwich pieces down on the hot pan, turned them over a couple of times, and flipped them on a dish.

"See, hot and heavy."

"My mom's cool?"

"Of course."

"Maybe I should talk to her. About the situation?"

"Are you sure you want to churn up old wounds?"

"You think I should forget about this whole thing?"

"It doesn't seem like you'll win. Everyone just seems to want to let it lie, even your dad."

"What about social justice? What we keep preaching about?"

Max bit into his sandwich.

"Well, no one had pointed a gun at you when we were preaching before."

The Talk

Several weeks passed. Stephen began to follow the new coronavirus outbreak in Wuhan, China, then on cruise ships, then in Italy, Iran, South Korea, and Washington state. The first confirmed case in New York, a lawyer in his 50s, was hospitalized in Westchester.

Stephen was busy at the library with the chaotic kids and disruptive customers: homeless, emotionally disturbed adults, trouble-some teens, and wannabe gangbangers. He hadn't pursued his findings or heard from Reggie or Gina, but the situation was still alive in his mind. Max continued to advise caution.

One day after work, he took an Uber to his mother's apartment. He waved at the brothers he grew up with as a kid, most of whom had been deadbeats and bullies, but he walked past them swiftly to avoid conversations.

He was buzzed up and entered the small apartment where he had grown up. There was a tiny hallway (small bathroom on the side) leading to a small kitchen, a table for a dining room, a living room with a ruffled pink carpet, a couch with a pull-out mattress where he had slept, some pictures of him and his mom on a dresser, and a medium-sized TV. There was one bedroom: his mom's. All windows had grates. You never know, as Gina had said.

His mother was watching the evening news: more people associated with the lawyer had tested positive for the coronavirus. She turned it off.

"Hopefully it won't get too bad," she said. They started to talk about family: she had spoken to Uncle Phil and Gladys. They were on board with the wedding, Brantly too. He wanted to get together with Stephen and Max.

"I haven't heard from him," Stephen said. "I'm pretty sure he has my number."

"He's got his own problems," she said. "But put him on the list for sure. Which reminds me, what have you two been planning?"

"We're still thinking about where to hold it, here or Montana. Or maybe destination?"

"Can you afford that?"

"Max's dad will probably be footing the bill, and he'd like it in Montana. We're strongly considering moving there and living on the ranch."

Ma's eyes went wide. "What? You'll leave the library?"

"I don't have so much seniority anyway. Pay's not great. The ranch seemed cool."

"You've gotta consider the pension."

"Max's dad will teach me the operation. Max would keep a stake in the brewery here, but Clay would run it."

"It does sound like you have a plan."

Stephen strolled around the apartment. "When I was a kid, this place looked majestic. Playing with Power Rangers and stuff. Now I realize how dingy it is. You deserve better, Ma. You should move to Montana with us."

"I've gotten so used to this place. I feel like I'll die if I leave."

"No, Ma. You'll be reborn. Like those Buddhist statues I saw over there."

"We're Christians."

"Dad's Muslim. You should have changed my name like he did."

"You were barely alive when he went away."

"Unjustly," Stephen said. "And you know it. Because you were involved in the coverup."

"What?"

"I know everything. About Reggie, Gina Cassidy, the NYPD's plot to murder Officer Kirkpatrick, a good man. And Turner Goodson."

Ma was shaking her head. "It was a different time—"

"I keep on hearing that!" Stephen yelled. "How in the hell was it different?"

Ma didn't respond.

"We're still being killed by cops now, so how was it different?"

"Stephen—"

"Tell me, what was your role? Did you plot against Dad too?"

"Stephen..." She paused. "When your dad found out we were going to have you, he did change. That's when he joined the Nation of Islam. He thought he had been a hypocrite. Now having a child, he thought he would teach you the right way forward for a new Black America."

"But he didn't. Because he got framed. And if he wanted to teach me, why didn't he reach out to me? Why isn't he even trying to get out?"

"You went to see him?"

"Of course. He's my father. I can see him, right?"

"He's matured and learned like all of us."

"Did you know?"

"Turner told me."

"He told you what?"

"He told me the day of the arrest that me and you would be okay."

"If you played ball."

"We learned a long time ago we shouldn't mess with the powers that be. Your father has learned the same thing."

"So Turner was in on it. Did he plant the evidence? Did he pull the trigger?"

"I don't know. But he was true to his word. Nobody bothered us. We've been taken care of."

"What does that mean?"

"Helping with rent, necessities. You don't realize how lucky you've been compared to the knuckleheads around here."

"Turner paid for that?"

"He set up a fund for us. Quietly."

Stephen was silent for a bit.

"How well did you know him?" he finally asked.

"He was a friend."

"How good of a friend?"

"We were all involved at some point. But I loved your father."

"Am I Turner Goodson's son?"

She shook her head. "I doubt that. We've never taken a paternity test, but you look like your father. If I had suspicions, I could have sued Turner for paternity. But I'm not interested in that."

"Considering he's paid for everything anyway. How did you get Section 8 for all those years?"

"The fund isn't exactly transparent."

"You didn't want to sue him because you didn't want to rock the boat. But—"

"Stephen, George is your father. Period. But Turner cares about our people. He's done a lot for victims of police injustice. And he's done a lot for us."

"Dad's been in jail for thirty years for a crime he didn't commit. I can't think of a bigger injustice."

"So what will you do? Go to the papers? Ruin Turner, me, former police officers, and, in the end, get nothing? Once the authorities think someone is a cop killer, they're stuck with that label. No one will let them out."

"I'll go to a podcast. They've flipped injustices. What could be a bigger story than corrupt cops and a famous Black politician colluding to frame a former Black Panther for murder?"

"I'm asking you not to, Stephen. You were taught it's a free country, but we'll never be free in America. We need to take what we can get. To survive."

"Things are changing."

"Are they?"

Stephen turned to leave. He was fuming. "Look, you have the option of going to Montana. We can be free there, trust me, and you won't have to rely on your killer boyfriend to pay your bills. Let me know what you decide."

The Virus

A day later, Mayor De Blasio said it was still safe to ride the subways, but people began to get nervous. The day after that, more cases in NYC were reported, most of them connected to the lawyer. The stock market had been crashing for weeks.

Max and Clay began to have conversations about how to orient the brewery in case of a city-wide shutdown. And Max and Stephen began to wonder if they should leave for Montana because they could be trapped in NYC for good.

On Saturday March 7, Governor Cuomo announced a state of emergency in New York. Already many establishments were canceling large events. Max decided he would take a quick trip back to

Montana before cases rose too high in NYC and it became impossible to leave. He took a red eye to Montana, wearing a mask on the plane just in case.

So far Montana had no cases. But the turbulence of domestic and international markets could affect supply and demand, meaning the prosperity of the ranch was uncertain too.

Stephen was unsure about the situation at the library. While he could quit his job at any time, his relative job security was now an asset. Max told him to stick it out a bit longer—he could always drive the Mercedes cross-country if it became necessary.

Max's departure led to a staffing shortage at the brewery in the evenings, so Stephen promised to fill in on some shifts after work. Staff were beginning to get antsy, but Clay tried to assure them.

The next day, Sunday, Stephen worked with Clay in the brewery to learn the ropes. Max texted him that he had gotten home okay and that he was discussing next steps with his dad. Stephen and Clay watched the news that evening: the city was now warning people about riding subways and buses and advising people to avoid large crowds.

Hundreds of customers a day came into public libraries, and afternoons were especially packed. Library staff complained to their union who said they were talking to the administration, but the mayor was concerned about closing schools and libraries since the underprivileged kids would have nowhere to go and nothing to eat.

Stephen drove to work that Monday in Max's Mercedes. During his morning toddler program, parents asked about a potential closure. Staff had gotten little guidance from the administration regarding Covid protocols, but when he watched the evening news at the brewery, he learned that sixteen cases were now confirmed in New York City.

The next day Governor Cuomo announced a containment zone in New Rochelle. Stephen worked at the brewery again that evening. Max called to tell him he might be in Montana for a few more days at least.

On Thursday March 12th, it was announced that restaurants and bars would have to cut their seating capacity in half, even though only days earlier the mayor had announced that it was still safe to keep dining at full capacity. Many bars and restaurants, especially in Manhattan, were already shutting down to safeguard themselves and employees. Clay spoke to Max: they decided to stay open for the time being, but they prepared themselves for a shutdown too.

On Thursday the New York Public Library announced that they would be closing. Brooklyn, a separate system more dependent on city funds, didn't make the same decision, but they did announce that they would suspend all programming until further notice.

The mayor hadn't decided yet to close city schools, and he was reportedly angry about NYPL's announcement. By then, though, Stephen and his fellow library staff had gotten instructions to space tables apart and cancel crowded children's programs.

On Sunday, Brooklyn Public Library decided to reduce its hours. By the late evening, when the mayor decided that schools would be closed, the library followed suit and closed too. Restaurants and bars were ordered to limit business to takeout only.

At first, Clay began to panic. Food was a small portion of their sales, and they would have to spend significantly on additional takeout supplies. Then it was revealed that bars could sell alcoholic drinks as takeout too, but only if the customer bought a food item as well.

Stephen worked from home for the library, but he would continue to get paid his full salary for the foreseeable future. Clay prepared for his takeout model, updating the website and spending money on implementing restrictions, including signage.

Clay also made the difficult decision to furlough much of his staff and curtailed his evening hours. He and Stephen began working most shifts, Stephen with a laptop near him for his library work and meetings.

One evening a week later, well after a stay-at-home order had been issued, Stephen, wearing a mask, was working the front table (a small screen was up to protect him), when he heard Clay yelling all the way from the back office. He knew Clay was planning to speak to Max about getting a loan from Max's father to help with the extra expenses, and also, to determine when he was returning to NYC.

Stephen waited until he heard the shouting stop, then asked one of the chefs to temporarily man the front table and phones. He made his way to the small, cramped office, where Clay was sitting at a desk piled high with invoices and other papers, his head in his arms, next to the old-fashioned office landline.

"Clay, are you okay?" Stephen asked.

Clay shook his head. "He's not coming back. Says the Covid rates are too high here. And he's not giving any money either. In fact, he might want to sell his portion to me. Not that I have the cash to buy it."

Stephen was shocked. "Are you sure? I'll talk to him."

They had been talking and texting almost every day and Max never indicated he wouldn't be returning to NYC. Clay left the room to man the front desk and Stephen called Max from his cell phone.

"Is this for real?" Stephen asked.

Max didn't respond for several seconds.

"Cases are high Stephen," he finally said. "People are starting to die. It's going to get worse. Here we've got the ranch and open land."

"You're just going to give up on the business?"

"We'll stay in if Clay can't afford to buy it. But the situation here is unsteady too. We can't afford to loan money we might not have in the future."

"I mean this was your dream, not mine," Stephen said, beginning to accept it. "But if that's the case, should I drive over there in the Mercedes? I should be able to get out, but I probably can't get back in."

Max hesitated. "It's probably safer to stay there at this point," he said. "You could get infected on the way. It'll be at least a couple of nights staying over at hotels. And forget about flying."

"What, are you worried I'm going to give it to you?"

"I just think it's more practical."

"You're hiding something," Stephen said abruptly. At first, he regretted saying it, but Max's continued evasiveness made him feel he might be onto something.

"We can Zoom," Max said. "I think it's safer that way."

"If you're quitting on Clay, there's no point in me exhausting and risking myself here. I'm getting paid at the library no matter where I am. I can do programming and reference online."

"I just don't want you to get here and then regret it."

"Why would I regret it?"

"Look, I'm not sure it's going to work. That's what I mean."

Stephen was silent himself for a bit. It started setting in.

"What? Are you breaking up with me?"

"Stephen, since I got here, I've started feeling that maybe New York was wrong for me, and this is where I need to be."

"We already agreed on that a while ago."

"I'm just not sure you're going to fit in."

"I fit in fine when I was there, Max. With your dad, Skylar, even Shawna. What the fuck?"

"Yeah," Max said. "There's someone else."

"Motherfucker," he said, after he had absorbed it. "You two-timing fuck."

"It just happened. I just realized..."

"What, are you fucking one of the tractor guys or something?"

"No, it's a she."

"Tessa?"

"We rekindled stuff. I just..."

"All this time, I should have known. You little mother..."

He slammed his phone on the desk. It fell on the floor. The screen cracked.

Stephen wept uncontrollably. He slammed his hand on the desk until he yelled in pain. He was delirious; at some point he heard somebody speaking to him. Then he was being held.

He got out of Clay's embrace.

"Just leave me alone, man. And tell that mother—"

He grabbed his coat and ran. He locked himself in the Mercedes and kept bawling.

The Aftermath

He stayed in the loft for a few days, alternatively crying and catatonic. Clay cooked for him, checked up on him, and worked all the shifts at the brewery.

Ultimately, Stephen had another conversation with Max where it was determined that Stephen could keep driving the Mercedes for now and stay in the apartment until the lease ran out. Max was apologetic but it didn't seem like he would change his mind.

"It's a little weird Max became bisexual in like a Montana minute," Clay said as Stephen ate some miso soup and vegetarian sushi Clay had crafted in the kitchen. "Not to mention a backstabber on multiple fronts."

"Fuck that asshole," Stephen muttered.

"Just goes to show, it always comes down to the moolah. And your roots."

"Are you heading back to Savannah or something?"

"I didn't say the rule applied to me, did I?"

Stephen shook his head. "Came out of nowhere. I should have fucking known."

"Don't blame yourself bro."

"I don't. I blame that backstabbing fuck."

Clay laughed. "Well, at least he's still paying his portion of the rent. And you can stay here. Just don't engage in risky behaviors with weirdos."

"Thanks Clay. I never figured you'd be the good guy."

"Life is funny, right?"

Relief

When the first Covid relief bill was passed on March 27th, things began to look a little better for the brewery. Clay believed he could get a forgivable loan to keep the business afloat and maybe even hire back some employees.

Stephen looked online for apartments in Bed Stuy so he could be closer to his mom, but the rent moratorium and stay-at-home order made those apartments scarce because that population had nowhere to go. The hipster areas became available as people fled, but landlords were cautious of renting them, especially to people of color, in case they couldn't pay or were bringing Covid with them.

He also investigated Turner Goodson's background and current activities. These days he was focused on cop killings of black men during traffic stops, showing up around the country wherever an incident occurred. Pandemic or not, plenty of incidents were occurring.

He hadn't heard anything from Gina Cassidy or Reggie, and he hadn't decided what to do with the voice recording. Since their fight, he had only spoken to his mom a couple of times, just to check in on her due to the pandemic, but neither had mentioned Turner, Montana, the breakup, or the murder conspiracy. They stuck to small-talk—she had to go to her branch occasionally for shifting, clean-up projects etc.—he warned her to take the necessary precautions of masking, distancing, and glove-wearing—he had mentioned it might be a good time to retire, without bringing up a potential move that could no longer happen.

But his mom called him in early April, and this time it wasn't the usual "How are you doing?"

"It's your dad," she said. "He has corona virus, and it's bad."

"How do you know that?" Stephen asked.

"I got a call from a mutual friend."

"Turner Goodson?"

"He said they closed Sing Sing to visitors weeks back but maybe the guards brought it in. There's no social distancing or even testing in that place, but Turner pushed and got it done. Dad's in the makeshift infirmary now in quarantine but word is he's having trouble breathing. They've already had one death."

"Motherfucker."

"The worst is that no one can see him. And we don't completely know what's going on. Turner is pushing to have him moved to a real hospital so they can put him on a ventilator."

"You better be careful yourself, Ma. Are you still going to the grocery store?"

"I've gone a few times."

"I told you, get it on Uber Eats, have them leave it outside the door. And sanitize the box maybe. Or as I offered last time, I'll get it from the brewery and deliver it in the Mercedes."

"I can take care of myself, Stephen. You take care of yourself. How is Max?"

He hadn't told her about the breakup. He couldn't bear to tell anyone.

"He's fine," Stephen said.

"You might want to go to Montana now while you can. I mean, it makes sense."

"I'm not leaving you, Ma."

"I could come with you, but I'm not used to it, obviously. Living on a ranch. It'll be weird."

This was the first time she had considered the possibility. He wondered if he should tell her. Moving to Montana wasn't an option anymore.

"Or you could retire and go live with Uncle Phil and Aunt Gladys," he said. "At least it's not in the city proper."

"No, it's not good for too many old people to be in one place. And anyway, it's probably there too."

"That's the reason we can't go to Montana either, Ma."

"Oh," she said.

"Yeah."

"So what's going to happen to your relationship?"

"Zoom, I guess."

"I see. This horrible virus has done so much to us. Damn Chinese."

"Don't scapegoat, Ma. It's not like they created it. It's this asshole in the White House who keeps saying it's going to go away."

"I know. He's so horrible."

"Anyway, what are we gonna do about Dad?"

"We just have to wait, I guess."

"For Turner to tell us?"

She was silent.

"Is he going to create a crusade about prisoner treatment at Sing Sing? Probably not since he wants Dad to die."

"Don't say that. He's the only reason Dad got tested. And why he's still alive."

Downward

For the next few days, Stephen became more obsessed with articles on Sing Sing's situation with the virus. He read an article by John Lennon in Esquire published on March 19th about how the prison had gone into lockdown on March 14th, disallowing visitors, going into "quarantine" but with few actual procedures in place to enforce it, other than prisoners cleaning the institution with some questionable fluid. A few days into it, he finally got the nerve to call the prison with the hope that he could speak to his father or maybe get some information about him.

He was passed around to several departments. He was hung up on. He called again, and once again was passed around. Finally, he got the warden, who transferred him to the infirmary.

A nurse picked up.

"I'm sorry to tell you," she said. "Your father is dead."

Stephen was floored. It couldn't be true.

"Are you sure it's him?"

"George Florence. Is that him?"

Stephen hung up. He called his mother, but she didn't pick up.

He called several more times and got more voicemail. He went to the brewery for his shift and then he got a call from Uncle Phil.

"Your mom's in the hospital," he said. "At Woodhull."

"What happened, did she fall?"

"She's coughing a lot. She called us and we called 911. Thank God that she called us. I'll never leave her alone again if we get her back."

"If?"

"She's alone now. We can't go inside."

"Does she have it?"

"We don't know. They suspect so."

Stephen began to freak out. He called Woodhull and was told that there were too many patients for him to get through to a particular one.

"We have patients lying on stretchers in the hallway," a nurse quickly told him. "Call again and we'll try, but we're busy trying to save lives. I'm sorry."

Death

It was only a matter of time, he felt, before he got a call that his mother had passed away too. He had stopped working at the brewery and holed himself up in his loft. He finally made a connection, after several calls, with the nurse who was caring for his mother, along with many, many other people. His mother wasn't doing well: hooked up now to a ventilator, still crammed into a corner of intensive care (at least she wasn't in the middle of a hallway anymore, but that's because enough patients in the ICU had passed away), since the isolation rooms were booked.

If he could talk to her one last time, he would ask her if she knew whether Turner was his father or whether it had been George or even someone else. Since he had been dealing with his mother's situation, he hadn't called Sing Sing for several days.

When he finally did call the prison to make funeral arrangements, he was told that since no one had claimed him and fearing the virus could spread from the body, George had been buried like so many other state prison fatalities about 45 minutes north up the Hudson in a wooded area near Fishkill Correctional Facility in Beacon. Stephen marked the spot on his Google Maps, but he hadn't decided to make the trip yet.

One day, as he was researching the latest BLM incident in Ohio where Turner had shown up, he got a call from the nurse.

"I think it's the end," she said. "Do you want to speak to her?"

Stephen said yes, but he began crying so hard he could barely speak. He heard the beeps from the ventilator and other machines and his mother's labored breathing.

"Ma," he let out.

"Take care, son," he heard vaguely. "Don't let them get you."

"Tell me what to do Ma. Dad is dead."

"Follow your—"

"What Ma?"

"—conscience," she said with great difficulty.

"Is George my father, Ma? Or is it Turner?"

Coughing and labored breathing dominated the line.

"Ma?"

"I don't know," he heard her say and then an extended beep.

Then the nurse was on the line. "Gotta go," she said and hung up.

He waited a long fifteen minutes, silent except for his occasional coughing from the salty tears engulfing his mouth, when she called him back.

"I'm sorry," she said.

Despair

He moved into his mother's apartment as he tried to make arrangements with a funeral home—every place he called was booked up for weeks, even months. He didn't want his mother buried in a mass grave in Hart's Island, and he was assured she wouldn't be. She was housed in a refrigerated truck until the funeral home he had finally selected in Middle Village, Queens, could take her.

He rummaged through her papers, but he ultimately discovered that her will had been left with an old lawyer—but as he himself was sick, the process was delayed, and they would have to go through probate too. His Aunt Gladys was annoying him about getting the process moving, but he had stopped caring.

He had started to hang out with his gay Queens buddies in Jackson Heights, even though it was a high percentage Covid spot. He was drinking excessively now, one reason Clay had politely asked him to move into his mom's place.

One day, a Saturday, he read that Turner Goodson was in town investigating an incident where a black man had been choked by a cop on Staten Island, although the man had not died. The echoes of Eric Garner reverberated, and in defiance of Covid protocols for mass gatherings, a masked crowd had gathered on the spot where Garner had died, demanding further action against any cop using the choke hold maneuver.

Depressed, Stephen had been drinking since the morning, but he had slowed down in the afternoon, enough to make a relatively sober drive to Jackson Heights, where for once he could find parking because of the Covid disruption.

He hung out with a trio of friends: Rafie, a half Cuban, half Ecuadorian Queen with a bong; Ronald, an Afro-Latinx of Puerto Rican descent with the stash; and Gerry, a white editorial assistant who lived in the hood too.

When he got there, he immediately started drinking shots of Jim Beam bourbon. Rafie told him to slow down, and they got the bong going too. Then came a mean game of four-way chess which Gerry won by teaming up with Ronald to beat Rafie who had already eliminated Stephen and then by back-stabbing Ronald to win.

They smoked again, passing around the bong, swapping saliva like nobody's business while watching the news and throwing paper balls and cups at Donald Trump and his retarded so-called Covid task force.

As they prepared for a game of strip Twister, Stephen started to complain about the whole conspiracy to frame his dad and shut him up, something his friends had heard a few times now and dismissed as depressed crazy talk. But this time, Stephen followed his whole spiel by taking out his phone and playing the recording of Reggie confessing.

"Shit," Gerry said, "Did you pay that guy to say it?"

"Nah, it's legit," Stephen said. "God's honest truth."

"That'd be a great book," Gerry said. "I'm gonna run it past my boss. Whatever you do, don't delete that fucking recording."

"You kidding? It's my lifeline. I'm gonna get back at those fucking murderers."

After strip Twister, they had group sex; Gerry immediately regretted it, and everyone expressed mixed feelings.

"We're gonna die anyway," Ronald reasoned. "This is our generation's HIV."

"You want danger?" Stephen asked. "Let's party in the Bed Stuy projects. You never know what gangbanger's gonna shoot up the place."

"Don't think that's our scene, Chico."

"What are you afraid of? A bunch of black people, you racist fuck."

"I vote for it," Gerry said. "As long as it won't disrespect your recently departed mom."

"No one cares about us anyway. No matter what happens, we suffer first and hardest."

"True that," Ronald said. "But taking the subway'll take forever."

"We got my Mercedes. Ride luxury."

"Any of us fit to drive?" Gerry asked.

"It's my car, I'll fucking drive," Stephen said.

"I wouldn't advise that," Gerry responded.

"I got more toke than bourbon in me," Ronald said. "I got it."

"You sure?" Gerry asked. "Do you even have a license?"

"This gringo asking if I got a license. Don't mean I can't drive from here to there."

Gerry shrugged. "I don't have a license in NY either. But I can drive."

"I got it, man," Ronald repeated. "I got less drinks in me than any of you."

So, it was decided. They all drank glasses of water, went downstairs and out, and crammed into the Mercedes, Ronald driving and Stephen riding shotgun, Rafie and Gerry in the back.

"What are we taking?" Ronald asked. "BQE?"

"I got my phone," Stephen said, turning on Google Maps and putting it in the holder.

"Just don't forget that phone," Rafie said. "It's gold for you."

They headed out, taking 32nd Avenue, then merging onto the BQE. Ronald began to swerve in the lane, prompting honks behind him.

"Be careful," Gerry said from the back.

"We're gonna die, aren't we?"

"Preferably not today. Preferably not this way," Gerry responded.

"Alright, I'll try to be good."

They exited onto Wythe Avenue and made it to Flushing Avenue. At the left on Norstrand, Ronald went over the double yellow line before making the left, and they quickly heard sirens behind them.

"You stupid fuck," Gerry said.

"Calm down," Ronald said, pulling over at a hydrant. "I got it."

"You're driving without a license."

"How about Stephen switch with me?"

"Too late now. Plus, he's plastered."

"I think without a license might be better than DUI," Stephen said, slurring his words. "But I don't fucking know."

"We're fucking screwed," Rafie said. "But I think I'm seeing things now at least."

Then there was silence in the car. "Rafie, you got a license?" Ronald asked, taking Stephen's phone from the holder.

"I think so. Somewhere in my wallet."

"Let's switch, Chico."

"They not gonna see that? And I got alcohol in my blood too."

"You a light-skinned Latino, man. That's better. But the white boy is the best, except he got no license."

"Just shut the fuck up," Stephen said, opening the door and getting out of the car. As he did, he turned towards the cop car.

The cop on the driver's side had just exited and pulled his gun out.

"Get back in," he yelled. Then the same command came from the robotic voice.

Stephen put up his hands and kept proceeding. "I just wanna explain."

"You better fucking stop where you are," the cop said.

Stephen did. The other cop got out too and drew his weapon. "Put your hands on the trunk of the vehicle," he said. Stephen turned right and did what he was told.

"Okay," the primary cop said. "Now I want the driver to open his door and get out too."

Ronald opened the car door quickly and got out.

"Slowly!" the primary cop yelled. "I wanna see your hands in the air."

Ronald put up his hands.

"What the fuck's that in your hands?" the cop yelled.

Ronald brought down his hands and stepped towards the officer. Then Stephen heard two shots. He instinctively went straight down.

A flurry of shots followed, one after another, some on top of others. It seemed like many minutes before the shooting finally stopped.

"Shit!" he heard someone yell. Then he felt someone on top of him, pulling his arms behind him.

"Check the vehicle!"

"Fuck!" the primary cop yelled as Stephen heard the door open. "They're not moving."

"Deceased?"

"Not sure. How about the flopper?"

Stephen let out a small groan, followed by a yell.

"He's alive," the cop on top of him confirmed as he put handcuffs on him.

Nightmare

The rest of the night was a blur. Stephen remembered that he had been on the ground for a while. At some point he felt a knee on his neck and thought he was a goner. Later he heard more sirens. They finally let him up and slammed him against the car. It was decimated with bullets; he observed Ronald on a stretcher, his chest destroyed, while Gerry and Rafie were still in the back seat, their heads visible, arched back like crash test dummies.

He had a headache; he was dizzy. At one point he was throwing up on the pavement. Then he was in an ambulance, handcuffed to a masked cop while an EMS worker checked his vital signs and otherwise made small talk with the cop.

Then he was in a hospital corridor; masked people were looking down at him. They were saying he wasn't too bad, but they had no room in the rest of the hospital. He looked around and saw stretchers everywhere, and some people attached to ventilators. He was dizzy still. He thought the night would never end.

Exam

He stayed overnight lying on a stretcher in the ER, a mask placed over his mouth, his left hand handcuffed to the stretcher. In the morning, a man wearing a hazmat suit, double-mask, and visor, came up to him. He showed Stephen an iPad—Stephen saw three men on a Cisco WebEx Meeting. One was in a cop uniform. Another was wearing a suit, and a third had on a pink shirt.

The man in the pink shirt told Stephen that he was Mr. Goldberg, Stephen's lawyer, paid for by friends, and that he should remain silent and let Mr. Goldberg do the talking. Stephen hadn't done anything wrong, had he?

"He was drunk and wasted," the cop said.

"He wasn't driving, was he?" Goldberg asked.

"No."

"The driver is dead," Goldberg continued. "Passengers deceased. All unarmed. The whole car was massacred. It's all over the news."

"The investigation is ongoing," the man in the suit said.

"Look, we want the entire report. I want him examined for all injuries and released. You don't have any room here and no place in the joint. We want him transferred to his home asap. And if you give him Covid on top of nearly killing him and violating every right in the book, we're going to make this even bigger than you thought possible."

Healing

He wasn't sure how long he had been in the hospital. Some doctors looked at him again. They moved him to another room and did some tests on him, including a Covid swab deep into his nose.

Then he was whisked away on a stretcher into another ambulance and driven to the Bed Stuy projects. He thought he was carried through streams of reporters, or maybe they were just gangbangers souped up with microphones and cameras, he wasn't sure. He was carried up to his mom's apartment and placed in bed.

The EMT gave him a buzzer. "Look, if you start feeling dizzy or nauseous or have any symptoms, just press this button. Remember, since you were exposed you've gotta quarantine for 14 days. Not that you can do much anyway."

"How am I gonna eat?" Stephen asked.

"Order delivery: Uber Eats, Grub Hub, whatever. Worse comes to worse, call us at Woodhull. But I was told that you've got people looking out for you, so they'll be in touch."

Stephen lay in bed most of the day. He still had a bit of a headache; his neck hurt, and his thighs and calves were sore, but he was able to stand up and walk around the apartment.

He sat on his bed again. He thought of his friends. He couldn't believe what had happened.

He ordered a taco and enchilada combo from a local Mexican takeout place through Door Dash, but he could barely taste it. He felt like a dead man eating. Then his phone began to ring.

He didn't recognize the number, but he picked up.

"Stephen," the voice said. It was a deep voice. It sounded recognizable but Stephen wasn't sure where he had heard it. "How are you feeling?"

"Okay. I have a headache. Who is this?"

"Your patron saint. Turner Goodson."

Stephen tried to process it. "Mr. Goodson. Finally."

"We should have met much earlier, Stephen. I'm sorry it had to be like this."

"You're responsible for my lawyer?"

"Among other things. I don't know if you've turned on the news, but this is big."

"I haven't had a chance."

"All the major networks want to interview you. I'd pick Anderson Cooper on CNN first. Are you up for it?"

"About what? I'm not processing anything."

"The NYPD murdered your friends. Including a black man. And injured you and violated your rights. During a routine traffic stop near a housing project in Bed Stuy during a fucking pandemic and a surging racial reckoning. What can be worse than that?"

"You set up my father," Stephen said.

"I am your father, Stephen," Turner Goodson said after a long pause.

"I don't believe you. My mom would have told me."

"Believe what you want to believe. I helped George during his final days."

"You didn't go on CNN to talk about the conditions at Sing Sing, did you?"

"We have to pick our battles. Maybe George was unable, but you will save our people, Stephen."

"How do I know you won't set me up like you did to my father?"

"That was a different time, Stephen. We must all do what we can based on the challenges of the age. Let me ask you: Do you care about your friends? Do you care about our people? Because if you don't, I'll leave you alone."

Stephen began crying. It started as a low groan, then escalated to uncontrollable tears.

"Let it all out, son," Turner said.

When he had finished crying, Stephen breathed heavily into the phone. Then he was quiet.

"Stephen..." Turner said.

"I want to ask you," Stephen replied, now composed, although his heart was beating rapidly. "How should I sound? Gay or straight?"

Turner laughed. "That's a good question. Now you're thinking."

"I'd say gay," Turner continued after a pause. "Further discrimination is better."

"We were a bunch of aimless queens on a joyride," Stephen said.

"You were a diverse group of friends driving in a black neighborhood," Turner corrected. "And Stephen, trust me, that made all the difference."

~ Day Four ~
Reaction to Rashan's Story

By the time Rashan finished his long tale, Ares and Rabia had added wood to the fire several times. Rashan had alternatively sat and stood, as had some of the audience, since the story had been so long—yet everyone had been mesmerized by it, especially when Rashan had acted out some parts.

"Motherfucker," Khassan said. "Don't tell me you didn't memorize that. Or maybe they invented some prompt that's installed in your brain. They can do a lot of things these days."

"Nah, I swear, I just started with the concept and made it up as I went along," Rashan said. "Don't think it was half bad, right?"

"It was fucking amazing," Lisa said. Everyone seemed to agree. Taylor was surprisingly quiet. He seemed to be ruminating on the story, shocked by its length and complexity.

Olive came up on stage.

"Wow, I don't know how our next storyteller will top that, but you'll have to try. It's always about getting better."

Everyone started getting up, stretching their legs and arms.

"I guess you'll have to vote," Ares said, reminding the guests.

Rashan surveyed the scene. He didn't want to be banished for the day. He hoped even his enemies would vote for him.

"You might get the sympathy factor, even though you're not Hayley," Ares said. Hayley and Pritesh weren't there, so there would only be nine votes. Everyone seemed to vote as an afterthought because most were either tired or still processing the story.

Olive got the votes and announced that he had received nine out of nine. Even Ricard and Nalini had voted for him.

"Thanks, everyone," Rashan said. "I didn't expect that."

Ricard approached him and shook his hand.

"Anything against the man," Ricard said to Cathy's smile behind him. Then Nalini congratulated Rashan too.

"See, I vote on quality," she said.

"I'm sorry for calling you a race traitor," he replied. "That was harsh."

"Yeah, well, I guess I did gum things up," she said, watching Ricard with Cathy. "What do I do now?"

"I don't know. Be yourself?"

Darnell approached Rashan.

"Thanks for telling it how it is, my nigga. I don't jive with that gay shit, but that story really made me think about my own life."

"No problem," Rashan said, a bit embarrassed. "Glad it worked for you."

Darnell play-punched him on his arm and returned to observing the scene—particularly Taylor and Angela. Meanwhile, Abeo whispered behind Darnell's back.

"I don't understand why you serve someone when you do not accept their lifestyle, Darnell," Abeo said.

"Why, you gonna fag out too, my nigga?"

"It does not exist in our culture," Abeo said. "But every culture is different."

"Yeah, I'm sure there are no fags in Nigeria. Get the fuck out of here. I respect all, nigga. And I acknowledge."

Abeo went back to mind the desserts. Nalini took the crème de manga and sonho as she poured Van Der Hum, the South African liqueur, into her Brazilian lemonade.

"That's what I call multiculturalism," Khassan said. "I think I saw you slurp down a few of those."

"Yeah, well, I'm eating too," Nalini said dismissively.

"Maybe we should all take a walk to the White House or something," Ares said.

"The woods are lovely, dark, and deep," Nalini muttered.

They took another trip through the woods, but this time they lounged near the pool. Maja and Zahra had the tokes, and they began smoking and drinking. Ares went inside the house to his room.

Khassan took a walk on the beach. Nalini could hear Maja and Zahra telling Lisa about Olive's behavior one time when he had come down to his room from a party on his roof. Maja had been cleaning his bed and had found a used condom.

"He joked like I should lick it. And he implied that he liked my ass and that I should join him in his orgies."

"Oh, my God, that's borderline harassment," Lisa said. "Nalini, are you listening to this?"

Nalini waved her hand as she looked up at the stars.

"What did he actually say?" Nalini asked.

"I don't remember the exact words, but it was something like that."

Nalini noticed Zahra was shaking her head at Maja.

"You probably dreamed it," Zahra said.

"Did you?" Lisa asked Maja.

Maja shrugged. "I am high."

"Maybe he did something like that to the other maids, but worse, and he had to fire them." Lisa said. "I should investigate."

"No, don't investigate," Zahra said. "Olive has been a good boss. We don't need to be fired."

"That's why you need a union," Lisa insisted.

Maja and Zahra got up and went inside the house too. Rashan said, "What I want to know is this guy's sex history. Maybe we set up a trap, for fun. I mean, I need to get laid as it is, and so far, it's not working with the help."

"The fact that he would sleep with Ares is evidence enough for me that he's suspect," Lisa said. "Trust me, I've had plenty of experience."

Lisa checked her phone. "Shit, it's bedtime."

"Why, do you have an important call early in the morning?" Rashan asked. "Chill, sister."

"We'll talk more about this later," she said, giving Rashan a kiss on the cheek and waving to Nalini. Nalini praised Rashan for his story, and they discussed it a bit, then Rashan went to walk along the beach. The maids approached Nalini and stood above her as she was lounging.

"I was wondering, Nalini, what are her prospects if Maja sues Olive for harassment?" Zahra asked.

"First you're defending him, now you want to sue him?" Nalini asked.

"It's just a question."

"Well, I'm going away from litigation and towards defense," Nalini said. "So if anything, Olive should be asking me for help."

She realized she had been out there too long. She should have been hanging out with Ricard. It was past midnight. She got up suddenly, her latest drink knocked to the floor, and turned, stumbling through the woods with a slick pace. She entered the Saggplex and ran up the stairs and started pounding on Ricard's door.

A few minutes later, Ricard opened the door, wearing a wife-beater and boxers. Clearly, he had been sleeping. She could see a figure behind him and then saw it was Cathy, in her pajamas.

"My Asian sister, right?" she asked. "This is what you fucking do to me."

"I'm sorry, Nalini, it just happened," Cathy said.

"And what about you?" she asked Ricard. "You fuck me last night, and now you're on to the next girl?"

"That's not exactly what we did," Ricard said. "Look, Nalini ..."

"Fuck you, loser," she said. She started to walk away but noticed Lisa's door was open too. And standing in the doorway with Lisa was Micah, shirtless.

"You fucking hypocrite," she said to Lisa. "Sleeping with the help, huh? It's a perfect storm."

She threw up slightly on the carpet in front of Lisa's room, then rebuffed Micah's hand of help.

She marched up to her room and locked her doors. Then she rolled up in a ball and cried for a long time.

~ Day Five ~

Ricard awoke to the singing of the whip-poor-wills just before dawn. That was strange because the Eastern whip-poor-will rarely sang that late. Its call was usually heard during the night. Maybe it was a sign of something.

For once he awoke next to an East Asian girl. The night before, an Indian girl and a suit, though in neither case had he "done the deed," as Nalini had implied.

It was ironic that he had come to The Getaway as more of a joke, to take a pause from his jobless reality, one step out the door at first, and now he was the envy of the house, maybe, with two ladies fighting over him.

He swiped his phone to see the pics of his two kids, Logan and Carter, cared for by his ex-ol' lady, Ricki, to whom he paid child support, though without work, he was behind. He looked back at Cathy, her mouth slightly open, so young and sweet, their new relationship so effortless despite their differences.

He put on his gym clothes and saw the card as he went to take a leak. He picked it up on the way back as he walked to the window and pulled apart the shade. The rain had stopped, but pools of water still soaked the grass and dirt roads outside. It was cloudy, but slits of sun rays pushed through, creating a kind of prism. Mostly robins and sparrows flew around—he saw one cardinal, but it quickly disappeared.

People assumed bikers were dumb, but Ricard had read a lot about ecosystems and how the diversity of birdlife had fallen, increasing the likelihood of viral transmission to humans from common birds with whom they had more interactions. Maybe Covid caught on that way, or perhaps it was a leak from the Wuhan lab, or from dead bats at a wet market, or the CIA pushing it, directed by the Free Masons. Either way, none of it was likely an accident.

He glanced again at Cathy. The slight light through the curtain opening didn't wake her. She was still sleeping, still snoring. She had to be strong to be his ol' lady, certainly stronger than the suit. The future wasn't clear, from the virus to lockdowns to the potential vaccines they were developing and everything else manufactured by the Man to deter freedom, but they could survive no matter what was thrown at them, with a little help from his friends if needed.

He went back to the door, picked up the card, and ripped open the envelope with his fingers. The card read:

> You've now heard many stories
> Of much hype and various types
> What will be your contribution to this scary
> And perilous moment of fear and division
> Where derision rules the airwaves
> Poisons the well of hope and paves
> Over any vision of a brighter tomorrow
> Will you be the fusion, further the fission
> Will you perform a circumcision?
> Or forge the creation of a greater mission?

"What the fuck?" Ricard asked. "Circumcision? Mission?"

Sounded like propaganda—maybe implanted by "the J," but more likely it didn't mean anything—more empty shit injected into the fake news media sphere by the Man.

He didn't mind bringing people together with his story, like Rashan's tale ostensibly had despite its dark subject, but that wouldn't be Ricard's goal. He wasn't even going to practice. He was confident he could tell the truth about the world without worrying about offending anyone.

Exiting the room, he walked past Lisa's room and looked down at where Nalini had thrown up and now only saw a small grayness on the carpet. Micah must have cleaned up. He took the elevator down to the basement, noticing that it shook as it stopped abruptly. Then it paused for several seconds before the door opened. Likely the mechanism was the problem—maybe the cylinders didn't match up or the equilibrium had fallen off.

He had noticed the elevator maintenance room in the basement—he could ask Olive or Sung if he could gain access and fix it. Maybe he could stay on after The Getaway to maintain it. At least the work would be stable, and Olive could afford it, right?

Still, how long would he be comfortable around suits? He felt less of the heebie-jeebies being around this set than before The Getaway, but how long would that last?

He found Khassan in the gym and did some lat and lunge exercises with him, saving the bench press for the next day. Taylor was being spotted by Darnell again. Astonishing, considering their rivalry over Angela.

In fact, Taylor was complaining that he and Angela had a fight the night before.

"Spanish girls be spicy, nigga," Darnell said. "If you can't take that shit, there are others that can provide ..."

"No thanks," Taylor said. "She's sweet, not spicy at all, unlike what you imagine."

"Yeah, I notice she on the defense. Not like most señoritas."

"Feel so bad for that bitch Hayley," Darnell continued, looking over at the treadmill, where she was a morning regular. "Hope she recover quick, keep killing it on IG and making those Gs, baby. Might need an OnlyFans otherwise."

"You should have killed that shark, Darnell," Taylor said. "Then Thiago could make hakari."

"What's that?"

"Nasty and toxic crap. Thiago threw it up on national TV."

"For real? Thought that nigga could hold anything down."

Ricard saw Micah in the security room. He went over to him.

"I'll say nothing if you put in a good word for me."

"Not sure what you mean."

"I saw the spot. I guess you cleaned up. But ..."

Darnell was suddenly behind him. "I cleaned up, nigga," Darnell said. "Saw it on that camera right there. I doubt Olive will mind. He was fucking Ares himself."

"What, you only enforce stuff when others are breaking the rules?"

"No rules against fucking the guests."

"You're supposed to be protecting us."

"That's the way we all got here, ain't it? What's wrong with that?"

"I just want a job fixing elevators. Yours needs work."

"And you expect to get this by issuing threats, my nigga, and by being a white supremacist on top of that?"

"I'm not a white supremacist. I'm for the People."

"Sure. And the Jews rule the world, right? You know, Micah's Jewish. And that guest, Lisa, I think."

"It's just certain ..."

He realized he was in a hole and quickly left the gym via the elevator.

"Some people, yo," Darnell said. "Don't see what the ladies see in such fucks."

"Thanks for sticking up for me, man," Micah said.

"I'll do anything for my boys. Good looking out." They bumped fists.

Taylor and Khassan had already gone up for breakfast. Soon Ricard was back in his room, hugging a cute Cathy, sleepy-eyed in her PJs, and wondering about his ability to tell an unfiltered story. Would he be banished otherwise?

Downstairs, Nalini was sitting with Rashan, Lisa, and Andrea, while Khassan was with Sylvania, Angela, and Taylor. Pritesh and Hayley were not there. Ricard ignored Nalini's glare. He and Cathy sat separately.

Breakfast seemed lighter today—according to Abeo, this was because the activity that morning was going to be physically strenuous.

They were mostly pastries from across the world, but centered around South America and Africa, building on the themes from the day before. Abeo introduced each item: Argentinian medialunas; a typical Brazilian breakfast of French bread, cassava, ham and cheese, and fresh papaya; Bulgarian banitsa with yogurt, ayran (a yogurt-based drink), and boza, a fermented grain drink; mandazi, a triangular donut from Eastern Africa; Nigerian kosai; tacaho con cecina, roasted plantain fritters, from Peru; Somalian canjeero; South African putu pap; and Venezuelan cachapas. In addition, they had puuro porridge with blueberries from Finland, Russian kasha, and muesli with fruit. There were different coffees like cappuccino and cornetto, Senegalese café touba, and Turkish coffee.

Most offerings were vegetarian or vegan, so it was acceptable for all palates, and everyone got a variety of dishes to try.

Pritesh finally came down—without Hayley. He sat with Nalini and explained that she was sleeping. He seemed tired, like he hadn't slept that night.

Olive marched into the dining room, wearing military fatigues with a yellow poncho on top and carrying what looked like a machine gun with a balloon on top of it.

Rashan and Andrea gasped, startled. Olive motioned for them to get up and follow him outside. Soon everyone had walked past the pool, steam bath, and barbecue station to the manicured field between the miniature golf course and the batting cage, where they gathered and waited for instructions.

"We had a down day yesterday, but the sun's shining now," Olive said. "It's still wet outside, though, so it's a better day to get down and dirty in the woods rather than lounging and flirting on the beach. So, let's play paintball—two teams as usual, but should I anoint someone other than Taylor and Lisa?"

Lisa said she didn't want to play, with Rashan and Andrea opting out too, even as Cathy tried to convince them it could be fun.

"If you opt out, you'll be on the losing side and will get what they get," Olive warned.

The three still didn't want to participate. Nalini and Pritesh were leaning towards opting out too but convinced each other to stay.

Since nobody volunteered to be a Team Leader when Olive

asked, Taylor took on his typical duty; then Sylvania and Khassan offered to do the same. Khassan won a coin flip. Taylor deferred to Khassan to pick teams, and Khassan selected Sylvania first.

Taylor picked Ricard, and Khassan took Nalini. Taylor didn't really want to pick Cathy, but he figured she was probably the best player left, so he did. That meant she and Ricard would be on the same team this time. Then Khassan selected Pritesh, and Taylor took Angela.

Suddenly they saw Ares and Rabia approach, carrying fatigues and equipment. Then, a couple they hadn't seen before came up too, holding guns.

"Introducing Nick Sorvino and Temple Mattina," Olive said, as the two took bows. "They'll be helping us with many activities going forward."

They were an odd-looking combination: Nick, of mixed Irish, Norwegian, Welsh, and Italian descent, standing 6'7" and appearing, on the surface, somewhat serious and straightforward; and Temple, half-white, half-black, standing at only 5'0" and constantly giggly.

"Bet they didn't have to quarantine," Nalini said bitterly.

"Actually, they did, Nalini," Olive said, "and they have agreed not to contaminate themselves for the next week and a half."

Nick and Temple taught the participants how to hold and shoot the guns. They, along with Olive, would spread out and serve as judges.

The rules were simple: whoever got hit would be eliminated, and the team with the last member standing would win. The teams could survey the lay of the land first before they began, and they were able to hide and maneuver using various strategies.

Taylor considered himself at a significant advantage since he had led troops into battle. Ricard advised him not to underestimate the other side, but Taylor took the lead in the huddle and formulated a strategy, to Cathy's chagrin.

Meanwhile, Khassan was formulating his own battle plan, but he was open to Sylvania's ideas too. Nalini and Pritesh gave their takes as well. Theirs would be a team effort; Nalini joked that this tournament was a battle between democracy and autocracy.

Each team was able to wander around the woods freely for five minutes before Olive blew a whistle and play commenced. Taylor and his team used a series of hand gestures to identify themselves and, more importantly, their prey. Once a prey was located, two team members would strategically surround them, one making sure the coast was clear of other enemies before the other made the kill shot.

Khassan's team played more defensively, using the trees and shrubs as barriers behind which they would hide and surprise their opponents. They also utilized a series of hand gestures for identification and guidance purposes.

Only a minute into the match, Taylor spotted Khassan hiding behind a shrub. He couldn't believe the Team Leader was the first one exposed. He pointed to Angela, who, by strategy, served as the watch woman as Taylor made the kill shots.

Angela looked around the perimeter. She gestured to Taylor that all was clear, and he could fire at Khassan. But Sylvania had climbed a tree and used their aggression as bait. She hit them both from the treetop, Angela on the ass as she was running away, eliminating them.

Taylor was embarrassed by the ambush. He knew it was easy to blame Angela again, but he couldn't help himself.

Meanwhile, Ricard and Cathy were still alive, gesturing to each other regularly, hiding behind two adjacent trees. Nalini and Pritesh were coordinating with each other too. They heard Taylor yelp and curse—unclear if it was a victory cry or one of frustration. Then Ricard noticed Pritesh run between two trees. Ricard fired but failed to hit Pritesh; now his position was exposed.

Nalini fired at Ricard from behind another tree, while Cathy returned fire from her tree. The four of them shot at each other off and on for a few minutes. Ultimately Pritesh got hit, and Ares, who was nearby, called him out.

Frustrated, Nalini went out into the open and fired a volley of balls at Cathy, but Ricard took this opportunity to blast Nalini, eliminating her.

Ricard and Cathy celebrated, but their celebration was short-lived. Khassan and Sylvania had been watching and waiting all along: they sprang out. Ricard was hit, but Cathy was able to escape behind some other trees, hotly pursued by Khassan and Sylvania on two sides.

Ultimately, they found Cathy lying behind a shrub. Khassan fired and thought he hit her as she screamed. But as he started to celebrate, Cathy got up and hit him—she had faked it.

Then Cathy turned to Sylvania. Sylvania was able to hit her first, eliminating Cathy and winning the game.

The whole skirmish was observed and approved by Rabia and Nick, the two judges on the scene. It had been a thrilling game. Taylor had been defeated again, as had Ricard and Cathy, though they had eliminated Nalini. The winning team was told they would get an extravagant lunch, while the losers would get the scraps and spend the rest of the day helping Ares and Rabia set up for the next event in the woods, which was zip-lining.

The losers technically included those who had opted out: Lisa, Rashan, and Andrea, but they were away: Andrea had gone to help Alexa and Rashadi tend to Hayley, while Lisa and Rashan were hanging out with Maja and Zahra, first watching them clean the remaining rooms at the Saggplex after half-heartedly offering to help, then accompanying them to the White House, where the two maids would finish their rounds in the staff rooms.

Relaxing on the patio before they went up, Maja and Zahra drank homemade mimosas and smoked cigarettes while Lisa and Rashan went inside the White House to use the bathrooms.

Lisa, staring at herself in a mirror, kept repeating Nalini's accusation in her head: was she a hypocrite for "sleeping with the help?" She could tell herself she was a cougar who had agency, but on the other hand, was she using her position as a guest to bed the younger, less experienced security guard?

It was basically the opposite of an episode she had blogged about that had ended her career in the art world. She had been blacklisted, and she became a Me Too radical—but was she now one of the exploiters?

She needed to end the relationship, she decided, but she also needed to redeem herself by investigating Olive, even if it made her feel like a hypocrite as Rashan found a laptop inside the White House lounge and started perusing through alt-gay sex sites. On one site, profiles could be searched sans account; he found a profile featuring a silhouette that often depicted the otherwise reclusive Olive online.

This individual, named Domhampton, allegedly lived in Bridgehampton and was a dom looking for a sub. So, Rashan created a basic sub profile—he couldn't see likes, but he could send and receive messages. He messaged Domhampton and offered to meet up.

"I don't have anything else," Rashan said. "Even if this isn't Olive, at least I'll get laid."

"And maybe get Covid," Lisa reminded him.

"Gotta live on the wild side," Rashan said.

"I hope we expose him," Lisa said. "Maybe it is him."

"He still hasn't done anything wrong," Zahra said, approaching.

"We're building a case, though," Lisa said. "A pattern. Ares, the used condom, the sexual overture, now this?"

"So he likes sex," Zahra said. "Proves what?"

"I want to see if there's a bigger reason behind the firing of the maids," Lisa said. "What if it was retaliation for a sex crime? I mean, look at Charlie Rose—so many people."

"Salem witch hunt," Zahra muttered as she saw Maja come inside.

"A union for all the workers," Lisa continued. "Counting the cooks, the chauffeurs, the doctors, you ..."

"The doctors aren't going to join a union," Rashan said. "I wish, but ..."

"What can I say, I'm an idealist," Lisa said. "We need to find out everything."

At the Saggplex, Khassan, Sylvania, Nalini, and Pritesh relaxed by the pool there and had their lunch: meat eaters got a New England-style combination of fish and chips, lobster rolls, and clam chowder with croutons and cilantro. The vegetarians were fixed a salad with mock grilled chicken, walnuts, kale, baby spinach, beets, avocados, croutons, and French fries, along with corn chowder and tomato broth. They were also served fresh iced tea and lemonade.

Andrea came down to get some food for Hayley, but Pritesh volunteered instead, beating out Thiago.

"Two for two," Thiago said.

"She can't miss any of your expert cooking," Pritesh quipped.

"I've had plenty of Chef Thiago's meals," Andrea said. "Time to get the peanut butter and jelly with the losers."

Hayley was a bit groggy from the meds, but she showed Pritesh a picture of a model on IG.

"Pretty, right? You want that?"

"No. Who I want is right in front of me."

"Don't flatter me, please." She kept fidgeting on her phone. "I had some time to think this morning. Why is it that you would still want to be with me?"

"I don't know. Because I love you?"

He leaned in for a kiss. They kissed briefly, but then he felt pain.

"Ow," he said, pulling back, realizing she had bitten his lip. He touched it, and it was bleeding.

"No, can't be that," she said. "Maybe you need a visa?"

"A visa?"

"You can't be too careful with the administration these days. Right?"

"I think the drugs have gotten to your head."

"You know, that Indian girl is pretty too. And she's a lawyer. Bright future."

"Yes, Hayley. Sure."

"You can ask her for legal advice. For me. For you."

He placed the salad on the counter. "I think I'll let you rest," Pritesh said. "I'll be back later."

He went to his room first and washed his lip, but he didn't have anything to put on it, so he asked Andrea for something when he got back.

"Lover's quarrel?" Nalini asked as Andrea went to get him some ointment. Pritesh didn't respond.

Lisa and Rashan arrived at the same time Nick and Temple did to round up everyone for the afternoon activity.

"This is just for fun," Olive said. "No competition."

They directed the guests to a different section of the woods than they had been in the morning. Entering a large, mostly empty field, they stopped at a wide intersection of two tall trees: one elm, about 100 feet high, and the other a tulip, about 90 feet high.

Next to the elm tree was a wooden platform about twice the tree's height, about 200 feet. One could climb up a long ladder or be pulled up in a small box.

Adjacent to the tulip tree was another platform, about 150 feet high. Between the platforms were the zip lines, with harness, carabiner, and pulley. On the elm tree platform, there was a bungee jumping cable too.

Rabia was on the elm tree platform, and Ares was on the tulip tree platform. At the base of each tree were golf carts filled with the equipment that the participants would need for the activities: helmets, tethers, gloves. Between the trees was a large safety net.

The losers were sitting at the bases of the trees, having their lunch after helping to set up, eating peanut butter and jelly sandwiches with Hi-C box drinks and bananas, served in brown bags from the kitchen.

Taylor and Angela had been sitting apart after Taylor had blamed Angela for their loss. Taylor, for once, stayed back, observing what other people would do. Angela was nursing a "welt on my culo," as she said after being hit in the ass by a paintball.

Cathy was excited and volunteered to be the first to zip line. Ricard shrugged and seemed more wary but ultimately decided he would follow his girl.

One after another, most decided to try the zip line. Lisa revealed that growing up in rural New Jersey, she had enjoyed climbing trees until one day her cousin had been attacked by a swarm of bees and killed. It took her a while to climb trees again, and after leaving her hometown to attend Bryn Mawr, she had just stopped.

"I guess that was the first of many traumas," she said, looking for Micah but not finding him. "But we've got to get over them."

After most guests, including Angela, had zipped across the trees without incident, Taylor announced he would be the first to bungee jump. He had bungee jumped and skydived in Dubai while on a brief leave during his army days, so this was like nothing.

"Good for you, man," Khassan said. "Maybe just leave it for other peeps then."

But Taylor insisted and completed the brief dive. Then Cathy and Ricard wanted to do one together. Olive was inclined to disallow it, but Nick and Temple said they should be able to bind them safely. Olive wrote up a de facto agreement. By signing it, they gave their consent, and then they were able to complete the dive without incident.

Nalini told Pritesh that was funny. "I'm surprised they didn't ask me to look over the agreement. I wonder why."

"Hayley mentioned something about that," Pritesh said. "How you were a lawyer so you could get her rich from this."

"I'm not personal injury," she said. "But I guess I can try."

Nalini and Pritesh both declined to bungee jump. Angela said the welt didn't get better with the zip line, so she'd forego the jump too in case she landed on her ass instead.

"Bigger the better," Darnell quipped to her arm-slap in response.

Then, everyone was surprised when Hayley was wheeled out by Alexa and Rashadi. Alexa apologized to Olive but said Hayley had insisted on coming out to try the bungee jump.

"It's risky," Andrea said. "But if it lifts her spirits, it might be worth it."

"I'm pretty sure we can secure her for the zip line," Nick said. "It would be safer than the bungee."

Hayley said she would try the zip line; Olive reluctantly agreed. Everyone clapped and cheered her on.

After Nick fit her helmet, Hayley was able to stand from the wheelchair, her wound covered with taped gauze, but Olive noted the wheelchair would fit in the box on the makeshift elevator, so she sat down again.

Alexa wheeled her inside and stayed with her while Rabia used the pulley to raise them to the platform. Then Hayley stood again and placed her legs, one-by-one, slowly into a body harness, with Rabia assisting her.

Hayley held onto the cable and teetered on the edge of the platform, looking down nervously. She was shaking. She glared at Pritesh, then Nalini. She stopped, then peeked again and closed her eyes.

Rabia told her it was best not to look down if she was freaked out but that she might miss the experience if she kept her eyes closed, so she opened them again.

Rabia counted to three, then released her. She zipped over, holding the harness tight, closing her eyes in the process. But soon she felt the motion cease abruptly. Ares was embracing her. She held up her hands triumphantly. Everyone was cheering and clapping for her, even, reluctantly, Nalini and Pritesh.

For that evening, Olive announced they would have their meal and their story on the Saggplex roof. He would unlock the elevator so the guests could access it.

Pristine tables with hookahs and lounge-like velvet couches were set up under flaming lights and disabled heaters. Pop music, a mix of 1980s to present, filled the air. Thiago and Abeo manned an open bar; next to it was a station for made-to-order items, operated by Rafael and Bom; and behind that, grills, ovens, toasters, fridges, microwaves, and anything else needed for cooking.

The air was fresh and relatively cool, the breeze just right.

Each corner of the rooftop provided a different view of the Saggplex and its surroundings—the forest, the creek, the path to the beach, the beach itself, the road, the "T" structure of the complex and beyond: the swimming pools, the baseball field, the racetrack, the Jacuzzis.

Viewing binoculars and high-powered telescopes allowed visitors the ability to explore in-depth, without needing to insert quarters, and next to them were brief descriptions of the ecological, geological, and architectural history of what they could see, as if it was a tourist site.

A marble fountain of Cupid spewed water from his mouth, and its foundation could be used for handwashing.

The scene evoked nostalgia in the first arrivals.

It reminded Lisa and Rashan of rooftop parties in Greenpoint and Red Hook, Brooklyn, and similar lounges in the Lower East Side of Manhattan, experiences they hadn't had in months.

For Nalini, it was like the roof of her apartment building in Hunters Point with a view of the East River to the skyscrapers in Manhattan and of parties she had attended in Murray Hill and Tudor City looking over the other way into Queens.

Hayley recalled the Boom Boom Room and the other elite clubs with millionaire patrons ordering bottle service and dinner for her and her fellow models at the behest of her initial promoters. For once she asked to be wheeled next to Sylvania and Angela.

"I know all about that," Sylvania said. "I was on top of the fashion world at one point. But I'm glad it came crashing down."

"Models never get paid for anything," Hayley said. "Only the promoters and club owners make money off the rich dudes and socialites who come to those things to feel cool. People with money want to be around beautiful women. I was warned about these promoters by my agency, but when my conventional career wasn't exactly taking off, I had no choice but to get free meals."

"So, we were opposites, darling. But now we're equals," Sylvania said.

Lisa sat down with Rashan on a couch and started smoking a hookah as Bom and Rafael came around with hors d'oeuvres: caviar and other fish eggs with brie and muenster cheese on crackers; miniature empanadas and samosas with various brown and green sauces and chutneys; miniature burgers and hotdogs; croquettes and a large variety of other small bites. They came around with various cocktails too: Lisa took a whiskey sour and Rashan a Jack & Coke.

"So, happened?" Lisa asked.

Rashan opened his arms. "Date night ..."

"You're kidding."

"Nope, got a hit."

"Gay guys have all the luck."

"Now I've gotta figure out how to get out there."

"Bridgehampton is right here."

"With a car, yeah. But it's like a 45-minute walk, yo."

"The skinhead could give you a ride."

"Yeah, sure. I'd never come back. Maybe I can hoodwink Ares."

As they figured out their plan, Ricard was nervously thinking about his story and about how he could approach Olive or Sung about a job opportunity. Nalini was standing next to the telescope, looking back at him and Cathy, wondering how her seemingly perfect plan to bed the biker had been thwarted. He should want to peer into the telescope to check out the birds, but he was just sitting there.

Pritesh approached her.

"How's the lip?" she asked.

"Healing. I think they've got Hayley on too many drugs. Maybe we can sue Olive for that."

"Very funny. Seems like we're both on the outs."

Pritesh noticed Hayley looking at him. She had eaten some caviar, other fish eggs, cheese, crackers, and samosas, but now she told Alexa that she felt tired and wanted to rest. She was wheeled away.

Dinner was served. When they saw the assortment was akin to an Indian wedding, Nalini and Pritesh acknowledged each other.

"Get ready for a ton of questions," Nalini said. "As if we're experts on all brownness. I'm not even Punjabi."

Punjabi and South Indian dishes included, for appetizers: pakoras, samosas, chaat with chickpeas, spices, cilantro, and yogurt; belpoori chaat which included poori bread; mirch, aloo tikki; tandoori tikki; aloo kebab nara dil; murgh chicken kebab; tikka chicken on a stick. For the main courses, they had aloo baingan, saag paneer, bhindi masala, paneer bhurji, gobhi nawabi, daal, mutter paneer and many meat variations of the same dishes, along with tikka and tandoori, chicken and lamb. There was chicken/vegetarian biryani and afghani pulao. Several salads, including fruit salads, and breads—naan, parantha, roti, poori. For desserts there were rasmalai, gaggar halwa, gulab jamoon, jalebi, mango, and malai kulfi ice cream. Included: raita.

Bom and Rafael manned two stations: one cooked South Indian masala dosas or uttapam upon request, the other idli samba.

Most offerings were vegetarian, some vegan, so everyone was able to enjoy the meal without needing tofu-meat variations of dishes, though one dish of mock chicken was cooked tandoori-style. Also, the hands-on nature of the eating requirements meant plenty of napkins were employed.

Everyone converged at once at the stations, where, as expected, questions about the food were directed at those of Indian descent. Pritesh was more helpful, as he was South Indian, whereas the American-born Gujarati Nalini was dismissive, even though she had been to tons of Indian weddings.

"Everyone's always asking me about 'Spanish' food too," Angela noted when Nalini expressed her frustration after sitting to eat. "We'll be at an Argentinian restaurant, and they'll ask my Ecuadorian ass about that shit. I was born in Ecuador, but I was raised in Corona, papi."

"I'm an Asian-fusion girl from redneck California," Sylvania said. "I state on the record I know nothing about bahn-mi, other than how good it tastes."

"No one eats Chechen anyway," Khassan said. "Terrorizer discrimination up front. Those not in the know might ask me about hummus or Turkish food, though."

Just one floor down, Olive was sitting on the bed, having escaped to his apartment down a secret hatch, when he noticed the elevator door open. He had given access to the staff—Zahra emerged, alone.

"So, how's it going at the lawsuit convention?" Olive asked as he was putting on the pants of a black tuxedo.

"They're trying to trap you," Zahra replied.

"Maybe I'll let them succeed."

Zahra glanced at a picture of Olive's mother, framed by an oval mixture of pearls, rubies, and emeralds, on a stand next to his bed.

"Maja said that's where it happened," Zahra mentioned. "The condom was right next to the picture of your mother."

"Fake news, like the con man says. I'm a fag, for God's sakes. I'm not gonna hit on a woman."

"Alcohol does funny things to a person."

"Maybe it was a joke. I know you're not allowed to joke anymore."

Zahra laughed. "Yes, your orgies were a joke."

"I used to like people. Didn't marry the limelight like Mark Cuban. Did everything I could to keep my picture out of the press and my name out of the papers, but I enjoyed my circle. I was wrong, though. When shit hits the fan, you realize who your friends are. Or if you have any."

"You fired Adelina and the others."

"They're getting unemployment, aren't they?"

"Even the ones without papers? The ones who live in Hampton Bays?"

"With this commie government? Probably. They'll get by. Look, they all worked on the side for my so-called friends. Only you and Maja were loyal to me totally."

"Yes, I remember some of your so-called friends being very demanding and nasty. I didn't think people could act that way in this country. I thought every rich person was like you."

"Well, hopefully, then, you'll appreciate me that much more."

"Adelina mentioned Maja's story when Sung told her she was let go, that you were trying to bury it by keeping her."

"You think I'm scared of Adelina? Or people like this Lisa character? I'm not. I brought her in for a reason. And she signed a contract. Let her 'investigate' all she wants. It's funny, really."

"I heard one of the maids got Covid and died. I don't remember her name."

"Am I responsible for every breath everyone takes? Most CEOs don't care about anybody but their family, not even their inner circle.

I've looked after you, haven't I? And we'll see about these guests. If they prove themselves worthy, maybe they have a seat at the table."

He took a black top hat from his dresser. "Now let's enjoy dinner. Don't you like Indian food?"

Upstairs, Ricard finally approached Sung and mentioned car and elevator maintenance work.

"I don't know if Olive wants or needs another full-time employee," Sung said. "I certainly don't need another security guard."

"Ha," Ricard laughed artificially. "There is a lot of space to cover and only so many shifts."

"Olive's the man to talk to. I'll mention it to him. Good luck on your story."

Ricard suddenly felt pressure to abandon his story so he could more likely get the job. But the story would portray a real American who was worthy of such an opportunity. And he always had the Micah card in his pocket, even though it might not be effective.

Speaking of which, he saw Micah emerge from the elevator and get some food. Darnell must have relieved him on Big Brother duty. But then he saw Darnell too and noticed Sung go downstairs. So much for his plan to isolate Micah with Sung and let the truth emerge organically.

Darnell went over to Angela, who was sitting with Sylvania, separately from Taylor, who was alone.

Lisa saw Micah and hoped he wouldn't come over to her. He glanced at her briefly and looked away.

Meanwhile, Nalini had answered the questions about the Indian food and had eaten. She saw Ricard and Cathy near the telescope now.

"You and the other Indian guy will be a better fit," Thiago said as he handed her a plate of gulab jamoon.

"Because you want Hayley for yourself?"

"Don't insult me, my dear."

She got up and went over to Pritesh, who was near the jalebis. She touched his lip.

"What Hayley did to you wasn't very nice," she said. She moved in and kissed his lip softly, like it was a boo-boo.

She made sure Thiago saw it. She wanted Ricard to see it too, but it wasn't clear if he had.

"Okay," Pritesh said, awkwardly. He wanted to kiss her back, but she seemed to push him away. She rejoined Angela and Sylvania.

Olive emerged from the elevator, arm-in-arm with Zahra, as if he were entering with Vanna White. He wore the black tux, carried a black cane, and was wearing the top hat.

"What's the occasion?" Micah asked.

"After giving his speech, he's visiting Gotham City," Khassan said, wiggling his fingers and speaking in a spooky voice. "To flood the streets from underground."

"Very funny," Olive said as Rafael and Bom came around with wet wipes. Some guests made their way to a marble fountain to wash their hands.

Everyone got closer to the front, sitting mostly with the people they had been around.

"I just thought our nightly story deserved a bit of a classy touch," Olive said, standing next to a disabled heater that suddenly became inflamed.

"Who's the storyteller?" Taylor asked. "Trump?"

"Talk about classless," Cathy said.

"He's in the Social Register with me."

"Every President is listed in the Social Register, whether they deserve it or not," Olive said.

"I've been meaning to ask, Olive, are you in it?" Taylor asked.

"Of course not. I made my money."

"Nobody has read that thing in like 50 years," Lisa replied.

"Yup, nobody cares about me," Taylor admitted. "That's why I'm sitting here by myself."

"You'll get some friends eventually, honey," Sylvania told him. "Just try to smile every once in a while."

"Looks like I've gotta change my gender, Sylvi. Kaitlin Jenner-style. The new wave of fame!"

"Honey, you're already living in the 18th century. Now you're getting sent back to the 14th."

"Seems like we're already there. With our Black Death."

Abeo was laughing uncontrollably.

"Could be a long night," Olive said to him. "Make me a Manhattan, would you? Hope everyone's got a drink, but don't have too much—I want you to pay attention to our next storyteller."

~ Day Five ~
Introduction to Ricard's Story

"**O**ne thing I was worried about when selecting people through my apps was getting too many of the same types of people," Olive said. "We talk all day about diversity, but our algorithms undercut our rhetoric. I don't just mean dating apps, though I take responsibility on that front.

"Certain dating apps have all hipsters, or all overly educated people, or all rich people, or all women or gays, or all Jews looking for fellow Jews, or whatever it might be. Even the mainstream ones are more likely to bring similar people together. Thankfully I own a lot of apps, so by integrating them and selecting from the pool myself, I was able to find a genuinely wide range of people—or at least I hope I did.

"I think the most difficult type of person to find, other than essential workers, was a common man from outside our blue cities. I hate to introduce you that way, Ricard because it sounds like I'm putting you down, but I'm really not. While you can tell whatever story you want, I picked you for The Getaway because I thought you could contribute something different."

"I'll try my best," Ricard said, shrugging.

"Like our last storyteller, Ricard Shaw is from Connecticut, but he's not what most people would think when they hear Connecticut. He's a biker living in a rural area who works as a part-time handyman and maintainer. He works with his hands, and he hates wearing masks. I have no clue about his ancestry—maybe he doesn't either. But I'll let him fill in the blanks.

"Everyone, please give it up for Ricard Shaw!"

Ricard got up and pumped his fists. Cathy slapped his ass. Khas-

264

san clapped fervently. Pritesh, Sylvania, and a few others lightly patted their palms. Nalini was silent.

Ricard stood right next to the flame, bent over awkwardly to the right.

"Okay, so, I haven't prepared much for this, but I've made some mental notes. It's the truth, so it's gonna come from the heart, whether people like it or not," he said, empowered by Olive's words to go the route he wanted to, but with a tremble.

"You probably don't know a lot about bikers. There's some myth that we're like gangsters or criminals, but truth is we're independent Americans, true Americans, who live by a code of honor and fidelity to our principles and to each other. But we're also ordinary people trying to survive day by day in the Land of the Free.

"I don't like to talk about or play politics. The whole political divide is part of this New World Order plan by the Freemasons and the Illuminati, financed by certain Jews, not all, to stir up uneducated people, especially Blacks, poor whites, and illegal immigrants, against hardworking people of all races. And that's what my story is going to show. There's a perception that bikers and red area folks are a bunch of hicks and simpletons, but we're not. We just like our freedom and don't want it to be taken away by a bunch of elitists from New York City or millionaire princesses from Fairfield County telling us what to think and what to do. It's not about race or money or anything else; it's about freedom and principles."

Most guests appeared aghast. Neither Cathy nor Nalini would look Ricard in the eye. Rashan and Lisa had their arms folded. Thiago was shaking his head. Even Taylor said his ancestors were Freemasons, and this was a bunch of baloney.

But Khassan was laughing and clapping. Sylvania insisted that he should be able to tell his story. Angela concurred that everyone should have their stories heard.

~ Day Five ~
Ricard's Story
(*AKA "MASON MAYHEM"*)

I

The Masons were meeting in the Great Masonic Hall in the middle of Manhattan, and they were angry. The Presidency of Donald Trump had shaken up their New World Order agenda and they were determined to stop it. They needed a way to both restrict freedom again and to create chaos in the streets so that their candidate would emerge to restore fascistic order, push a Leftist agenda on the people and unleash a large swath of illegal immigrants and Muslims to flood the nation, destroying it in the process.

Why not, they decided, unleash a great plague upon the nation and the world?

They sat around a great table: bankers, lawyers, political advisers, intellectuals, wearing their Masonic hats and their pins, uniforms, and robes passed down by generations of Masons. They had ruled the world through divide and conquer for centuries. Now that this was being threatened and they could no longer control the American government, who else could they work with to achieve their goals?

Of course, the easiest and wealthiest alternative was the Chinese government who could control their population and already controlled many other countries through debt. They would also work with the WHO. They could unleash a great plague and send it on airplanes across the world, and no one would know until it was too late. The WHO would cover it up, and they could use draconian tactics to control it in their own country. It was enough of a benefit and worth the risk of a worldwide Chinese government takeover.

The Masons took a vote. They decided it was best to work with China. And then they decided to celebrate by practicing a Satanic ritual of Brotherhood. They made their signs, then they took out their knives and passed around the Golden Chalice. They all slit part of their hands to pour blood into the cup as it went around the table. Once it was filled, each Mason drank the mixed blood from the chalice.

Now it was time to offer a sacrifice to their god Jahbulon. They got up in succession and descended into a secret lair where naked children were chained to a stone wall. The children were crying, begging the Masons for help, but the Brother Masons were only further excited by their fear and terror.

The Master Mason, after saying a prayer to his god, unchained an unlucky few. In front of the other children, the Masons disrobed, sodomized, and molested the children, then slit their throats and laughed like hyenas as the blood drained from the poor children into rivers that flowed into buckets dug into the floor. The buckets were then collected, poured into a large vat, and then into each Mason's individual chalice. Then the Masons drank the blood to finalize their sacrifice to their god Jahbulon.

II

The great American road is a wondrous thing. Nowhere on Earth do you have such a free-spirited pathway. And the biker is the symbol of American exceptionalism, of individualism and the triumph over regimentation and fascism.

But as with any family or groups of people, there can be conflicts and disagreements, as is natural.

I transport you to upstate New York several months later, where three bikers are cruising along. They're part of the Danson club, a small tradition of bikers who like riding and celebrate the freedom it brings.

As they were riding along a section of road they had never explored, they saw the Danson sign on a cafe and decided to stop. The individual in front of the pack, Jake, made their sign with a thumbs up, and gestured towards his mouth. Then he pointed to the right, and the others concurred, so they parked and lined up their bikes in front.

Jake dismounted from his bike and made sure his fellow riders were secure. As they headed into the café, he looked around at the landscape. It was a desolate and open area of Americana, filled with dust and open air, with the beauty of the trees beyond and birds flying above. But directly across from the café was another club that looked like a large trailer, with blackened windows and a steel door. It was shut. But that's not what attracted his eye. While there was no club sign, menu, or nothing else describing what this establishment was, mounted in front was a confederate flag.

Jake was immediately angry. He rushed into the café where they had parked. It was a small place that sold everything from postcards to hats to biker paraphernalia and had two small tables on the side near a window where visitors could sit.

On the other side of the counter was the owner, a man wearing a T-shirt and small vest. He was short and balding, but he had a pleasant smile.

He was speaking to Jake's fellow bikers at the counter, but Jake rushed up to him.

"What's that place across the way?" he asked. "Those a bunch of traitors?"

"They're assholes, I gotta say."

"They riders?"

"Nah. Some of 'em ride, for sure. But mainly they're a bunch of pickup truck-driving drunken assholes."

"The Confederacy lost. This is America. Maybe you should remind 'em."

"Why don't you?"

"Jake," one of the bikers named Fletcher said, "it's a free country. They can fly their flag."

"I'm sick and tired of seeing that shit up here. This isn't the South."

"No, but a lot of southerners live here now," the owner said. "Or they adopted that tradition. Anyway, besides being dickheads, they're not really bothering nobody."

"I guess."

"Jake, I don't like that flag either," Parker, the third biker, agreed. "But they're free, and they can fly the flag they want. I can't tell them what flag to fly or what to say, and they can't tell me. That's the American way. We want to preserve our freedom too."

Jake accepted that and sat for a bit and drank some coffee as they gazed out the window. Then, before leaving, he bought a Danson pin for his mom. As he pulled out onto the road, he saw a truck pulling into the club next door, but he ignored it.

III

The clubhouse is part holy land and part hangout parlor for the Danson boys. It's the place where they always go for their meetings and big get-togethers, where they can celebrate Danson traditions and be themselves at the same time, forgetting the problems of their other lives.

They were having a meeting and family get-together, where a lot of members brought their wives and kids. There was a barbecue and a cookout and all the rest of that outside on the grounds.

Jaylan, the club President, was presiding over a meeting in a room the members called the Great Lounge since it was filled with all kinds of Danson symbols and ancient lore including a big book that had been in Danson tradition from its founding in the 19th century, back when Danson boys rode buggies and bicycles. Sometimes Jaylan or one of the Dansons would read from this book. And yes, Dansons can read.

In this instance, though, Jaylan was conducting a regular meeting with an agenda and bullet points on old fashioned paper, and at the end he collected member dues. Fletcher passed along a great jar and everyone put in their portion, and it came back to Jaylan. Then he announced that a large portion was going to the family of Gerald "Bubba" Hanson, an older rider who had contracted and died of that vicious coronavirus.

Everyone concurred that it should go to his widow, and they bowed their heads and remembered the rider in a moment of silence. When they awoke though, Parker got to complaining about Cuomo's restrictions. It was one thing to promote mask-wearing, social distancing, limiting businesses, and confining people in their homes in New York City where people were on top of one another, but in the real open America, it was treason.

"Agreed," Jaylan said. "God can take any one of us, and Covid took Bubba, unfortunately. But this is a free country, and this ain't the big city. Albany politicians and other liberals don't understand that. The cure can't be worse than the cancer."

Everyone started arguing about that but most agreed with Jaylan and Parker. Meanwhile Jake paid his respects to their President and set off on the road towards his home.

IV

Jake pulled up at his home. It was a large trailer, kind of like the one with the confederate flag, but with windows and an easy door.

Lots of people look down on trailer homes, but it's a good way to live because you can also pick up and leave if you need to. That way you stay free and don't put down your flag too firmly. In Jake's case, they owned the land too so no one could raise their rent or nothing, but they had wheels so they could decide to sell the land and get out if they thought it was necessary. Not to say regular home ownership isn't as American as apple pie; it sure is, but there's something about mobility that's also irresistible.

His mom was watching TV with his brother in the big room. It was a TV their dad had bought them, but not too big so it wouldn't fall if they moved it. His brother was twitching a bit, and Jake asked his mom if he should be worried.

"Just ate PB&J, Jake. You know peanuts sometimes give him the jitters."

"So why doesn't he eat it with just the jelly or jam? Or the butter?"

"You know milk stuff makes him cough. So we'll leave it to the lighter brand."

"The jitters just make me think he's going to explode. That makes me nervous."

"He hasn't shaken for a few years now. You're getting paranoid."

"I don't work three jobs and pay my Obamacare bill so he can raise my rates. At least tell him to be careful."

❧

I'm giving you this bit of dialogue to "show" not "tell" what Jake's brother, Pete, is going through. But now I'm just gonna tell it. He's got epilepsy ladies and gentlemen, but that's not all: cerebral palsy too. Jake's real protective of his little bro, especially since his big bro is in prison for murder.

I don't wanna make this into a whole exposé on OxyContin, I mean you hear about all these people being addicted and stuff, but it's true. His bro got hooked on that shit when he hurt himself lifting something at his construction gig and later started using the stronger stuff. Then he started dealing it, thinking it would make him some extra dough because this was when their father first divorced their mom and left, and he thought he was the big bro and he had this obligation. So he was dealing and he got addicted. It was a vicious cycle that could only lead to ruin, and it did one day when he got into it with a difficult customer while he was hopped up himself.

Long story short, he killed the guy, panicked, and tried to hide the body but got caught. He was doing life in Sing Sing and Jake was ashamed enough that he wasn't a big fan of visiting. He loved his bro and admired him for trying to help Pete, but he also blamed him for not being able to control himself and failing the family that way.

It was a strange combo of emotions Jake felt because the responsibility of his family landed on him suddenly and without warning when he was used to a life of freedom. He took that responsibility seriously, but he felt bitter about it too. And that bitterness was not just towards his big bro but also his dad, and of course at the doctor who had hooked his brother, the pharma industry as a whole, and the federal government too.

But it also meant Jake had dedicated himself to a life of self-control, using that Aryan dictum from the Hindu great men. That meant becoming a vegan and sticking to it. So he didn't mind having that PB&J sandwich himself, especially when he had ground the peanuts and made the jam with fresh ingredients and the bread was fresh-baked.

"I knew you'd make that sandwich yourself," his mom said while watching some real shitty reality TV show. "And you're criticizing your bro?"

"I'm not addicted to it, Mom," he said. "Better than your dinner."

His mom didn't have the same self-control. He knew she'd make steak, eggs, and corn or something for dinner using lots of butter and oil, and he couldn't control that. She was a big woman, she had diabetes, high blood pressure, and chronic heart issues, but she still hadn't turned it down.

That's why, even though he didn't believe in the hoax and didn't wear a mask when riding or when around his brothers, he still did when shopping because both his family members were high risk, and he wanted to protect them from the plague in case it wasn't a hoax. And he wore it when he got really close to his mom and brother.

But he was in the kitchen now, so he was far enough away even in the small trailer, he thought, but his mask was in his pocket just in case. He knew they didn't really work, but he felt that responsibility.

His cell rang, and it was Regina. Now here's where the story gets complicated. Regina was his dad's second wife, but they were already divorced, and his dad had a third wife, Becky, whom he was still married to. Except Regina was, at this point, Jake's former girl too, and she had two young kids, who Jake's father thought were his but who Jake and Becky suspected were Jake's.

And it was Becky who was putting the screws to the situation because Jake's dad was still paying child support and she thought Jake should be paying it, or at least Jake's dad could take the kids and raise them with Becky's kids who they already had. She was much younger, but she was blond and Christian, and she thought they would give them a better home, you know how that kind of woman is.

You got all that? I thought so.

Point is, Jake's situation was complicated, and he didn't feel like taking this call, especially since he was kind of anticipating that crunchy-creamy buzz of the PB&J and cherry jam. He had ignored so many of Regina's calls, but eventually he decided to take this one, and he left the trailer and stomped down the short stairs and said hello.

"Jake, she's done it this time. The devil-bitch."

"What'd she do? You got a court order?"

"Not yet, but she sent me a text that Stevie's gonna cave soon and do it. She's saying at least give them partial custody without having to go to court, our kids over there part of the time, some shit about raising them in Christ's house; what a pompous little bitch."

"Alright, let me talk to Dad. I wanna see if this isn't smoke and mirrors."

"I don't wanna lose my kids, Jake. And I can't afford to lose Stevie's child support either."

"Okay, let me handle it. I'll talk to him soon."

He hung up and headed back in. He put the sandwich together finally and bit in.

"That Gina?" Jake's mom asked, "or the landscape man?"

"Don't worry about it, Mom. Just watch your TV and let me handle it."

"News is on now. All Corona, all the time."

"Turn it off. So depressing. Can't let us live in peace, ever."

"I'm all in. Gonna admit, I'm addicted."

"What aren't you addicted to, Ma?"

The news made him angry. He was listening to it while eating, but it got to him. He remembered Bubba and how the China virus took him. He wasn't angry against Chinese people or anything like that, but that government had to be suspected.

"I'll be back," Jake said as he finished his sandwich and cruised out the door.

"Tell Stevie's he's still shit!" his mom yelled.

Jake decided to take an impromptu trip to see Bubba's relations. Mainly it was because he wanted to pay his respects but also because he didn't want to think about his family situation for a bit. So he cruised down some roads till he got to Bubba's home, which was a small house on the edge of a park.

He turned into the gravel road leading to the house, parked there and put down his kick stand. He put on his mask too because he didn't know if the family still had the China virus.

He knocked on the door. He figured Bubba's wife, Marcy, would answer, but instead it was his younger son who was a pock-faced middle schooler he called Little Bubba.

"Your mom home?" he asked, and he got the typical call to the back of the house where he heard an annoyed thunder and then got an apologetic rumble towards the door from Marcy.

"Oh, heyah, Jake, what are you doing here? Come on in!"

"I don't want to bother you, just thought I would pay my respects..."

"No bother, come on in, I'll make you some coffee."

So it turned out he ended up sitting in Bubba's small living room looking at his Danson paraphernalia and at the picture of his daughter who he had heard lived in the big city; she was kind of cute. Meanwhile little Bubba was forced to sit with him and was squirming a bit from the assignment. Little Bubba mentioned that the other one, a bit older at 17 or so, was gallivanting with some friends, who knows where. (Yes, I know some big words too—fuck you!)

"So how have you been, Jake, how is your family?" Marcy asked as she brought in two cups of coffee, one for each of them. Little Bubba was bereft, I guess.

"Oh, you know—the same."

"Yeah, how is your brother?"

"Which one? Good one's watching TV as we speak."

"Come on, don't be too hard. We all have our demons."

"My demons didn't land me in the slammer. Anyway, I wanted to see how things were. China virus got Bubba, I'm so sorry about that."

"Yeah, well, seems there's no rhyme or reason who God takes with this strain. We all had it too and we didn't have it bad at all."

"It's not fair. Someone's gotta be held to account for this plague."

"I don't think we can hold God to account."

"I mean the people responsible for it. How do you think he got it anyway? It's not too prevalent in these parts."

"Well, he made the mistake of going down to the big city to visit our daughter, Pearl. I think that's how he got it and then we got it too."

"Didn't they have a lockdown?"

"We're coming from in-state. So no, we're not restricted."

"I knew it was something from the city. This great plague is coming out from the devil's house."

"I told Pearl not to go to New York, but you know how these kids get it in their heads from school and stuff that it's the place to be. She can come home now that we're all better, but she says she's only coming up for the funeral and then heading back down there again. She told me she lost her job, only God knows how she's paying her rent with everything shut down."

"Rent moratorium. Ridiculous libtards, taking from one to give another. Homeowners got bills too."

"Well, I certainly appreciate all the Dansons have done for us. Jaylan came by earlier with your support. I didn't want to accept it, but you know we're hard up now. I'm looking for a job but there aren't no takers."

"Don't worry, we'll help out until you can get on your feet. Don't need no government for that."

He drank his coffee quick while he kept looking at that picture of Pearl. It's strange how the biggest rats look the best, he thought.

Anyway, before he left Marcy, he got kind of emotional. Little Bubba had gone to the other room so he hugged Marcy, and she cried in his arms, and he tried to comfort her the best he could. He was good at that.

Then he got going and took off to take care of the business he had put out of his mind for a while. It was only a ten-minute ride to his dad's place on a big property he'd bought after the divorce with his mom, the bastard.

He knew the first person he'd see when he approached that big-ass house was Becky the witchy blonde in her summer dress even though it was spring. She'd have at least one kid sitting on her lap in the rocking chair on said house's porch and that's what he saw, except she also had the other kid with his arms around her neck, kind of straddling her, the lioness always working and scheming while the lion lay back except when there was a big decision to make or he had to put his foot down and then he did it, proudly and with precision.

So there were some crazy birds flying ahead too, and I'm not going to say they were ravens, though they probably were. Weird since most of the birds have vanished with the deforestations. She did a short tight wave to him as she saw him come up, this mechanical little gesture that he responded to with a short, "Hey," as he rushed past her and the kids, into the house where the lion resided.

Except Becky informed him with a yell that the lion was actually out back. He expected his dad was landscaping as usual, so he tore through the house and out the open back door. He saw the king standing on the ledge of his mower, just staring out into his big backyard. Jake assumed he was figuring out how to carve the property further. Why he had to after so many alterations were made really bedeviled Jake, but this is how the big boy's mind worked, he guessed.

"Hey Dad, looking to keep 'scaping the property?"

"Nah, actually I was thinking about another property in my accounts. So what brings you by? Mom needs another check?"

"We haven't asked any money from you."

"I imagine you're here for a reason, huffing and puffing as you are."

"You know why."

"I have made up my mind regarding Gina. It's gonna be the part way."

"You're not gonna go to court, are you?"

"Do I look like I need that kind of trouble? Just tell the woman to make a compromise, and we'll keep a deal outside of that court. Because she knows she'll get crushed if we go."

"I'm not so sure. She's the woman."

"And she's poor, and she's relying on me. Look, I don't wanna make life difficult for her, I love my kids, even if they're yours, I don't care. I'll keep paying that support, but she's gotta put them in Becky's hands so they get raised a little right."

"You know Gina's not bad. She's got her moments of dysfunction, but..."

"Kids can't afford moments of dysfunction from their damn mother. Look at what happened with Danny. You think he would've gone down that road if I had been in his life as normal."

Jake shook his head hard. "For you to be saying that ... after you left ..."

"Look, we're putting out an olive branch," Stevie said, looking out far beyond his land. "If we take that test, and they're yours, you're on your own. And I know you got Pete to look after."

"He's your son."

"So was Danny. Now the govt's got him. You know I'll never let Pete starve. But while that woman ain't working, I ain't lifting a finger either. Not sure why you do."

"I love him. It's called love."

"Yes. Sure. That's why you've wasted your life too? Should've finished school like I told you, or at least found a trade, not this mercenary crap. Then you'd be set. But you never listened, just like your momma."

Jake was incensed. He saw a cleaver in the dirt. He had dark thoughts, but he tried to control himself.

"I don't know why I bother coming over here. You're such a prick."

"You shouldn't a done Regina after I left her. You should've known she was shit for that."

Before he did something stupid, Jake turned around and rushed back into the house. Behind him, he heard his dad's call.

"You tell her, you hear? Compromise is the best bet, for every-one's sake."

He rushed back through the house and past Becky on the porch even as she was calling his name. He realized only when he got on his bike that he'd been wearing his mask the entire time.

"We're not contagious, Jake!" he could hear her yelling. "Christ will provide!"

V

Regina lived in a trailer home bigger than Jake's but set on a man-ufactured housing lot; it didn't have wheels. She had moved into it with the kids soon after Stevie had decided to divorce her, buying it but renting the land; now some conglomerate had bought up the trailer park and increased the rent share, and started charging for the water, trash removal, repairs and some other things that were never on the bill before. That meant Jake might have to pay for that stuff if he was proven the father of Regina's kids, which only increased his financial woes and his burden.

Stevie had been smarter in his second marriage and had signed a pre-nup, so she didn't have a claim on the big house (they had owned a smaller one before, but he had sold it) and so it was just the child support that was his due. Jake's mom had gotten half of Stevie's stuff when he'd divorced her, but he wasn't as rich then; he'd learned from his mistake.

Jake knocked on the door. There were pluses and minuses to the trailer being in a bigger lot that had tons of neighbors; there was more socializing but less privacy. Still, Jake preferred his own setup, on which his neighbors were distant. He also owned the land and the unit both, so even though it depreciated, the leeches, whether it was the conglomerates or the government, couldn't possess it without a fair price.

He got frustrated that Gina wasn't answering so he knocked hard. His son Brennan opened the door instead. At least he thought it was his son since he had the same shape of the nose and the auburn hair, though his granddad had some of those features too, so it's possible they were just one generation removed.

Brennan was nine years old. He was conceived probably at the end of his dad's marriage or at the beginning of Jake's affair with Regina, which happened about the same time. So that's why it wasn't clear whose kid it was.

Brennan was excited to see Jake, who had taken off his mask and no longer looked like a monster. He jumped on Jake and hugged him around his neck and Jake picked him up and swung him around like one of those amusement park rides where the boats go up and around.

His daughter, Meghan, was behind him. She was Brennan's twin so not clear on the parentage either, obviously. Still, the Lion hadn't questioned this parentage because he didn't want to overburden Jake when he had taken responsibility for Pete around the time Danny got caught up with the drugs and took things too far.

But now that the Lion felt he needed to raise the kids right at this critical juncture, he was going to use that issue as a press. And Jake felt it was in his best interest to convince Regina of the same thing, for both their sakes.

That might be a challenge for that woman though, as he was going to find out now. He heard her calling to Meghan and Brennan. Sounded like she was also in her backyard, so Jake took the shortcut and went around the trailer to find her hanging the washing with wooden clothespins.

Her black hair was out and crazy-like, there's no other way to put it, and her eyes wild as Jake approached her. But still, she shook her head and then got on him and they started making out.

He had to push her away by her big hips and then he started talking.

"He's serious," Jake said. "You've just gotta deal."

"Deal? The devil-bitch is gonna brainwash my kids!"

"What are you, Wiccan or something? You don't believe anything she doesn't."

"I don't constantly talk about Jesus and believe that sinners are going to hell just because they don't believe the same damn thing I do. Wake up, Jake!"

"Dad's got money, he's got a big house and a big backyard. Brennan and Meghan are gonna have some better memories than just living in this place. At least they'll have some different experiences. Anyway, don't you get it, if we get a paternity test and they come back mine like we know, we're screwed!"

"That's because you won't man up and get a real job."

I gotta admit this, even though I don't want to, but Jake struck her. Got her clean across the face, and she pushed him back. It wasn't the first time this scenario had occurred between these two, but this time Jake got scared and frustrated. He knew with this Me Too stuff she could put anything on him if she wanted. So he backed up and ran away, hopped on his bike and rode off.

Now he was enraged but it wasn't just at her. He started to go back towards his home but instead he veered off and went back to Bubba's place.

He didn't bother putting on his mask this time and just started banging on the door. Marcy answered and that was enough to trigger a pretty intense session of lovemaking, age be damned.

Afterwards, in her room, he got to talking with her about how Bubba got pinched since she clearly felt guilty that she'd gotten it on with another man, a much younger man at that, with Bubba not even buried yet.

"It's the plague," she said. "It's getting us crazy, even in these parts."

"The devils are in the city. You know what? I'm gonna go down there to investigate."

"You'll get it too. Are you crazy?"

"I need to know what got Bubba. What's getting all of us stir-crazy like these socialist city folks?"

"Wear your mask, at least."

"It don't work but I'll wear it. Don't you have to, anyway, down there?"

She kind of reluctantly gave him her daughter Pearl's address in Brooklyn.

"If that Welch could investigate Pizzagate, then certainly I can go and figure out this devilish-ness. Bubba deserves it."

She tried to talk him down a bit, but that made him more determined than ever. And he set off on his bike to the land of the devils.

VI

Now look, every man has a time in his life when he feels like God or some supreme being has called on him to do something special for humanity. Every man has his moment. You know, like that song from the 80s: that "St. Elmo's Fire" or whatever.

Jake felt this was his time. It was all these things bubbling in him and he wanted to figure out why Bubba was dead and why the world had gone so crazy. Just like that Welch had decided it was his time to save the children at the devil-worshipping pizza parlor in DC, despite his imperfections, so too Jake thought he would go into the pit of darkness to see how the China virus spread to his community.

He got over these crazy bridges named after Washington and Kennedy and these other great men now being cancelled and he made his way down to this address on the route his Google Maps-GPS showed him. He went through this slick neighborhood with these so-called brownstones but then he got to the ghetto area where the homeless guys came up to him to beg for change, and he felt bad, so he gave it to 'em.

That's where he found the address, in one of these areas, in some apartment building. He rang up. At first there was no response, so he rang again. This time someone else was coming in so he thanked and passed 'em, climbing up the rickety stairs, where he smelled some rank weed.

He came up to the apartment and knocked.

At first, he figured she wasn't home and that he might have to camp out, but then he heard someone's voice ask who it was.

"Your momma Marcy sent me," Jake said through his mask, "on account of Bubba's passing."

There was a pause; he figured she was trying to assess the situation. Then he heard her say, "What's your name?"

"Jake, ma'am. I'm a Danson."

"She didn't tell me any Danson was coming."

"I just talked to her. You can call her if you want."

He heard a pause. He was getting frustrated. He was used to women going easy.

"Okay, she just texted me. I guess you're clear. Let me put on my mask."

He waited again. Seemed like for a century. Finally, the door creaked open, and Pearl appeared in the crack. She was wearing an N 95 mask and holding up her phone, apparently recording the interaction.

"Don't try anything funny, or I'm gonna send the video to the news."

"Sure," he said, leaning easy with a stiff-arm against the cracked and grimy wall.

"So what do you want? To get money from me for the funeral?"

"No, you can do that yourself when you go up. Club already gave our share to your mom through our President Jaylan, including mine."

"So then, why are you here?"

"To investigate. Figure out how Bubba got exposed to this deadly disease."

"Well, I got tested and I don't have it, so it wasn't from me."

"Really? Because Marcy's convinced you gave it to him. Or at least that he got it on his trip down here."

"He might have gotten it on his trip, but it wasn't from me."

Jake stopped leaning and put out his hands.

"Do tell."

She stopped recording and put down her phone.

"Look, are you really here to investigate, whatever that means?"

"Yeah. And then I can give you a ride to the funeral if you want. Don't have to rent no car or take no crazy public transportation which will take you here or there."

Pearl shrugged. "Show me the sign."

Jake showed her the complex Danson sign and she seemed to let her guard down a bit.

"I'm still watching you," she said, but she closed the door and then opened it again, this time wider, and he came in.

"You're the only one who's been in here since Dad," she said as they stood in a tiny space that was the kitchen, dining room, and living room combined. "Only other people who come are the delivery guys, but they leave my food on the floor."

"Tough life. I heard you still wanna stay in this hell hole."

"Well, I lost my job. Can't get another one. But the unemployment's enough to help me with essentials, and the savings from my last paycheck will get me by for a bit. I wanna come back; I'm trying different ways, but I might end up moving back. Haven't told mom yet though. Don't want to give her false expectations."

"Sure. So you got no money but thought I was here to get money from you."

"Why else would a Danson come all the way down here?"

"We've got pride. We take care of ourselves and our own. You know that. If anything, I might have come down to give you money, since you're so destitute."

"Yeah, because you really look like you're loaded."

Jake smiled. "You're right, I'm not. I got lots of burdens and little cash. But I feel bad about Bubba, and I wanna make it right by your mom and figure out why the fuck he's in a casket instead of shooting the shit in the club with us."

She opened her arms wide. "Well, what do you wanna know?"

"Who else was he with when he came down here? I mean if you didn't give it to him, as you claim, then who? Did he go play basketball with a bunch of Covid-infected slimeballs?"

"No, he's not that dumb. But...I told him something when he was here that might have exposed him a different way."

She started breaking down suddenly, and she sat down on a stool in the kitchen portion. Jake went close to comfort her, like he often did, but she stuck her arm out and glared at him wildly.

"Don't you dare touch me," she said. "Just stay back."

"Alright," Jake said, backing up, his hands out and displayed. "Just thought I'd comfort you."

"I've had enough comfort. I can't believe I was so mean to Dad when he came. Last time I saw him, the fuck."

"What happened?"

She shook her head as she wiped her eyes. "We were arguing, you know, about me living down here, with so many people and opportunities; it's so horrible, of course. He started quizzing me on my relationship with my then boss, this film producer, Kent Holder. And I guess I let it slip that Kent had come onto me right before the pandemic hit."

"Dad flipped out and wanted to confront him. So maybe that's what he did, I don't know. I was one of the few employees Kent had kept on payroll during the pandemic, and we were working through Zoom calls and everything, and suddenly he lets me go, just a few days after Dad's visit. Dad got sick right after so I never got to ask him, but maybe he did talk to Kent before he left the city. I was such an idiot for telling him."

"This Kent Holder, what did he do to you?"

"I don't wanna say, you fucking pervert."

"Alright, sorry. Sounds like a regular douche. But it's a lead. Where can I find him?"

"What are you gonna do? You're gonna get the virus too."

"He's probably over it by now. Anyway, I'll wear my mask."

"What's so important about finding out how Dad got it? So many people here are dying of it. No funerals for them, they're just flipping them into holes. Jesus, you need to get out before you expose me. It's approaching ten minutes since you've been in here. That's the exposure time, they say."

"Alright, I'll go. But I'll find this Kent Holder, with or without you."

He stormed out, shutting the door as he left, and marched down the stairs and to his bike. Then he looked up this Kent Holder on his phone. He found a site where he could pay to get his address. He had one credit card for emergencies, and he used it.

VII

Jake cruised into Manhattan and got to this Kent Holder's apartment, which was in some fancy-schmancy neighborhood. He took out a knife he had for special events like this one and got ready to go on an offensive.

It was one of those security guard buildings, but the guard was busy tying his shoelaces, so Jake got past, and he slipped onto the elevator and pressed the button to the floor, and then he realized it was the only loft on that floor because this douche was a suit. He cursed when the button didn't work because apparently you needed a special code to get to that floor, considering it was the only apartment on it.

He figured he was screwed but then luck got on his side when the elevator opened up and a Chinaman delivery guy got on with a package, and he pressed the button for the loft too. This time it worked because apparently, that security guard had activated it from his end.

So the elevator went up and stopped on the floor, and the door opened up directly to the apartment. He heard a voice telling the delivery guy to leave the package on the table near this white couch and get going.

The Chinaman did that and gave Jake a funny look as he came into the apartment and lingered, but he didn't say nothing and minded his own business because it was New York City where no one cares about no one.

Jake took out his knife after the elevator closed and waited kind of awkwardly around the delivery, which was this folded paper bag, probably Chinese food—typical right?

Suit came out wearing a bathrobe and Jake pounced. Kent Holder put his hands up like a coward.

"Whoa whoa whoa, take it all!" he yelled out.

"I don't want nothing but the truth," Jake said. "For America."

"What?" called the coward.

"Did you give the China virus to my buddy Bubba?"

"Who?"

"Don't who me! You know Pearl, right? The girl you laid off since you're a pervy producer type? Was her dad in here, giving you the business?"

"Oh," he said. His hands were shaking while they were still up, and now Jake was behind him, the knife at his throat.

"Yeah, look," he said. "Some crazy guy comes up to me while I was approaching the building. He grabs me and says he's Pearl's dad, and to stay away from her or he'll kill me. All this out in broad daylight."

"And what'd you do?"

"I gave him what he wanted. I let her go. Better than keeping her on and her accusing me of more stuff I didn't do. That's significant liability."

"Sure, you didn't do it. How long was he around you?"

"Maybe a few minutes. But he was right up on me."

"And you gave him the virus?"

"I don't know. I had a slight cold around that time, but it wasn't like what they're showing on the news."

"Who'd you get it from? That Chinaman who did the delivery?"

"No, I never see him."

"You been around anybody else?"

"Not really. Only my brother."

"And he is?"

"Bill Holder. William Holder."

"Who's that? He famous too?"

"He's a banker for Goldman Sachs."

"High up there, huh? I knew you were all connected. Where can I find him?"

"You're not gonna hurt him, are you?"

"Not if he comes clean like you."

It's weird how when it comes down to it, these suits don't got much loyalty, even for family. They'll turn on their own quick when it comes to preserving themselves.

This Kent Holder told Jake his brother William's address uptown and even his habits. After convincing Kent that speaking up about this visit would get him axed in the head one day, Jake went down and out and took his cycle up to William Holder's place.

He hung out outside the building knowing this William Holder always went out around this time for some "constitutional" crap. His brother Kent even provided Jake a picture via text so he recognized the snake as soon as he left the building. Then Jake started following.

Except this Bill Holder didn't go far: he went straight to the Masonic Hall and using a key and showing some signs, he went in.

It was early evening now, so Jake guessed the Masons were starting their usual meeting. He had never seen any Masonic Hall or Grand Lodge before, but he knew the sign of the Masons and had heard of their Satanic rituals, so he figured he'd have to find an alternative way to investigate and not get caught like Welch.

He checked around the building and found one of those manholes uncovered so he jumped inside. It was dark and dank. He heard some water splashing and rats scattering but he had his cell phone flashlight and would try to get inside the building someway if he could.

He went down some dead ends, almost lost his footing a couple of times and the rank smell almost knocked him out, but he got through. As luck would have it, he was squeezing through one pipe when he heard some whining and whimpering and thought maybe it wasn't rats but possibly humans.

He followed the sounds. It was tough: sometimes it would get so narrow he'd have to slouch down and crawl, and the echoes in the pipes made the direction of the sounds sometimes difficult to locate. But he was determined to follow the cries until they got closer and fresher. Finally, he could tell they were the anguished pleas of poor children.

VIII

And then he came into the light, or at least the shine of the medieval torches that lit up the stone walls of the dungeon like out of a Poe story. There they were: naked children chained to a wall, shackled, struggling and crying, while a minder was hissing at them and baiting them while licking his lips and thinking about what his fellow Masons would do later in the night. It made Jake so mad, when he thought of his own kids, Brennan and Meghan, and about Pete and all the children and folks who were weak and couldn't protect themselves. But he kept his cool, went up behind the Mason, put his hand over the Mason's mouth and slit his throat.

The blood gushed out of his neck, and he went down without a word or a sound, and Jake put his finger to his lips to calm the children so they wouldn't make any unfortunate sounds. And then he climbed up the steps himself and opened the door a bit so he could silently watch the proceedings of the Masonic meeting.

The banker Willian Holder was there, wearing his strange hat, the robes and ornaments and all the rest, but another man was holding the gavel. He was the mayor of the city, and city council people were there too, and so were prosecutors and attorney generals and entertainment people and media leaders and military men. The whole swath of the upper crust.

And they were laughing about unleashing the China virus on the population and how their fellow New Yorkers were dying. The mayor then changed the conversation to when they should unleash the vaccine, which they already had, so they could manage the virus. That is, once enough chaos was created to make the fascistic control of the country permanent. The banker William Holder said he still wanted to kill certain people with it, but the virus was this finicky thing; he had slipped it to his brother because of this slight that had happened when they were kids, but his brother had only gotten a slight cold and didn't die like Bill wanted him to.

Now Jake got really hot because he knew now that William Holder was responsible for Bubba's death specifically and that the Masons had given it to the whole country and all of humanity. And then he watched as they got the Chinese premier on the screen and discussed with him how the next few months of the virus would go. They decided to keep the lockdowns here and extend them to the rural areas so they could slowly convince the people it was receding in the city and rising in the rural areas. This would give them the impression that the city slickers were responsible, and the country hicks were dumb, until everyone was controlled. And then the vaccine would be the permanent fix; it would rewrite everyone's genetic code so that everyone who got it was controlled by the Masons and Chinese telepathically. They would be turned into politically correct, drug-reliant zombies like in Huxley or *1984* or something.

Anyway, once this decision was reached and the Master Mason, the mayor, slammed his gavel, the Satanic ritual was completed and everyone delighted in going down to torture, molest, and murder the poor children. But Jake had another idea.

He ducked behind the stairs, and as they descended, he stabbed each one in the heart. They screamed, doubled over, and died. Thankfully one of them was William Holder, so Jake was able to get his revenge.

Once three of them went down, the others got wind of the situation, locked up the door and fled out the main lodge entrance. At that point, Jake hurried to the dead body of the minder, got his keys, and freed all the children. He pulled the robes off the dead Masons, cut the fabric and tried to cover as many of the naked children as he could. Then he led them through the sanitation pipes, using his cell phone flashlight, and tried to remember where the open hole was.

After some stops and starts, he was able to find the open hole by the streetlight and called up. An ordinary ma passing by heard him, and told others nearby, and Jake was able to apprise them of the children down there that needed saving. He was able to hoist the children up and the people pulled them through. Then finally he jumped up and was pulled out also.

He saw a cop car there and a couple of EMS workers and they were doing CPR on one kid, who was exhausted, and it didn't seem like he would make it. Then Jake realized the cops would never believe him and probably worked for the Masons too. So, with the children saved and everyone focused on them, he ran to his bike and jetted off.

IX

Jake biked back to Brooklyn and to Pearl's apartment. He rang her and she let him in. He apprised her of the whole tale. Considering how much blood was on him and his rank smell, she believed him.

She thought they should call the police and report it all, but Jake said the police and the media were controlled by the Masons too. And sure enough, when they turned on the TV, the media was reporting about the children being saved from the sewer, but the story was spun so that they thought maybe it was a pedophilic ring of subway workers who were enslaving and molesting the children.

He took a shower, and to his surprise, Pearl got in with him and washed him off and then they made love. In bed, she told him that she agreed there was nothing they could do because the world was controlled by the worshippers of Jahbulon.

So, the next morning she packed what she could in a small bag, and she got on the back of his cycle, and they rode back upstate. He dropped her off at Marcy's place; she was real happy to see Pearl, not knowing of the awkward relations.

But it worked out. They had a socially distanced funeral a few days later, though people barely followed the regulations, and afterwards at the wake, Jake made it known to Marcy that Pearl and he were going to be an item going forward. Marcy wasn't happy but she accepted it, knowing that Pearl was nearer to Jake's age.

So, Jake saw Gina only so often, and she decided to accept the Lion's offer to give partial visitation of Brennan and Meghan to the devil-woman in exchange for not outing Jake as the father. And Jake started frequenting Marcy's place anyway because that's where Pearl was staying, and they'd make savage love in the bedroom knowing that Marcy and the teen could hear them; but it was all right, there was no other way.

X

In sum, Jake was an ordinary guy who stood up to an extraordinary situation. Nothing much changed in terms of his life; in fact, it got a bit more complicated, but still, he found a good ol' lady and I gotta admit, he got her pregnant too. Not having no means of income, she started taking pics of herself and putting 'em on a site; she heard a lot of girls were doing that to pay the bills, supplementing the unemployment. Unfortunately, it didn't go so well because Pearl was a bit of a bigger girl but still, she made the effort and Jake appreciated that.

Jake still watched TV with his mom and Pete in the trailer like old times. He was eating PB&J when he saw the update about the subway pedophile people being captured, and he wondered how the Masons had schemed to frame them. Thankfully, they hadn't tracked him back to town, at least not yet. He had saved the children and got his girl. Not bad for a biker from upstate. He wondered still when they would come out with the vaccine to brainwash the people, but he knew that, when they did, he and all the folks he knew wouldn't be getting it.

~ Day Five ~
Reaction to Ricard's Story

Most guests had sat in silent disdain during the story; all the chefs except Thiago had walked out, and Rashan had almost left but had doubled back; only Khassan and Sylvania had laughed at various moments throughout.

Once it was clear that Ricard was done, the torrent of opposition started.

"That was the most ignorantly racist, antisemitic, sexist, homophobic piece of shit story I've ever heard in my life," Lisa said. "What the hell is wrong with you?"

Ricard was a little shocked. "It wasn't any of those things," he said, shrugging.

"My ancestors were Freemasons," Taylor said. "They teach good men to be better men. It's got nothing to do with the Illuminati. It's hicks like you who are ruining our country. And it's got nothing to do with Trump either. I think he might be a Mason, but let me check—"

"And what the fuck is wrong with you, with this anti-Chinese shit?" Lisa asked. "Your girlfriend is Chinese!"

"She's Taiwanese American," Ricard corrected. "She hates the CCP too."

Cathy hadn't looked up at Ricard the entire time. Now she quickly got up and went to the elevator.

Rashan stood up also to accompany her, but first he said, "I didn't wanna disrespect you by leaving Ricard because you stayed through my story. I think you're a nice guy, but your perception is whacked. Makes Taylor's story seem sane. All this QAnon conspiracy crap is nuts, man. Let me ask you, have you been to Brooklyn or Manhattan? It's not this psycho-socialist reality you red hicks have made yourselves believe it is. And even worse than that, it lightens the load Covid has put on all of us. It's not some hoax invented by the elite. It's very real. Ask Andrea; let her tell you."

Rashan marched to the elevator to follow Cathy. Ricard watched him go, then turned to Andrea, but she shrugged in response.

"I already told my side through my story," she said.

Khassan defended him. "It was funny, it was imaginative, it was different. You guys gotta lighten up; this is storytelling! It's fiction."

"Did you forget him mentioning that a flood of Muslims is going to ruin the country?" Rashan shouted as he approached the elevator.

"Hey, if it's true ..."

"And when he's making light of a disease that has killed tens of thousands of New Yorkers, and the reason why we're all here—" Rashan shouted from the elevator before getting on.

"How's he making light of it?" Khassan asked as the elevator doors closed. "A dude died of Covid in the story. He's explaining its origins from his perspective. I don't know if it's true or not, but it's an explanation. And it works fine as a story of triumph over insurmountable odds. Can't tell you what to think, but it worked for me."

"It's typical blood libel, antisemitic racist shit from like the 1930s about how the Jews are ruling the world through the Free Masons and capitalism and communism combined," Lisa said. "I wish we had hate speech laws like in France and Germany so this shit couldn't be circulated."

"He didn't say the Jews rule the world, even though they do," Khassan said.

"Fuck you, Khassan," Lisa said.

"I don't mean you, Lisa, I just mean ..."

"Who, then? I'm Jewish."

"I know, but he doesn't mean all Jews, just the Zionists," Khassan explained. "Anyway, he was talking about the Masons, not the Jews."

"He mentioned it in the beginning," Darnell said, "but I'll defer to my Jewish brother."

Micah had gone back down to the basement to talk to Sung and had only returned recently to hear the end of the story.

"Whatever, I don't care, man," Micah said. "I barely caught your story, but it's a free country. We probably shouldn't hang out, but I'll still protect you if you get stabbed or something."

Thiago, Ares, and Rabia were silent.

Pritesh said, "On the positive side, I have to say it gave us a good picture of how some Americans live in areas outside the city and some real issues they face, from divorce to extended families and economic woes. I also appreciated that Jake was vegan. That changed things up, since I don't think you are, Ricard."

"I have to agree with that," Taylor said. "I was also surprised by your vocabulary and knowledge of literature. You quoted some classics."

"All white, cisgender, heteronormative literature, Taylor," Lisa said.

"Alright, so it wasn't all bad," Khassan said, ignoring Lisa's comment. "I mean, I'm from an ethnically diverse suburban area outside Boston, and we have a lot of the same issues there too. So, the subject is pertinent."

"Big word," Lisa teased.

"Conspiracies do exist, chico, though you know nothing about the City or diversity," Angela chimed in. "Entertaining story, but totally ridiculous."

Ricard shrugged. "I'm sorry you guys didn't like it. I was nervous about telling it, but I didn't think it was going to be hated so much. I thought you would like it more than the elite."

"That's your problem, Ricard," Lisa said. "People like you don't think. That's why you believe this Pizzagate bullshit."

"It's all over YouTube," Ricard noted.

"Thought it was entertaining too, honey," Sylvania said. "I agree with Khassan; you all have to lighten up. We're going to get all types of perspectives here; isn't that the point?"

"Yes," Olive said, coming to the front. "I know a lot of people were offended, but we're not censoring anybody's stories. If we do it to one, we've got to do it to all. I know some of my staff weren't fans, so I guess I'll have to deal with that. Thanks for coming. We'll have the tally, and then you can enjoy the rooftop for as long as you want."

Ricard said it was clear he would lose and be banished to the North Shore Complex the next day; he said he would go back to his room and pack his stuff so he wouldn't be too bored.

"Who knows, you might win," Khassan said. "Mad people have left."

Only Rashan and Cathy had left. Hayley wasn't present either.

The tallies were done. There were eight votes. The tally was 4–4.

"Who does the tiebreaker?" Khassan asked.

"I hadn't thought about that," Olive admitted. "I could do it myself, but that would be problematic."

Olive noted much of his staff had left, but the ones who had stayed could form a tie-breaking committee.

"I don't care what they say," Ricard said, heading towards the elevator. "Need some time to myself anyway."

But even in absentia, Olive asked Ares, Rabia, Darnell, Micah, and himself to vote. That would, theoretically, break the tie since it was an odd number combination. Micah hadn't heard the whole story, so he wanted to abstain, but Olive insisted he vote too.

Ricard was banished by a vote of 3–2.

He was already gone. So were many others.

Nalini hadn't commented the entire time. She did appreciate a non-elitist perspective, and now that Cathy had walked out, Ricard didn't seem as out of reach. Maybe she could have explained to him that she was sorry about her behavior the night before. He did say he would be in his room.

But Nalini was feeling the drinks again. She thought it might be better to call it a night rather than embarrass herself again. And anyway, she had a plan. She wanted him to be banished. That would work in her favor.

"Only the white people are offended," Angela said to Darnell. "Guess brown people got tough skin. Or actual problems."

"You're looking pretty white to me, girl."

"Brown-lite."

"He didn't have time to mention everyone he hates. Blacks and browns are the lowest, right?"

Angela shrugged. "What white people in the sticks think got nothing to do with me keeping my salon open in Queens."

"Valid point. I guess. But you know we dying out there, right?"

"I watch the news. But I see fools fighting and gangbanging in the streets too. Know plenty of amigos gone to Rikers. Take a trip to Corona, chico. Illegal central. Hate crimes too. We're #1."

"Illegal, legal—what's the difference? Knuckleheads do what they do."

"You can't go to Mexico and come back like it's nothing, though."

"Let's agree to disagree. Now what about that injury? Can I rub that away?"

"You think I'm gonna let you in after this ignorance?"

"You playin' too much with me, girl. Got me irritated."

"You need exercise, go to work on it. Stronger wrists, guaranteed."

"Come down to the security room with me. We can hang out while I working."

"There are cameras, right?"

"You don't trust me?"

"Not the way you talking like a perro."

"Alright, I behave myself. I protect you."

"Maybe for a minute."

She looked around for Taylor but didn't see him. They went down the elevator.

Meanwhile, in the third-floor den, Cathy was crying. Rashan was already there, while Lisa and Andrea had joined her after voting.

"I can't believe he used 'Chinaman' like it was nothing," Cathy said.

"Forget about him," Lisa replied. "He's the worst of the worst."

"But he's not like that," Cathy insisted. "He's sensitive and sweet. Just an idiot sometimes."

"You can't just forgive that kind of hate," Lisa said.

"He's ignorant and stubborn," Rashan said. "Not unchangeable. Better to work from within."

"You'll feel better tomorrow," Andrea told Cathy, rubbing her back. "Let's go to bed."

"Talking about going to work," Lisa said to Rashan on the staircase as they went down one floor. "How about Domhampton?"

"Got my ride."

"Ares?"

Rashan smiled without responding. Then he left.

"I guess I'll remain in suspense," she said.

~ Day Six ~

Nalini woke up at 5 a.m., took a shower, and did her makeup before realizing that the envelope was for her.

> We just got a wacky weave
> Of tall conspiracies told with ease
> Will you be able to lower the flame
> Or blow the top off the game?

"Blow the top off the game, baby," she thought to herself. She immediately took the elevator down to the garage and examined her options. She wasn't sure if she could ride a motorcycle—a bicycle would be a better bet, and based on her calculations, it would take her two and a half hours to ride out to the North Shore Complex in Jamesport, the address divulged to her by a Rashan text—how he got it remained a mystery. But she felt better about her biking skills than her motorcycle skills, since she didn't know how to turn.

It was a challenge and an exhaustion, taking on major bike lanes and major roads, massive inclines including one that was 43 feet. But by 8:30 a.m., she had made it there, only half an hour before Ricard was supposed to arrive.

She was surprised that she was able to get into the complex easily, through a slight passage between security gates. Then again, it was even easier to get into the Saggplex.

Up the driveway, the initial building appeared like an outsized medieval German inn. The external structure was hewn of sand, limestone, and brick masonry with a white-painted stucco surface and carefully crafted vines coming down it. The interior wall was brick, and its chimney stuck up high.

Directly adjacent to it was a smaller cottage. Gigantic stones of melded limestone and granite formed its structure, and vines covered them both inside and out. The cottage led to the courtyard and then the vineyard, with the bungalows spaced out on either side of the latter.

Nalini found both doors locked, but she was able to go around the building anyway and make her way into the courtyard, where she waited patiently, her bike stashed on the side of the smaller cottage, invisible to an onlooker.

Around 9:30 a.m., Ares pulled up in his limousine with Ricard inside, since Olive had forbidden access to a motorcycle. It was supposed to be a punishment, after all.

Ricard emerged from the back seat of the limousine, his arms clasped like he was in cuffs, even though he wasn't. Ares pressed a button on a remote control.

"Doors are open for you," he said to Ricard. "Enjoy the land."

Ricard shrugged and pointed to the larger building. "What's in there?"

"You'll find everything from wine to beer and hot chocolate. Go make yourself a mocha."

"Some punishment."

"It's punishment for the rich, my dark friend."

Ricard shook his head.

"Tell me, you're an immigrant, right?" Ricard asked. "How long do you plan to be in this country?"

"As long as they'll let me."

"I heard you think America is sick."

"Well, it is. But it's still better than Finland."

"Meaning you'll make more money."

"Yes."

"And, especially with how you are."

He rolled his eyes. "Actually, Finland is one of the most LGBTQ-friendly places in the world. Look, if there's anything else you need, I'll give you my number."

"Sure, I would love to have that," Ricard said nervously, "from you of all people."

As this was transpiring, Nalini saw the cottage door open, and there was Rashan.

"What the fuck?" she gasped.

Rashan told her the story of how he had tried to meet Dom-hampton the night before but had found himself in a trap instead. He had scootered to the location, but instead of a dom gay man, he was met by Ares.

"They're serious about spreading," Rashan said.

"No shit. They quarantined me the first day. And you called me a spreader."

"Yeah, well, I was just frustrated. Sorry. It wasn't what I anticipated. But Ares was a good lay last night. Said I had to stay in here all night until I was trusted again."

"A good lay? Are you serious? Did Ares force himself on you?"

"Nah, it was my call. Just happened, I guess, and better than nothing. In fact, I got a 2fer."

"A 2fer? Who was the other guy?"

Rashan pursed his lips.

"Oh my God," Nalini said. "You're kidding me."

"Don't tell anybody, please. I think I love both of them."

"Fucking freak. Lisa's gonna have a field day with that if she finds out."

"I feel higher than I ever have in my life, baby," Rashan said, spreading his arms. "Maybe better than when I met Josh."

"They brainwashed you, dude. Well, I'm glad it worked out for someone. An eager and willing slave."

"Fuck off. I'm not the one sneaking out to see a desperate crush. They'll find you too, guaranteed, but, whatever, if you don't say anything, I won't."

"I'll be back in time for lunch. Just got lost."

"Sure. There are cameras everywhere, but sure."

He waited until Ricard was inside the inn, and then he ran out and went into the back of the limo, winking at Ares as he went past.

Ricard had made himself a black coffee and was drinking from a mug when he saw Nalini approach.

"Am I dreaming?"

"Maybe it's a nightmare."

"What are you doing here?"

"Trying to figure out what went wrong between us? Between Sag Harbor and DDR and that fucking whore."

Ricard put down the cup.

"Well, she's not a ..."

"A suit. I know. A suit. I'm tired of hearing that. No, I'm not a suit; I'm a person. I was brought up in one reality, you were brought up in another. How is that a lifetime confinement?"

"Even if you choose defense or whatever, won't you still be a suit?"

"You want to live in the buttfuck countryside your entire life? Working odd jobs and paying child support to your worthless ex-wife? If she's anything like the ladies in your story, I feel doubly bad for you."

"You know, you can't even process that life. Or the fact that I wouldn't want to move out of it. At least Cathy gets that."

"Cathy walked out on you. She wants nothing to do with you. I understand you. I respect your love of nature. Remember that walk in the woods? Remember cuddling, necking, in Sag Harbor?"

"And petting in your room. But that's all it was. You made it seem like ..."

"We fell asleep. It would have been."

"Why do you even like me? I'm everything in the world that you despise."

"No, you're everything that I've missed."

She approached him. They embraced, then kissed. But as their lips parted, the kiss felt hollow to both of them.

She said, "Oh, my God. Why do I hate my life so much?"

"I don't know, Nalini. Maybe take a look in the mirror and see what you don't normally see."

"Everyone else sees beauty and brains. All I seem to see is darkness."

She moved towards the door. He followed her out.

"Look, you can stay here with me," he said. "I don't really want to be alone."

"You don't?" she countered. "Isn't it you against the world? The world has oppressed you bikers so much. But you don't oppress anybody, right?"

"Where is that coming from?"

She put on her helmet. "It's pretty clear that you'd prefer to ogle the birds and the vines more than spend a second with me."

"I never said that."

"Good luck going through the world alone, Ricard. It's funny, I can actually help you with your child support situation. Not that you ever had the brains to ask."

He reached out for her arm, but in a flash, she was on the bike and gone, riding through the slit in the security gate. Ricard rolled his eyes and tried to think of how he was going to spend the day here.

Meanwhile, at the Saggplex patio, Pritesh was sitting with Khassan, Taylor, and Sylvania, trying to avoid Hayley and wondering where Nalini was. Taylor noticed Angela wasn't there either. They were served a Middle Eastern and North African breakfast, including shakshouka, a dish with poached eggs in a spiced-up sauce including tomatoes; falafel with baba ganoush; scrambled eggs and tabouli; dhal (lentils) in zhoug, a spicy sauce, and eggplant; chickpeas, cucumbers, and dates in tahini dressing; fried eggs smashed up and served with hummus, fool medames (fava beans), and pita. The spread also included several types of fruit, including kiwis, guavas, grapes, strawberries, papaya, and mango with yogurt and rose water dressing; and for a light dessert, an orange blossom semolina pudding with date and honey purée.

Everyone enjoyed the breakfast, and they were ready to get going for their activity, with the sun shining brightly and the humidity being moderate, the cicadas singing in a low volume.

Lisa checked in briefly with Rashan regarding Domhampton. He told her no one showed up at the site, and he went back home. Lisa expressed disappointment but said she would press on.

Olive appeared, this time wearing short shorts and an orange T-shirt.

"We're going back to the beach today. We'll play some volleyball. How does that sound?"

Everyone was excited. They had become sick of the rain, the house, and the woods too. But it was going to be Hayley's first time back on the beach since the attack, and it wasn't clear if she was ready or cleared.

"I'm going!" Hayley proclaimed, reacting against Alexa's head shake. "I'm playing!"

"How about this?" Alexa suggested. "You can play as long as you're in the wheelchair. I want to be safe."

Alexa looked at Olive, who shrugged.

"Fine," Hayley said. "But if I start falling asleep, you're gonna give me some Adderall, right?"

Alexa rolled her.

"Kidding, doc. Compromise. I'm for it, I guess."

"Like the last two times, everyone can make their way down like they choose," Olive said. "Kayaking, biking, paddleboarding, walking, whatever. I'll see you there, and we'll form teams then."

As the crowd left the patio, Hayley insisted she wanted to kayak. Andrea told her she could get her dressings wet or, worse, fall in the water, potentially infecting her injury and delaying or altering her recovery. Alexa had also called Rashadi down, who advised Hayley of the same thing.

"Fine, if you're all against me," she said.

"I'm not against you, honey," Andrea said. "I'll roll you down to the beach; how about that?"

Meanwhile, Taylor decided to bike, racing Khassan and Sylvania. Pritesh was standing next to the kayaks wondering who he should ask to kayak with him—he saw Angela appear from the area near the croquet court. He asked her if she wanted to kayak to the beach.

"I'm sorry about how Hayley treated you, chico," Angela said in the kayak. "I heard from the grapevine anyway."

"I don't want to talk about her anymore," Pritesh said. "Let's talk about, I don't know, you."

"What do you want to know?"

"Like where you were right now. I didn't see you at breakfast."

"I was on a detour, chico. A funny detour."

"On the croquet court. I guess it's much different than life in Corona."

"Yes, much different. Spanish guys don't know how to treat a lady. Half of them are illegal anyway. Think we're just Barbie dolls. They toy with us, and they discard us, and no one says anything."

"I see. I guess that's happened to you?"

"More than you know."

They talked about their various backgrounds, finding commonality in their immigrant origins, even though Angela had come to the U.S. from Ecuador much younger and through family. But before they knew it, it was time to dock. They could see the volleyball net was set up in the distance as they gathered around Olive near the White House.

"We're going to change it up a bit," Olive said. "I randomly picked the teams out of a hat. Since Ricard is at the complex and Nalini seems to be missing, they will be replaced by staff: Darnell and Thiago, since Ares and Rabia are otherwise occupied, and Abeo wants to take the reins on lunch. We'll have four teams of three."

He took out his phone.

"Team 1: Darnell, Cathy, Angela. Team 2: Thiago, Khassan, Hayley. Team 3: Taylor, Sylvania, Rashan. Team 4: Lisa, Andrea, Pritesh."

Angela noticed Darnell come around the corner of the White House.

"Hey girl," he said nervously. "Looks like we're on the same side."

She shrugged and turned towards Cathy.

Cathy realized she could live with Darnell—at least it wasn't Ricard. She would have to figure out what she thought about Ricard after last night, although she was simultaneously missing him too. Khassan felt his team was crippled by an actual cripple, and who knew how good Thiago would be; Taylor was ecstatic about Sylvania and could tolerate the weak link Rashan. Lisa accepted her teammates; at least they weren't assholes.

The first game was between Team 1 and Team 2. Cathy and Khassan naturally took charge, even though there weren't official captains. Cathy set up their strategy: a triangular setup of positions, with anyone able to do bumps, sets, or spikes. Meanwhile, Khassan assigned roles. Thiago would man the back and hit the arm bumps if the balls went his way. Hayley would perform the sets at the front and Khassan the spikes, unless the bump was out of Hayley's reach, in which case Khassan would set up either Thiago or Hayley.

The game went better than expected for Team 2, with Hayley able to accomplish some sets and even a bump, and Thiago getting most hits in the backcourt. Angela was surprisingly effective at bumps and even the occasional set, despite pain from the welt in her ass, which caused Darnell to flinch along with Angela every time she had a hitch.

Ultimately, though, Hayley's lack of mobility hamstrung Khassan's team. Cathy's beautiful setups of Darnell's spikes into dead man's land propelled them to a 25–18 victory, after which the three participated in an awkward group hug.

The next match seemed unfair due to Taylor and Sylvania's athletic prowess, but Lisa had a more formidable team than she thought, as both Pritesh and Andrea had played volleyball before—Pritesh during corporate team outings, both in India and in the U.S., and Andrea for fun in Queens and on cruises. Lisa's team assigned zones so anyone could react depending on where the ball was hit. But Lisa ended up hitting most of the spikes for her team. Team 3 played a combination of zones and roles: Sylvania manned the front zone and was the primary spiker due to her height and long arms; Rashan was responsible for most sets; and Taylor for the bumps and some spikes.

Initially, it was Sylvania's blocking ability that put Taylor's team out in front 6–1. But Lisa's team was able to adjust, with Lisa and Pritesh lifting their spikes or bumps over Sylvania's outstretched arms. Eventually, they decided to exploit Team 3's weakness, Rashan, hitting it towards him whenever possible. Taylor adjusted by trying to play Rashan's zone for him, but it wasn't always possible.

So over time, Lisa's team came back, and it was 25–25 after fifty points. The first team that scored two in a row would win.

Taylor served to Andrea, who bumped up towards Pritesh. He faked like he was going to set for Lisa but instead sent the set over the net to Rashan, faking him out. The ball hit his left arm as he swung, but it went awry. Taylor was furious but didn't say anything. Down 26–25, Taylor served again. This time the serve was bumped by Lisa, set by Pritesh, and Andrea bumped it over. Rashan was able to bump this one, and Taylor set it—but his set was behind Sylvania, who had to tap it backwards towards the upper net. Lisa blocked the shot with two hands straight up, and the ball hit the ground on Team 3's side, ending the game.

Taylor had screwed up the last point, but he was still steaming at Rashan. He didn't say a word as he dumped himself in the sand to watch the final match: Team 1 vs. Team 4.

Both teams played zones, so everyone hit the ball over the net in a variety of ways, making the match tense. It was close for much of the way. With Lisa's team up 22–21, she confronted a backwards bump from Darnell, sailing slowly towards the net, with a titanic spike that hit him in the face. He screamed and held his hands over his nose.

Angela ran over immediately. The other team sauntered over too, but Darnell told them he was fine—he didn't think his nose was broken.

Being up 23–21 now, Team 4 was in a good position. But Pritesh's serve was intercepted near the net by Cathy, not with a spike but with a soft set, which Andrea couldn't handle. The next point went back and forth 11 times until finally Lisa's block of a bump by Angela was bumped back by Cathy, then spiked by Darnell between Pritesh and Andrea, tying the game at 23–23.

Pritesh served into the net, giving Team 1 a match point at 24–23. His next serve was bumped by Angela right back to him.

He was able to bump it up. Lisa set it over the net, trying to fake out Team 1, but Darnell blocked it, and Andrea's return bump went awry, giving Team 1 the victory.

Olive thanked everyone for a great tournament. Then he announced that the winning team, Darnell, Cathy, and Angela, would be given a special lunch and musical performance at the White House swimming pool deck. Nick and Temple rode up in their van and unloaded various musical instruments, including a cello, bass, guitar, French horn, saxophone, and harmonica.

The three other chefs arrived in a different van driven by Ares and Rabia, who then unloaded the food—both for winners and losers.

The winning team was served iced sangria, tea, lemonade, mimosas, Bloody Marys, and any mixed cocktail they wanted. The food was primarily French: heated baguettes with a variety of cheeses, fresh salami, ham, pepperoni, and their vegan counterparts, accompanied by jams, spicy homemade sauces, and other accoutrements. Meanwhile, the losers had grilled cheese and onions. Everyone was told that dinner would be far more extravagant.

For the winners, Nick and Temple played a mostly eclectic mix of 1920s jazz, 1950s bebop riffs, and classical melodies, as well as some of their own mixed concoctions. Olive, Ares, and Thiago occasionally helped out by playing various instruments too.

Angela started dancing to the music, but when Darnell started to move in on her, she fended him off and sat back down. He backed off and danced a bit with Cathy. Angela went off toward the beach, where Taylor intercepted her.

"You're acting strange," he said. "What's up?"

"Nothing, chico. What are you going to blame me for this time?"

"Look, I'm sorry for being a dick."

"You don't need to apologize for the same thing each fucking time, chico. I get it already. Maybe you just need somebody on your level physically."

"Is Darnell on your level physically?"

"You would know; don't you lift with him every morning?"

She walked away. Meanwhile, Olive announced there would be no afternoon activity and that they were free to frolic and do whatever they wanted. Lisa was on the patio with Maja and Zahra as usual and noticed that Rashan was heading towards the path back to the Saggplex.

"Something went on last night," she said. "I can feel it."

"Maybe you should just mind your own business and get on with your life," Zahra said.

"I know you've aligned yourself with power," Lisa said. "You even came in with Olive last night like you were his maid-in-waiting."

"If he really did something bad, I would be the first to say it," she replied.

"Maja, you're on my side, aren't you?" Lisa asked.

Maja appeared embarrassed. "I mean, it wasn't anything. Just something weird."

"How about what he did to your friends?" Lisa asked.

"I mean, he chose us, didn't he?"

"Loyal to the end. Chalk it up to ass-kissing."

"How about you?" Zahra asked. "Are you a perfect person?"

Lisa noticed Micah in the distance, patrolling near where Andrea was wheeling Hayley around the beach. He glanced her way once in a while.

"I'm not in a position of power," she said.

Meanwhile, in her room back at the Saggplex, Nalini was building her story. Her primary experience with writing and storytelling was at Yale Law, when she had argued cases as both a prosecutor and a defense attorney at various mock trials. More recently, she had taken on some interesting cases in pro bono briefs for her boss, Miles Glorioso, and done witness interrogation and some courtroom prep.

But she had a different mission now. She looked up biker narratives: movies like *Easy Rider* and *Sons of Anarchy*; books like *Hell's Angel* by Sonny Barger and *Hell's Angels* by Hunter S. Thompson; murder mysteries and John Grisham; even Joan Didion and Nathaniel West.

She knew she had the tendency of making her stories sound like a brief, so she rewrote it several times so it wouldn't be too technical but still contain legal realism. But that wasn't even the point. Her story would have purpose and serve as penance.

Rashan stopped by and knocked on the door. She was too busy to talk. Work was her mantra. It was like she was back at the firm, as much as she tried to shirk it.

"Want me to get you some food?" he asked. "Might be some back in the kitchen from breakfast."

"I'm good. Gone days without it if I was really bombarded."

"Shit. I thought teaching was tough."

He went up to the sixth floor and then up the special staircase to a door that entered Olive's apartment. Ares had given him a special code that he started to put in, but it wasn't necessary, as Olive opened it for him.

"Thanks," Rashan said, entering the abode. He looked around.

"I feel like I'm in a boat," he said, noticing all the circular windows.

"That's the idea," Olive replied.

He noticed old globes, nautical maps, round windows, even drawers underneath the frame of the large bed. A library of books surrounded it, and workout equipment was in the corner. Most furniture, including the desk opposite the bed, was made of black ebony. In the middle was a ladder leading to the rooftop, a hatch sealed by a round locked door.

"You really like Poseidon," Rashan said. "But I didn't think you actually would be Domhampton."

"I wanted you for Ares. But I'm not sure he's so into you. I guess he could go either way."

"I see," Rashan said. "So that's why you didn't put any other fags here?"

"It's funny how things work out. I just wanted the best for everyone. Especially for my staff. I kept the ones I cared about. Who I felt cared for me. You see, my friends abandoned me. It's a long story, but they all bailed when the pandemic hit. So, this is all I have left. Rashan, I'm sick."

"Sick?" Rashan asked, stepping back a few steps. "Like, in the head? Or, like, you have Covid?"

"Worse, I'm afraid. And no, you don't need to worry; I don't have AIDS or anything. Not that someone of my wealth couldn't mediate that. No, I have a brain tumor. Diagnosed, and only so long to live."

"Wow," Rashan said, hesitating. "You're kidding."

"I'm afraid not. See, this was not just about bringing in people for everyone else but also about my staff. They are all single too."

"And you think everyone will match with someone?"

"I can only hope, can't I?"

"That's a pretty harebrained scheme."

"I became rich somehow, didn't I?"

Back at the beach, Andrea had wheeled Hayley around long enough. She wanted to get off the wheelchair and lie on the beach like a regular girl. Thiago came over and put out a towel for her.

"We can even get you a lounge chair, princess," he said. "A shade too. Whatever you desire."

She could see Lisa from afar, sitting on the patio.

"I'm still hotter than her, even with this," she said, pointing to the bandage on her side.

"You will always be what you are," Thiago pronounced.

She began laughing, but the laugh went on so long that Andrea stared at Thiago.

"I'm going to get some more sunscreen," Andrea said, heading towards the patio.

Thiago sat down next to Hayley on the sand.

"See, you are brave. You have confronted the beast. You can look out at the ocean and say, 'I conquered you.'"

"I haven't gone in it yet. Who knows if I ever will?"

"You will, my dear. When the doctors say you are okay."

"The doctors. Yeah, they know best, all right. The best pills to take. Just like the Park Avenue docs who fill blues and reds just because. Always right."

"You need to be patient, my dear."

"I know plenty of models who were patient," she said. "But what's the difference?"

"Actually, thinking about it, what is the difference a few days make?" she went on. "A few days ago, I would have been telling Pritesh to take pictures of me."

"I can take pictures of you if you please. We will Photoshop some bits."

"Where is he?"

"Who?"

"My boy toy."

"He is not your boy toy anymore."

"Why not? I just nibbled his lip a little bit."

"You're not the only one."

Hayley stared at him sharply.

"What do you mean?"

Thiago paused. "I'm sorry. I should not have said anything. I did not think you cared at this point."

"I have nothing else to care about," she said. "So, tell me. Who nibbled his fucking lip?"

"Who else is pretty in this place?"

"Man, he really is Valentino."

Thiago laughed. "It's always the unsuspecting ones."

She scanned the beach and finally spotted Pritesh, flipping a Frisbee with Khassan.

"The bitch is writing her story, I think. Or maybe she even went to stalk Ricard."

"You think so?"

Hayley nodded. "She's a lawyer. Always playing all sides. I wonder if I still have a play. Find a way to get him over here."

"A way? I could just tell him you want to talk to him."

"That'll be very suave."

Thiago shook his head, got up, and left. Meanwhile, Andrea came back with the suntan lotion and began rubbing it on Hayley's back.

"You're a nurse, right? I think someone else can do that."

Soon Pritesh had wobbled over, his hands out.

"Thiago said you wanted something?"

"Yeah. Rub my back for me."

Andrea handed him the cream. He reluctantly took it.

"Are you serious?" he asked.

"I bite your lip; you get me bitten by a shark. Which is worse?"

"Fuck you," he said. He threw the sunscreen at her and marched away.

He went past Angela, who appeared uncomfortable, and Lisa noticed too.

"Guess that went well," Hayley said to Andrea.

Soon it was time for dinner. Ares drove Ricard via limo directly to the beach. When he arrived, Khassan asked Ricard for his thoughts on his brief prison term.

"Lots of good coffee, chocolate, wine, beach. And birdwatching especially. More warblers about there."

"Maybe relocate."

"Maybe."

"Did you do a lot of thinking?"

"Yeah. Some of that."

He noticed Cathy kind of hovering around, trying to approach him but hesitant.

"You can approach, my lady," Ricard said. "I don't bite. At least, I don't think I will."

As soon as she came up, he kissed her. She tried to push him away, but he stayed engaged, and soon it became a passionate smooch session.

Just then Nalini walked by.

She had memorized her story, she was all set, and now she tried to pretend what was in front of her wasn't happening. She had rejected him, right? She had won. So why did she feel so heated?

Pritesh, Rashan, and Olive were right behind her, with Hayley watching everything from her wheelchair as she and the others enjoyed the dinner at tables the staff had set up. The bonfire was not yet lit.

Dinner was a seafood extravaganza of fresh lobster, clams,

crabs, mussels, fish cakes, shellfish, octopus, fried cod, fish and chips, scallops, and endless sauces to go with them, including tartar, blue cheese, and lemon butter. They had shark fin soup, fried and scrambled blue shark with wild rice, and a steamed shark head. For the vegetarians and vegans, there was mock fish, including imitation shark fin soup and vegan crab cakes, and these sides: sweet potato fries, mashed potatoes, macaroni salad, and coleslaw.

Available were a wide range of light beers, including Summer Shandy and Blue Moon; a wide collection of ciders; sangria and margaritas; and other cocktails/mocktails. Desserts included key lime pie, yogurt parfait, mango ice cream, fruit salad, and orange sorbet.

"A fucking shark?" Hayley complained to Thiago. "You want to re-traumatize me or something?"

"It's meant to get you over your fright, my dear," Thiago insisted.

"Yeah, we all know how helpful you are," Nalini said to him. Thiago rolled his eyes and walked back to the spread.

"Ready to tell your story?" Hayley asked her.

"How'd you know I'm telling the story?"

"Maybe I can just read lips?"

Nalini looked towards Thiago. "I see somebody's been talking."

"Don't worry," Hayley continued. "Since the biker didn't work out, you can have Pritesh. I have a new perspective on life."

"I'll think about boys when I'm done with my story, thank you. Still retelling it in my head, hoping I don't fuck it up."

"Well, I'm curious about the shark head," Andrea said to redirect the conversation. "I've never eaten it, and I eat all kinds of meat."

Nick and Temple played soothing, light romantic music as everyone ate heartily after the rather light lunch, with the meat eaters and pescatarians opening the raw crabs, clams, mussels, and lobsters with pliers and hammers (getting help from others if they didn't know how), finding and devouring the meat where they could, dipping it into the sauces, and drinking their beers, sangria, and cocktails or, in Hayley's case, mocktails.

Cathy took Ricard's hand and led him to the newly created bonfire. Ares surprised Andrea and asked her to dance; meanwhile,

Maja and Zahra, Lisa and Rashan, and Angela and Sylvania got up and danced too in a mock-ballroom style.

Darnell watched Angela dancing; Taylor watched Darnell. Nalini tried to avoid Ricard and Cathy and to keep track of Pritesh. Pritesh watched Hayley. Hayley ignored him.

Olive, now wearing a striped, purple suit and yellow pants, the same outfit he wore during the first story, was back up to introduce Nalini.

~ Day Six ~
Introduction to Nalini's Story

"I'm happy to introduce our storyteller this evening, Ms. Nalini Shah, Esquire. Nalini is a litigator with a major law firm in New York City, where she represents major corporations and, occasionally, regular people through pro bono work. She's also a trained Bharatanatyam, Kathak, and Bollywood dancer and singer—she has performed Britney Spears, Katy Perry, Lady Gaga, and others. I was intrigued by this combination of skills and experiences. I thought she might tell an interesting story, so I took her on board. I was a little surprised that she didn't dominate our karaoke competition a few days before, but considering I haven't seen her all day, hopefully she used the time to practice a great story. I'm intrigued by what she will tell us today."

Everyone clapped as Nalini waved to the crowd. Ricard and Cathy were cuddling—she tried to ignore them.

"Thanks, everyone. As Olive mentioned, I'm a corporate litigator, so I focus on briefs and motions, but I also work on pro bono cases and have done some limited trial work as well. I might switch to public interest or defense because I'm a little tired of filing briefs and defending rich people, but it's not exactly a good time to switch, so who knows what I'll do. I did do some mock trials at Yale Law, so my story will have a trial aspect, but I'm going to try to steer clear of legal jargon and boring details.

"I'm originally from Fairfield County, Connecticut. That's where I quarantined during the lockdown, which you might have heard about since I got a raw deal when I got here. But otherwise, I didn't exactly have a difficult upbringing except for the tiger Asian parents. Yes, my parents came to this country with nothing, but my dad now works in finance; I went to Yale, and I work for one of the most respected law firms in the world. But recently, with everything going on, I've been reevaluating my life and trying to feel more sympathy for people who haven't had it as good as me, who've had to struggle like my parents did when they first got to this country, so that's what I'm going to try to convey in this story.

"I hope you'll enjoy it."

~ Day Six ~
Nalini's Story
(AKA "LOVE LIABILITY")

Introduction

The jury appeared stone-faced to Nisha as she took the stand, raised her hand, and swore an oath that she would tell the truth, the whole truth, and nothing but the truth.

Out of the corner of her eye she noticed one juror, an older, Black man, wipe away a tear with a handkerchief. It was red and embroidered with the images of small cherry blossoms that reminded her of so much.

"I understand," she thought he was saying. Someone, at least, was listening.

Apparently, he had been moved by the testimony of the prior witness, a forensic pathologist who had described in detail Nisha's injuries and those of her assailants. That was good because overall, the forensic evidence was scant. Most trials rose and fell based on the science, but her case hinged on her word against those of her rapists. That and the testimony of her boyfriend, Peter, whom she pictured sitting in the audience.

But he was not actually there. Instead, her father sat in the spot where she focused; the lead prosecutor taught her to concentrate on someone she loved to keep herself calm. The problem was that her father was stone-faced too. That was just his way—the stern Indian man, outwardly serious but inwardly compassionate, worried about his little girl being sucked into the world of the "working white wackos" as he called them.

Peter was at an undisclosed location somewhere in Fairfield; the prosecutors and Peter's attorney had strongly discouraged him from being there when he wasn't testifying so he wouldn't be triggered by his smug former friends sitting at the defendant's table.

Peter had already testified for an entire day about what had happened from his perspective. He had become infuriated on cross. Using his anger, the defense had reserved their right to call him again as their own witness, a hostile one, to support their theory of the case.

This was unusual, as normally all questions would be asked at one time, but Peter's hostility had persuaded the judge to potentially allow it.

Whether he testified again or not, Peter had told Nisha that, on the day of the verdict, guilty or not guilty, parents or no parents, he would pick her up outside the Bridgeport courtroom on his motorcycle, and they could finally drive west, all the way out to Colorado, or Oregon, or California, living free again.

Nisha's World

Breaking from the trial, let me bring you into Nisha's world because you cannot understand this case unless you understand her.

She is only 19 years old, and the experience of the last year has changed her immeasurably. She's grown into a woman faster than anyone should have to because of trauma, but that pain has also solidified a love that is, arguably, the only thing worth living for, more important than trials or briefs.

She dared to spread her wings outside of the life laid out for her, and for that she has paid a hefty price but also garnered an enormous reward.

Picture a world of privilege—a large house with high ceilings, a massive yard mowed and manicured by hired hands, and a deck for summer parties or daily relaxing. Imagine an idyllic setting in suburban Connecticut, a community where Nisha grew up. The worst thing she ever had to endure was a group of girls deciding to be mean to her in junior high school because she was a little overweight.

But she lived in that world. She felt those micro aggressions. Those slights hurt, and she resolved to change herself. In high school she started running track and lost weight; she got more involved in the local Indian community, learned traditional Hindu dances mixed with contemporary rhythms, and performed at weddings and other gatherings. She also started planning and practicing dances based on popular songs by Katy Perry and Kelley Clarkson; all the while, she did well in school.

Her parents wanted their daughter to build on their American dream, to become a doctor or marry a doctor, and to own a house bigger than theirs. They had built this fairy tale world for their daughter on purpose. They had achieved the American dream in less than a generation, so of course, they expected her to fulfill her part, and she intensely felt that burden.

But when she looked out into the world, she was curious about its possibilities. Before her was a summer of daring and transition before the cage of college.

She had already been accepted to Yale; she had already visited; she had already received an old-fashioned letter (yes, a letter!) from her prospective roommate, who lived somewhere in Illinois. And every day that summer, she drove out to the local hospital where she was volunteering at the behest of her cardiologist father.

Normally, the roads were empty; only the occasional car passed. She knew the meandering pathways; she felt as one with the dense woods.

She loved nature. She enjoyed school field trips, science experiments, and exploring ponds and marshes. Secretly she dreamed of being a scientist. She had begun a Regeneron Science Talent Search project before regretfully abandoning it because her college applications and AP classes took up too much time.

And like all young women, she fantasized about her prince, the one who would sweep her off her feet into a life of freedom where she wasn't just another peg in someone else's dream. Returning from the hospital in the late afternoon, she would stand in the path leading from her house to the road, daydreaming about the handsome, tall, rugged yet wealthy man who would take her on adventures all day, make love to her all night, and make sure she didn't have to work again. Sure, she had her interests and ambitions, but let's face it, every woman has that fantasy, and Nisha would indulge in the full range as she peered out at that mostly barren road.

One afternoon, she was doing just that when she heard an unfamiliar noise. It wasn't actually unfamiliar because, in fact, many motorcycles, even gangs of motorcyclists, had driven by before, but she had never actually seen them, just looked past them. So, when the engine roared, she didn't pay much attention until she heard the skid; then she saw the motorcycle flip and the body fly onto the road.

Shocked, she put her hand to her mouth; she wasn't sure whether to run forward or backwards, but she was propelled ahead when she saw his blond mane of hair, his thick motorcycle jacket, ripped denim pants, and the skid of blood mixed with broken glass and debris on the pavement leading from the motorcycle that lay on the double-yellow divider. She hoped the blood came from his knee or his leg, not his head or his heart.

She rushed back to the house to call her father. He was the most reliable man in her life, the most helpful man she had ever known. He was busy fidgeting with his calculator as he analyzed data on his computer, hard at work as usual with a wisp of curiosity as always.

As soon as she rushed in, he was up at once, ran to the road, took the man's pulse, and began examining vital signs and injuries. Meanwhile he told Nisha to call 911, which she did on her cellphone.

The man had appeared unconscious, but under the care of her father, he seemed to come to. Faintly, he asked where he was. Her father told him to relax and stay calm: his vital signs were stable, and he didn't need CPR. He had likely suffered a concussion. The blood was from a scraped knee.

The ambulance would likely arrive soon; in the meantime, her father returned to the house to get materials to tend to the wound. He didn't want to risk moving him, so he asked Nisha to watch traffic and to talk to him so he would stay awake.

Nisha talked to him. She asked him what his name was (Peter), where he lived (Oxford, Ansonia), how he felt (bad, he said), and whether anyone knew he was there (his biker bros). Nisha assured him help was on the way. She stroked his hair.

A car came up; she ran to the car and asked the driver to go around; the lady pulled down her window and asked if she could do anything. Was he okay? By this time her father came rushing back with the materials, and then they could hear the sirens in the distance. Nisha knew they would take care of him.

Nisha's Testimony

Back at the trial, Nisha was being guided through her testimony by the prosecutor based on their pre-practiced dialogue. He was asking her how she got involved with the biker gang called "The Duplexers."

Nisha's Testimony:

Nisha
After he got out of the hospital, Peter came to my house
to give me flowers. They rode with him.
Maybe they were passing anyway; I'm not sure.

Prosecutor
Peter, who is now your boyfriend?

Nisha
Yes, it was very sweet. It was only a week after the accident.
They were tulips and daffodils.

Prosecutor
Did he knock on your door? Where were your parents?

Nisha
No, I was outside. I usually came home around that time
and watched the road just to relax.
That's how I had seen Peter when he crashed.

Prosecutor
How did he know that?

Nisha (laughing, shrugging)
He didn't. I guess we were connected from the beginning.

Prosecutor
You're saying it was true love from the beginning?

Nisha
Absolutely. From the moment he crashed in front of
my house, I knew he was the one.

Prosecutor
How did his friends react to him giving you flowers?

Nisha
A few were staring. I felt a little uncomfortable, but I was
focused on Peter. Later, when I got to know them better,
I realized they did have a problem with it.

Prosecutor
Did they, or he, say anything to reveal why
they had a problem with it?

Nisha
Yes. Peter told me himself that they didn't like "suits"
and didn't generally associate with them.

Prosecutor
Suits?

Nisha
They mean anyone who isn't of their class.

Prosecutor
Meaning the working class?

Nisha
Anyone with a professional or managerial job.
Anyone who didn't embrace freedom or their lifestyle.

Prosecutor
I see. Do you think your race had anything to do with it?

Nisha
I didn't at first. But later, I was having a conversation with one of
them, and he mentioned that it was too bad I wasn't pure because
the Dravidians mixed with the Aryans thousands of years ago.

Prosecutor
What did you take that to mean?

Nisha
That they were white supremacists and didn't like
that a person of color was dating one of their own.

Prosecutor
Was the individual who made that comment
one of the defendants who attempted to rape you?

Nisha (pointing to one of the defendants)
Yes, it was Clarence. Lymey is his nickname
because he's originally from Lyme, CT.

Prosecutor
I see. And all the Duplexers were white?

Nisha
Yes.

Prosecutor
Did any of the defendants make other disparaging
comments about people of color?

Nisha
Yes. Nellie and Stoney (pointing) once said Black people
in Bridgeport and New Haven were almost
as bad as the suits because they chose to be subjugated.
And they made a racial epithet that I won't repeat.

Prosecutor
Please, I know it makes you uncomfortable,
but can you tell us what it was for the record?

Nisha
They called them "coons."

*Prosecutor (shaking his head and looking at the jury,
as they took notes; some also shook their heads)*
I see. Any other controversial racial statements?

Nisha
Anti-semitic stuff. About how they rule the world and all that.
And just conspiracy stuff in general.

Prosecutor
Now let's go to the attempted rape itself. Can you describe
the exact details surrounding it, in your own words?

Nisha
Yes. I had started living with Peter at his house near Oxford. It's up a rural road near Kettletown State Park. We lived in the basement of his mom's home, and we were very happy living there. His mom was happy too, and we thought we would get married soon. Occasionally we would go to the Duplexer club to hang out. It's closer to Ansonia, but still in a rural area near Route 334. The other men would bring their girls, and I was expected to hang out with them while Peter and his friends had their meeting in the den of the main lodge. We girls would be in the kitchen and dining area, kind of typical. They were a, let's say, rougher crew than I was used to, and they mainly liked heavy metal, but we did have some things in common. For example, they got me interested in sewing. They were mostly older, though, and a few seemed protective of Peter and were concerned that I might try to take their men, so I was mainly comfortable when I was with Peter.

Prosecutor
I'm sorry to interrupt, but can you describe who seemed to be jealous and/or protective?

Nisha
It was mainly Vicki, Terri, and Tammy.

Prosecutor
For the record, these women were the significant others of the defendants accused of attempted rape?

Nisha
Yes.

Prosecutor
Thank you. Please continue.

Nisha
After the meeting we would hang out together in

the den and garage, and even outside for a barbecue,
so sometimes I would speak to the guys.
And that's where I heard them say some of those things.

Narrator:
Nisha continued to describe the details of her life with Peter and the Duplexers, but I won't get into the specifics of every aspect of her life so as not to bore you. I'm going to move on to where she describes the actual incident.

Prosecutor
Please take us to the day of the attempted rape.

Nisha
Peter told me he had gotten a job at Shop Rite in Milford. He was working a sixteen-hour shift, including the overnight shift, because one of his coworkers was at the hospital as his wife was having a baby.

Prosecutor
Did you know that Peter previously testified that before his shift,
he was meeting with the leader of the Duplexers,
Claude, to solidify a drug sale to another biker gang?

Nisha
No. I didn't know anything about the drugs.
I didn't know they did anything illegal.

Prosecutor
So what happened that night, before the attempted rape?

Nisha
Vicki, Lymey's wife, called me at Peter's mother's house and said
the ladies were having a backgammon night at the club and that

they were inviting me because they knew Peter had the long shift.
They said someone would pick me up and drive me.

Prosecutor
And you agreed?

Nisha
I was hesitant, but she seemed to really want me to come,
and it was true, I didn't have much to do without Peter.
His mother was visiting a friend.

Prosecutor
Did you tell Peter?

Nisha
I texted him, yes. But he didn't respond right away.
Which was odd, but I guess he was busy.

Prosecutor
Who picked you up?

Nisha
It was Lymey.

Prosecutor
How did he seem?

Nisha
Nice. Unusually so, I guess.

Prosecutor
And he drove you to the club?

Nisha
No. At first it seemed like he was going that way,
but then he diverted into a side road.

Bad Americans: Part I

Prosecutor
Did you question him about it?

Nisha
Not at first, but we were really in the middle of nowhere, no
streetlights or anything, so I started to get nervous. I asked him if
we were on the right road, and he said that we were taking a side
road because of construction. That didn't make much
sense to me because even the road to the club was rural,
but I wanted to believe him. Maybe five minutes later,
I saw a couple of motorcycle lights, and as we got closer,
a couple of men in front. (Nisha wiped away some tears.)

Prosecutor
Please, when you're ready.

Nisha
When we stopped, I asked Lymey what was happening.
I could recognize Nellie and Stoney now. They rushed
towards me, grabbed me, and pulled me off the bike.
Lymey got off the bike. The two were holding me,
each clutching one of my arms. They were holding them tight.
I said it hurt; what did they want? I was crying. I was scared.

Prosecutor
And then?

Nisha
Lymey came up to me slowly, with this smirk on his face.
I'll never forget it. I could only see it partially because of the
darkness, but I could see it in the motorcycle lights.
He grabbed me suddenly by the top of my hair. He said,
"We're going to teach you not to mess with us."

Prosecutor
Did you know what he meant?

Nisha
No. I had no idea. I was shocked. I said, "What do you mean?
What are you talking about?" Or something like that.

Prosecutor
And what did he say?

Nisha
He said I had influenced Peter to betray them. I can't remember
how he said it, but he said something like that.

Prosecutor
Are you aware that Peter has already testified that these three were
unhappy and that Claude had favored him over them to make
the drug deal since they were senior to him in the gang?

[The Defense objected, claiming the Prosecution was testifying, and
the judge sustained the objection.]

Prosecutor
What else did he say?

Nisha
He said that Peter had become "uppity" since he had started
dating a "suit" and that they were going to "gang me proper"
to show me my place and that I should never
try to influence him again or they'd kill me.

Prosecutor
And you still had no idea what they were talking about?

Nisha
No.

Prosecutor
What next?

Nisha
Lymey started to tear off my clothes.

Prosecutor
I'm sorry, can you be specific for the jury?

Nisha
He ripped off my tank top and tore off my bra.
Then he started fondling my breasts.

[The prosecutor paused and looked at the jury. After a few seconds, he continued.]

Prosecutor
And then?

Nisha
He started to pull off my pants too. But while he did that, I kneed him in his balls, and when he jumped back, I kicked him in his face.

Prosecutor
Have you always been that brave?

Nisha
I didn't think about it: I just reacted. I used to dance,
so thankfully I have strong legs.

Prosecutor
What happened then?

Nisha

I guess one of them, Stoney I think, was shocked, so he let go of my arm. I took the opportunity to bite the other one's arm. He screamed and let go too, and I ran into the woods.

Prosecutor

Do you consider yourself lucky?

Nisha

Yes, very lucky.

Prosecutor

And then?

Nisha

I kept running. I didn't look back. I knew that if I did, they could catch me. I couldn't see anything, so once I ran straight into a tree. That knocked me back, but I got up quickly and kept moving. I could hear noises behind me. I think I was lucky I didn't have any light, so they couldn't find me.

Prosecutor

How long did you run?

Nisha

I'm not sure. I had no idea where I was; I couldn't see anything, so I ran for a while. When I was tired of running, I stopped.

Prosecutor

And then?

Nisha

I was shivering; I was shocked. It was the end of summer, so thankfully it wasn't really cold, but it was creepy. I lay down for

a bit, not moving for about who knows how long, waiting to hear
any voices or see any lights. But I didn't. So, I finally got up. My
cell phone, keys, everything had been in my purse, which I had left
attached to Lymey's motorcycle. So, I had nothing, no flashlight, no
time, no way to communicate, and I was naked from the waist up.

Prosecutor
Can you please describe your time in the forest
and what happened after?

Nisha
I was terrified of being caught by the Duplexers or being eaten by
some predator, so feeling around in the dark, I was able to rip out
some plants, weeds, and grass, and I covered myself with them
and tried to sleep. I might have slept a bit, but I'm not sure.
It was this weird middle road between sleeping and waking.
I had some terrifying dreams that I can't remember. Anyway,
after a while it became light. I listened for sounds, for people.
I figured they might still be looking for me. I lay like that for what
seemed like hours, but I don't know how long it was. Finally,
I got up and started wandering in the woods,
looking for a road where I could stop somebody.

Prosecutor
And did you find this road?

Nisha
No. I kept walking, but I didn't know where I was, so I couldn't
orient myself. I could tell what approximate time of the day
it was by the sun's position, but it was also cloudy sometimes,
so I lost that too. Directionally, I could tell west and east
because of the sun's rising and setting positions, but again,
I didn't have a starting point, and sometimes there was no sun,
so I was cautious. I certainly didn't want to go back
to the place where I was, either, that's for sure. One

time I heard footsteps, so I ducked behind a tree and hid.
It turned out to be a deer. I laughed to myself,
I remember. It was so absurd.

Prosecutor
Any other animal encounters?

Nisha
I was afraid of bears, but thankfully, I didn't see any the first day.
Other than a road, I was looking for a lake, or trail, or something.
But I didn't want to move too much. And I know it isn't a very wide
area of forest, but I didn't see anything or anyone that day.

Prosecutor
Did you get hungry? What did you eat?

Nisha
Midday I started getting hungry but ignored it until around late
afternoon. When I would pass plants with berries of any type, I
would pick and eat them. I avoided chokeberries
and holly berries because I had learned they're poisonous.
Mainly I ate mulberries and elderberries.

Prosecutor
Do you think your knowledge of nature saved your life?

Nisha
I don't know about that. But I didn't know when I would find
somebody, so it was essential for me to keep up my energy.
I had no water, but I had to keep going.

Prosecutor
Then what?

Nisha

When the sun started setting, I picked a tree, made a blanket of
leaves, plants, weeds, and grass, and slept under it again.

Prosecutor

And you were okay?

Nisha

I woke in the very early morning. I kept going.

Prosecutor

Did you see anybody the second day?

Nisha

First, I came across a lake. It was a small lake and not something
touristy. But that's where I saw a bear. I was afraid,
but I was far enough away that he didn't sense me.
I took my chances and bent down for a drink of water.
Carefully walking away from the bear,
I ran into a trail that led me to a house.

Prosecutor

Was anyone home?

Nisha

Yes. I climbed up the steps and knocked on the door hard. A young
man answered. I covered my breasts with my hands. I was crying
and describing what had happened to me. He looked shocked, then
called back to someone. An older man came out. He gestured for
me to come in and had me sit in the kitchen. Then they both left.

Prosecutor

They left?

Nisha
Yes. They said they were calling the police.

Prosecutor
And did they?

Nisha
I thought they were. I finally felt safe. But then suddenly
I saw the younger man run at me with a pair of handcuffs.

Prosecutor
Oh my. How did you react?

Nisha
I struggled with him. He got one handcuff on, but I was able
to elbow him in the face and run out the door, screaming.

Prosecutor
And what happened?

Nisha
I got down the stairs and started running towards the woods,
but the older man appeared and started chasing me.
He was on his cell phone.

Prosecutor
And are those two in the courtroom today?

Nisha (pointing to two more defendants)
Yes, it is those two.

Prosecutor
Going back to the chase, did the older man grab you?

Nisha
He was about to, but then I heard a familiar voice.

Prosecutor
Who was it?

Nisha
I turned around and it was Peter. I couldn't believe it.

Prosecutor
He saved you?

Nisha
Yes. He had a gun in his hand. He told the older man he would
shoot him if he laid a hand on me. I ran into his arms.
He hugged me, and then we backed up to his motorcycle.
He put his jacket on me, and he drove me to the hospital.

Prosecutor
Were you shocked?

Nisha
Yes. It was a miracle.

Prosecutor
Do you know how or why he was there?

Nisha
He told me that the two men from the house, Kyle and Larry,
were inactive members of the Duplexers. When Peter
found out I was missing, he decided to search for me.
Terri had given him a tip that I might be in the woods,
so he had gone to their home since they lived near the woods.
He didn't know Lymey and the others kidnapped me
until I told him on the ride to the hospital. Later I learned

that Kyle and Larry informed Lymey that I was there
and tried to keep me in the house until they could get rid
of Peter.I guess they planned to take me away and finish the job.

[The Defense objected that this was speculation, which the Judge sustained and informed the jury not to consider it.]

There is a bit more to this testimony, but let's fast forward and give you some more juicy details. The Prosecutor asked Nisha to identify all six defendants again, who were facing various charges from attempted rape and kidnapping to aiding and abetting these crimes, namely the three bikers, the father and son who tried to assist them, and Vicki, Lymey's wife.

The jury saw them clearly, Nisha thought, but who knows? Now it was the Defense's turn to cross-examine her, but it was late, so they adjourned for the day.

Adjournment

The Prosecutor had warned Nisha that the Defense had a completely different theory of the case: on cross, they would attack her character and allege that she made up the rape to make herself into a celebrity since she had lost her social status when she had started living with Peter.

She was willing and ready to face it, as long as Peter remained in her life, which he did, at least via text and phone. In fact, that night, they spoke to each other, and he comforted her after her difficult testimony.

After taking her to the hospital that day, Peter had called the police and made a deal with both Federal and State prosecutors for his testimony to avoid drug charges on both levels.

In addition to Nisha's trial, Peter agreed to testify against Claude, some of his associates and members of the other gang who were facing federal drug trafficking charges in a separate, concurrent trial at the U.S. District Courthouse only a few blocks away. He was set to give testimony there in a few days. They had moved the State trial to Bridgeport, also, because they wanted a neutral territory, as well as some jurors who were people of color, and for convenience.

Since the Duplexers could try to silence him, Peter and his mother had been moved to a secret location in Fairfield County. Nisha lived with her parents again in their house in Fairfield County, with a police presence to deter a revenge plot. But the Defense would apparently use even that move to discredit them, saying that they made this all up for their own benefit.

The next morning, the trial was delayed when the Defense made a motion, and both parties went into the judge's chambers. When the lead Prosecutor emerged, he appeared distraught and took Nisha into a room along with a female ADA.

"Do you know someone named Fipp in Colorado?" he asked.

"I don't know anyone in Colorado," she said.

"Defense presented new discovery to bolster their theory of the case," he said. "Usually, the judge wouldn't allow that at this late date, but the Defense says the evidence was already there in Peter's texts on his phone, which they subpoenaed earlier to review his communication with you and the other Duplexers. Their attorney says they just put together the pieces while reviewing it yesterday. We'll have to review it again. Apparently this Fipp was a former member of the Duplexers who was banned by Claude and moved to Colorado. Based on the texts, the Defense is alleging that he may be the reason Peter betrayed Claude and that you were in on that."

"I don't know who that is," she said.

"Okay. I asked for a continuance, but the Judge wouldn't grant it since we already have the evidence, and the Defense says it doesn't plan to call Fipp or any new witnesses. He says we can redirect if we want. I'll have the ADA review the texts now. Just answer as best as you can. I'm here to object if necessary."

"I still do what we practiced?" she asked.

"Yes. Do the best you can."

Nisha was frazzled by this development, but the clerk came in, and they had to enter the courtroom again. I won't go into the entire testimony. It's not like *Law & Order* or *Matlock* or something where these things are quick. Testimony can last hours, especially if it is a crucial witness. But like those TV shows, I'm going to give you a quickie, pint-sized version of the question-and-answer dance.

~ Nisha's Testimony ~
Cross Examined by the Defense

Defense
Let's go back to the period when you first met Peter, so we
can get some context for the situation surrounding these
allegations. You say you started living with Peter and his mother at
his home outside Oxford that summer. What caused you to
leave your parents' home in Westport to live with Peter?

Nisha
I wanted to be with Peter. I love him.

Defense
And your parents were okay with this?

Nisha (shrugging)
Not really.

Defense
I wouldn't think so. Am I correct that, not only were you
volunteering at a local hospital in Fairfield when you met Peter,
but you were also slated to attend Yale that fall as a freshman?

Nisha
Yes.

Defense
And that you were then only 18 years old?

Nisha
Yes.

Defense
And your parents didn't mind that you were living with a 26-year-old man, a biker in a motorcycle club no less?

Nisha
I told you they did.

Defense
What did they do about this?

Nisha
They couldn't do much. I'm an adult.

Defense
Isn't it true that you quit volunteering and weren't going to attend Yale in the fall after you decided to move in with Peter?

Nisha
I did quit my volunteer job. I was still deciding about Yale.

Defense
Were your parents still going to pay your tuition?

Nisha (trying to avoid looking at her father)
If I decided to go, yes.

Defense
But not if you kept living with and seeing Peter, is that right?

Nisha (after a pause)
Yes.

Defense
So essentially, you were choosing your relationship
with Peter over your parents' wishes that you attend Yale.

Nisha
I guess.

Defense
How long after you met Peter did you decide to move in with him?

Nisha
Two weeks.

Defense
Two weeks? That's fast.

[The Prosecution objected that the Defense was testifying. The judge
sustained the objection and struck the remark.]

Defense
I apologize, Your Honor. Can you characterize your
relationship during this two-week period after Peter
gave you those lovely tulips and daffodils?

Nisha (shrugging)
Characterize?

Defense
Isn't it true that you started cutting your shifts at your volunteer
job to spend time with Peter and his Duplexer friends?
Isn't it also true that your father caught you in bed with Peter,
at your house, and that led to him kicking you out?

Nisha
No.

Defense
I can call your father to testify, miss.

Nisha
I mean the last part is not true. He didn't kick me out. He grounded
me. But I told him I was 18 and he couldn't control what I did or
who I loved. So, I snuck out one day and started living with Peter.

Defense
And your parents didn't report you missing?

Nisha
I texted my father and told him. Then both my parents
called me. They were angry. I think they went to the
police, and yes, the police visited Peter's house,
but I told them I was there of my own volition.

Defense
I see. Isn't it true then that you were more involved
with the Duplexers from the beginning of your
relationship with Peter than you let on?

Nisha
More involved? No. I hung out with Peter, and if he
happened to be around his friends, then I was too.

Defense
Here's what I'm trying to clarify: if what you claim is true,
that his friends were angry that you had turned Peter
against them or had made him "uppity" or something,
to the extent that he had moved ahead in the gang
above them, allegedly, why would they think that?

343

Nisha
I don't know. Maybe they just hate women, or Indians,
or rich people, or want somebody to blame.

Defense
So you didn't influence Peter at all in his dealings with the gang?

Nisha
No.

Defense
I see. Tell me, you say you were uncomfortable at times
hanging out at the clubhouse, and among the wives and the bikers
themselves—that they were racists and misogynists, and apparently
potential rapists—yet you hung out with them regularly
and from the beginning of your relationship with Peter. In fact,
within two weeks of meeting Peter, you had given up your family,
your volunteer work, and your future at one of the world's best
universities to live with a poor biker working at Shop Rite
and involved with an allegedly drug-dealing motorcycle gang.

Nisha
I told you; I love him. You can't control love; it just happens.

Defense
Isn't it true that you were attracted not only to Peter but to the
outlaw style that the bikers represented, and that you were, in fact,
more involved in the club and in motivating Peter than you claim?

Nisha
No.

Defense
Are you attending Yale now?

Nisha
I decided to postpone my enrollment for a year.
While I figure things out.

Defense
So you can be with Peter after the trial is over?

Nisha
Yes. But that doesn't mean I won't attend Yale.
My parents are more open to Peter now.

Defense
Are they? So, they will pay your tuition if
you decide to stay with him?

Nisha
They haven't said they won't.

Defense
Isn't it true that you have no intention of attending Yale?
That you intend to live with Peter again and perhaps
travel out of state once the trial is over?

[The Prosecution objected to the relevance. The Defense insisted it supported their theory of the case. The Judge accepted this explanation and gave the Defense some leeway.]

Nisha
It's possible.

Defense
Possible. Let's shift to your relationship with the defendants and,
more specifically, the significant others of some of the defendants.
Did you not tell Tammy Love, girlfriend of Stoney,
that you thought Peter was getting "gypped," as you said,

by Lymey and Nelly in the hierarchy of the gang,
and that Peter did so much more for Claude than they did?

Nisha
I don't remember saying that.

Defense
She'll testify to it.

Nisha
Then she can. She would be lying.

Defense
Do you know a Phillip Fippinger, aka Fipp,
who lives out in Colorado?

Nisha
No. Why would I?

Defense
Isn't it true that you and Peter plan to move to Colorado after the
trial is over to live with Fipp and his Duplexer outfit there,
where Peter will have a more senior role in their operation
and get rewarded handsomely for his loyalty to Fipp?

Nisha
I don't know what you're talking about.

Defense
I'm talking about your plot with Peter to frame my clients for this
bogus attempted rape accusation, so you and your boyfriend can
lead the life you want with a silver cushion in Colorado.

Nisha
This is crazy.

[The Prosecution objected that the Defense was testifying again and should produce some evidence to support its theory.]

Defense
We plan to recall Peter to ask him about his relationship with Fipp, which is supported by some of his text messages, and about the timing of his deal with Federal and State authorities.

[The Judge sustained the objection and reminded the Defense to ask questions, not make statements. But he allowed the line of questioning to continue.]

Defense
Isn't it true that Peter told you he had a close relationship with a man named Fipp who was pushed out of the gang by Claude with help of the defendants and who later moved to Colorado with his loyalists but who wanted to frame Claude and the defendants for crimes in return for a monetary and loyalty reward?

Nisha
No.

Defense
And that this aspect of the frame was expected to work because an upper-class Indian girl from Fairfield County, possibly headed to a top university, would be believed while a bunch of rugged bikers would not?

Nisha (screamed)
No. I'm telling the truth!

[Nisha began crying. The Prosecutor asked for a continuance, but the Defense said it was done with its examination of this witness for now, though it reserved the right to redirect if the Prosecution did the same.]

[The Prosecutor then asked for adjournment until the next day to reassess the evidence and decide whether a redirect was necessary. This time, the Judge did grant it and ended the day's proceedings.]

Another Adjournment

The Prosecutor asked Nisha's father to wait outside for her and then took her back into the private room.

"Are you okay?" he asked.

"Yes," she said, shrugging.

"The ADA is still examining the texts. This Judge is a dick: he should allow us more time to prepare, but whatever, I'll have to talk to Peter. Looks like the Feds might know more than they're letting on, too, if there's any truth to this. Is there anything else you're not telling me?"

"No, I swear. They tried to rape me; I don't know anything else!"

"Okay," the Prosecutor said, tapping her on her back lightly, careful not to touch her too much. "Let it go. Your testimony is done for now, so relax."

She thought her father would grill her about these new revelations, but he didn't say anything on their drive back home. As they pulled in, she saw the police escort in the corner of the driveway, only feet from the spot where Peter had fallen many months before.

Once inside her room, she called Peter. He didn't respond, so she texted that he should call her, before remembering that their texts might be monitored.

An hour later, after frantic worry and tears, he finally did return her call, and she told him about the Defense's questions.

"Let's meet," he said. "I've been dying to see you anyway."

"How? The cops are here. And my parents won't let me go anywhere."

"Sneak out the back. Like the time when your dad caught us. I'll be there, and we'll go somewhere."

She remembered the time her father had caught her and Peter

making love in her bedroom. Her parents were supposed to have been at a friend's house for a family friend's pre-bridal ceremony, the Ganesh Pooja, where only her parents were invited. Nisha was expected at the mehndi ceremony and the Garba the next day, as well as at the wedding and reception the day after.

In her bedroom, she showed Peter the ornate Panjabis and Saris she would be wearing and described some of the wedding events as they sat on the bed. He admitted they were beautiful; he regretted not being born into such a sophisticated culture.

She gave him all the right signs, but he still sat there, bent over, looking shy and unsure. The saris on the bed, the giggling, the direct look of desire—these hints he didn't understand. Boys were so dumb. She had to put her hands on his—thankfully, pre-mehndi—before he finally acquired the courage to look her in the eyes and kiss her.

One thing led to another, and they became one. What she hadn't counted on was her father forgetting his cell phone and coming back to the house. Of course, he saw Peter's motorcycle. He went upstairs to explore. He opened the door and witnessed their lovemaking. He closed the door immediately, shocked. When he opened it again, Peter was struggling to put on his clothes, and Nisha was still under the covers, screaming for her father to leave.

He didn't leave. He threatened to strike Peter, then to call the police. He did neither; Peter fled, forgetting his jacket in the process. Nisha returned it to him when she snuck out that night to meet him in the far corner of the property. He picked her up, and they fled to his mother's house, where she lived for the next few weeks until the fateful episode.

She missed the wedding ceremonies; she never again wore Indian clothes. The first week, she borrowed Peter's mom's clothes; then Peter's paycheck paid for a chic biker outfit from an Ansonia shop. She got used to the biker world, but that was nothing new for her: she had never felt totally comfortable in her former life either, even as she danced and wore bhindis and got great grades and did everything a good Indian American girl was expected to do. But she loved Peter just as she loved her parents, so she tried her best.

Now she was back in her room, and her parents were confronting her again. Déjà vu from the emergency meeting they had the day she was caught when they grounded her for weeks and forbade her from seeing Peter. She couldn't even volunteer anymore, they said. Yale was the main thing: she would meet better people there.

Dr. Vivek and Aarti Patel were parents extraordinaire, whom she loved to the moon and back but also loathed for controlling her life without end, for trying to direct it into the perfect Indian American chronicle, minus the medical school education.

Her mother started, as always: "Nisha, what is this about you running away to Colorado with that Peter? I thought you were going to attend Yale like we talked about."

Nisha: "I was just interrogated about the attempted rape, and now you're interrogating me again?"

Mummy: "We want to make sure you do not run away again, that you do not ruin your life with that drug dealer. We are your parents; don't you understand?"

Nisha: "I thought you were open to me being with Peter. That I would decide about Yale?"

Mummy: "When did we say that? We thought you would take a year off because of what happened. And then you would regroup after the trial was over and attend Yale."

Nisha: "So you're banning me from seeing Peter? Again?"

Pappa. "Beti, please. Don't you understand what kind of people these are? After all this, you still don't understand? What we've worked so hard to give you—this amazing American life. What you've worked so hard for, to get into the best school in the world? And you're going to throw it away for this criminal gora?"

Nisha: "I knew you weren't on my side."

Pappa: "Did you know anything about this Colorado man?"

Nisha: "Of course not. And it's probably not true. Why don't you give Peter a chance? Let me see him and he'll explain everything. Yes, I'm actually asking you this time."

Pappa: "Absolutely not, Beti. Stay away from him until the trial is over. Don't you know that a defense lawyer could use that against you, against him? Don't you see what they've already done? Live your life right, Beti..."

It went on like this for a while, as you can imagine. But Nisha stood her ground, and she was determined to see Peter as she had planned. So, she did sneak out late that night and met him in the same spot. After a few miles he stopped on the side of the road and they made wild love in the pitch dark, tasting and biting each other like it was their last time.

Then they headed to an all-night diner where they each had a black coffee because it was simple and pure like their love.

"Is it true?" she asked.

"I don't exactly have prospects, working at Shop Rite in Milford."

"So it is true."

"I wasn't born with a silver spoon in my mouth. With two parents in a great culture."

"I know."

"If you want to stay with your parents, I'll stay with you until they accept me. But if you want to move to Colorado, Fipp's going to give us a big reward and a good position in the club."

"Are you still going to sell drugs?"

"No way. He's got a better outfit: a restaurant, a bar, and a few stores selling motorcycle shit. It's all on the up-and-up—not suity, but real. That's why I worked with the Feds to bring Claude down. They pushed Fipp out; they were ruining the ideals of the Duplexers. This was for our benefit."

"Not for mine."

"That's not true, baby," Peter said, putting his hand over hers. "I had no idea Lymey and them were going to do that to you—as soon as I found out you were missing, I rushed to find you. So lucky I was in the right place at the right time. I wish I could've gotten justice myself, but that wouldn't work in our favor. Now we're going to put away those bastards for good."

"And go to a better place?"

"I don't want to take you away from your parents. You know I never wanted that."

"Yeah, but I did."

She leaned across the table, and they kissed. Then again outside, they kissed more. And Peter dropped her back home right before the sun rose; she crept upstairs and lay in her bed like she had never left.

Peter's Testimony

The next day, the Prosecution decided not to redirect on Nisha and rested. The Defense recalled Peter as a hostile witness. Peter's attorney had already spoken to the State Prosecutor and the Feds the day before. They had agreed he would testify regarding the texts and Fipp and still be covered by the plea deal, so he wouldn't have to take the Fifth Amendment.

Defense
Can you describe how you became an informant for the DEA and decided to frame Claude for the drug deal with the Axios gang?

Peter
He committed the act. So, he wasn't framed.

[A couple of Duplexers jeered from the audience, but the Judge quieted them and warned that further disruptions would result in their removal from court.]

Defense
In any case, how did you first encounter the DEA?

Peter
Two agents approached me in the Shop Rite parking lot as I left work one day. They identified themselves with badges. They drove

me to an office and showed me pictures. They said if I
didn't help them finger Claude, I'd be the one behind bars.

Defense
Did you wear a wire to the meeting with Axios?

Peter
No, they check for wires. I told them the meeting spot,
and the DEA put cameras and a recorder in the back room
of the bar. Sometimes we'd change up the spot at
the last minute, so it was a risk, but this time we didn't.

Defense
And you knew the spot because Claude had appointed you as his
right-hand man recently, over veterans like Lymey?

Peter
Yes. He trusted me, and he thought I was smart.

[The Prosecutor objected that this line of questioning was irrelevant
to this case. The Defense promised to tie it into their theory of the
case. The Judge said he would allow some leeway.]

Defense
How did it feel to betray that trust?

Peter
Not good. I wouldn't have snitched if I didn't have to.

Defense
Yet you've made a concurrent deal with the State
prosecutor over this case to avoid State drug charges
in return for your testimony against five other comrades.

Peter
I don't want to go to jail.

Defense
You won't have to now.

[The Prosecutor objected that the Defense was testifying. The Judge sustained the objection and struck the remark.]

Defense
Do you know Phillip Fippinger, aka Fipp?

Peter
Yes

Defense
Are you in touch with him?

Peter
From time to time.

Defense
Even though Claude expelled him from the club?

Peter
We remained friends.

Defense
Why did Claude expel him from the club?

Peter
As far as I know, they disagreed.

Defense
About what? Isn't it true that Fipp felt the Duplexers shouldn't be involved in drugs or other criminal activities? That it was corrupting the original ideals of the Duplexers?

Peter
You'd have to ask Claude why he expelled him.
But yes, Fipp does believe that.

Defense
Do you believe that?

Peter
I think that criminal activity, especially dealing drugs that could
affect children and lives, is an unfortunate necessity when you need
to raise funds to support families and large numbers of people.

Defense
Beats working at Shop Rite?

Peter
I still have to, obviously.

Defense
So ideally, you would not be involved in dealing drugs?

Peter
Ideally, no.

Defense
Yet you volunteered, even persuaded Claude, to be the point
man in the drug deal, when you knew Lymey, Nelly, Stoney,
and other senior members of the Duplexers could do the same.

Peter
Claude thought I would be a good fit.

Defense
You could have declined, right?

Peter
How would that look?

Defense
Haven't you discussed with Fipp, via text and phone, well before
the drug deal, that you didn't like being involved in the drug trade
and that you preferred to move out to Colorado with him to be
part of his newly formed and legally abiding chapter? Before you
answer, what if I told you we have the records to prove this?

Peter
Yes, I have. I told you; I never liked the whole drug thing.
It didn't thrill me like some other guys.

[The Defense held up papers, including text conversations between
Fipp and Peter, reiterated the evidence number and passed it along
to the jury.]

Defense
And wouldn't Claude have expelled you too
if he knew you were texting Fipp about all this?

Peter
Again, you'll have to ask him.

Defense
Did anyone else in the club know you were in touch
with Fipp and felt this way?

Peter
You'll have to ask them. But I don't think so.

Defense
This is what I don't understand: if you were texting
Fipp about your dissatisfaction with the drug culture

and talking about joining his chapter well before the drug deal,
why would you agree to be the point man in a drug deal
and then conveniently be the one to snitch on them?

Peter
What's the question?

Defense
Let me rephrase. Wasn't it your plan from the beginning to bring
down Claude in a drug deal to please Fipp so you can become his
second in command at his Colorado operation following this trial?

Peter
No. And there are no texts that can prove that.

Defense
You're right. Very crafty.

[The Prosecution objected; the Judge sustained the objection.]

Defense
But you are planning to join Fipp in Colorado after the trial?

Peter
It's possible. I haven't decided yet. But I can't
exactly hang out here anymore.

Defense
Will Nisha be going with you?
Peter
I don't know.

Defense
Does she know about Fipp?

Peter (paused)
No.

Defense
She wasn't part of your plot to frame Claude, Lymey, and everyone
in the club so that you could decimate it for your mentor Fipp and
get your reward from him after this is all over?

Peter
There is no plot, so no.

Defense
And you and Nisha didn't make up this whole rape incident to
frame Lymey and all five defendants at Fipp's behest, knowing that
you would be immune from prosecution, and she would be believed
as a sweet Indian girl from a wealthy family in Fairfield County?

Peter
No, that's fucking crazy.

Defense
Seems very convenient that you were outside
that house just when she needed you.

Peter
I went looking for her. I love her.
And those two were going after her.

[Peter pointed to Kyle and Larry. The Prosecutor objected that if the
Defense had any actual direct evidence of a conspiracy, they should
produce it. The texts just showed a relationship between Peter
and Fipp and how they felt about the gang's culture. There was no
evidence Nisha knew about Peter and Fipp's relationship, let alone of
a greater conspiracy.]

[The Judge agreed but said that the Defense could question Peter further on a different topic or call witnesses to rebut his testimony. The Defense decided to conclude their questioning of Peter.]

Rest of the Defense

Peter was dismissed from the stand; as he passed, he glanced at Lymey, who snickered briefly before turning away. This time Peter stayed in the courtroom, sitting across the aisle from Nisha and her father.

Next the Defense called Tammy Love, Stoney's girlfriend. She testified that Nisha tried to integrate herself into the biker lifestyle from the beginning and expressed anger that Lymey and Nellie had more influence than Peter in the club. She saw Nisha talking to Claude, possibly about giving Peter a bigger role.

On cross, the Prosecution accused Tammy of trying to protect Stoney, and that even if her testimony was true, it just bolstered the defendants' motive to rape Nisha.

Next Kyle and Larry testified that they did not try to handcuff or hold Nisha. They admitted to calling Lymey to inform him that Nisha had been found but claimed that she ran out only when she saw Peter. They had ridden away together with no drama.

The Defense noted that no handcuffs were found at the scene; the Prosecution countered that the handcuffs could have been thrown in the woods or in any number of other places. And what about Larry's injury to his face? His claim that a baseball accidentally hit him off his father Kyle's bat seemed preposterous.

The Defense wanted to recall Terri, but the Prosecution objected, and the Judge sustained the objection, saying that the Defense had already had the opportunity to cross-examine her. However, he did allow the cross-examination to be read back to the jury.

Terri had testified earlier about tipping Peter off about Nisha's whereabouts after hearing Nellie mention that she might be in the woods while on the phone with an unidentified person. The Defense had countered that it was a typical place where someone could go missing, so it didn't really prove anything. It also showed that Terri wasn't involved in any conspiracy.

The Defense could have called the other defendants, Claude, the Federal agent in charge of the drug investigation, or Fipp from Colorado. Instead, they motioned that the charges should be dropped, noting that the Prosecution had never located the site of the attempted rape and had no real physical evidence, other than Nisha's word, and that they had shown enough reasonable doubt that Nisha had made up the rape for her own benefit.

The Prosecution countered that they had presented plenty of forensic evidence in addition to Nisha's verifiable testimony. The forensic pathologist testified that the bite mark on Nellie's arm matched Nisha's teeth, and other injuries to the defendants matched Nisha's testimony exactly; that Nisha's condition did match someone being out in the woods for an entire day and two nights; and that the way her shirt was ripped indicated that someone had ripped it off her.

The Judge decided not to dismiss the case, but he told the jury that they could consider the Defense's argument. The Defense said that in that case they would call additional witnesses the next day, including a forensic pathologist who would rebut the State's expert.

Nisha's World Part II

Nisha was back in her room, wishing she could talk to Peter and wondering about her future. Accusations that Nisha had faked the rape made the pain and memory of the experience that much worse; now the Defense was primed to call even more witnesses to build their absurd theory.

Nisha had cried the entire way home. Her father had tried to console her, but later, in her room, he had reminded her again why they had created this cushioned life for her away from the harsh realities of the everyday world.

"Live your life right, Beti. Attend Yale; meet some other boys. First love is dated; it is futile; it is doomed. It isn't like in the pop songs. You are young, and you will grow. Don't throw away your life on your first experience."

And he had held her, rubbed her hand, cried himself, reminded her of how he had taught her to read when she was a young girl, how her mother used to take her to the playground, how they allowed her to have a rather perfect mix of American and Indian experiences, to play with all kinds of children, to have a wide group of friends, and even to eat meat on occasion. They never put her in a box, but they didn't want her to experience unnecessary pain either. Now the damage was done, life had been lived, and she could not undo it, but she could move on. Family was the most important thing, and Peter was not family.

Yet, when she was left in her room for hours to think, she worried about Peter—wasn't he supposed to testify the next day in Federal Court? Could he be targeted beforehand, not just for being a witness but now for betraying the club on the orders of an ousted member?

When she called Peter, he told her quickly, "Same time, same place." She assumed he was afraid his calls were being monitored.

She waited for what seemed like an eternity for the hours to tick off her grandfather clock, which had been left by whoever owned the house before her parents. She kept glancing at her phone to confirm it or to check if a text might call the meeting off.

Standing in the dark, she peered out the window to the far corner of her property to see if a figure on a motorcycle appeared, a motionless silhouette thinly lit under the lone streetlight against the vast darkness, waiting for his true love.

Finally, a little after 2 a.m., she saw a figure. But could she be sure it was Peter? What if a Duplexer had listened to the call, murdered Peter, and was waiting to punish the last traitor? She remembered seeing Lymey on his motorcycle, feeling uneasy but ignoring it; climbing on the back, putting her arms around his torso like she did with Peter but then thinking better of it, placing them on the handle behind her; the shock and terror when she realized that she had been duped; Lymey's grimy hands against her breasts after he had ripped off her shirt.

She wanted Peter to saw off Lymey's hands, to torture and destroy the others too. Thoughts of violence and revenge, which she'd never had before the incident, engulfed her now and again. But at this moment she also felt dread. Lymey and the other four defendants were incarcerated pending the verdict, but other Duplexers roamed free. They could act.

But she put aside her fear—she wanted to be with Peter. She snuck out again and ran across the long backyard. She was ready to turn around if she suspected a trap. She slowed down, trying to define the figure. But she knew her Peter before she was even close and hugged him fiercely when she converged on him.

Only a few miles down the road, she tugged on his jacket. She needed to make love like last night, in the same way, in the same woods; despite her trauma in that setting, she was hungry for its protection under the cushion of her man, her hero, protector. and knight.

At the diner, Peter was talking.

"I mainly talked to Fipp on the phone, so the texts don't tell them anything. Now I'm going to avoid either. I'll get a new phone in Colorado."

"They're making it seem like I did something wrong."

"I doubt the jury will buy it. But what's the difference? Once we're in Colorado, it'll be difficult for them to get at us even if they get off."

"They still could," she said, her legs shaking. "Why didn't you tell me about Fipp?"

"I told you we would go out West. I didn't want to complicate things or put you in a tough position on cross. You've been through enough."

"Dealing drugs, setting up Claude. It's a lot."

"I did it for us. So we could be free."

Did she want to be free? It sounded like Peter had plotted with Fipp to bring down Claude even before the FBI approached him.

Part of what the Defense attorney had said was true. That probably motivated Lymey and his friends to commit the assault. Was he her hero, and did she really know Peter like she thought she did?

"After I testify tomorrow in Federal court, we should be home free," Peter said. "Unless they reserve the right to recall me or the cross goes longer. I think we can go at the end of tomorrow. Who cares what the verdicts are? I've done my part, and Fipp should be happy."

"They won't call me again?"

"Calling me again was a special circumstance. My lawyer says he's shocked that they allowed it. So, I don't think so."

"What will they do tomorrow?"

"I don't know: what did the prosecutor say?"

"They'll call some bogus forensics 'expert' to say I made up the assault and created my own injuries. Maybe they'll call Lymey and them if they agree. And Claude, the FBI agent, Fipp, they're on the list but not clear if they'll go through with it."

"They could call the whole cavalry and argue all the bogus shit they want. This is why I wanted to bring them down."

She checked her phone again. She scanned texts she had ignored from her friends: Laxmi, Karen, Lori. All wanting to wish the best in this tough time; she could call them if she wanted to talk.

She had friends she could lean on, family she could trust. What was she doing?

"Can I count on you?" he was asking. "Will you be ready tomorrow?"

"I don't know, Peter. It might be too soon."

"The verdict is irrelevant. We have each other."

"Yes, Peter," she said after looking at her coffee clouds for a long while. "I'll be ready."

Love

We think of first love as some kind of ridiculous fairy tale from romance novels or movies. We're told that it's a kind of illusion that will fade with time when we enter the "real world" and build a career, have children, buy a house in the suburbs with a white picket fence, and mow our lawns, live the "good life," and make a better world for our children.

But for those of us who have followed the straight path of career and capital, who've done what our parents wanted and never felt the touch of true love, a passion as deep and animal and inexplicable as first love can be, doesn't this pandemic teach us that love and freedom are more important than we were led to believe, that we should embrace it before life is taken away from us in a flash, or perhaps more painfully, while trying desperately to breathe with the help of a ventilator?

Before we've wasted our lives on an endless list of meaningless work?

Nisha had already faced this dilemma at a young age. She had already suffered for it. She knew the pain of love; its possibilities and unexpected consequences; she had experienced too the micro-aggressions of the supposed real world of the Joneses.

She had a choice. Was she ready to make it?

Choice

Peter did get to Federal Court the next day and testified; on cross-examination, Claude's defense attorney used a similar theory as had the Defense in Nisha's trial, claiming that Peter set up the drug deal with the Axios gang in order to frame Claude with the assistance of the Feds. Initially, Peter claimed not to remember if the Feds had contacted him first or the other way around, but ultimately, he repeated the same story as in Nisha's trial about the Shop Rite parking lot visit.

Claude's Defense called one of the Federal agents and asked him how and why they had approached Peter; he claimed that they were surveilling Claude and had noticed that Peter was young and malleable. The Defense tried to push the idea that Peter had contacted them first, but the agent stood firm and repeated Peter's version.

Then the Federal Prosecution laid out more evidence against Claude, including phone calls they had recorded between Claude and the Axios leader before the deal. In the meantime, Peter left the courthouse and headed over to Nisha's trial. Sitting again on the other side of the aisle from Nisha and her father, he listened to Nellie testify about how Nisha had bitten him as a prank that evening at the clubhouse; Vicki, Lymey and Stoney had already testified to the same before him. How Lymey had driven Nisha home that night, dropped her off at Peter's mother's house, and had returned right after, everything seeming fine.

The three defendants testified that they didn't harbor animosity for either Peter or Nisha, and that their injuries had occurred during rough housing at the party. They even claimed that they knew nothing about the drug deal. All this had been countered strongly by the Prosecution.

Next, the Defense called a forensic pathologist who testified that Nisha could have ripped her own shirt, based on its patterns in evidence. This baffled Nisha but hardly surprised her after the other nonsense.

She looked at Peter, then at her father. She looked at the jury. The Black man was rolling his eyes, holding the cherry blossom handkerchief to his ear. She thought maybe she would be okay.

She glanced again at Peter. This time he met her gaze; he nodded. She looked at the witness again, then whispered into her father's ear that she needed to go to the bathroom. She left the courtroom, but she could feel her father, through her rearview mirror eyes, staring at Peter.

She walked down the hallway, went to the bathroom, and re-lieved herself. She washed her hands and walked back out into the hallway. Then, instead of entering the courtroom, she turned to leave the corridor.

She went through the doors of aluminum and glass, into the short entry hall with the coffered ceiling of terra cotta tile, past the brick walls and the metal detectors, and through the exit. At that moment, she saw him pull up on his motorcycle in front of the road. She headed down the short staircase and met him. Then turning back, she saw her father come out of the courthouse exit, too.

She hesitated. What she was doing crossed her mind. But she turned again just as fast and went on, climbing the motorcycle and putting her arms around Peter's torso.

Ahead of her, she saw someone on a motorcycle, helmet on, visor covering his face. He held something in his hand, but he was coming fast, so she couldn't tell what it was.

Peter accelerated too at that moment. She thought of warning him, but then she thought better.

She trusted him. This was his domain. She would live with the result.

~ Day Six ~
Reaction to Nalini's Story

By the end of her story, Ricard could not look at Nalini. Cathy was crying. So was Andrea. Even Hayley was a bit teary. Nalini's hands were shaking.

Then Rashan started clapping.

"Bravo," Rashan said. "A thought-provoking and moving story of how love conquers all; normally that would be corny, but you made it powerful and real with all the details, including the courtroom theatrics and legal particulars. Still not as good as my shit, but hats off to you."

"Good job," Andrea said, wiping her tears. "I really liked how you focused on Nisha's choice and the romantic relationship over the courtroom stuff, even though they were present too."

"It wasn't anything special," Taylor said, yawning, "but I was vaguely entertained."

"I thought it was funny and cool," Khassan commented. "And like Ricard, you focused on rural America, outside of our deep blue cities, which was unique."

"Good descriptions of Nisha's recurring trauma, girl," Sylvania said. "Courtroom testimony was intriguing."

Nalini had noticed Lisa roll her eyes during parts of the story. Lisa avoided eye contact with Nalini now, but Nalini couldn't help herself, so she asked Lisa point-blank what she thought.

"I just felt Nisha had no agency, Nalini," Lisa said. "She was so reliant on this creepy older guy who duped her. I mean, she was only 19 years old."

"I'm sorry, Lisa," Nalini said. "I wanted to make it real, but I understand my responsibility to be a role model for women too."

"I get Lisa's point," Cathy said, avoiding eye contact with Nalini now. "But let's face it, the biker criminal is pretty seductive for most women."

She elbowed Ricard, who rolled his eyes. Nalini didn't say anything, and after an awkward silence, Olive came forward.

"Thank you, Nalini, for telling a great story," he said. "I guess we should vote now. I think everyone is here this time."

The votes came in fast—only one was against, and one person abstained. Nalini wouldn't face Ricard's fate.

Nalini felt a hard slap on her shoulder. When she turned, she saw it was Angela.

"Thanks for that," she said. "It's a tough world out there for women."

"You're welcome," Nalini said, "I think."

Angela went off down the beach towards the darkness.

A minute later, she noticed someone was following her. She turned.

"Yo, girl," Darnell's voice said. She stopped suddenly and saw him approach. "What's up?"

"I can't believe you would try to follow me in the dark. Is this another round?"

"Why you frontin', girl? I just wanna make sure we're cool."

"No, why would we be cool after last night? After I said no several times and you were still touching me and grinding on me."

"You know, Spanish girls be different."

"Well, I'm not different, Darnell. Look, I can't be around you. I just can't ..."

She started to walk back towards the bonfire. Darnell spread his arms but wasn't sure if he should follow her.

"I'm sorry," Cathy said to Nalini after approaching her, with Ricard in the background. "I didn't mean for this to happen. I know we were sisters. I hope we can still be."

Nalini ignored her. She was looking at Ricard.

"So, what did you think of the story?" she asked him. "Are you the one who abstained?"

"Glad you're trying to win me over by portraying bikers as rapists and criminals," he said.

"Well, I did my research."

"I think that's the problem," Ricard replied, snickering. He kissed Cathy on the cheek. "You two try to make up. Think I'll finally bother Olive himself about that job I'm after."

Meanwhile, Hayley asked Pritesh for a cider as he walked past.

"Get it yourself," he said. Hayley smiled defensively. Then Pritesh noticed Angela rushing by.

"Are you okay?" he asked. But she continued to go forward, past Ricard and onward to Olive, who was discussing something with Micah.

"I need to tell you something, Olive," Angela said.

Darnell had been tailing her, but he stopped when he saw who she was talking to.

Taylor noticed the intrusion too. So did Lisa. And they heard Angela's words.

"He assaulted me," she said, pointing to Darnell. And that's all they needed to hear.

Acknowledgments

I often call *Bad Americans* a book that's "of the People, by the People, and for the People." This is partially because so many individuals from all walks of life assisted in the beta reader process to make sure *Bad Americans* was as accurate and realistic a portrait of the Pandemic Era as possible. These readers included people of every conceivable background: profession, race, sexuality, ethnicity, age, gender, location, political preference. Others assisted by commenting on style, form, point of view, and many other aspects of the art of narrative.

Among those I would like to thank are Vanessa Levine-Smith, Ditiksha Desai, Manny Figueroa, Jaymi Grullon, Lawrence Hestick, Molly Collins, Bahar, Rickin Desai, Brienne Walsh, Josh Youman, Bianca Sultana, Anasuya Desai, Matthew Allison, and David Martin.

A special thanks to Ingrid Anderson for her detailed edit and critique of the massive original manuscript (which she read thoroughly at least twice), as well as for showing a couple of her stories to her book club for their feedback; W. Lance Hunt, for also giving the original manuscript such a thorough evaluation; Ishy Christine Degyansky, another *super* beta reader; Rachel Luria, who took me around the Hamptons twice, gave me multiple suggestions, and answered rounds of questions on that crucial setting.

Several people gave me tours of locations in the past that were eventually used as settings in the book. These included Nomita Ramchandani, Betty Cunningham Templeton, Jignesh Desai, and the Quinn Family (RIP to Robin Brown and Kieran Quinn). Todd Sullivan, Jhankhana Naik, "Big Bill," and Malena Reyes also introduced me to worlds that triggered some tales.

Major props to my tireless cover designer Fena Lee, copyeditor/proofreader Barbie Bowen, designer Christine Keleny, my marketer Michael Beas, and publicist Dar Dowling.

The New Wei Collective has been an inspiration: William McGee, Chris Stylez, Annette Brown, Lynley Shimat, Lancelot Schaubert. My buddies Kacper Jarecki and Vijay R. Nathan.

Raj Tawney, you're the man. Thanks too to the ESRT crew—Fred Gitner, Selina Sharmin (and Elma!), Wilma, Jay, Simone Wellington, Madellen Garcia, and many others.

Robert Ballard and Heather Heathren, I love you. Bayard, Alex, Issie, Jamie! Billy and Law: let's get back to karaoke nights. David Wang, my man. Andrew Barfield, Christiana Parish, Monika, and the rest of the crew. Jessie Rothschuh, I miss you; let's hang out soon!

My QPL Family; my Flushing bros, including my basketball buddies, especially Tommy and Mr. Liu; my barbers, including AT; you guys are some of the best storytellers around; my PS 163, Bronx Science, Wesleyan, and QC friends; South Asian media peeps and Asian American writers.

My parents and my entire extended family, you've been such an amazing support and inspiration. I wouldn't be who I am without your adventurous spirit and sacrifice.

To America itself, my nation through thick and thin, without you I wouldn't be who I am, and this book wouldn't be what it is.

To my readers, I hope you enjoy this florid tale of tales!

About the Author

Tejas Desai is the author of the Amazon #1 bestselling international crime trilogy *The Brotherhood Chronicle* (2018-2020), which has won 17 literary honors and has been praised as "awe-inspiring," "breathtaking," "riveting" and "a must read that will keep you guessing." His panoramic portrait of American society, *The Human Tragedy*, includes the award-winning *Good Americans* (2013), which was hailed by *Kirkus Reviews* as "a solid collection of rare caliber" that "speaks volumes about the human condition and modern life in America," and the groundbreaking pandemic novel with short stories *Bad Americans*, which is being released in Parts throughout 2025 and 2026. The founder of The New Wei Literary Arts Collective & Movement, he has been profiled by numerous publications including *HuffPost*, *Buzzfeed* and *The London Post*. He attended Wesleyan University, University of Oxford and holds two master's degrees, including an MFA in Creative Writing, from CUNY-Queens College. He was born, lives and writes in New York City, where he works as a supervising librarian for Queens Public Library.